★

The corpse was stiff as a board, dead long enough for rigor mortis to have set in. He squatted to peer at the man's face. The bruising was apparent even in bad light. Then Ben jerked upright and gasped. He swallowed a couple times before squatting again beside the body, and continued to stare at the top of the man's head. There was no skin across the frontal lobe. A chunk as big as a man's fist had been ripped away—no, cut away; this was not the work of an animal. The skin had been pulled forward, separated from the bone, then sliced along the hairline. The man had been scalped.

★

"Susan Slater scribes a strong story that will leave readers wanting more Ben Pecos tales."
—Harriet Klausner Internet review

Previously published Worldwide Mystery title by
SUSAN SLATER

THE PUMPKIN SEED MASSACRE

YELLOW LIES

SUSAN SLATER

WORLDWIDE®

TORONTO • NEW YORK • LONDON
AMSTERDAM • PARIS • SYDNEY • HAMBURG
STOCKHOLM • ATHENS • TOKYO • MILAN
MADRID • WARSAW • BUDAPEST • AUCKLAND

YELLOW LIES

A Worldwide Mystery/June 2002

First published by Intrigue Press.

ISBN 0-373-26422-4

Copyright © 2000 by Susan Slater.

Printed in U.S.A.

To my friend, mentor, fan, Norman Zollinger—
I will never stop "hearing" your advice:
"Susan, learn to edit!
Develop an ear for the crap and leave it out!"
You will forever continue to make me a better writer.
I will miss your enthusiasm for writing,
zest for life and unending support.

ONE

THE COYOTE HOWLED four times. Salvador Zuni laughed, realizing he was holding his breath, then waited for another long piercing wail—*hoped* for another. In the old days four cries was the signal for the gathering of witches. Did he believe that today? He wasn't sure. But if he didn't, why had he paused? He sighed and still waited, but there were no more yippy songs from the mesa. That was just his luck. When he needed everything to be going his way, there was this omen.

It wasn't that he felt threatened, just vaguely uneasy—more like he was being warned by the shadows that whispered behind him, followed him. He'd feel someone watching, but he'd turn and find no one. At night, dream-strangers dressed in the costumes of his ancestors would ring his bed and chant, mouths open in soundless harmony. Usually, Atoshle, the ogre *kachina* came. Sal's skin prickled with a fine coating of sweat. Was it the work of the *hadikanne,* the witch society? Maybe he should see a shaman. But that wouldn't be cheap.

Four staccato barks burst through the silence, coming from somewhere to his left, a half mile, maybe a mile, behind him. In answer to the first four calls? They could be. But he'd have to believe that a witch could turn itself into a coyote and call other members of the society together. And he just wasn't certain about that.

Sal leaned against the bark of the cottonwood. He'd wait, watch, just to be sure. If it was coincidence, he'd get to work soon enough. He liked to visit the river at dusk and watch the night come alive with its creatures. No one had followed him—even knew he was gone for that matter. But he couldn't be too careful. No need to arouse suspicion. He'd parked his pickup a quarter mile back in dense brush and carried his tools with him, the sacks of Mason jars, small nets, pins, a vial of formaldehyde. He needed the cover of darkness to hunt his tiny prey.

And it wasn't like what he was doing was wrong—not really wrong—the type that could hurt someone. This wrong was more of a lie. But Hannah always said he worried too much. How would people find out? Raid his workshop? He kept the one room behind his trailer locked. And there wasn't a pile of the stuff anywhere. At least, not for long.

Hannah had found an outlet, a local trader who traveled, someone they could trust. Sal wasn't so certain about this last part, but Hannah was confident. As soon as Sal got twenty pounds ahead, she'd pack it up and send it off. The man sold almost all of Sal's raw material out of state. Hannah only kept his carved pieces at the trading post—and then just a few. They hadn't been careless. Unless this trader, Ahmed, told…

Sal hated the pressure. He was an artist, a carver in the old tradition. He'd been against Hannah's plan at first. Hannah had the idea, asked him to try different recipes, said to trust her. She knew it could be done, actually had been done before, but those people had been careless, had gotten caught. She felt the reservation offered good cover, different jurisdiction and all, sort of put them above suspicion.

And she had played her ace. The one thing she knew he'd help her with—keeping her son in that special school. "A short time, Salvador. I'm only asking that you make amber for a short time. The school is so costly. You want Harold to be successful, don't you?"

Harold. Always Harold when she wanted something from him. Unspoken but insinuated that perhaps the child was his. Sal didn't know for certain, but he supposed it could be true. There had been indiscretions, the hapless encounters outside a loveless marriage.

So, he'd agreed to make amber. And his work was good, something to be proud of. No one could tell the difference between old and new. The formula was his. It was not for sale and not for sharing. Even Hannah didn't know how he did it.

How he made this golden, prehistoric sap—fabricated the ancient jewel of the woods right down to its enclosures.

He'd learned to mix resins, add color, encapsulate a leaf, twig or insect and no one suspected—not even using a magnifying glass. He dried the animal/vegetable inserts in a vacuum cylinder, sucked their juices carefully from their forms and left them exactly as in life, perfect, with only a hint of their former coloration. His amber was a work of art.

People paid big money for his discovery, his handiwork. Hannah was sending off more and more of it in its raw form. Egg cartons filled with irregular golden balls the size of peas, marbles and golf balls left the trading post, some by United Parcel; others waited for the middleman, this trader, to pick them up. Fat checks came back in return—five thousand here, ten thousand there. His shed held the makings of a fortune.

Animated voices floated above the river's song and poked at his consciousness. Kids were out drinking beer. The early evening was warm, unseasonably hot for June, and swarms of pesky mosquitoes buzzed around his ears. Hannah had helped him adjust the new hearing aid, but its hum rattled in his head, getting louder if he nodded. When he turned the thing up, it made the mosquitoes sound like dive bombers. He dug in his ear until the tiny plastic oblong, the size of a flesh-colored beetle, lay in his palm. And the quiet returned. Now that was interesting, if you didn't hear the coyotes, did it mean their message had no impact?

But that sounded decidedly like Father Leget's lesson on "if a tree fell in the forest…." He had thought about that until his brain hurt. And when he couldn't figure it out, he'd asked the priest about its meaning. And the priest had laughed and slapped his shoulder and told him to keep working on it. But he hadn't. He knew when he was bested.

Sal waved away the mosquitoes, fretted with his loose cotton shirt until its tail flopped out over his jeans and then carefully pushed the tiny bit of plastic back into his ear. Maybe, if he concentrated on the river… He didn't mind the hearing aid, not really. It was free from the Government. And his loss of hearing had gotten him out of the military on disability, out of uniform and home to his artwork with a monthly check. That had been over thirty years ago.

The full moon seemed sluggish in the heat and rose slowly, unfurling silver light across the river's wet rocks. Sal gazed at the slippery shine that spread along the shallows and sought him in the shadow of the cottonwood. Hot, moon-bright, summer nights were the best to gather the tiny insects for his work. He'd gotten a book from the Library on Wheels that had pictures of hundreds of insects native to the Southwest and had circled the pictures of ones he liked. He tended to lean towards anything with pinchers, but iridescent wings ran a close second.

Snatches of conversation floated across the water. Playful banter that meant someone would probably get laid later on. Sal winced. How long had it been since he'd approached Hannah? A month, two months? He'd have to make sure that the drought ended one of these days.

He let his thoughts stay on Hannah, a tall, bony Anglo woman with stringy blond hair tied back at the neckline of some shapeless, ankle-length dress in checks or faded flowers. And always those same sandals—with thick socks in the winter when there was snow on the ground. Even if her legs, covered with downy-soft hair that had never known a razor, turned blue with cold, she never wore anything different, no slacks or heavy skirts. She'd come to the reservation in the sixties every weekend, an anthropology student from Maine doing work at the University of New Mexico. And she'd met her husband, the owner of the trading post.

Only he'd been a lot older—maybe by a full twenty years. And when Ed Rawlings dropped dead one spring day leaving a thirty-something widow and a five-year-old son, everyone on the reservation expected her to leave. Pack up, close the trading post, sell the inventory to another Anglo and never be seen again. But that wasn't the way things happened. Hannah stayed, stayed and struggled to make a go of things. The odds were against her, alone like she was.

Sal had felt beholden to help. Because of the child? Maybe.

He didn't try to figure out why. Yet, at the time he had hesitated, waited six months before he'd offered himself, made her realize that he would do whatever she needed, odd jobs, help with the trading post. He told her he could move out there, board with her. She allowed as how she would feel safer. It was Hannah who had come up with the trailer, made his lodging part of their deal. She couldn't thank him enough, said she'd had no one else to turn to.

But what she needed was much more of a personal thing. She wanted to sleep with him, continue a relationship that, at best, had been a handful of one-night stands. Was this the real reason he'd moved out there? Could be. Hannah was young, vulnerable, pretty…and she'd come at him like a she-wolf. Deprivation. It was a primal hunger like he'd never seen and had been almost too much that first time. He'd had difficulty performing.

But he had to respect her. She was fair to his people, a good businesswoman, and she took care of her son. Once a year after she'd visit the boy in that special, year-round school in Albuquerque, she'd travel back East and sell. Business was always second. Sometimes reservation artists would go with her. At first, that had made Sal jealous. But again, it was like the tree in the forest—if you weren't there to hear it fall… He stooped to turn over the rotting end of a log and deftly caught three scavenger beetles. All had neatly formed pinchers. He'd put them in separate jars. He was beginning to consider himself an expert on insects and could discuss original hosts, larvae, and parasitical control of pest infestation at the drop of a hat. Only that wasn't very often because Hannah warned him that he shouldn't seem so knowledgeable. It might arouse suspicion.

His stomach's gurgling broke his reverie. He hadn't eaten since lunch. Maybe he should get his pickup and drive into Gallup for some KFC, or maybe Chinese, and take some by the trading post. Hannah loved pan-fried noodles with her chicken chow mein. He could be there by eight-thirty.

He gathered up the jars he'd set beside the log. There was never any waste. What insects he didn't use, he'd give to Harold, who was home this summer for the first time since he was ten. He'd been released at the age of twenty, not cured exactly, but able to cope, help his mother, anyway.

Sal smiled. Nobody but his mother called him Harold; he'd been .22 so long only a few remembered why—remembered that old Ed hadn't owned a twelve-gauge, the usual choice of firearm for a man to shoot in the air to commemorate the birth of his first son. So, it had been a .22—a rifle pointed skyward in celebration. But had he known that his only son wouldn't have made a twelve-gauge proud? That he would be…what did Hannah call it? Learning impaired?

It was odd to see .22 almost grown. But for all his size, he was still a little boy—and a handful. Hannah had to keep an eye on him. Sal helped when he could, took .22 fishing, or collected toads and frogs with him. At least these amphibians ate any leftovers Sal had after he'd picked over his catch. It made Sal feel better to think that nothing was needlessly killed; nothing went to waste. And .22's little green friends were fat and happy.

The trip back to the truck took longer than he'd expected. He couldn't move too fast on account of all the glass jars in grocery sacks; he tried to keep them from knocking together. He had two ice chests in the bed of the truck, and he'd put his catch there where all the Mason jars fit snugly with cardboard in between and only squeaked against the sides of the Styrofoam when he turned a corner.

He was intent on this business of fitting the jars into their resting place for their ride home and was singly aware of how his stomach repeatedly grumbled now—ever since he'd thought about food, promised it something to grumble over. He put the last jar in place and leaned over the tailgate to inspect his charges—some kept prisoner with nothing more than wax paper and a rubber band over the jar's mouth.

A twig snapped. Somewhere barely thirty feet to his right, something had moved. He straightened up and listened but didn't look that way. Had a shadow flitted along the edge of the trees? Something subliminal had registered on his brain, seen only by his mind's eye. He used to carry a rifle in a gun rack that hung in the back window of the cab. But the gun disappeared. It was too difficult to remember to lock the truck every time he parked; so, it had tempted someone to just reach in and take it, a pump action Remington, a reminder of his seventh birthday. There had been a time when someone's property wouldn't have been touched on the reservation.

He moved towards the cab of the truck and stuck one arm through the open window. Still staring ahead of him into the darkness, he fumbled for the switch to the headlights. He pulled the knob quickly and then without waiting walked to where the two beams of light thrust into the trees and seemed stopped by the dense foliage some thirty feet dead center. A buffalo moth began a series of drunken loops edging closer to the circle of light before falling away to begin the spiral all over again. Sal pushed past the rim of light and stood in waist-high grass.

Nothing. He wished he could trust his hearing, but he couldn't. Sometimes he could hear a leaf fall, other times like now he strained to pick up any sound that didn't belong. Even as his eyes adjusted, the too-bright headlights masked rather than revealed his surroundings. They weren't any help. He told himself that it was his imagination. The cries of the coyote had made him edgy, ready to jump at his own shadow. He turned back.

As he neared the truck, it didn't dawn on him at first why one headlight would be turning pink, but he stooped to find out and put his hand in liquid that was spreading languidly from a pool between fender and hood. He jerked upright and held his hand in front of the light. Blood. But he hadn't needed to confirm it by sight. His brain registered blood the moment he had felt the slightly congealed warmth and smelled its peculiar metallic odor.

He willed his heart to stop pounding. Then after a deep breath, he blinked away the temporary blindness from the headlights, moved his eyes to look for the source, and focused on the hood of the truck.

The body sprawled spread-eagle, head propped against the

windshield. Eyes wide, mouth open as if in surprise. A splash of red splotched the whiteness of his shirt. Why? Who could have done this? From the void of shock came a jangling flood of questions. But the worst? The most sobering thought of all— he knew this man. It was the trader, the one who sold his amber—the one outsider who knew about the fraud.

Sal held his bloodied hand away from his body. Already his fingers were beginning to tingle and the palm of his right hand grew hot. Then his fingers began to swell. He didn't wait but ran crashing through the brush towards the river. He had to wash the blood away or be tainted forever by the dead.

Slipping on the rocks he fell headlong into the shallows and pulled himself forward on his elbows until he could immerse his arm up to the shoulder. And then he lay there oblivious of the wetness that penetrated his jeans, lapped against his neck, soaked the toes of his ropers. And prone he waited, felt the water gently cleanse him, lull him into breathing steadily—deep breaths forcing oxygen into his depleted lungs.

The moon was now high overhead. He'd lost track of time, but things seemed normal finally. Frog songs trilled into the night. He waited, then pushed to his hands and knees, still listening, then upright to stand in the bright darkness—silhouetted in the sparkling shininess of the moon's path across the water. His hand was clean with little washboard puckers across his fingertips from its immersion.

He slipped off his shirt, wrung it damp-dry, then twisted it into a roll and held it to the base of his neck before bending over to splash more cold water on his face from cupped hands. He smoothed his shoulder-length, black hair straight back. The moonlight bleached his bronze skin, and he couldn't suppress a shiver as a breeze skipped across his chest, thin and sinew-taut with the bare outline of ribs—taut as the runner he'd been in high school. A wall full of trophies at his sister's house said he had been pretty good.

He was beginning to feel better, slowly beginning to regain strength. At least his head was clear enough to think of what to do. The persistent breeze was cooling as it sucked away the last of his feverishness and restored order. He was surrounded by the loud, insistent, but calming chirp of night creatures. This would have been a good night to collect, but he had no heart for it now. He walked back toward the truck.

He'd leave the truck, hike to the highway, and call Hannah from the One-Stop. Or maybe he'd call the police first. The police would have to come. Sooner or later, they would have to know. But what questions would they ask? How could he explain the man being found on his truck? Would they think there had been a fight? Would they discover the business arrangement? Sal shook his head. What a mess.

The headlights shone somewhat dimmer, but clearly. Hidden from their brightness, Sal paused at the edge of the thick brush, then stepped into the clearing and stopped again. He blinked, stared…it couldn't be. The hood of his truck was clean, bare of any trace of blood, let alone a body. He looked to the dense underbrush on either side. There was no evidence of a disturbance, no trail of where a body had been dragged away. The calm was mocking—nothing was out of place. The moon floated free of the clouds as a light breeze fanned the tall grasses. Could he be losing his mind? No, there had been a body and blood. He started forward; there was too much to do—and then he saw it.

Sitting on the scratched paint like a hood ornament was an amber fetish, maybe two inches tall. A sphinxlike rabbit, inset eyes of polished turquoise looking into nothingness, ears taller than its golden translucent body, which held captive several tiny insects. Sal turned away and slumped against the truck's side. The rabbit was made out of amber from his shed, his laboratory. Amber he had made. Insects he had caught. His lungs ached as he gulped in air, tried to get his breath. Someone knew, had found out the lie. Killed because of it. And now warned him.

He roused himself to look in the truck's bed. The Styrofoam cases were gone—Mason jars, their inhabitants, everything. First, there was a body, then there wasn't; now, in addition, he'd lost a night's work. Clearly someone didn't want him making amber. Could it be the ancient ones? The ones who crowded his dreams? Had he sinned against nature with his lie?

He found a stick and knocked the amber rabbit off the hood and poked it under the left front tire, then pushed a flat rock against it. He'd smash this fake to powder, and then he'd talk with Hannah. He'd feel better then. Sal hoped there was enough battery left to turn the engine over.

"SALVADOR. OH, MY GOD, what happened to you? You're soaked." Hannah jumped up from the big oak table in the corner of the boarding house kitchen, a pile of bills scattered across the floor. She threw her arms around him, a quick hug of relief when he'd said that he was all right. Then, he'd told her as best he could about the body but felt foolish adding that it had disappeared.

"Show me where it happened. We need to go back and look. A body just can't disappear. And if it's who you say…well, we've got some thinking to do."

Hannah first insisted on looking at the truck. She opened the hood and wiped a rag around the inside edge. "A bleeding body would have left a trace. There's nothing here. I've never seen this old truck so clean."

"Yeah, maybe that's the point." Sal was getting tired of the hocus-pocus. Maybe he shouldn't have told Hannah. She was acting like he was crazy. He should have just gone home. But he had to tell Hannah. It was one more reason to stop making amber, stop the lying. .22 was home now. Soon the school's bills would be paid. The money wasn't needed anymore.

He didn't want to go back to the river, but Hannah said she'd drive. He didn't even change clothes, just rolled down the window on the passenger side and let the warm air dry them. He was quiet, and Hannah respected his silence.

The truck's headlights picked up little more than the width of the two-lane highway. Yet, the night was lighted by the now-high moon in a cloudless sky. Calming, peaceful—already he was having second thoughts about what he'd seen. Leaving the highway, Hannah maneuvered the ancient truck down the steep incline where two tracks led to the river. They bounced along in silence. Hannah chewing on her lower lip, cursing when the truck slipped sideways over slick rocks, throwing them around before the tires gained dry ground.

"How do I know this isn't your imagination? You've talked a lot lately about bad dreams, Atoshle, and all. Isn't there a chance that you *thought* you saw a body, but there really wasn't one?"

"I know what I saw." He felt angry now like someone had played a joke. "There. That's where the truck was parked. Pull straight in."

Hannah nosed the truck to within twenty feet of the thick wall of rushes, cut the engine and sat a moment listening.

"You're coming with me. I don't like this any more than you do. But I won't investigate alone." She left the headlights on and walked to the front of the truck. Reluctantly, Sal followed.

"Tell me again what you did. What happened before you saw the body."

Sal mimed looking in the bed of the truck, hearing a sound, walking into the high grass, then turning back and seeing the blood dripping across the headlight.

"And the body was like this?" Hannah hopped up on the hood and dangling a leg across the fender leaned back against the windshield.

"Get down." He'd lost all patience. She was mocking him. She didn't believe him.

"I'm sorry. That wasn't funny. Salvador, look at me." Hannah slipped down from her perch to take his hands in hers. "I just don't think you saw a body. How could you? There's no evidence that this place has been disturbed. For someone to have dragged a body—"

"It could have been carried."

"Ahmed isn't exactly slight. It would have taken two strong men to move him let alone hoist him up here." She patted the hood. "You would have heard something, saw something. They would have left a trail, trampled the grass. Sal, I'll call

Ahmed's store in the morning. You'll see, this is all some fabrication.''

''I know what I saw. It's a warning. I'm not supposed to be making amber.'' Sal was looking on the ground for some trace of the amber rabbit that he'd smashed under the tires. But again, nothing, not even fragments of the golden ornament. Had he imagined everything? He was feeling slightly sick to his stomach.

''You know this could have been some kind of prank. Someone pretended to be dead, then got up and walked away, leaving the rabbit.''

''Maybe.'' He couldn't deny that as a possibility. He hadn't examined the body, just took off scared out of his wits. ''Should we call the police?'' Probably, he'd already decided not to, but he needed to ask.

''And tell them what?''

''I don't know.''

''We don't even have the amber rabbit to corroborate your story. I really think this was done by someone from the village. A jealous carver, perhaps.''

''Or Atoshle—''

''You know I don't believe the same way you do. My practical side says someone you know has set this up. Hired someone to scare you into giving up the amber.'' She leaned her elbows against the fender. ''I just can't believe that word has gotten out. Certainly, everyone knows that you excel at carving amber. Your work is some of the best that's ever been done. But no one knows that you make it, too.'' She frowned, causing her forehead to wrinkle. Sal always thought this was the only clue to Hannah's age. Otherwise, her clear pale skin pulled smooth around her eyes with only the hint of laugh lines to betray her fifty-some years.

''Is the notebook safe?'' she suddenly leaned towards him to whisper.

Sal nodded. Everything he knew—had learned about the making of amber was written down, carefully noted in a small pocket-sized spiral binder. It had been Hannah's idea and a good one. It represented a lot of work and a lot of money—too much of both to trust to memory. If it were to fall into the wrong hands…

"What would we do if someone were to steal it?" Hannah voiced his thoughts.

Sal shrugged. He started to tell her he was stopping anyway, but she rushed on.

"I'm talking about someone duplicating our work or worse—exposing us." She was biting her lower lip now. "Salvador, give the notebook to me. It's incriminating—points a finger at both of us. And I'm not willing to go to jail." She leaned towards him waiting. He liked the way her eyes glittered. They were the most unusual deep blue. "I'll put it in the safe at the trading post."

"I can't." That sounded better than he didn't want to.

"Why not?" He could hear the start of anger in her voice.

"I use the notebook. I make corrections. Add things all the time. Look up what I've done before. It needs to stay with me."

"I'm worried. Maybe, this was a warning. What if these people won't stop at a harmless prank? What if they are willing to kill for it?" Her hand was on his arm. "I couldn't bear to find you dead somewhere." Her eyes glistened with tears caught just behind lower lashes.

"I don't think you have to worry."

Sal had thought about his death. But he wondered if tonight's warning came from the elders—those in the village who could call upon the *kachina* to show him his errors—not to kill him but to give him a vision of what could be. Maybe if he appeased the priests, showed them that what he did was really not so harmful. He could tell them he would stop by the end of the summer. Yes, that was it. If they knew he was quitting soon…

"You know, we're in such a good position." Hannah was staring into space, tears blinked back—any further search for the body apparently forgotten. "I've spread rumors about a new vein of Baltic amber, one just discovered. No one ever questions me. People are clamoring for the good stuff. And ours is perfect." Suddenly she grabbed both his arms and faced him, her eyes narrowed. "I don't want anything to happen to that notebook. Or to you. Do you understand me? I don't want you taking risks."

"It'll be okay. I'm going to stop."

"What?" Her arms fell away.

"By the end of the summer, I'll be finished when the last of the school bills are paid."

"But I've just started repairs on the house. We talked, don't you remember? The house is Harold's inheritance. I can't just let it go. The plumbing is terrible. I've just had the place painted—I still owe for that. I'm talking thousands. Salvador, are you listening to me? I've committed myself, signed contracts."

"You'll have enough."

She stared up at him. He couldn't tell what she was thinking, only that she was angry. Then she stepped away and leaned back against the truck.

"I want to help. I want to keep you safe. Don't throw that back in my face. All our years together—they have to mean something. We had a deal—a business contract. I expect you to honor that."

He didn't say anything.

"You're afraid, aren't you?" she finally asked.

He shrugged. How could a man answer that?

"All the more reason to give me the notebook. Don't give someone the chance to kill for it."

Sal didn't answer. The notebook would stay with him. There was no argument. He reached out and pulled her to him. "I'm glad you care." He said it brusquely and felt her relax.

"It's like the old days. You and me by the river. I hate it when you fight me about the notebook. Sometimes I just might know best." She leaned back to look at him, chin defiantly thrust forward. But her eyes were smiling. "You know, as long as we're out here we could walk to the river. The night is beautiful." Hannah slipped a hand in his and pulled him to follow.

Some sixth sense perked up and sent a message to his brain.

Maybe he was about to get lucky. Sal thought fleetingly of the kids who had been out there earlier. They'd had the right idea. He drew her back and put an arm around her waist.

THE SUNLIGHT ricocheted off the trailer's silver siding and sought entry through the kitchen window. It was too early. Sal wadded the pillow and buried his face. He wasn't anxious to start the day or remember the night before—well, maybe the sex, but not the other. In the morning light it was difficult to believe he'd thought there had been a body on the hood of his truck, let alone an amber rabbit. He pressed his hands to his forehead. Hannah was right, things like that didn't really happen outside your imagination. He needed to forget about it, get on with his life.

Today, he was minding the store and there were deliveries— early ones—gas tanker from Shiprock, bread truck, Sysco Foods. He threw the pillow on the floor and swung his feet over the high plywood side of his bed, then stood and stretched.

He had never paid rent; he helped out. And that made it all right. This trailer in back of the trading post wasn't charity. He pulled on the pair of jeans he'd thrown onto the top bunk and rummaged around in the cupboard above his head for a clean tee shirt, then started out the door. His bathroom and shower were in back of the deli-mart, the one room grocery attached to the trading post and piled floor to ceiling with racks of canned goods, paper products, and toiletries. An upright cooler of cold sodas took up a part of the south wall. Fresh food was frozen mostly, unless you counted Hannah's vegetables that she sold during the summer.

He should probably mist the bins of vegetables before he went to the bathroom but more likely than not, the leaves of lettuce would slowly wilt anyway even under the fine spray of water that he applied twice a day. Cabbages became shriveled and hard in less than a week and reminded him of shrunken heads that he'd seen on display once in a museum. Now there was a unique approach to preserving the enemy. The year Hannah had raised Brussels sprouts had been singularly bad until kids discovered they made good ammunition for slingshots.

He unlocked the storeroom and the front doors. Today he would mop the plank flooring worn brown and smooth after years of traffic. He'd opened early for deliveries, but Frank Yazzie was late. Usually the big white Sysco Foods truck was waiting for him. Of course, sometimes Frank saved them for last, on his way home to Window Rock for the weekend. The company let him keep the big truck overnight as long as he wasn't carrying anything that would spoil.

Sal wiped out the hot dog cooker, the clear plastic cylinder with rotating spokes that sat on the edge of the counter. He could count on Frank buying two—smothered in Texas chili. He'd have to remember to scrape the dry crust from around the edge of the brown mass in the crock pot, maybe add another can of Wolf-brand and set out the Tabasco.

He sighed as he got four wieners out of the walk-in cold storage to fill the cooker. Fill was a misnomer. Hannah instructed him to put in four dogs and space them so that it looked like they'd sold the other eight. Sal threaded the wieners onto different rungs of the cooker each morning. Almost always they sold all four. But when he asked Hannah to let him cook a couple more, she'd given him an emphatic, "No." Eight dollars in the pocket was better than the possibility of two wasted.

He waved to the driver of the Navajo Gas and Oil truck and walked outside to watch him pump fuel into the underground holding tanks. A splash of gas was evaporating on the driveway. Sal pulled a hose from the side of the building, turned the spigot and aimed a spray of water at the spill then filled the mop bucket. The tanker from Shiprock would top up the reservoir of fuel rated eighty-seven octane. There were two pumps in the drive but nobody paid the extra fifteen cents a gallon for the ninety rating except Hannah, but then she didn't pay exactly. She filled her aging Buick once a week with the expensive stuff. Sal couldn't keep his mind from dwelling on last night. Hannah had said later she thought it might be his wife paying someone to scare him into sending more money. He'd given that some thought as he lay beside her on the soft sand of the river's bank—exhausted by what they had done so well for so many years.

Could it be his wife and not the ancient ones? She had ways of finding out what he was up to. He needed to give that some thought. When he'd moved out all those years ago, the unspoken agreement was that he'd give her money as regularly as he could. There were no children. Over the years he'd kept his part of the bargain. Among his tribe adultery wasn't a crime; infidelity might lead to divorce, but, unlike Anglos, no one considered his rights violated. Not that there weren't some things expected. More because of the Catholic religion and the intrusion of Anglo laws—like property rights, restitution, an eye for an eye.

Just last month his wife had asked him for money. And when he'd said "Maybe," she'd hinted that a man who had all that amber must be rich and could afford to meet his obligations. How did she know what he had? He'd just shrugged but gave her the Indian courtesy of listening. And she could talk. He wasn't sure he could remember a list of faults that long unless he recited them every day. But, maybe that's what she did. They had certainly been committed to memory in a perfect, unchanging order. Sometimes he'd try to pay attention just to make certain that nothing new had been added.

"Hey, you need this *'bilagaana nik'os'* or not?" Frank Yazzie leaned in the door.

Sal stood the rag mop in the bucket and pushed it into a corner beside the freezer. Frank must have the ten cases of Spam that Hannah had ordered. Navajos referred to the pink luncheon meat in the blue can as "whiteman's neck." Probably wasn't a bad name as names go.

"Over here."

Frank maneuvered the loaded dolly down the last row of shelves and headed towards the storeroom.

"You know Shiprock City Market sells 1,400 cases every three months of this stuff and there's twenty-four cans in a case. They got an entire aisle that's just Spam. They won a prize last

year as the southwest territory's top consumer. Spam people
gave 'em a banner.'' Frank disappeared through a swinging
door.

Sal didn't say anything. He often wondered how Frank could
rattle off these facts and sound proud of something like Spam
gluttony. Personally, he hated the stuff, and it wasn't because
Hannah railed on about its salt and fat content. He just didn't
like it—not its looks, not its taste. But shelf life was a different
story. The company referred to it as "unlimited." How could
a perishable not perish? But then maybe Spam was like Twin-
kies.

One time in grade school his best friend had left a Twinkie
on a plate above his bed. The first month nothing happened.
They'd poke at it and its yellow cake sides would bounce back
fresh-like. Three months into the experiment, the thing suddenly hardened but didn't lose its rounded oblong shape. Then
one month later it was back to its springy freshness. Sal accused
his friend of replacing the original. But he swore he hadn't.
This time his friend's sister said it was witched and made them
take it out of the house and bury it. Sal always wanted to go
back and dig it up but he'd forgotten where they'd put it.

"Hot enough for you?" Frank walked back through the
swinging door.

Sal didn't answer. It was like the stuff Anglos said all the
time; it didn't need an answer. It used to bother him that Frank
could sound so Anglo. But Sal guessed he had to. Someone
had told him that Frank was up for promotion, some desk job,
manager of the west territory. Maybe he wouldn't even be driving a truck much longer. Sal took the papers Frank held out to
be initialed.

"Want me to add on the usual?" Sal pointed with his chin
at the hot dog cooker. He'd slip 'em in the microwave to get
'em warmed through the center and heat the chili.

"Yeah, and make sure I can see the chili for a change."
Frank laughed. Sal knew he liked to tease.

"I hear we've just about seen the last of you. I should be
thankful. Profits should go up on hot dogs," Hannah teased

back as she came through the door and crossed the store to stand behind the counter. She took over the making of the hot dogs. It was subtle. She never out and out accused him of not minding the profits, but it was there. Sal knew she'd put on less chili than he would have.

"We're supposed to have a busload of tourists in here before noon." Hannah didn't look up from making change for Frank.

"Good season this year. More write-ups in the *Albuquerque Tribune* get the newcomers out this way." Frank began eating one of the dogs.

"Are we going to be ready for them?" She didn't glance his way, but Sal knew that Hannah wasn't referring to refilling the hot dog cooker. It was time for him to get into the cage. At least that's what he called it, the wire enclosure at the front of the trading post that kept a workbench and tools from becoming too tempting—and separated the artist from the masses.

Out on the highway—the first billboard was on the four-lane just before Gallup—a series of signs about five miles apart invited the public to view an Indian at work. A real Indian. As versus what, Sal always wondered. But it brought people in. Mostly vacationers in the summer but they did a stiff trade in December around the time of the *Shalako* festivities.

It was the only way he sold his artwork anymore—the tiny animals that he carved then strung into strands of birds, bears, wolverines or mountain lions in coral, turquoise, malachite…amber. And his work sold well. Everyone wanted to buy something from an artist he knew. Tourists would crowd around his work space, faceless, pressed against the wire, sometimes asking questions.

Hannah encouraged him to be more talkative. Like she was an authority on Anglos. He preferred to keep quiet. It gave him time to think and, today, he needed silence to figure out what was going on—find the true meaning of the body, then the amber rabbit on the hood of his truck. But more importantly, he needed to know what it would take to keep these things from happening again. Should he speak to his wife? Or assume it was Atoshle and pay for a ceremony to keep him away?

The bus pulled into the shade close to the building. Sal bent over his work but watched the double-file group of tourists walk his way. Q-Tips. Twenty of them, or more. One time a tour bus driver had told him he'd looked in his interior mirror and all he saw were cottony-white tops of heads bobbing behind high-backed seats and for all the world it looked like a busload of Q-Tips. It was a good name.

A sandy-haired man appeared to be the guide mainly because he looked forty years younger than anyone else. He hopped off last and followed the others, quickening his steps to catch up with a couple who motioned for him to join them just inside the door. Sal wondered if being a guide was a hard job, putting up with little old people and riding backwards all day.

"I understand you have a rabbit."

Sal almost buried the Dremel in the palm of his hand. He shut the small power tool off, set it down carefully and took a deep breath before he glanced at the speaker.

"My daughter has a collection. Over five hundred, I think. All kinds. Paper. Ceramic. Stuffed." An elderly woman peered at him, standing so close to the wire of his cage as to touch her nose.

"No rabbits."

"But I asked the guide. He assured me that I'd find some here. Look. In this book on your people's fetishes by Bennett, it says…" She thumbed through the pages, backed up, turned one more forward and stopped. "Here it is. 'The rabbit is a trickster comparable to the coyote. He's a representative of the world of illusion and double meanings. He's often prone to acting impulsively, giving himself away, and thus turning his worst fears into self-fulfilling prophecies…sometimes causing his own destruction.'" The woman snapped the book closed. "Is that true? I mean, in your religion do you consider the rabbit—"

"No." The word sounded strangled, forced, overly loud. Had it come from him? He glanced quickly at the Q-Tip again, then away. Were her eyes glowing? Was she pointing at him with a bony finger, the other hand with blood-red nails holding the book, and hanging on the wire of his cage like an arachnid, its parchment legs clasping the wire? Whatever she was going to say was lost to Sal because he pushed back from the bench and abruptly opened the gate to his enclosure and left.

He saw Hannah glance his way, pause in her explanation that they were temporarily out of hot dogs. He didn't even smile. He didn't care if she lost money because she wasn't prepared. It probably didn't matter anyway. She was setting up a dinner for all twenty-some tourists for that night. Sal walked past her.

"Oh, Salvador? I called Ahmed's store this morning. Ahmed left for New York two days ago. He'll be back a week from Friday. What'd I tell you?"

TWO

BEN PECOS HAD CHOSEN to drive from Chicago. Hindsight had proved that to be foolish, but who could have known the temperatures would reach record peaks across the Midwest in June and that vapor lock would stalk him from St. Louis to Albuquerque. His belongings could have been shipped. He could have braved the separation. It wasn't like he had bonded with the thirty-five cartons of books, box of kitchen "things," another box of bathroom "things," a broom, a cantankerous Hoover, two sets of bed linen and assorted clothing.

There wasn't a lot that defined his existence—maybe the storyteller, the clay doll that sat holding the eager child with an upturned face. It was a sample of his mother's best work, done when she was sober a few months before she died. He had turned four that summer. And his grandmother had let him be adopted by Mormons. She thought it would be the best for him. Who was to say it wasn't? So, this trip was another homecoming. This time to pay back Indian Health Service for his education.

It could have been worse. He could have been assigned to a

reservation in Montana or Oklahoma. This way he was only a hundred miles from his mother's pueblo, maybe another fifty miles from Albuquerque. He'd be the psychologist for the Hawikuh tribe in western New Mexico for two years, longer if he wanted.

To someone who didn't know New Mexico, it was difficult to explain how the landscape could differ so completely— within a few short miles of a neighboring state. But he knew exactly—before the welcome sign—that he was home. And he did consider New Mexico that. Mountains emptied into deserts, wooded areas gave way to cultivated fields, mesas loomed at the edge of canyons—and somewhere in the Tewa Pueblo, his mother had buried his umbilical cord assuring he'd always return.

I-40 from Albuquerque towards Grants and Bluewater passed in the shadow of Mt. Taylor. Black boulders of volcanic ash lined the highway for some fifteen miles, a testament to prehistoric devastation. Then the flat land gently rose pulling the highway up and through low hills and rocky embankments. The farther west he got, mesas seemed to pop up as if pushed from below, red sides steep but with a dusting of greenery. And the sky was a backdrop—startling blue filled with mound upon mound of cumulus clouds.

The interstate was fast. Eighteen-wheelers, piggyback transports, and campers crowded almost bumper to bumper, but no one was doing under eighty. At least there was a break in the weather. By the time he had picked up Highway 53 out of Grants, the temperature dipped to a respectable ninety-four and continued to drop as he entered the sparsely wooded Cibola National Forest. It seemed to qualify as a "forest" only in spots where pines, juniper, piñon, or desert cyprus spread thickly to block the sun. But these clumps were randomly spaced. Many of the two-story pine's hovered by the side of the road without a companion.

The temperature fell to an almost brisk seventy-three as he crossed the Continental Divide and continued to climb. The rocky edifice of El Morrow loomed in the distance vaulting some two hundred feet straight up from the fields. Some day he'd visit the information booth and view the signatures of Spanish explorers from the 1600's, but not today.

He was looking for a boarding house about five miles from the village, and rounding a curve, he abruptly braked. There it was. This had to be it, but the boarding house looked out of place—a big rambling Victorian with a wraparound screened porch whose bric-a-brac in salmon and yellow stood out against the sage green of its clapboard sides. The paint job was fresh. They might not be his choice of colors, but the house looked cared for. He pulled up at the end of the drive and sat a moment.

Maybe it was the surroundings that threw him. Someone had carved a niche out of the woods some two hundred feet from the highway and to the right of the house was a trading post and convenience store, behind that and almost hidden in the trees was a small mobile home with attached shed. It was a miniature community about five miles from the reservation proper.

He slipped the pickup into gear and eased his way towards the house. When he had agreed to take this position with Indian Health Service, someone in Albuquerque had suggested his rooming at Hannah Rawlings'. He might have preferred living closer in but, for now, it would do. He'd have plenty of time to make a move later.

He parked the truck in front of a brick path that led to the front porch, but it was difficult to tell front from back because of the darkness of the screening—yards of grayness that loomed above him. A scruffy yellow lab lumbered to his feet from under a large cottonwood behind the trading post, took a look and sprawled out on his side again. Must have decided it'd take too much energy to make friends, Ben thought.

The place looked deserted. Yet, he had the oddest feeling that he was being watched as he stepped from the truck and started up the walk. From the porch? He couldn't tell. Surely Hannah wasn't going to be the type of little old person who spied on her borders. Nonetheless, it was difficult to suppress a shiver. His grandmother would say someone had walked on his grave.

"You must be Dr. Pecos." The screened door whined open, and the closeness of the voice startled him.

"Yes. Hannah Rawlings?"

The woman stepped through the door and stood on the top step. At first, Ben thought she was an albino, silver-blond hair, eyebrows and eyelashes almost too light to show up against pale skin; her body, neck to wrists to ankles, covered by a cotton dress. But the eyes were blue, an icy, deep azure, and he thought of the puppy he'd wanted to keep, but his uncle had looked into those same eyes and called it a "chicken killer."

And she didn't seem to be embarrassed by staring at him openly, a hand shading those penetrating eyes. She loomed above him blocking the door. He felt awkward, but he had started to take another step up, holding out his hand when suddenly something grabbed his ankle throwing him off balance.

Ben jerked forward, arms flailing in the air before he landed hard—the palms of both hands stung from striking the top step's edge. His right shinbone smarted with the promise of a bruise. It had happened lightning fast. The rough hand that had thrown him still grasped his ankle—a hand that had shot out from between the slats at the back of the steps and belonged to someone hiding under the porch.

All Ben could see were creased, suntanned fingers, dark brown with nails bitten to expose a soft pink cuticle streaked with dirt. The stubby fingers and square palm connected to a thick, sturdy wrist. Still pinioned, Ben squatted to see its owner and found himself eye to eye with a troll. At least that was the first word that came to mind. Scabs dotted the hairline of his shaved head and freckles melded in patches to give him spotty color on his cheeks and across his nose. It took very little imagination to think of a creature who lived under bridges and probably porches; a creature to scare children, who had done a pretty good job of doing just that to him.

He stared, and the crouched owner of a slack jaw and bland expression didn't flinch. Just returned his stare, then said, "My toad gone. He there. No there now.'' The voice, stilted and singsongy, had the whisper of a lisp.

Ben looked at the step. What was he talking about? What toad? It must be ''gone'' because he didn't see anything. Ben had expected to see a child under the porch, but the pair of watery blue eyes that stared back at him from the darkness belonged to a much bigger individual. This boy is almost grown, he thought. He's big enough for serious harm if he decided to do more than trip people on the steps.

Suddenly, the boy stuck his other hand through the slats, and opened his fist to show a perfectly carved toad fetish in amber.

''That's a handsome fellow. You better be careful or he might try to escape again,'' Ben said.

This time there were giggles, and Ben felt the pressure on his ankle release.

''Harold, this is Dr. Pecos. Can you come out and say hello?'' She waited a moment then added, ''My son is shy.''

. Son? This hunched figure under the porch belongs to the landlady? The only thing they seemed to have in common were those arresting blue eyes. How odd that there were no excuses, no apologies for Ben's fall—just a simple he's ''shy.'' Ben waited but thought any further exchanges with Harold probably wouldn't occur any time soon.

''Harold is a special child. He won't bother you. He's just curious.'' Hannah turned abruptly and motioned for Ben to follow.

The hallway was cool. That was one thing the porch did— besides provide Harold with a hiding place—keep the house comfortable in the summer. Ben didn't even hear the sound of a swamp cooler.

''Your rooms are on the first floor at the back behind the kitchen.''

Ben wasn't certain that a reply was necessary; he just followed her. But strangely, Hannah had suddenly become talkative and went on without his offering any encouragement.

''I don't know what you were expecting. I suppose you're used to reservations and all. This one's no different. My husband's family came out here in 1912 and kept a trading post going through wars and a depression. Well, here's your place. Those double doors open onto the porch. Kinda gives you extra living space. Private bath…'' She'd stopped to twist an antique brass doorknob that reluctantly turned. ''There's politics in the village and at the clinic. It's never easy for a newcomer. But, then, that shouldn't be a surprise.'' She stepped aside so that he could see the bathroom but not before she had given him another of those thoughtful, sizing-up kind of stares. ''You don't look like someone who's going to have a problem getting along.'' And she smiled, then looked away. The smile almost made her pretty, Ben noticed. Softened the point to her chin, kept her face from seeming so gaunt.

''Oh, I almost forgot. You've been getting mail here for the past week. I'll be right back.''

The quiet allowed him to look around. The first room was a sitting room. A couple bookcases and it would become a study. The room beyond was dominated by a four poster bed with thigh-thick posts in dark walnut. The matching dresser was equally imposing.

''What do you think?''

He hadn't heard Hannah return. ''It'll do fine.'' He absently rubbed his shin.

''Mornings you want to join us for breakfast, just give a holler the night before.''

Ben had no idea who ''us'' might be—Harold and a pocketful of toads, maybe.

''Thanks.''

''Don't mention it.'' She handed him a packet of mail neatly trussed with a rubber band and pulled the door shut behind her.

He started to toss the mail on a table but the letter on top stopped him. He extracted it, looked at the return address but made no move to open it. A breeze pushed through the porch screen bringing the scent of honeysuckle, and he walked out to view his ''extra living space,'' the letter still in his hand.

The truth was he didn't want to know what was inside. Or maybe he was afraid what he found himself hoping the letter would say wouldn't be what he'd find. It had been four years since he'd heard from Julie. That was a lot of time—growing up and apart. This was silly, stupid even. Abruptly, he tore away the flap. The note was brief. She was spending some time in Santa Fe on assignment, a series for *Good Morning America* on Native American symbols. She'd tried to reach him at school to get names of Pueblo people she could interview and found out he'd graduated and was moving back, that he'd be in New Mexico by the time she got there. Did he believe in coincidence? Could he call her? She was staying at the La Fonda on the plaza. Maybe they could get together.

Ben checked the postmark. She'd be arriving tomorrow, a week after she'd written the note. He pulled up a wicker armchair and sat facing the panoramic view of the woods but couldn't keep Julie's face from floating across his vision—red hair, freckles, dark brown eyes that crinkled at the corners when she concentrated.

Did he still care? Yes. Had he had a serious relationship since she left four years ago? No. But then school saw to that. So what were his feelings? Wasn't he sitting here trying to ignore the excitement that had leaped up unexpectedly when he saw her handwriting? An excitement that he didn't trust, maybe was afraid to? Would he call? And if he did, what did he expect would happen?

"Join us for dinner?" Hannah's paleness grayed through the screen as she peered up at him, her face dwarfed by a floppy, wide-brimmed, cloth hat. He hadn't noticed before, but she appeared to be standing in a garden just beyond the porch.

"Yes. Thanks."

"Six-thirty, then."

He watched her go back to picking leaves of lettuce and placing them in a colander. All of a sudden, company sounded great. He folded the note and put it in his pocket.

He shouldn't have worried about missing dinner because someone, probably Harold, struck a gong with enough vigor to wake the dead. Ben had finished moving in, unloaded the boxes of books from the truck, left the hot plate boxed after reading the list of "don'ts" posted on the bathroom door, hung his clothes in the closet, and placed the storyteller on the faux mantle. Home. His life had a "just add water and stir" quality. And he was still a long way from anything permanent.

With a prick of conscience he thought that that was why Julie wasn't with him or he with her. They were two strong-willed individuals who had put careers first. But he was going to be thirty-one in August. Did that make a difference? Was it time to think differently?

He followed the sound of talking and found the dining room. No one among the twenty-odd people was seated yet. Harold towered behind what was evidently "his place," folding and unfolding his arms, his gangly body almost too much for him to control. Probably had just gone through a growth-spurt and was relearning control, Ben thought.

Harold was the bumbling, beefy sort. An oversized tee shirt, the football insignia now unreadable from many washings, covered but didn't disguise a massive set of shoulders—even rounded as they were and sloped forward. His head and neck pushed away and out and gave him a stooped look—a turtle poking out from its shell frozen in bland inquisitiveness, red-rimmed eyes blinking repeatedly.

The shaved head added to the turtle image, but Ben supposed exposed skin was easier to take care of. Tufts of straw-colored stubble popped up between scabby sores only to be glued flat by a yellow, probably medicating, salve. There was every possibility that a recent infection caused the broken skin. He should wear a stocking cap, Ben thought, at least, at the table. As if he knew Ben was thinking about him, Harold made some attempt to wave, but then Ben guessed he had been wrong when Harold's other arm shot out from his body before falling back to dangle by his side.

Two plank picnic tables had been pushed together end-to-end, their knotty-pine roughness sanded and varnished to a mirror slickness. No tablecloth or place mats diminished the shine. A large vase of orange and pink zinnias sat on a doily in the middle of each table. Cutlery was wrapped in a napkin and bundled on a tray at the end of the second table next to a stack of plates. Only Harold had dinnerware in place—the speckled white on blue, deep dish enamel-on-tin plate and squat cup that made one think of going camping.

Hannah, looking flushed from the heat of the kitchen, motioned everyone to sit. At a distance she looked like a teenager, Ben thought, decidedly pretty with the hint of rosy cheeks and damp hair curling around her face.

"I'll hand off things from this corner. Help yourselves across the table." Hannah left a pitcher of ice water and returned to the kitchen.

Ben copied the line in front of him, picking up a place service before he sat down. Ben was beginning to see why Harold was seated at what would be the end of the food line. Long before the heaping dishes and platters reached him he was banging his cup on the table and no matter what was left, he dumped it all on his plate and mashed and stirred until potatoes and roast and gravy and lime Jell-O salad melded into one mass. Ben felt a little guilty that he was glad to be sitting at the first table.

Most of the people in the room seemed to be part of Hannah's bed-and-breakfast trade, travelers passing through after a day or two on the reservation taking advantage of what was supposed to be the best home-cooked meal within miles. He'd seen a bus parked alongside the trading post. But some of the people probably boarded there, too. It was hard to tell. They all had that madras-bright, too-new jeans look of well-heeled transients. Some of the group exposed knobby bent knees and the bluing of varicose veins with Bermuda shorts. But it was the men's argyles, socks with cuffs pulled straight up, and worn with sandals that gave the group that "tourist" flavor.

"So, you're a psychologist?" The questioner was a seventyish woman who sat next to him.

"Yes." Ben handed off the plate of rolls covered with a red checkered cloth.

"It seems so strange to me, I mean, that you would even need to be out here. I can't think that Indians would have the same problems that the rest of us have. And wouldn't they prefer to have their own people cast spells, exorcise their demons—or whatever they do?'' Reaching for the salt, the elderly woman leaned across Ben. "A handsome young man like you should work where there's some wife material—not hide away out here in nowhere land among strangers.''

"Ben is Indian." This from Hannah as she began filling glasses with iced tea. "His people live east of here.''

"I'm sorry. I didn't mean…it's just that you don't look very…your skin isn't as dark as mine." The elderly woman seemed truly flustered as she put a tanned arm next to his.

"My father was Anglo." Ben left out the "probably"; that would only compound the confusion. Instead, he gave her an all-is-forgiven smile and geared up to discuss problems shared by both populations. Public relations. Isn't that what his adviser would call it, a little PR to inform the masses?

Dinner was pleasant enough. He'd been popular. There were curious questions, not malicious just an honest quest for knowledge. Hannah announced a break of forty-five minutes before dessert and coffee. Some left the table to smoke, dragging chairs into a semicircle on the screened-in porch. But all promised to return for fresh-baked cherry cobbler.

Ben watched as Harold carried his plate to the kitchen, then didn't return. The boy was a puzzle. Or should he say man? Ben thought he'd be over six foot if he stood straight. That was a pretty big "boy"—only an inch or two shorter than Ben. Clinical curiosity on his part, Ben thought, but he might question Hannah sometime, get a little background when the time seemed right. Ben picked up his own plate and pushed through the double doors that opened off the dining area.

The kitchen was one of those farm-big rooms with a commercial stove and oven in one corner next to an industrial-sized refrigerator. There was an oak island in the center with four high-backed stools and an old-fashioned round table in an alcove or breakfast nook surrounded by windows that faced the forest from the back of the room. The Indian man eating at the table was someone Ben hadn't seen before. In his forties somewhere, maybe fifties, it was hard to tell; but he was handsome with high cheekbones and an angular nose. One of those who would take on the look of a venerable elder early in life.

Hannah was busy spooning cobbler into rainbow-hued dishes on the counter next to the sink.

"Salvador, I want you to meet someone. This is Ben Pecos. He's going to be working at the clinic. He works with crazy people. Has he come to the right place, or what?" Hannah gave a short laugh, almost sounded exasperated, Ben thought. Should he say something, soften her description of his work? He looked towards the table. The man didn't actually look up, just bobbed his head and reached for a bowl of mashed potatoes. Because of her slightly raised voice, Ben thought the man might be deaf.

"Shy." Hannah gestured toward the man. "Won't talk unless he absolutely has to. And he hates it when I won't call him Sal. But he knows I abhor nicknames." Hannah took a swipe at a strand of hair that had escaped the rubber band at the nape of her neck and continued to talk like Sal wasn't there but loud enough so that he couldn't miss a word. "He embarrassed me this morning, ran out of the trading post like something bit him. And what was I to do? Try to explain some crotchety old Indian to a busload of tourists?"

Ben couldn't tell if this was playful goading by two old friends or something more serious. Was Hannah upset? He wasn't going to get the chance to find out because the man rose, put two slabs of roast beef between the halves of a hard roll and left by the back door. Ben watched as he disappeared into the dusk.

"You'll get used to him. Or him to you." Hannah was setting bowls of cobbler onto two large metal serving trays. "He helps out around here. Harold considers him his best friend."

Well, that was in the man's favor. Harold probably didn't have a lot of friends or male role models. Ben helped Hannah clear the dishes from the dining room table and load the dessert trays. He filled the coffee maker with fresh grounds and added water before he carried cups, saucers and spoons to a sideboard.

He didn't mind helping. And Hannah could use it. She seemed genuinely touched that he'd offer.

Eventually, somewhere from the hall the gong summoned everyone back for the last course. It wasn't any less loud the second time, Ben noted as the sound hummed in his ears.

Everyone seemed relaxed and continued chatting and milling around the large room with the stone fireplace at one end for another ten minutes until Hannah motioned for them to return to the table. Each place now had clean salad forks and spoons.

"Where's Bernard?" A small elderly woman with blue-white hair seemed reluctant to take her place at the table.

"In the john, probably," a man offered as he pulled out a chair across the table from her.

The woman sat down next to Ben but seemed reluctant to start without Bernard. "He was out petting that dog. He misses our little Rocky. At home we have a Yorkshire terrier, just the cutest bit of a thing. The two of them do everything together. Could you check in the bathroom? He's probably washing his hands." She peevishly pleaded with the man. "He's been gone over fifteen minutes."

Was this what it was like when you got older? Not letting each other out of your sight? Each worried that something might happen? Ben wondered.

"Aw, Delores, give it a rest. Maybe he's hiding from you."

Only the men found this hilariously funny.

"It's not funny. He's been diagnosed with…with…" She broke down in sobs.

Ben guessed that she was going to say Alzheimer's.

"I'll go." Ben surprised himself. He knew he was reacting to the stress of the elderly woman, but the man across the table struck him as needlessly unkind. He pushed back from the table. The elderly woman whispered, "Thank you," then placed a saucer over his cobbler to keep it warm. Hopefully, it wouldn't take long to find the errant Bernard.

The bathrooms were in the hall about halfway between the front door and his rooms. He could see before he got to it that the door of the men's was standing open. And there was Harold with toilet paper stuck to his hand and his fly open.

"Hello, Harold. Maybe we should wash those hands before you go back for dessert." Ben turned Harold towards the sink and turned on the tap. "Let's use some soap on these guys." Ben lathered up the heart-shaped guest bar and handed it to Harold before he rinsed his own hands. "Better not catch a chill." Ben pointed to Harold's fly and noticed the drying spots on the crotch of his chinos. It would be a challenge to have a child like this.

"Keep lizard warm." Harold zipped up, then patted his crotch before drying his hands so that two new stains stood out sharply—one stretching almost to his knee.

Ben smiled and patted him on the shoulder. "Better hurry. Someone just might eat your cherry cobbler."

Ben stepped back into the hall. A quick look up, then down confirmed that no one else was there, so he headed for the front door. Should he check the bus? Maybe the man had gone back to get something. The hydraulic door was open, and Ben stepped up into the passenger well beside the driver's area. He stood a moment checking the seats. Nothing. No one was in the bus, but to make certain, Ben quickly walked the length of the aisle before hopping back down onto the driveway. What next?

Dusk made it difficult to see clearly. With any luck the old duffer was back by now. He had just turned towards the house when he thought he saw movement by the trailer. He paused. Maybe he was mistaken. He didn't see anything now. But it wouldn't hurt to check. Ben waited another moment, then started in that direction, breaking into a trot to cover the fifty or so yards quickly.

The trailer was dark and other than a light breeze and the chirping of what was probably frogs, there was no sound. Then he heard it, a faint cry for help. Ben sprinted around the front of the trailer and almost tripped over the old man sitting on the ground hunched over a body.

"Bernard?" Ben squatted beside him. There was no indication that he recognized his name. "Let me take a look at your friend."

Ben eased the body onto its back. At first, Ben thought it was the man in the kitchen, Sal something-or-other. Had Hannah given a last name? The yard light in back of the trading post did little to clearly illuminate the area, but the man was dressed like Sal, white shirt and stiff jeans. They would both be about the same height, dark-skinned—only this man was probably a Middle Easterner. Yet, it was odd. The corpse was stiff as a board, dead long enough for rigor mortis to have set in.

He squatted to peer at the man's face. The bruising was apparent even in bad light. Then Ben jerked upright and gasped. He swallowed a couple times before squatting again beside the body and continued to stare at the top of the man's head. There was no skin across the frontal lobe. A chunk as big as a man's fist had been ripped away—no, cut away—this was not the work of an animal. The skin had been pulled forward, separated from the bone, then sliced along the hairline. The man had been scalped.

Blood oozed from the wound in a solitary trickle above his ear. The scalping hadn't killed him. The cut was fresh, probably done within the hour. If Ben's guess was right, some twenty-four hours after death. A brownish stain down the front of the man's shirt suggested a stab wound.

"I don't think he's moving." Bernard leaned over Ben's shoulder. "What should we do?"

Ben rose and guided Bernard away from the body. "We need to get back inside and call the police."

THE TRIBAL POLICE were prompt. They were the closest—coming out the five miles from the village. Law enforcement out here was more about helping those who needed help and worrying about jurisdictions later, Ben thought. That could be sorted out when it was determined if there had been a murder and where it might have occurred. Right now there was just a body with a chunk of scalp missing. And if it could be proved that there had been no foul play, wasn't it still against some law to deface the dead? Ben wasn't sure.

Hannah had gathered everyone in what she called "the parlor." An old-fashioned word but one that suited the big room that held a grand piano in one corner against a backdrop of oval walnut frames circling photos of stiff, bearded men standing beside women in long black dresses. Two couples stood in front of a one-room building with Trading Post written across a five-foot-high marquee—evidence that the Rawlings had been there for some time.

"I know how upsetting this must be," a young tribal policeman was saying. "It is very unusual for a crime to happen this close to our reservation, especially a death with such unusual circumstances."

They had been waiting over an hour in the stuffy parlor. Hannah had offered seconds on cobbler but there were no takers. And now the cop was saying that a crime had been committed. Ben didn't find this very reassuring. The officer was speaking to a roomful of pretty spooked tourists—some of whom probably had preconceived ideas about Indians in the first place and didn't need a scalping to verify them.

But the cop made a nice appearance. His thick black hair was trimmed razor-smooth almost to the occipital with only the front long enough to stand upright. The tan uniform was neat, starched and pressed with perfect trouser pleats. But there was the beginning of a slight roll above the belt, that telltale bulge that hints of a too sedentary life of fast foods. The real badge of most law enforcement officers, Ben thought, unless they were careful.

"My partner will take statements from each of you. This is strictly routine. Give your name, address—yes, where you can be reached after the tour—and a brief accounting of where you were during the break between dinner and dessert. I want to know if anyone saw anything—even if you think if can't be helpful, let us be the judge. I promise this won't take long. I thank each of you for your cooperation."

Even amid the obvious distress, the young man was thoughtful and exacting. He was young enough, looked like mid-twenties, to have gone for training off the res. Ben thought he'd probably had a dose of Psych 101.

But he didn't seem to be as gentle with the morose Sal, who remained in the kitchen and made the young interrogator go to him.

"You the new Doc?" Ben walked beside the officer down the hall.

"News gets around fast."

"Hey, it's the res. I'm Tommy Spottedhorse. Sorry this had to be the first impression of your new home."

"Spottedhorse?" Odd name for this part of the country, Ben thought.

"Mom was a rodeo groupie. About the time I came along, she split with her bronc rider but tossed his name my way."

The grin was genuine. Ben knew he was going to like this man.

"Were you telling the truth in there a minute ago about how this sort of thing doesn't happen very often out here?"

"Yeah. First homicide this close to the res since I was in the mission school." He paused. "Just in case you were going to say something smart, that's been a year or two. I'm twenty-four." He grinned.

"But homicide? Are you saying the man was killed where we found him?"

"No, couldn't find any evidence of that. It looks like he was killed somewhere else and the body was stuffed under Sal's trailer. About the only thing I could tell for sure tonight is that the body has been lying face down for at least twenty-four hours. *Livor mortis*. It accounts for all the discoloration in the face. Cells break down, die off and blood settles to the side of the body against a hard surface."

Ben was impressed.

"I guess the question is how did one person drag the body out from under the trailer and leave it where the tourist found it. It wouldn't have been easy."

"You think two people were involved?"

Tommy shrugged his shoulders, "After you." Then he pushed the kitchen door open and followed Ben into the room.

Sal sat at the oak table and didn't look up.

Tommy took a chair facing Sal and motioned for Ben to join them.

"I'd like to question the two of you together—establish time of discovery. Sal, I need to know your whereabouts when the tourist was calling for help. Ben, how 'bout you starting."

Ben retold his part of searching for the tourist's husband, of thinking he saw something or someone move by the trailer, of hearing a cry for help and going to investigate, and finding the tourist bending over the body.

"And, Sal, where were you during this time?"

At first Ben thought Sal wasn't going to answer. But even if it took awhile, Tommy wouldn't break the silence. It was the Indian way. Sal was an elder, maybe a relative on his mother's side. It would be difficult policing the place where you grew up.

"In the trailer."

"Tell me what you heard."

This time instead of answering, Sal took his hearing aid out of his pocket, showed it to Tommy, then slipped it back into his shirt.

"Hearing aid not in," Tommy interpreted and made a note on his pad.

"Let's start with the discovery of the body, Ahmed's body. Can you help me out, Sal, with why the body of the trader was behind your trailer?"

Still staring at the tabletop, Sal shook his head.

"For that matter, can you give me a reason why the tourist was out there? Had you ever seen this man before? Or his wife?" Ben thought Sal flinched. "Let's see," Tommy consulted his pad, "someone reported that you had been rude to the wife earlier in the day. That so?"

"She wanted a rabbit."

"I see."

Ben didn't, but he knew enough to question Tommy later and not show his ignorance now.

"Let's go back to Ahmed. What kind of relationship did you have with him? He ever buy your work?"

"Sometimes. Not for a while."

"When was the last time you saw him?"

Now, Ben knew it wasn't his imagination, Sal blanched and looked away. He was pretty sure Tommy noticed Sal's reaction, too.

"Maybe two weeks."

"And maybe not?"

"I don't remember."

"It might help you to work on that memory of yours. I think it's safe to say after a preliminary investigation, the tourist simply discovered the body by accident. There is no indication that he was involved other than that. We have no idea why he was wandering around behind your trailer, but it's been reported that his thinking may not always be clear. Ahmed, however, is a different story. Here we have a clear case of murder—murder and disfigurement by removal of hair and skin covering the man's frontal lobe."

It would be easier to just say scalping, Ben thought. But Tommy already had a penchant for the legalese required in most court reports.

"I don't know how you figure in all this, Sal—or even if you do. I just don't want you disappearing. We clear on that?"

Sal continued to look at the floor but reluctantly nodded.

"While we're here, we probably need to take a look around. I'd like to check the trailer and the shed out behind."

If he found evidence would the search be legal? Ben's train of thought was interrupted by an emphatic, "No." This time Sal was visibly upset.

"What do you mean, no? What are you so afraid I'll find? What do you keep in that old shed anyway?"

"Tools. Some carvings. Not much of value to anyone but me."

"It won't hurt to take a peek. I don't want any more bodies showing up."

"No need. I looked. Everything was okay."

"It won't take us a minute. We'll just take a quick inventory. Maybe we'll find an old knife. Something about the size that got poked into Ahmed in the first place."

Sal was anxious, more than edgy, Ben thought. He watched him play with a thread sticking up from his cuff. Finally, wetting thumb and forefinger, he curled it back to lie flat.

"Something I noticed that might be important…"

Tommy focused his attention on Ben. With annoyance? Ben thought there was just a shade of something for letting Sal off the hook, diverting the discussion.

"What's that?"

"You know at first I thought the dead man was Mr. Zuni. I mean they look somewhat alike. The trader was wearing a white shirt and jeans same as Mr. Zuni is now; they're approximately the same height, hair long, coloring just a shade different. It could be that—"

"Anyone out gunning for you, Sal? That you know of, that is?" Tommy swung abruptly back to Sal.

Sal shrugged, not a yes, not a no and returned to pick at his sleeve.

Tommy laughed. "Maybe, you put the horns on someone."

This Ben recognized as the old way of saying cuckolded, but it was difficult to imagine this dark slight man sneaking around with anyone's wife.

"One thing seems sure, you had a crowd of Peeping Toms out there tonight. Footprints all over the place under the trailer windows—front and back. Two sets of prints are pretty clear. One matches the victim, and if that coating of dirt on your ropers is any indication, I'd bet one set is yours. What are the chances that if you rethink this a little bit, you'll remember that you were out there tonight after all?"

Sal sat stone-faced, even the fraying cuff was forgotten. "I've told you all I know."

"For some reason, I'm not real sure about that." Tommy

reached in his pocket. "This yours?" Tommy held a heavy padlock in his hand. "Twisted off the door to that shed, most likely. I'm surprised you didn't see it earlier."

Sal looked up quickly and reached for the lock. There was real alarm in his eyes, Ben thought.

"I better check my tools."

No, "Are we finished?" or, "Can I go now?" Sal simply pushed back from the table and stood, then rushed out the door.

"I thought you said you'd already checked. Maybe you need some help?" Tommy yelled after him, but he was grinning. In all likelihood Tommy had already been in the shed but wanted to bait him, Ben decided. "Don't go too far away in case I need to find you." But it was doubtful Sal had heard as the screen door banged behind him.

Tommy sat at the table opposite Ben, made another notation in his notebook, then leaned back.

"I'm not sure how Sal figures in all this. It's tough to think he'd kill someone. I've known him since I was a child. It's more likely someone was trying to set him up—dump the body by his trailer, implicate him. But why? Still, I have to keep an open mind. Sometimes that's the hardest part about being a cop—in your home territory." Tommy ran a hand through his bristlestraight hair. "You know? 'Bout the worst thing Sal does is bang the landlady once in a while."

"The landlady?" That was a shock. Ben was trying to imagine Hannah and Sal in the throes of passion. It was difficult.

"So they say. But you know how people talk. Sal moved out here to the trading post shortly after her old man died." Tommy was flipping through the pages of his notepad. He stopped, read for a moment, then looked up. "Tell me what you know about .22?"

"Twenty-two?"

Tommy explained Harold's nickname then pressed on, "I guess I'm wondering if this kind of bizarre killing, the scalping and all, could have been done by a kid like .22." Tommy paused to make a circular motion with his index finger pointed at his head. "He could have dragged the body from under the trailer. He's big enough to wrestle a grizzly."

"True. But what reason would he have?" Ben thought of being tripped on the steps. That was a childish prank, not murder. He didn't see Harold as malicious. He was more of a gentle giant.

"I dunno, crazy or something, maybe he wouldn't need one. Isn't that your specialty?"

"Are you asking me for a diagnosis?"

"Naw, not really. Just thinking out loud." Tommy stood. "If I have any more questions, I'll catch you at the clinic. I'm sure you'll hear from me."

It was almost midnight before Tommy and the other officer pulled out. Understandably, the busload of tourists had left first. They would spend a couple nights in Gallup. The body of the trader was taken by hospital van to the Office of Medical Investigation in Albuquerque. What a puzzle. A scalping. The brutality of it was numbing.

SAL SAT AT THE fold-down table in his trailer. He'd made instant coffee with tap water but couldn't drink it. He watched as a glop of brackish-looking scum adhered itself to his spoon. He walked to the sink and poured the liquid down the drain, then swished water around the porcelain to make certain there were no leftover stains.

He should go to bed, but he wouldn't sleep, not after what had happened. Why hadn't he called Tommy last night? Or told him tonight that he'd seen Ahmed's body on the hood of his truck down by the river? Sal knew why—Hannah. She wouldn't want him to. It would raise too many questions. They had to be careful because of the amber. He might make the stuff, but she sold it. And that made both of them implicated in wrongdoing. And he couldn't do that to Hannah, take a chance on getting her in trouble.

And how could he explain that the body had somehow managed to follow him home? Wouldn't he have to have a pretty good explanation for that? And who would believe him when he said he knew for a fact that it was Atoshle? That he had seen the great *kachina* go past his window carrying the body... No, he wouldn't be believed. Silence was better, safer.

"YOU KNOW IN the old days they even had a scalp house." Hannah sat across from Ben at the kitchen table. The clock in the hall had just struck twelve. She'd offered him a cup of tea that tasted like mint. They were both too wide-awake to go to bed.

"A what?" Ben thought he hadn't heard her correctly.

"It's true. There was a guardian, a scalp chief, and an elaborate ceremony when an enemy scalp was brought back to the village."

"Was that often?"

"Maybe not too often, but I remember my husband's father talking about it. Seems there was a certain amount of sexual license practiced during the celebration. I was always intrigued." One corner of Hannah's mouth turned up in a wry smile.

It was difficult to think of this angular woman as being interested in sex; she seemed so "contained," Ben thought, but what had Tommy said about Sal?

"The scalp was placed on a pole and dances were held round-the-clock," Hannah continued. "Later the scalp would be washed. But this part of the ritual had to be done at a place where the water wouldn't flow back into a stream that people might drink from. Contamination with the dead brings death, as you probably know."

She was looking at him expectantly. Was this a good time to confess about not being very Indian? Not knowing the ceremonies of his own tribe, let alone others. Ben could hear the admonishments of his grandmother.

"After watching you with the deceased earlier, I don't think you believe that way." Hannah poured milk into her tea and offered him the plastic pitcher.

"I was adopted at four by Mormons. I only spent summers on the reservation."

"Figures."

Ben didn't ask her what she meant. He still wasn't at ease with this woman.

"Too bad the murder had to be discovered here," Ben said.

"Oh, I don't know. Maybe, I should have tee shirts made. First excitement we've had in a while."

Was she being sarcastic? Ben didn't know. It was hard to figure her. Could she really be thinking of capitalizing on this tragedy? He pushed back from the table. Tomorrow was his first day at work. He needed some rest.

"I'll skip breakfast."

Hannah nodded but didn't look up. She was staring fixedly in front of her, lost in thought as she took small sips of tea. The scent of mint floated around her. Some of the bunches of dried herbs hanging from the ceiling must also be mint, Ben thought. The odor was so pungent.

Ben continued out into the hall that led to his room. He had almost passed the staircase before he saw Harold huddled, arms around the banister.

"Are you okay?"

"I don't do." The young man was visibly shaken. His eyes seemed to plead with Ben and fastened unblinking on Ben's face as he moved to sit beside Harold on the stairs. Harold's leg twitched spasmodically, gently thumping against the wood.

"What don't you do?"

Harold made a quick slicing cut with stiff, straight fingers across the top of his head.

"I know that."

"I go there."

What was he talking about? The police had been over this with Harold earlier in the evening, but it seemed like he had more to say.

"Did you see something?"

"You no tell?"

Ben found himself making a sign that vaguely resembled something he thought a scout would do.

"You come. We go find." And Harold stood looking at him expectantly.

Ben listened for Hannah in the kitchen. Shouldn't she be the one to handle this—whatever it was her son wanted? But she had turned on the tap at the kitchen sink. It ran for a while. Then there was nothing. No sound. He could see light coming from under the door and guessed she must be doing dishes.

Harold was tugging on his hand, pulling him towards the front door. It was too late to change players now. Harold dropped his hand once they had cleared the front steps. He ran ahead with the short choppy gait of someone neurologically impaired, but he still covered ground amazingly fast.

The full moon of a couple nights back had shrunk to a lop-sided globe, the right side falling away sharply. As Ben stumbled over the brick walk, he regretted not having a flashlight. Wherever they were going, Harold had been there before and had the advantage.

Before he reached the trailer, Harold slowed to a walk and approached from the front. Then he ducked his head under the metal awning over the wide window and looked in.

"Sleep." He tossed the word over his shoulder and continued to walk hurriedly towards the woods.

Ben assumed that he meant Sal. Maybe that's why he had the honor of being the escort.

Harold had plunged into the brush about one hundred feet to the west of the trailer and deli-mart, and Ben jogged to catch up. Harold was moving quickly, following some kind of path. Not one that was used often, Ben thought as he ducked a branch that had invaded the path's space. This was more like a trail someone had cut out years ago and didn't keep up.

The moon's light was filtered and severely limited by the tall pines—but only in spots. Just when he couldn't see a thing, the trees thinned to only a cluster of ten-foot piñons. Then sometimes nothing for several yards, just hard-packed sandy soil. Ben tried to estimate how far they'd come. He thought about a half mile, and Harold hadn't slowed even though Ben could hear his breath coming in raspy gulps. Then Harold stopped.

At first, Ben thought he was just trying to catch his breath as he slumped to the ground, and Ben squatted beside him.

But Harold started crawling forward towards a fallen log and pile of brush. He dug away rotting vegetation and pulled out a white sheet and then a mask—one of the wooden masks of the *shalako*. Ben looked at it closely. He wouldn't swear to it, but he thought it was a fake, clever, but not real. Yet, the eye slits were precisely carved, a black fringed material was tacked to the lower edge, the portion that would hide the neck. The wood was new, and even in this half-light the paint looked shiny— too bright and fresh. This mask had not been used in the winter ceremonies. The question was, what had it been used for?

"No more."

Harold had been rummaging around in the indentation under the log.

"Were there others?"

Harold looked puzzled. Had he not understood? Ben pointed to the mask and then to the hole.

"More?"

"Not now."

"More yesterday?"

Ben had no idea what word would stand for elapsed time. And for all he knew, Harold might visit the cache daily. But yesterday seemed to work because Harold held up four fingers, his thumb doubled back against his palm.

"Four more?"

Harold nodded and seemed pensive, then he pointed to the mask.

"He did."

It took Ben a moment to figure out what Harold was saying. "What did he do?"

Again, a stiff fingered slice at the hairline. There was no doubt, Harold was telling him that the fake *shalako* had scalped the trader.

"How do you know?"

"Me know."

Ben sat back on his heels. He'd run out of questions or more accurately, Harold had run out of answers. But he believed Harold. The boy was guileless and obviously disturbed by what had happened that evening.

"We need to get some sleep. Let's go back to the house now."

"Take?"

"We need to leave these here." Ben wrapped the mask in the sheet and placed it back in its hiding place. Tommy Spottedhorse needed to find it where they had found it. Not that the hiding place wasn't disturbed now. Harold's furious digging had probably erased any clues. But Ben felt uncomfortable removing evidence.

"You tell?"

Ben nodded. "I have to tell. Tomorrow I'll call Tommy Spottedhorse." Harold hesitated. He seemed uncertain about giving up his find. "It's the right thing to do," Ben said.

Reluctantly, with Ben's hand at his elbow, Harold started back towards the house.

THREE

THE FLAT-ROOFED, pale green, cement block building housed both the clinic and the hospital, taking up a good quarter block on the corner of Third and Riverbed. Recently, a covered walkway had been added to connect it with the senior center and civic auditorium. In the back and to the side, a four-car garage housed an ambulance, a fire truck and a snowplow. The last space contained a pickup with the tribal seal on its doors.

Ben parked on the west in a space marked staff and sat a moment contemplating his new place of work. It was more than a stopgap but less than a full-blown health care center. Indian Health Services strategically placed units like this at the edge of pueblos to fill immediate needs—broken bones, immunizations, prenatal care and short-term inpatient care such as stabilizing someone's diabetes—all problems that could be addressed in a twenty-bed hospital. Anyone needing sophisticated tests or long-term hospitalization would be sent to the modern, usually well-staffed research and medical complex in Gallup.

Ben would be the first psychologist to be in residence in Hawikuh. He was joining six doctors, five nurses, a caseworker, a lab technician, a pharmacist, secretary/receptionist, and three maintenance people. It wasn't like he'd be by himself, but he couldn't help thinking that after five more years of school, he was back in the sticks.

Dowa Yalanne, or Corn Mountain, loomed in his rear-view mirror. Majestic, commanding, its white-striated sides and wind-whipped pinnacles gave it an air of mystery. He couldn't fault the "sticks" for being ugly. The steep-sided mesas to the north and east warmed as he watched to a rich violet in the morning light. But the beauty of the countryside did little to assuage his feeling of being alone.

He thought he might be the first one in, but the woman behind the receptionist's desk could have spent the night. Her rumpled short-sleeved cotton blouse looked slept-in. She was almost hidden by a stack of folders, and she was pulling more from a bank of file cabinets along the wall.

"You're Ben something-or-other, the new shrink."

"Pecos."

"Yeah. I remember now. Are you Indian?" She had stopped her frenzied digging in the files to look at him.

"Supposed to be. How 'bout you?" Ben meant this as a joke since the woman's pumpkin-round face and brown skin assured a Pueblo heritage.

"Humph. Full-blood until my next period. You got enough blood to be registered somewhere?"

"Tewa."

Now she was leaning on the counter giving him her full attention. And after a once-over, she nodded her approval.

"You got any idea what you're in for?"

Ben was smiling, "That good, huh?" He was finding himself starting to like this straightforward, fortyish woman, graying black hair cut into a bob.

"I'm the caseworker. Only this week I'm the caseworker/receptionist/secretary 'cause Yellow Skin ran off another young girl who just accidentally cut him off in the middle of a phone conversation."

"Yellow Skin?"

"Clinic Director, Dr. Lee. You must have met him last night. He did the pre-limn on that poor trader found out at the trading post."

"I didn't get a chance to meet him."

"That figures. Amenities are not his strong suit. But you'll get to love the rest of us." This time the smile was sincere.

"Any idea where my office is?"

"They bumped maintenance and put you at the end of the hall, next to the back door. Here's a box of odds and ends. Pencils, pens, stapler… I'm Rose, holler if I can help."

Before he could say thank-you, Rose had turned back to opening and banging shut the file cabinets behind her, adding to the stack of folders on the counter. He followed her directions and carried his box of supplies down the hall.

The office was on the north side—probably why there was a space heater in the corner. He looked around. A gunmetal gray desk, a matching battered file cabinet which seemed empty but locked, two folding chairs, and a private phone were the room's only occupants. Sparse. Maybe he could come up with some artwork.

"Hope you weren't expecting anything plush. Welcome, I'm Dr. Leland Marcos, Dr. Lee to you." A smallish Filipino man stood in the door. So this was old "Yellow Skin." Ben found himself looking closely at him.

"The office is fine."

"Good. Young people expect too much nowadays. They want everything to be like television." He stepped into the room, looked around like he was taking inventory then turned back to Ben. "We tried mental health out here five years ago. It didn't take, too much resistance. Don't know why the tribe insisted we try again. 'Course, might be better with one of their own.'' Dr. Lee looked up át him with squinted eyes. ''Didn't I read that you're Pueblo? Tewa tribe?''

''Yes. My mother's people.''

''I see. Well, you'll need every break. It won't be easy.'' And he was gone, out the door, and down the hall in quick hurried steps.

Yellow Skin didn't waste time. No handshakes, ''see you later,'' help you settle in—in fact, he'd sounded skeptical about Ben's even being accepted.

''This program *will be* successful,'' Ben said to four empty walls.

''Gee, this isn't a good sign. I thought you were supposed to cure people who talk to themselves not model the behavior yourself.'' Rose laughed as she entered the room. ''Don't worry. He gets to everyone.'' She placed a half-dozen patient folders on the desk. ''Look these over. Maybe we can talk after lunch. This will give you some idea of what you're up against.''

''Thanks.''

''Don't mention it. Remember, you have friends.'' She pulled her eyes into a slant and pursed her lips so that her two front teeth showed—a close likeness of Yellow Skin. And then she left.

Ben picked up the phone and got a dial tone. That was promising. He'd called Tommy Spottedhorse from the house before he left. He told him what Harold had shown him last night and what he'd said about a masked person being the murderer. Ben promised him that Harold had agreed to take Tommy to where the mask was hidden. He'd check with Tommy later but now he needed to call Santa Fe—more accurately, call Julie at the La Fonda.

Was he surprised, disappointed, or simply hurt when the reservation desk clerk said she'd checked out? He'd gotten his hopes up. The clerk added that there was no message, and no forwarding address or phone number. Ben asked twice to make sure she had gone and wasn't out working. He had probably sounded foolish making the man repeat himself. Ben couldn't believe that there didn't seem to be any way to catch up with her. Maybe she'd try to get in touch with him again. That's about all he could hope for. And, yes, he had been looking forward to seeing her—more than he'd realized.

He settled back to look at the folders Rose had left. She could help him get started, suggest how it might be best to approach people, maybe even visit families with him. He wanted to build confidence. He wouldn't rush in. He'd begin with those suspected of having chronic mental disorders, throw in a few alcoholics and then hope his practice would fill with the less pressing—those with errant teens or wayward spouses—the ones who could meet him here during office hours.

By noon he was famished. When he suggested the Taco Train, a railway caboose disguised as a restaurant a block from the hospital, Rose wrinkled her nose.

"Ptomaine Trolley."

"Is that a joke or for real?"

She shrugged and snapped the top off of a Tupperware container. "I usually bring my own lunch. I have to watch the phones this week. We're going to try another sweet young thing for this job but not before the end of the month. Maybe the next one will last more than five days."

"I'd be glad to give you a break sometime."

"That'd be nice." Rose smiled up at him, full cheeks pushing her eyes into sparkling dark slits in brown skin. He felt a camaraderie, more than just a friendly face—this woman wanted him to succeed.

Ben walked out to the parking lot and the warmth of the day radiated around him. They hadn't spared the expense on asphalt. Someone even kept it freshly striped though he doubted that the fifty or so marked spaces would ever be filled.

He hadn't planned to go back to the boarding house for lunch, but he wasn't sure of his options. He'd take a chance that Hannah would have something on hand.

SAL HAD SLEPT IN. Not on purpose but because he'd tossed and turned getting twisted in the sheets, finally throwing the top sheet on the floor about four a.m., and all this activity had kept him awake—wide-awake for most of the night. But at least, Atoshle hadn't returned to admonish him for his sins. But, then, why should he? He had already done something far worse. The *kachina* had scalped a man, probably killed him, too.

He agreed with Hannah's new border. Sal had been the one the *kachina*, the murderer, sought. Even now, the skin on his neck prickled as he thought about it. Why had Atoshle brought the body to him if not in warning? To show him a death that so easily could have been his own.

But the padlock was broken off the shed's door. That was sure evidence that someone knew about the amber. Could this someone be the *kachina?* Could the *kachina* want to destroy his lab—keep him from making the amber, and keep him from selling?

He let the tap run a full minute before he filled a glass with water and drank. It was better that way—less sediment. Sometimes the wells could be a problem. He swirled the water around and around. It helped him think. He'd made some decisions that morning.

Just before dawn he'd gone up to the boarding house. He knew Hannah would be starting breakfast. Her greeting was cool.

"I didn't tell them anything," he said as he poured himself a cup of coffee. "But it doesn't make me seem so crazy finding a body by the river." He gave her a sideways glance.

There was no response. So he told her what he feared—about the trader being killed as a warning, about the dreams, about the ancients cursing everyone who had anything to do with the false amber—how they had sinned against nature. How he'd seen the *kachina* dump the body behind his trailer.

And still Hannah hadn't said anything, just continued to roll out biscuit dough, cut the inch-thick pad into circles and fill the tin baking sheets. Then, she broke the silence.

"Did you kill Ahmed?"

Sal was startled. How could she think that?

"No." He couldn't say more or the anger bubbling below the surface would spill over.

"I'm sorry. I know I should trust you. But under the circumstances... You understand, don't you?" She walked to the table to stand in front of him, then impulsively touched his cheek with a floured hand. "I'm afraid for my life, too. Have you ever stopped to think of that? It's true. I'm involved as much as you are. It could be my life next."

"I would never let that happen."

"But you aren't taking precautions. The notebook, for example—"

"I won't talk about the notebook."

"Okay. Then, do this for me. Move your work, it's too tempting where it is. The shed isn't safe. I have a better idea, something I've been working on for a while in case we needed it."

"Where can I go?" He thought the mischievous grin made her look impish, elfin, even. But he was intrigued. It was a good idea to move his things.

"Now don't ever think I don't care about you." Hannah tugged on his hand. "Follow me."

SHE LED HIM TO the pantry, switched on the light and showed him the trap door that lowered stairs to the floor below when she pulled a brass ring. The cellar was small, twelve by twenty feet, and smelled musty. Its walls were solid rock blasted out before the house was built over it. Generations had stored root vegetables, beets, turnips, potatoes, in the tin bins along the wall. They would even have kept butter and milk down here, Sal thought, and pumpkins and squash.

But the place wasn't going to be used for vegetables anymore—Hannah had set up a lab. Three rows of fluorescent lights hung from the ceiling, and a new aluminum workbench was pushed against one wall. It was cool with a hint of clamminess. The limestone walls felt slightly damp to the touch. Hannah showed him where there had been containers for ice—deep rectangles chipped out of the rock floor and lined with metal. One block supposedly kept for three days without refrigeration seventy years ago.

It wasn't ideal but, all in all, Sal felt better. Especially when after the biscuits were out of the oven, Hannah had helped him carry his equipment from the shed to the cellar. Under the protection of the graying light of dawn, they walked back and forth across the wide yard carrying boxes, some requiring the two of them together to lift or push forward. And then when they were finished, Sal went back to the trailer and slept.

So now at ten o'clock, he felt refreshed. He wouldn't have to worry about the shed. He'd continue to do his carving there. Dust and shavings would be kept out of the cellar even though Hannah had outfitted the underground room with circulating fans that would draw in fresh air and expel the stale, replacing all the air in the room every three to four hours.

He still had a few jars of live insects in the shed. Possibly, natural light was better for them, but he didn't know. He'd spend the rest of the morning weeding out the inferior specimens and transport the ones to be preserved to the cellar after dark.

He'd saved his pride and joy until last—the Jumping Sumac beetle. He'd amassed quite a good collection of them. The three-leaf variety of the low sumac bush was abnormally susceptible this year. His little colony sat on shelves along one wall in quart Mason jars. He held each to the light and then twisted the caps off and stuffed fresh sumac leaves inside.

He'd read about sumac—the anacardiaceous genus *Rhus,* cousin to mango, pistachio, and cashew trees, with its "pyramidal panicles of crimson drupes"—he'd had to have Hannah help him with that one. She said that all it meant was the berries were red and hung down like cherries. He'd memorized the English words and sometimes, like now, would play them over again in his head and wonder at their strangeness. "Pyramidal panicles..." for all his growing up on the reservation, he'd only needed to know which type of sumac was poisonous and which leaves to gather for tanning hides.

The larvae of the beetle were a different story. They had been a puzzle and difficult to work with. Sal had collected the tiny yellowish-green slimy worms and then had found them impossible to preserve. Any attempt to dry them did just the opposite—they'd turn to mush. One time he dehydrated several hundred in a solar convection tray only to find several hundred greasy spots when they were supposed to be done.

They were peculiar for other reasons. To the naked eye it looked like they wore hats. He studied them under a microscope but still couldn't figure out what they had on their heads. Some did, some didn't; but most of the time the majority of his catch had globs of something stuck right between their eyes. And then he ran across it in a book—they wore shit on their heads. Their own, the book presumed and went on to speculate that it was most likely a camouflage technique, some kind of protection from predators. And the only thing that kept running through his mind was the lecture by the forest ranger who said that everyone could learn from nature, that if we emulated nature, mankind would be better off.

It had become a private joke with Hannah. She'd say, "How you doing today, Salvador, you look a little peaked." And he'd say, "Oh, you know how it is when you carry shit on your head." He smiled. Maybe that was what was wrong with him now.

"My cousin back in Oklahoma collected lightning bugs as a kid. Don't think I've ever seen a grown man collect bugs."

Sal whirled around so fast the Mason jar slipped from his hands and landed with a thud on the dirt floor. But he had left the door to the shed wide open. He had nothing to hide and maybe Tommy Spottedhorse could see that.

"You feed these things?" Tommy picked a jar off of the shelf and held it at eye level.

"Yeah." Sal had regained his composure.

"I know there's got to be a good reason, but for the life of me, I can't figure out why you keep these things. You want to help me with that, Sal?"

"Bait. Fishing bait." Sal handed Tommy a pickle jar crammed with the beetles preserved in an alcohol solution. "Crappie can't resist. Bass and trout are about the same."

"You pulling my leg?" Tommy had stopped turning the jar

back and forth and now peered at him. Since Tommy had been known to wet a line now and then, this was a good test.

"No." Sal busied himself with straightening several jars of live beetles on the shelf.

"It seems like they're kinda small."

"It takes up to a half dozen on a hook. Supposedly when you cast them out, the impact of hitting the water makes their wings fan out. I think that's what the fish see."

"No shit?" Tommy looked at the pickled collection again turning the jar so that the beetles sloshed against each other. "Any money in this?"

"Keep me in six-packs 'til Christmas." Sal grinned. Since everyone knew that Sal had been on the wagon for almost twenty-five years, it was just another way of saying no.

"More like keep you off the streets and out of trouble—which isn't too bad, either." Tommy put the jar down. "You happen to see .22 around?"

Sal shook his head.

"Kid's supposed to show me something he found last night."

"Check the house."

"Did that. Miz Rawlings thought he might be with you. Oh well, I'll keep looking. Don't let the bedbugs bite." Tommy was almost out the door before he turned back. "What kind of bugs are those?"

"Beetles. Jumping Sumac beetles."

WHEN BEN DROVE UP to the boarding house a little after noon, he was surprised to find Tommy Spottedhorse leaning against the reservation patrol car, a bathtub shaped Caprice in white. But the only way Ben knew the car's color for certain was to check the roof—the rest hid beneath a generous dusting of reservation caliche, the hard-packed clay that made the backroads passable, unless it rained.

"Thought you promised .22 would take me on tour?"

Tommy sounded good-natured about it, but Ben was vaguely upset that Harold had promised, then didn't deliver. He started to say how sorry he was, but Tommy waved aside any apologies.

"I was smart enough to come about lunchtime, anyway. My mama didn't raise no dummies," Tommy added. "But I think I see another reason that coming out here was a good idea. Look at that."

Ben followed Tommy's nod. A young woman was taking suitcases out of the trunk of a car about thirty feet from them. The sun seemed to meld with the strawberry-blond hair piled on top of her head. The white, barebacked sundress showcased a tan and ended above the knees—considerably above the knees as she leaned into the trunk.

"That's heaven," Tommy murmured.

No, Ben thought, that's Julie and he took a full minute to let it sink in that here she was after four years. It was hard to believe—harder yet to keep from running over, taking her in his arms...and then what? He wasn't sure what the reception would be. And wasn't it always better to go slow?

"Maybe we should help her." Tommy was obviously eager to meet her. "You coming or not?" Ben waved him forward and watched as Tommy straightened his badge and tucked in his shirt before sauntering across the parking lot. Ben followed a few paces back.

"Hiding behind the law isn't going to work, Ben Pecos." Julie had closed the trunk and now leaned back against the car and watched the two of them approach. Tommy quizzically looked over his shoulder at Ben then stepped to one side.

"I called Santa Fe and found out you'd tried to reach me this morning. The clerk even said you sounded concerned." She stepped forward and took one of Ben's hands in hers, squeezed it and let it drop. But the gesture wasn't lost on Tommy, Ben noticed.

"You know if you hadn't called, I would have turned around at Grants."

"Hey, I didn't know you two knew each other." Tommy looked at Ben then back at Julie.

"Tommy Spottedhorse. Julie Conlin." Ben made the introductions then added, "Most recently of *Good Morning America,* right?"

"Wow. I knew it. I knew I recognized you." Tommy's enthusiasm seemed boundless. "My mom would love to meet you."

"I'm impressed. I'm only a fill-in on the show, but that will change in the fall. I'll have a regular spot highlighting Americana starting in September."

"How long can you stay?" Ben asked.

"Two weeks, a month, it depends. But I'm here with the show's blessing. This seems the logical place to gather background on Native American symbols. I'll start with fetishes."

Ben relaxed. Tommy's being there saved him from any awkwardness, any decision of whether to kiss her or just keep it neutral. Ben felt relieved when neutral won out. He wanted to give it some time. He needed to make certain that she was there because of him—not just for the show.

"Who's the Mia Farrow look-alike?"

Hannah waved from the porch.

"That's your landlady. Tommy, grab a bag and let's get some lunch."

It was just the three of them until .22 showed up for dessert. He seemed agitated and fidgeted with a bowl of ice cream, twirling the frozen lumps of vanilla and chocolate until he had produced a cool soup which he proceeded to slurp with a serving spoon. Hannah preferred to ignore this. Or so it seemed, Ben thought. Maybe over the years his behavior had become so commonplace, she simply didn't notice.

"We talk." Ben and Tommy had helped clear the table while Hannah showed Julie to her room and now .22 had cornered them in the kitchen.

"What do we need to talk about, Harold?" Ben asked.

"You call me .22."

"You didn't keep your part of the bargain, .22. You didn't show Officer Spottedhorse where we found the mask."

"It's gone."

"What's gone?" Tommy stood in front of .22 and seemed to be struggling to keep his voice even. "Can you show me?"

"No good."

"Let me decide that. I need to see where the mask was hidden." Tommy was clearly frustrated by the boy and turned to Ben. "Can you find the place again?"

"I think so. It was just off a path of some sort that starts behind the deli-mart."

"Do you want to come?" Ben watched as .22 seemed to consider the invitation then vigorously shook his head.

THE WOODS WERE cool and inviting in the daylight. A canopy of pines shaded them part of the way before opening onto bare rocky spots covered hit and miss with yellow button-round flowers. Under the trees the thick brush muffled the sound of their footsteps. They reached the log that marked the spot and Tommy uttered an expletive. There had been recent tampering—probably .22 trying to find the mask.

"I'm kicking myself that I didn't bring the stuff in last night. Guess I was thinking I'd be removing evidence—that you'd need to see it exactly like we found it."

Tommy didn't comment. He was on his hands and knees, one arm buried to the shoulder in the hole under the log. But when he sat back, he didn't have anything in his hand.

"Tell me again what you saw."

This time Ben described in detail the multicolored mask and piece of white material the size of a bedsheet—more than likely it was a bed sheet, if he remembered correctly, and had been used to transport the mask.

"No one has reported any artifacts missing." Tommy seemed to be talking to himself. "Every other year or so, someone tries to buy or steal ceremonial paraphernalia. But you said the mask seemed new?"

"I had that distinct feeling. It was less than a year old, probably. The cuts in the wood were rawlike, fresh and rough, and the painting was only fair. I'm not a good judge, but it struck me as a fake."

"And .22 said a person wearing a mask—the mask you found for sake of argument—did the scalping?" Tommy acknowledged Ben's nod. "He didn't happen to say he'd actually seen the scalping?"

"No. Not exactly. He just said that he knew that a masked person did it. Or something like that. It was a combination of gestures," Ben copied .22's slicing motion at the hairline, "and words. We're not talking a large vocabulary, so I could be mistaken."

"He wasn't much help when we interviewed him last night." Tommy kicked at a piece of rotten log with the toe of his boot. "You know my people believe the movement of a mask is an omen of death. It's maybe the most common hallucination. They think supernaturals do it, then put the blame on humans." Tommy looked over at Ben; the start of a grin played around his mouth. "Lucky you. You'll be treating this sort of thing soon. I hope you have heap strong medicine."

Ben fought a sinking feeling. There was so much to learn; it was so easy to take a wrong step.

"See this?" Tommy had stooped to pick up a few strands of some pliable vegetable matter at the base of the log. "Tobacco. It could have been left as an offering to supernaturals."

"Or someone, like .22, sat here and shredded a cigarette for no apparent reason."

"Guess it depends on how you see things." Tommy didn't look up. There was no clue as to how Tommy "saw" things. It was always difficult to figure the younger generations. Not all of them followed the old ways. Ben hoped he hadn't offended Tommy, but the young man appeared distracted, not angry.

"This mask thing bothers me. If it was real, this could have been its true hiding place. Masks are handled with great reverence. Usually, people are afraid to touch sacred objects."

"Outsiders wouldn't be."

"Like the trader, Ahmed. I was just thinking of that. Suppose he was dealing in stuff he shouldn't have been? That's a real good reason to get killed. If this was his cache, then it explains why we found his body nearby.''

"But if the mask is a fake?''

"Still doesn't rule out Ahmed being involved somehow. He could have sold copies. If the elders found out—''

"You're not saying they'd kill because of that.''

"No, today they'd handle a problem like that legally, go for restitution.'' Tommy looked pensive. "This isn't much to go on—testimony of a retarded kid and your description of a mask that's since disappeared.''

"What else do you have?'' Ben asked.

"That's about it, more or less zero. Everyone on the bus has an alibi, but frankly, I don't see a contingent from Ohio getting into scalping.'' He grinned ruefully at Ben. "You and Hannah were in the kitchen. Sal was in his trailer, which places him at the scene but not necessarily involved. .22 disappeared, but sometime during the break between dinner and dessert, he put clean silverware on the table leaving him very little time to dump a body, slice it up and get back to the house—that'd even be pushing it for someone who wasn't impaired. Seems to make a case for outsiders, doesn't it? But why?''

Ben knew it was a rhetorical question. He let Tommy think out loud.

"I guess I don't have to tell you I have a supervisor breathing down my neck. Anytime a person is killed near a reservation, it's messy. But this trader…I'm not saying he was unpopular in the village, maybe, just not trusted; but he was a member of the community. Outsider withstanding, his kids go to reservation schools, his wife is liked.''

Tommy squatted; again his eyes searched the area around the log. "There's talk about his family back in New York causing a stink. Ahmed took off for there three days ago. His car hasn't been found. Supposedly, he was on a selling trip so there might be a robbery angle. But I have nothing concrete to tell them.''

"I don't suppose the tourist who found the body was helpful.''

"Naw. Old guy means well but drifts in and out.''

"Still, he must have seen something or he wouldn't have been behind the trailer to start with."

"I agree with you. He was over that way for some reason."

"What about the run-in Sal had with the man's wife? Something about a rabbit? Could he have tried to find Sal? Maybe confront him?"

"That's interesting, but I don't think the squabble was anything more than just a misunderstanding. Sal's not going to take kindly to someone telling him what he should carve—especially an animal he's forbidden to touch."

"Religious beliefs?"

"His society."

"But I've seen rabbit fetishes."

"Whatever brings in the moola. Religious meaning is usually secondary, today. Most artists pay more attention to supply and demand economics than taboos."

"Then what do you make of the scalping? I would think that's a taboo."

"A hundred years ago if an outsider was involved with stealing or copying artifacts? I'd expect that reaction. But not today. I can't believe that if we had to have a murder, it couldn't just be a plain old shooting without embellishment."

"Have you heard from the lab yet? Do you know how this Ahmed died?"

"I got a call this morning. A little early for all the particulars but looks like a stabbing."

Tommy didn't look happy as he stood and dusted off his uniform. The silence seemed to last overly long before Tommy said, "I suppose if someone came to you with information about the murder it would come under patient/therapist protection? You wouldn't be able to talk about it?"

"Probably. You think that might happen?"

"Who knows? Some villagers would be bothered by knowledge of the dead. They might seek relief, want to talk about it." Tommy looked at him with a grin, "Maybe you should just give me all the names of disgruntled women—a man who's taken a scalp can't have sex for a year."

Ben ignored the humor. "Let me decide what I can say when the time comes." And found himself hoping he wouldn't be faced with that decision.

FOUR

IT RAINED THE FOURTH DAY. In itself, this wasn't a big deal, Sal thought. If there hadn't been substantial rains by the first of July, crops could be in trouble. So, some June rain was expected, needed. But rain the fourth day after a death indicated something else. That rain belonged to the deceased. He pushed the pedal under the workbench and started the whir of the grinder. A three-inch square of grayish marble was taking the shape of a horse, not a standard Hawikuh fetish, but a much sought-after figure among tourists. Even Sal, a master craftsman, carved what would sell.

But he couldn't keep his mind on his work. It kept straying to the rain. When he was little, his grandmother would point to white, fluffy cumulus clouds stacked high on top of one another on hot summer afternoons and say, "Look, the grandfathers are coming." In the desert, rain was sacred. Those who died went to the place of water and returned wrapped in sheets of rain.

But would this be true for someone like Ahmed? Someone from another country entirely? Sal didn't know. Since he died on Indian land, would his ghost follow Indian rules? Probably not. So, Sal shouldn't let it bother him. But that was easier said than done. He still feared death—any death. This was one of the most difficult beliefs for outsiders, for even Hannah to understand—that death was both revered and feared. But because it could be brought to earth by the dead, and water being an attribute of divinity, rain was a blessing bestowed by the divine.

And so long as the recent dead remembered life in this world, there was danger that they would long for those they had left behind, appear to them in dreams, trouble them during the day, make them sicken and die.

Sal felt a sharp pain in his side when he breathed in. Had he pulled a muscle moving his equipment or…? He shouldn't take chances. He was vulnerable. Why had the body of the trader been on the hood of the truck? Or found behind Sal's trailer. Death was stalking him. Sal knew he was marked in some way, and he needed to make atonement.

There was a place called Wide River, a piece of the river's bank cut away over time that was the special place of supernaturals. Sal would go there that evening and sprinkle black cornmeal to erase the path of the dead. Sal would make certain, be extra careful to cut their spirits off from the living—from himself.

"Is this a good time to talk?"

Sal's foot slipped off the pedal and the grinder abruptly stopped. He glanced at the doorway to the shed and blinked into the sunlight that outlined his visitor. He noticed the narrow waist and bare midriff between the cutoff jeans and halter top.

"Come in."

"I appreciate your letting me interview you."

The woman was pretty, Sal thought, pretty but with too many spots on her face—the problem with Anglos who had red-gold hair. But the breasts were nice. Large, but not too large for her slight frame and wide shoulders. He had watched younger men, Tommy Spottedhorse and Ben Pecos, look at her—with their tongues on the floor. They weren't looking at her spots. He almost smiled. There was a time he would've looked, too. Maybe that's what he was doing now, granting an interview so that he could look. But he knew better, he was talking to her because Hannah told him to—told him it would be good for business. He'd be on national television maybe. His work would double, maybe triple in price. He rose to empty a woodenbacked chair and drag it closer to his workbench.

"Do you do all your work in here?" She stepped into the room and stood looking around.

Sal nodded, "Most." He caught his breath. What did she

mean by that? No one knew about the underground lab. "I like it here. It's private."

"But there's very little natural light. I mean, I wondered if you did any real work down at the trading post. I'd hate to be on display like that."

Sal smiled. "It's not so bad." He motioned to the chair. "Anything in particular you want to know about fetishes?"

"I'd like to start by talking about their meaning. Do you mind if I use a tape recorder?"

Sal shook his head and watched Julie place the tiny black box between them. She sat on the chair and leaned forward, elbows on his workbench. Her eyes were large, hazel, fringed with thick dark lashes. She wore a fresh scent like a breeze carrying rain. It was difficult to concentrate as its clean crispness floated over him. He looked to the side but took in a deep lung-full of its headiness.

"Can you tell me about the origin of fetishes?"

He smiled. He liked this story. "Some say that in the beginning, the world was made of ooze, and animals huge and deadly roamed freely before the coming of man. The first man was no match for his surroundings—not the muck, not the animals; so, the children of the sun decided to help. They dried up the land and with bolts of lightning sought to stun the animals and turn them into stone. The mountains in this valley are testaments of this help. Some animals were missed and live with us today."

"And today," Julie asked, "how are the carved figures of animals used by your people?"

Sal gathered his thoughts again, leaned back and, staring straight ahead, heard himself talk about fetishes as the talismans of hunters. A fetish was used to aid the hunter's imagination—help him see the hunted, smell it, hear it. How the hunter could communicate with the spirit of the hunted through a replica. How he could ask its permission to kill it. Much like he did with the insects, Sal thought to himself. He prayed for the tiny lives first before he collected them and asked to be forgiven his killing.

"Your people have always been carvers?"

"In the beginning people collected rocks, bone, branches—things that already looked like a particular animal; a carver just enhanced this image. It wasn't until later that they produced images."

"Was this a problem with the church, with Catholicism? I mean, was it thought that you worshipped 'graven images,' that sort of thing?"

"At first missionaries thought they were idols until they realized that we honor the spirit. A fetish cannot be more than the animal it represents."

"Are fetishes only used in hunting?"

"They are also used in healing—illness, being out of balance with nature, drought, sometimes infertility…" Was it his imagination or did Julie's cheeks flush pink? Strange this pretty woman didn't have children. Maybe he could do something. He pushed back from the table and went to a chest at the back of the shed. Here he kept a surplus of carvings, the ones ready to be offered for sale or ones dear enough to keep.

"Fetishes don't have to be only animals." The carving he placed beside the tape recorder was four inches tall. It was a maiden who seemed to be emerging from an ear of corn. The meticulously sculpted shucks and tassels completed her shawl and curled about her black hair, embedded pieces of obsidian. Sal had outlined the kernels that made up her body in coral and turquoise, tiny inlaid pieces of stone that set off each small square in sharp contrast to the amber base.

"It's exquisite." Julie studied it, then walked to the door and held it to the light. "This is a beautiful piece of art."

"Corn is our life. The corn maiden gives life. I want you to have it."

"No, I couldn't." Julie seemed genuinely shocked. "It's too expensive." She walked back to the bench and placed the fetish in front of him.

"She suits you. She's been waiting for her new owner."

He watched as Julie once again picked up the statue. The maiden seemed to fascinate her. But isn't this what he wanted?

He wanted this woman to have something of his—something that was his best work. "Take her. She will be good for you."

"How can I thank you? I'll cherish her." Once again, Julie held the statue to the light. "Look, there's an insect of some sort, preserved next to the stalk. All you can see is a dark outline. What do you think it is?"

Sal took the figurine that she held out but didn't have to look at the insect very long.

"Looks like our Jumping Sumac beetle."

"To think it lived thousands of years ago, maybe, millions. Amber is fascinating, don't you think?"

Sal nodded. Yes, amber was fascinating. He gave the maiden back, aware that Julie's fingers had brushed his hand.

"Am I interrupting?" Hannah hadn't waited for an answer but moved quickly into the shed.

Sal sat up straighter. This wasn't good. How long had she been listening? He was going to be in trouble for this.

"We're just finishing. Look, isn't she beautiful? And there's a beetle caught inside. There." Julie held the maiden towards Hannah, who had taken a step backwards as if threatened.

"Lovely, but if you've seen one, you've seen them all." She gave a short, harsh laugh, "I've been out here too long. I'm getting jaded. But how nice of Mr. Zuni to give you a piece of his best work."

Not even Salvador, but *Mr. Zuni*. If the two of them hadn't been blocking the door, he would have bolted.

"Would it be possible to talk again tomorrow?" Julie was putting the recorder back into a carrying case.

"Probably." Sal wasn't committing to anything right at the moment.

"Good. I'll check with you after breakfast."

And then with a dazzling smile and one more thank-you, Julie left. At first the silence was overpowering, oppressive. Waiting for doom was putting a lot of pressure on him, Sal thought. Should he speak first? But, he didn't have to.

"You can't put an insect in every piece." Hannah's voice was a hiss of anger, barely above a whisper. "How do you think I can explain perfect amber—every piece with some little tidbit from the past, little iridescent wings, the veins in a leaf—all perfect. It causes suspicion.''

Hannah was pacing. Sal waited. This wasn't really the problem. He felt certain of that. He'd seen this before.

''And giving one of your best pieces to that reporter.''

Now the real reason for the anger was out—too much attention to someone else.

''It was your idea that I talk to her.'' Sal instantly wished he could grab the words back.

Hannah whirled towards him, leaned across the table, her face a foot from his. ''My idea? Just mine? Don't you want to be successful in this? Is it all my doing? Am I the one who has to take all the chances? Worry that in your stupidity, you'll tell all or give away the shop?'' She took a breath. ''And since when has talking equated with gift-giving? Just a little something that's worth an easy four or five hundred dollars. What a nice thank-you for a little chat.''

Anger had given her face color and made her eyes flint sapphire, but spittle bubbled at the corner of her mouth and she was shaking, panting, her warm breath puffed against his face.

It was his cue, remembered from the past, perfected over the years when too-pretty young tourists crowded to see his work, pressed close to him, touched him while Hannah watched from behind the cash register.

She would wait until they were alone then rant and rave about male posturing. How he had encouraged the flirtations, welcomed them, flaunted them in front of her. The first time she had torn his shirt and broken a nail on his belt buckle. All in a frenzy to couple, regain what she thought of as hers. But he knew the first move was really expected of him.

He reached up and steadied her arms, then drew her closer, sliding his hands up until his fingers laced behind her neck and pulled her lips to his. He let his tongue push into her mouth, just two or three short exploratory darts before he sat back, saw her anger turn into an animal wanting. Then he stood and moved to close the door.

JULIE HEARD THE DOOR to the shed slam shut before she had gone a hundred feet. She felt sorry for Sal. She wouldn't like to be in his place. There was absolutely no doubt that he was getting yelled at and she was, somehow, innocently to blame. She wondered if it would help if she went back and tried to help him, maybe, stick up for him. But what would she say? It was probably best not to interfere.

Besides, she had looked forward to some time alone to reconstruct her notes from the interview.

And, if she were being truthful, to think about Ben. It hadn't exactly been an auspicious reunion. But what had she expected? Crashing waves, a clash of symbols? More or less. And one thing she was fairly sure of; she was the only one who heard the sound of anything. He had made no attempt to touch her. No kiss. No handholding. Nothing. Right after lunch, he goes running off with that police officer, then back to the hospital. If she wasn't here on business, she'd think of going back to Santa Fe. But her story was here—out here in the sparse forest and mountains and on the reservation. She was already planning to shoot her first show from the boarding house. She could look in any direction and see beauty—the kind that photographed well—pines, and jagged basalt rising out of the desert floor against a backdrop of deep blue. And the serenity—her audience would be able to experience that.

Besides, she wasn't ready to give up on the relationship. She almost laughed out loud. There it was, the truth. She was so disappointed in Ben's reaction because of what she was feeling. But she'd have to go slow. If she had a chance, this was her second one. She'd blown the first one. She'd chosen to leave Chicago when a promising career offer came along. Could she blame him for being a little gun-shy? And if she really wanted to be honest, had anything changed? He was in the sticks. She was in New York. He couldn't break his contract, could she break hers?

"You wanna feel?"

Julie came crashing back to the present. Twenty-something

was holding out a toad. She hadn't even seen him sitting on the back steps.

"I'll pass."

"'Fraida warts?"

"Maybe." Julie bent down to inspect the animal and was struck at how dirty the boy's hands were.

"Could be prince. You kiss?"

Julie couldn't keep from laughing. She could be passing up the chance of a lifetime. Someone must have read him that story, and guessing at his limitations, maybe he believed it. She instantly sobered. She didn't want to appear to make fun of him.

"I already have a prince." Now, there was a lie.

"Who?"

"He lives far away." Another lie, as she thought of Ben. Her prince was right here for all the good it was doing her.

"In a castle?"

"In a big castle." As long as they were on fairy tales, she could only hope her nose wasn't growing.

"You come." He grabbed her hand, and she almost reflexively jerked away. But she didn't—out of sheer will power and trying not to think of germs or whatever else hands that handled frogs might have on them.

"Where are we going?"

"You see."

When he stood, he towered above her. He had to be six feet tall—what an odd child. But was child really a correct term? He was an impaired young man. Lack of motor control left him with nervous ticks. Her hand that he held was bobbing up and down; she knew he couldn't control those spasms. And mentally? It was hard to tell. But she wasn't frightened. He was so earnest. She didn't want to disappoint him.

"Is this a surprise, Twenty-one?"

"Two." He mimed shooting a rifle complete with sound.

"If you're named after a rifle, why aren't you called Remington or Browning or Winchester?"

His face went blank. It hadn't been a good question, Julie

realized as he became agitated. It was beyond him. He really was limited. She patted his hand. "It's okay. I like .22 for a name."

His smile just about pushed his ears back as he tugged on her arm and turned to go up the steps. Whatever it was, it was in the house.

His room was on the second floor towards the front. When he reached the door, he motioned for her to wait in the hall. He left the door open a crack, and Julie almost gagged on the dank odor that hit her in the face. She wasn't at all certain that she wanted to see this "surprise."

"You come now." .22 threw open the door and Julie stepped in. At first she couldn't believe what she was seeing. There was shelving everywhere, floor to ceiling with cutouts around the windows. But it was what was on the shelves that stunned her—aquariums with elaborate covers and lights, some huge— one hundred gallons, maybe more—and all held some type of amphibian.

"Friends." .22 made a sweeping movement to include his collection. "You like?"

"It's…awesome." It's also creepy; it stinks in here, and it's too hot. But, she kept her opinions to herself.

"You hold?"

He had swiftly grabbed a large toad from the aquarium nearest them and held it out. Julie started to decline but then decided to be a sport. So what if this was a little fifth-grade déjà vu?

"Oh, no." She quickly held the toad out away from her body but not before it had peed down her leg.

"He go pee-pee. He sorry." .22 quickly put the toad back in its house and turned back looking absolutely stricken.

"Don't worry. He didn't mean to." She pulled a couple of Kleenexes from a box on a nightstand and dabbed at her leg. The room, other than the aquariums was almost bare. A single bed, the nightstand and a plain wooden rocker—that was it. And the room had to measure six hundred square feet. There was no outside light. All the windows had been shuttered. The light came from fixtures in the aquariums, eerie little fluorescent tubes gleaming from the underside of metal lids that kept hundreds of frogs and toads from escaping.

"You hungry?" Not waiting for an answer, .22 snapped the lid off of a fifty-gallon plastic drum marked "dried flies," reached inside and grabbed up a handful of something brown, popped the whole thing in his mouth and started crunching.

"Oh, my God…"

"Yum. Yum." He stood facing her, chewing in an exaggerated manner with his mouth open. Julie felt faint. Then .22 convulsed in giggles and fell choking with laughter onto his bed. Julie looked into the dried fly barrel and pulled out a box of cereal—Grape Nuts, to be exact.

"Trick. I trick you," .22 shouted between whoops of laughter.

"You did. That was a very good trick." I'll never eat Grape Nuts again, she thought, but the trick took some thought, some planning. And it showed originality. She was certain that somewhere, some instructor of the impaired would feel he had accomplished something.

"A practical joke. You played a practical joke on me."

From his sudden frown, joke and trick were not synonymous. So Julie smiled, crossed the room and patted him on the shoulder then whispered, "I'll see you at supper. We're having your favorite—dried flies and peanut butter." She could still hear his laughter when she reached her room.

SAL DIDN'T FORGET his promise to scatter black cornmeal that night, to go to the place called Wide River and sever any ties that the dead man's ghost might have with him. So when the last of the sun's light faded pink into yellow across the horizon, Sal set out.

He'd skipped supper, fasted, leaving his thinking clear. The coming night was muggy and vegetation glistened from rain. The usual rapid cadences of insects were slowed by the drop in temperature. Their melodies lulled him into thinking of his work. Maybe Hannah was right. Maybe he should produce plain amber for a while empty of enclosures. But it would take

the fun out of it. His masterpieces, his challenge, were the myr-
iad of winged creatures frozen for all time. Thin filmy clouds
floated over, then away from the sliver of moon. There wasn't
much light. In addition to his medicine pouch, he carried a
flashlight and walking stick. He felt in his pocket for the offering he had made, cut the red willow, notched a face on one
end and tied the feathers before painting. The stick measured
from the tip of his middle finger to the palm of his hand. The
supernaturals would use the feathers for clothing.

Sal was walking in the shadow of the sacred mountain to
where the river spread out flat and languid, its waters skipping
over small rounded rocks worn smooth many years before the
Spaniards—maybe many years before his people came here. He
would skirt the ruins. The place where his people first lived.
He wouldn't disturb the ancestors.

He didn't bring the truck tonight but walked as part of his
pilgrimage. And he wasn't in any hurry. Lightning zigzagged
across the horizon to the west. There would be more rain. He
paused listening for the thunder, the rolling of rocks across the
sky, but there was none. The rain must be far away, not an
immediate threat, anyway. He needed the flashlight now to keep
from stumbling on the uneven ground. Cold, damp air settled
around him, and the brush was getting thicker. He must be near
the river.

He thought of Hannah, of the afternoon, the luck that brought
her to him before the ceremony that he had to perform, because
tomorrow and for three more days, he would have to abstain.
The severity of the need to do this kind of ceremony would
make him stick to its restrictions—no sex and only certain
foods. A general feeling of taboo, *teckwi,* would hang over him
for four days.

He slowed his steps. There were no roads out here, no footprints of man or animal after the rain. He felt alone but not
lonely. And he knew the difference. The five miles out and
back would have a healing effect; he was feeling better already.
He splashed into a puddle left by the afternoon rain and fought

back a curse. Now his feet were wet, not something he considered pleasant.

He stopped and removed his socks, stuffing them into his pockets. The running shoes were damp but drier without the bunch of heavy sodden cotton whose cuffs acted like wicks and drew the dampness up his ankles. Two frogs had hopped from the small rock-lined pool but waited close by probably hoping he would go away. Children of the *U'wanami,* the rainmakers or water spirits. He thought their protruding eyes followed him as he picked his way carefully around their neighbors' watery homes.

He was in the trees now, crossing a stretch of forested land that would eventually break before an expanse of marsh at the river's edge. He paused and took a directional sighting off the stars. He should be almost there. Before the trees parted, his nostrils filled with the smell of the river—wet earth, mud and vegetation, faintly acrid, sometimes sweet. He breathed in the dampness of this place of life and felt refreshed. Wide River, the sacred place he sought, would be a scant one hundred yards to his left if he had calculated correctly. He skirted the marsh and kept to the water's rocky edge. Shallow pools formed beside the river, their quiet waters stagnant, cut off to be fed only by the rains.

It wasn't sound that stopped him, but there had been something—even before he saw the flickering lights—something that he had seen caused a cold sweat to bead along his hairline. He stood quietly. The lights were directly ahead of him, their source concealed by the brush and young cottonwoods. If he'd thought, he would have realized that he was looking at a bank of candles, not the glow of a supernatural. But he wasn't thinking clearly.

He was mesmerized by the shadow of a dancer who leaped and twisted, causing the still air at the river's edge to swirl the flames of light; smoky wicks plumed upwards in the darkness disturbing the night. He crept closer. The dancer was chanting as he stopped to kneel at the edge of a still pool.

"Now, indeed, the enemy,
In a shower of war clubs,
With a bloody head,
The enemy,
Reaching the end of his life,
Added to the flesh of our earth mother.
Beast bow priests,
With their claws,
Tore from the enemy
His water-filled covering.
i'nakwe te' 'ona
to' wa ci'wan an u'lo'nakwi
o—''

It was the prayer of the scalp dance. Sal tried to look away;
he couldn't. It would be useless to try to run. His legs did not
have the strength to carry him. He slumped to the ground; his
eyes never leaving the tableau twenty-five feet in front of him.
Was it a man or a woman, the one in ceremonial dress who
now dipped and scrubbed the scalp? Yes, a scalp. He knew that
for certain—the dark scrap that was being immersed, shaken,
and stretched had once covered the front of a man's skull. He
knew what would come next, and he wasn't disappointed.

The scalp washer roared, squatted on his haunches, waved
his arms like paws and batted at the air around him. Holding
the scalp high, he slowly lowered it and bit it. Not once, but
many times he sank his teeth into the leathery piece of human
hide to receive the power of the beast gods. As an animal he
would be immune to any contamination, any taboos regarding
the dead. He did this to save his life.

Now it was an animal who dragged the scalp through the
shallows of the standing pool. It snorted, huffed, growled but
worked busily at its chore of cleaning. Sal stared without blinking. This was his every nightmare come true—to view the
washing of a scalp the fourth day after a death.

He felt queasy, faint even. Everything looked fuzzy. The
scalp washer-animal moved in and out of focus. But Sal

couldn't have turned away. Trancelike, he watched the finish of the ceremony, the breaking of a bowl containing food and the scattering of that offering on the ground. Then the scalp washer skewered the scalp to an eight-foot sapling, bending the young tree while he tied the scalp firmly in the upper branches. Then he let go and the tree sprang upright to weave back and forth before going still with its new burden.

Mechanically, Sal reached into his medicine bag and drew out three kernels of black corn and placed them under his tongue. Would this be enough to prevent being pursued by the ghost of the man who was scalped? He was viewing a ceremony that he should never have seen.

Next came the planting of the prayer sticks. But then the scalp washer did a strange thing. He rose and turned to stare in Sal's direction, locking his eyes on the exact spot where Sal crouched. How could Sal be seen? Only supernaturals could pierce the darkness and know his presence.

Supernaturals. Could it be? The costume was from his people. Had the old ones, the ancestors, come back to treat this scalp and keep the trader's spirit from doing harm? Sal felt the blood drain from his head. The lightness caused spots to swim and dance before his eyes. He reminded himself to take a breath but couldn't seem to find enough air to bring into his body. He opened his mouth, gasping, eyes bugwide, his hands involuntarily clawing in space.

Then came blackness and nothing. As neatly as if a hood had been slipped over his head, Sal lost consciousness and sprawled on his back in the dampness of the rain-fresh earth.

"YOU HAVE A PATIENT. Waiting on the doorstep when I opened up, 6:30 a.m." Rose paused, "I put him in your office. Hope that was okay?"

"Sure." Ben checked the counter for the person's folder. "No one was scheduled. Have you had time to pull his file?"

"No file. This one's a virgin."

"Never been seen before? For anything?"

"Never."

"Who is it?"

"Salvador Zuni, the carver. He says he knows you."

"I've met him." Ben's curiosity was piqued. The taciturn Sal in his office? That was interesting. Rose had left his office door open and Ben could see Sal's mud-streaked pant's leg before he stepped across the threshold. And the rest of Sal wasn't much better. Mud was caked along the right side of his neck, his shirt was streaked a red-clay brown, and on the crown of his head, dried blood matted his hair.

But it was the eyes. Sal looked petrified, scared to death. Ben had learned the hard way not to boom out, "Looks like you've seen a ghost." More often than not among his people, that was the truth. He closed the door and waited. Then walked behind his desk, sat down, took out paper and pen before he said anything, all the time feeling Sal's eyes follow him—not staring, but looking respectfully to the side.

He wondered why this man was here now when he'd never come before. He knew that Sal was aware of Ben's profession. Hadn't Hannah told him he treated "crazies"? But Sal looked like he might need medical attention. Should he offer to have a doc step in and take a look? At least at the cut?

"Some say you're half-Indian, half-Anglo?"

What did this have to do with anything? Ben wondered, but nodded.

"Would that give you power from both worlds?"

Ben paused. God, he wished he knew where this was going.

"Some would believe that. It gives me knowledge of both sides." That wasn't entirely a lie.

Sal seemed satisfied and continued to stare ahead of him. Ben waited. Whatever it was, it was important.

"What happens to the ghosts of non-Indians?"

Ben took a breath. So that was it. This wasn't going to be easy. "Are you thinking about the trader?"

Again, Sal nodded but didn't look up.

"Sometimes Anglos believe that spirits of the dead can stay with the living before crossing over." Crossing over? Where had he gotten that term? "But there's usually a sense of closure with burial or cremation. I don't know what religion the man followed.''

''Would being scalped make any difference?''

Ben thought a moment. ''How do you mean?''

''Would the spirit come back? Or stay here seeking this 'closure' if a part of him had been left here?'' Sal suddenly turned in his seat. ''What if the scalp was tended in the Indian way? Would that make a difference?''

''How is that?'' Ben risked showing his ignorance but he needed to know exactly what Sal was thinking.

''Washed by a scalp dancer.''

''In water that would not contaminate the drinking water of the village, wouldn't expose others to death?'' He remembered what Hannah had said, and it helped him sound knowledgeable.

''Yes.''

Ben moved from behind the desk and dragged a folding chair opposite Sal. This man was in torment. Something had happened. He knew something.

''Can you tell me why you need answers to these questions?''

''Do you cost?''

''My services are free to members of the Hawikuh tribe.'' The answer seemed to be what Sal had wanted to hear. He visibly relaxed and leaned back in his chair.

''Should we have someone look at that cut on your head?''

''No.'' Sal seemed oblivious to discomfort, and Ben decided not to press it.

''If I knew where the scalp was, should I tell someone so that it could be sent to the dead man's family? In the white man's way, would this give his ghost rest?''

Ben thought a moment. ''In the white man's way, the scalp would be evidence. It would have to be reported first. The police would have to get involved.''

This seemed safer than trying to second-guess how Ahmed's widow might receive a part of her husband's skull covering. Rumor was she'd gone back to New York. How would you send a scalp, second-day express in a bubble pack? Not funny,

Ben admonished himself. The man in front of him was dead serious—not a good choice of adjective, but true.

"I know where it is," Sal said.

"The scalp?"

Sal nodded.

"How do you know this?"

Sitting in front of him, Sal began to tell how he took sacred black corn to Wide River the night before to break the spell the trader had cast on him. He needed to appease his ghost, keep him from appearing to him at night. Instead, Sal stumbled upon the ceremony of his ancestors, a scalp washer completing the fourth-day ritual. Sal took a breath, then mimicked the growls and cries of the ancient one who had become an animal.

"In punishment for my watching, he stole my breath and threw me down on the stones beside the river."

That explains the mud and head wound, Ben thought. But ancestors? Supernaturals? It was obvious that Sal believed what he had seen.

"I think we need to share this information with Tommy Spottedhorse. Do you agree?"

Sal seemed to be thinking this over but finally said, "Will he lock me up?"

"He's not going to lock someone up who hasn't done anything wrong. Trust me on that. Can you take us to where you saw the scalp?"

Sal nodded. Ben dialed the Hawikuh tribal police station. It was still early; he hoped that Tommy would be in. The third ring got a receptionist who said that Officer Spottedhorse was on another line. Ben told her to tell him he was on his way over with an emergency. A little melodrama couldn't hurt. It would capture Tommy's interest.

WHEN THEY PULLED UP in front, Tommy was leaning against the Caprice. "So what's so all-fire important at quarter to eight in the morning?"

Ben filled him in.

"Shit." Tommy didn't seem very pleased about what he

heard. "What do you think? Any chance Sal is hallucinating? Or whatever?"

"I can't be positive. I believe that he is being truthful when he says he saw a scalp washer."

"If this is another wild-goose chase... Sal get over here. We'll run out to check your story in my car. Just try not to get mud on the seats."

No one spoke other than Sal giving directions. Tommy gunned the Caprice over mud and slippery rock snagging its undercarriage on brush as he fishtailed down embankments. Ben was thankful for seat belts.

If they had been on any other mission, Ben would have enjoyed the scenery. The greens of young trees and newly sprouted grasses were made vibrant by the recent rain. Indian paintbrush was a scarlet splash against outcroppings of gray rock. He would have sworn the flowers hadn't been there yesterday. This overnight awakening was miraculous. Worshiping rain in the desert had always made sense to him.

"Can we walk in from here?" Tommy had stopped the car and turned to look at Sal in the back seat. They were probably still about a half mile from the river, Ben thought.

"Yeah. Stay to your right past the red rock then go northeast towards the river."

"You going to go with us?" Tommy asked.

Sal shook his head.

"Thought so." Tommy sounded ticked.

The two of them walked in silence. Ben wished he knew what was bugging Tommy. He was almost antisocial, not his old wisecracking self. There must be some problem.

"There." Tommy was pointing towards a stand of young cottonwoods.

He motioned to Ben and plowed on ahead. The brush was knee-deep in spots and slowed their approach.

"Well, I'll be damned." Tommy was looking at an eight-foot cottonwood. Something dark, wadded to the size of a fist was tied to the top of a sapling. "He could be telling the truth. You want to help me get a closer look?"

Ben nodded. There must be some taboo for Tommy—something that said he shouldn't touch this part of the dead. He wondered how religious Tommy was.

"Shit," Tommy said.

Ben had pulled the young tree over, and Tommy held it as he inspected the small brownish mass tied to its trunk. He was careful not to touch it, Ben noted. Then Tommy broke the branch below where the scalp was tied and turned towards the car.

"I've got all I need. You want to see if you can find a plastic bag in the trunk. I need to speak to Sal." Tommy handed Ben his car keys as the two walked back. Tommy held the branch of cottonwood away from his body—as far away as he could get it. He laid it in the grass before he confronted Sal.

"Guess you know what this means, pal."

Sal nodded but kept his eyes averted.

"I'm arresting you for the murder of Ahmed Sahd."

"You can't do that." Ben slammed the trunk. Had he heard correctly? He rushed from behind the back of the car and stepped between Tommy and Sal. "What's wrong with you?" He was yelling in Tommy's face now, but he didn't care. "You can't arrest someone who has just led you to a valuable piece of evidence completely of his own volition." Ben didn't try to hide his anger. Sal had trusted him. Hadn't Ben promised that nothing would happen to him?

"Or put the evidence there because he's had it all along," Tommy yelled back. "Have you ever considered that? That this man took the scalp in the first place? Mr. Zuni here, if you remember, just happened to be at the scene without an alibi that night. He very probably was moving the body he'd hidden under the trailer when he was surprised by the tourist."

Ben glanced at Sal, who leaned against the car and studied a rock some two feet away. Sal wasn't going to say anything. Who knew what the consequences were going to be, but this man was not going to say anything in his own defense.

Tommy stopped abruptly and his anger seemed to dissipate. In a more normal voice he added, "This isn't the only thing that makes him look guilty.'' Tommy took a deep breath. "In addition, Sal here gave Ahmed's widow a bag of amber worth around two or three thousand dollars the morning after the body was found. He just up and drove into the village and presented the woman with a bag of riches.'' Tommy turned to Ben. "The Indian way says that a murderer must pay the family of the one he's killed—a substantial payment of all or most all of his worldly possessions. I'd say that sack of amber came close to being just that.''

Ben was floored. Would he have called Tommy if he had known this? He didn't know, but he stepped back. He was certain that Sal hadn't killed anyone. But how could he prove it? Ben had to admit it looked bad. He watched numbly as Sal held out his arms, wrists together and winced when he heard the snap of cuffs. Was Sal going to be charged with murder?

"You're making a mistake.'' It was all Ben could think of to say. Tommy gave Ben a look of exasperation and slid behind the wheel.

FIVE

IT HADN'T BEEN a good morning, and the afternoon was worse. Ben offered to pick up some personal articles for Sal back at the trailer and tell Hannah. He wasn't looking forward to that—not when he felt so responsible for Sal's sitting in a jail cell. And he'd ignored Julie. He hadn't said two words to her in as many days. That definitely had to change.

He pulled up in front of the boarding house, but his usual parking space, one shaded by a hundred-year-old cottonwood was taken. There were ten other spaces to choose from, and someone took this one. The newish blue station wagon wasn't one he recognized, more tourists, probably. He pulled in beside it, noticed the Century 21 insignia and wondered what an agent was doing out here.

And then he saw it—the For Sale sign stuck in the ground

to the right of the brick path, halfway up the slope to the porch. For Sale. For some reason it jolted him. He'd just moved in—maybe that was it, the thought of trying to find another place to live on top of everything else.

Did Sal know? Somehow, Ben doubted it. So while he's rotting in jail, his belongings would be tossed in the street and Hannah and son would move on. Ben took a deep breath and chided himself for being a little melodramatic. But was he too far from wrong? He doubted it. Somehow this made the job of telling Hannah even more difficult.

"It won't bite," Hannah said.

Ben started. He'd been staring at the sign, leaning against the steering wheel and letting his thoughts stray. The women, Hannah and the agent in a gold blazer, stood beside his truck. They must have walked over from the trading post.

"I'm surprised," Ben said.

"Oh, the time's right. Gloria promises me it is." Hannah indicated the woman beside her.

"The time is perfect. It couldn't be better. I've had two calls this week about income property—retirees coming this way from the Midwest. There's such an opportunity here. And with the market taking off in this state, you better pack your bags. Oh, look at the time, must toodle." She lightly pecked Hannah on the cheek, smiled brightly at Ben and slipped behind the wheel of the wagon.

Ben watched her pull out of the drive before he got out of the truck. "This seems sudden." Ben couldn't help the note of peevishness he heard in his voice as he walked Hannah to the house.

She shrugged. "You might say I've been planning on it for twenty years."

"Should I assume you haven't been happy out here?"

"Happy?" Hannah's laugh was hard. "Happy...what a joke; I've hated every minute of it. I've scraped together enough money to keep it going—support it in the style to which it was accustomed. But it's sapped me. It's taken everything I've given and demanded more." She made a half-circle sweep with her arm that took in the boarding house, trading post and deli-mart. "It's like getting stuck with a bad lover, only he's the only man on the island." This time the laugh was hearty. "Everything you see depends on me to make it go, absolutely everything. And I'm sick and tired of it. Simple as that, I want out."

"Why haven't you sold it before? It's probably none of my business, but twenty years is a long time."

Hannah paused as Ben watched. He thought she was struggling to find the right words, or decide how much she should share?

"My husband loved this land. The business has been in his family since the early 1900's." Hannah's gaze softened. "Only one other thing he loved as much and that was his son. And he didn't care what he had to do to make sure each was taken care of."

Did he detect bitterness? An awkward silence settled between them. Ben waited, hoped she would continue. But she didn't. She just pushed ahead of him, up the steps and pulled open the screen door.

"Hannah, there's something else we need to talk about." Ben caught up with her and held the door open. "Sal's been arrested." If he had struck her, she wouldn't have reacted any differently. She grabbed his arm for support.

"Arrested? For what?" She barely whispered the words.

"The death of the trader."

She stared at him a moment, then scoffed, "He didn't kill anyone." Her voice was gaining strength. "He couldn't have."

Ben told her what evidence Tommy Spottedhorse had.

"He gave a bag of amber to Ahmed's widow?" Anger now replaced incredulity. Hannah had whirled to walk back out across the porch and tucking her skirt beneath her, she sat on the top step. "I can't believe it." She didn't try to cover the anger. "Two or three thousand dollars of amber?"

"That's what Tommy says." Ben sat down beside her. "He thinks it represents most of Sal's worldly possessions."

"You know, maybe the little shit deserves to rot in jail."

Hannah absently worked a strand of hair, twisting it around her index finger.

"Why do you say that?"

"If he's going to act guilty, he might as well be treated as guilty."

"I think he was being thoughtful. He felt responsible somehow because the body was found by his trailer."

"And who's responsible for what happens to his job here? Where do I go to find someone to help out?"

Ben noticed the strident tone but decided to get it over with. "Did Sal know you were selling?"

There he had said it and caught Hannah off guard from the look on her face. He felt that Sal wasn't being treated fairly by this woman. He'd bet a paycheck that Sal was in the dark and from the twitch of muscle in Hannah's jaw, he'd already won that bet.

"I've never felt it necessary to get the approval of the hired help before I make a decision." So much for thinking the two might be lovers. This woman had no feelings. But then, in fairness, maybe feeling wasn't the only criteria for sex, Ben thought. Still, there was a coldness.

He was put off by it.

"You know how tough it is to be smart and capable and be treated like an idiot because of your plumbing?"

"Plumbing?" Ben wasn't following.

"That." Hannah leaned towards him and pointed at his crotch, her index finger an inch above his fly. "One of those. The preferred plumbing of the masses."

She turned back to stare in front of her. "You think I'm some kind of hard ass, don't you? But look around you. You know what the price was for maintaining all this? Slavery. I've been chained to one spot, no life without the trading post, boarding house, or deli coming first. And then there's Harold." She sat quietly a moment, and sighed. "I didn't deserve that."

"Sometimes we can't choose—"

"Do you think I'm pretty?" She'd turned abruptly to look him in the face.

Now it was Ben's turn to be taken off guard. Where had that come from? Better yet, where was it leading? Hannah had cocked her head towards him and peeled the errant strand of white-blond hair off of her cheek and pushed it behind her ear. He hadn't noticed before but her nails were bitten to the quick.

"And don't give me any of that 'for your age' crap. Either I am or I'm not." Her gaze was intense, eyes boring into his. He wasn't good at this sort of thing. But he'd have to say something.

"I don't think you can just dismiss age. Do you want to be pretty, which has frivolous connotations or would you rather be seen as savvy, or chic, a perceived elegance that's usually reserved for the older woman? And unattainable to the younger?" Ben mentally crossed his fingers. He needed to get along in this community and starting with his landlady made good sense.

"You're a bullshitter—an absolute, topnotch, first-rate one, but a bullshitter." She was laughing and seemed to relax.

"So, what are we going to do about Sal?" It was probably time to bring the conversation back to the problem that needed solving, Ben thought.

"Let him stew for a while. I can get him out by the end of the week, maybe sooner. I'll look into tribal representation, something he doesn't have to pay for now that he's given away his worldly goods." The laugh was derisive.

Ben stood and offered a hand to help Hannah up. Without dropping his hand, she stood on tiptoe and kissed him lightly on the lips.

"That's for being nice and having all the right answers. Oh, I forgot to mention your boss is coming to supper." With that she disappeared into the house.

JULIE SAT AT the table waiting for Hannah to finish passing the usual bowls and platters of food. Everyone was taking seconds. It was more of a private dinner tonight, Ben, his boss, .22 and Hannah. At any other time, she would have liked the intimacy, a chance to interact with Ben more. But she couldn't forget what she'd seen that afternoon. The kiss had probably meant nothing. It was more like a peck, an afterthought even. Julie knew that Ben and Hannah hadn't seen her coming around the house. And hadn't Hannah said something like the kiss was for "being nice"? Ben could have done some chore for her.

But rationalizing didn't make Julie feel any better. Something was going on. Ben had hardly spoken to her. He was preoccupied with his new job; that was understandable. But he was avoiding her. She was sure of it. The whole idea of coming out here to rekindle a relationship after four years had been stupid. Oops. She'd have to watch it. She almost dropped the bowl of green beans that she'd handed him across the table. He was seated next to his boss, Dr. Lee, an odd smallish man with protruding front teeth. Hadn't someone mentioned that he was from the Philippines? Strange to think of how different his country must be from where he was now.

She glanced at Ben, who looked up long enough to smile and comb the shock of dark brown hair away from his face with his fingers. She loved that smile, and probably a few other things if she was into admitting. He was leaning towards Dr. Lee, giving his boss his undivided attention. She knew that profile by heart—the high cheekbones, aquiline nose, a perfect, not too prominent chin. His chambray shirt was open at the collar, sleeves rolled up; he was muscular and tanned...if they could just have some time alone.

"Dr. Lee has a collection of masks—copies, but all first-rate." Hannah spoke loudly from the end of the table where she sat next to .22, who was bent over his plate pushing two pieces of chicken around in a pool of gravy, a fork in each hand. At least tonight, he wore a bib.

"An anthropologist couldn't have done better," she added.

"As long as I'm out here, doesn't hurt to take advantage of the native arts." Dr. Lee reached for the peach preserves. "There's a gold mine in artifacts. I've supported more than one trip back East by taking along a few things to sell."

"Are masks your specialty?" Ben asked.

"You might say that. Of course, as Hannah said, they're only copies.'' He dropped two rounded spoonfuls of preserves on his plate. ''My collection of fetishes isn't bad, either. Hannah helped me with it.'' He gestured towards Hannah with his fork. ''Now, there's the expert. You should have gotten that degree, done more scholarly work out here. There's a need for it.'' He speared a chicken leg from the platter in the middle of the table and began to cut the meat from the bone.

He must be single, Julie thought. That was his third helping of chicken and a quarter of his plate swam in peach preserves. There was probably an entire generation of men in that age group who could be reached through their stomachs. He looked like a prime candidate, maybe she shouldn't have been so quick to judge Hannah. She seemed to have something in common with this doctor—more than artifacts. Julie thought she'd caught an exchanged glance or two, a quick lowering of the eyes. Not that she thought of Hannah as a femme fatal, but living out here anything could start looking good. Even small doctors with protruding teeth.

''Julie has a prince,'' .22 boomed out.

Was that her fork that hit the table? What was he talking about—that absurd interchange yesterday on the back steps?

''How do you know Julie has a prince?'' Hannah asked.

''She tell me,'' .22 said smugly.

''How nice. Are you engaged?'' Hannah turned to Julie.

''No. I—''

''Her prince lives in a castle.'' If possible, Julie thought, his voice seemed louder. Again, all eyes turned Julie's way. She could feel her cheeks flaming. ''She's sad. He lives far away. She wants him visit. He no can. His work important,'' .22 finished in a falsetto.

Thanks for the interpretation, Julie thought, but what was she going to do, admit lying to the retarded? She forced herself to look at Ben.

''I think I'm being misinterpreted.'' She tried to say it low, under her breath, just for Ben's ears but .22 seemed to guess she was contradicting him.

''No. You tell me.'' .22 shrieked and then started to bang

his tin cup against the side of his plate. Milk sloshed onto the table.

"I'm certain that Julie didn't think you were lying. I'm sure that's what you thought she said." Hannah wadded her napkin and rose to mop up the milk, but not until she had given Julie a withering look. "He takes everything literally. It's not funny to play games with him. I'll thank you to leave him alone."

Julie opened her mouth to say something in her defense, but Dr. Lee beat her to it.

"Hannah, don't be so quick to judge. No one has hurt your son. I'm sure all this can be explained." He fastened exceptionally small dark glittering eyes on Julie. "Now then, what was all this about?"

Julie couldn't look at Ben. She couldn't believe that his boss was stepping in to help her save face. And she had nothing to say. She wasn't going to lie again. She pushed back from the table and arms akimbo faced .22.

"I think somebody needs to be fed a cup of dried flies and sent to bed." She waggled her index finger in his direction. Her tone was exaggerated but got exactly the response she wanted. Giggles. .22 put down his cup and said, "With peanut butter. Yum. Yum." Now his laughter was almost maniacal.

"What are you talking about?" Hannah was irritated, and tried to hush her son.

"Our little secret. Right?" Julie watched .22 nod vigorously.

"Me sorry." .22 looked contrite as tears welled in the corners of his eyes.

"That's okay," Julie said. "Want me to help you clear the table?" She was relieved when .22 pushed his chair back.

"You help." The grin was huge. All was forgiven. And that's the last time I kid with someone who can't kid back, Julie promised herself. But had the damage already been done? Did Ben think she had this man somewhere waiting on her? This whole thing was becoming a less than auspicious beginning to the reunion she'd looked forward to. Should she make the first move and ignore what she saw with the landlady?

Dessert was chocolate cake, three one-inch layers with icing in between. Dr. Lee just about had an orgasm, Julie thought, and helped himself to the biggest slice, beaming at Hannah and smacking his lips with every bite. There was something gross about the man. Julie wasn't sure his table manners were much better than .22's.

She could feel Ben's eyes on her. What was he thinking after that fiasco with .22? She took a deep breath, looked up and smiled—and got the result she wanted—a smile. She'd try to talk with him after dinner.

"I'll take two of whatever it is that smells like heaven."

Tommy Spottedhorse didn't wait to be invited to sit down; he just covered the room in three strides and pulled a chair up next to Julie.

"Hey, you outdid yourself this time." Tommy had slipped a slice of cake off of the serving platter and held his plate up in a toast to Hannah.

"Eating while on duty should be a misdemeanor," Hannah said with a laugh.

"You survived my growing-up years, and it didn't break you. My mother used to clean for Hannah and drag me along sometimes. She's the best cook this side of the Continental Divide, as God is my witness."

"Never took you for being religious, Tommy. And I don't think chocolate cake dragged you all the way out here." Hannah was expressing a curiosity they all shared, Julie thought.

"Sal talked me into coming out this way for his tools. Says he can finish some projects while he's there." Tommy paused to swallow. "Frankly, I think it's a good thing. I'd like to see him keep busy."

"I'd like to see him out of there." Ben sounded curt.

Julie had overheard Hannah talking with Dr. Lee about Sal being in jail, but she hadn't realized that Ben would feel so strongly about it.

"I agree," Hannah added.

"Okay, guys. Back off. I'm not saying he committed a crime or didn't at this point. We'll know more by the end of the week. But for now, he stays put." Tommy seemed adamant.

"Can his therapist visit him?"

"Sure." Tommy put his fork down and looked at Ben. "I was hoping his therapist would consider doing that tonight and give me his professional opinion on whether he thought Sal might be suicidal."

"Do you suspect he might be?" Ben sounded concerned.

"Maybe. I got somebody with him now. I'm not taking any chances. In the old days that would be laughable. It was absolutely unknown in the tribe. But now…" Tommy looked at Ben and shrugged.

"I'll go."

Well, there goes the evening. Julie suppressed a "damn" and tried to keep her disappointment from showing. She'd dig out that book she'd been trying to find time to start. Maybe she'd help Hannah with the dishes.

SAL SAT ON THE EDGE of the metal bunk. There were no mattresses. Tommy promised to locate one before nightfall, but he hadn't come back with one yet. The plumbing was another matter. It didn't work. So the deputy, a kid Sal had known since birth, let him out to use the one marked "employees only" at the end of the hall. He wasn't going to go anywhere. The kid knew that.

Grease from a helping of KFC extracrispy had saturated the paper towel it was wrapped in and now was stuck to the top of the metal tray on the floor. He hadn't been hungry. He'd tried to think, but it was difficult to organize his thoughts. Tribal police had brought in two drunks from Gallup. Navajos trying to get home to Ramah. They'd let them sober up here and send them on their way in the morning. But it meant he wouldn't get much sleep. The two were banging on the bars with the dinner tray now. Maybe they'd pass out, but Sal guessed they were loud drunks with just enough booze in them to start a fight—probably what got them picked up at some bar in the first place. There'd be more noise before they gave it up for the night.

Sal hoped that Tommy had found Ben. He liked the young

psychologist. Sal didn't blame him for his being here. It was important that Ben knew that. Tommy was just doing what he had to do. Sal had known the minute Tommy found out about the bag of amber he gave to the widow, he'd come looking for him. The scalp just nailed it. And maybe he was guilty. That was the bad part. There were a couple things he hadn't told Tommy—about how he'd first seen the trader's body and about that night after supper before he went back to his trailer to rest. He wanted to talk about that with Ben.

"You want anything before I leave? Tommy just turned in the driveway." The kid didn't even have a uniform, just a frayed denim jacket and stained tee shirt. Must be more of an errand runner, brings in supper, then leaves, Sal decided.

"I could use a Coke if you had one." Sal knew there was a machine in the front office. Maybe another of those "employees only" things, but he thought the kid would come up with a couple quarters and treat him to a cold drink. He wasn't wrong, but it was Ben Pecos who handed the can through the bars.

"I've talked Tommy into letting us meet in his office for a while." Ben had to yell. The noise coming from the other cell drowned out normal conversation. Tommy was saying something to the two, and they quieted before he let Sal out to follow Ben to the front of the building.

The office looked official and well used. There was a map of the reservation on one wall, a map of New Mexico on the other. Two flags commingled in an oak stand to the right of the desk, a yellow silk rectangle with a red Zia symbol and a Stars and Stripes. Sal was pleased that there were no wanted posters. He had recognized someone's picture in the post office once and had done nothing about it. He hadn't even told anyone the guy's real name. It wasn't like he knew where the guy was, but just knowing who he was and not saying anything made him feel guilty. He'd wondered if he could have been jailed for that.

"This going to be all right?" Ben dragged two chairs to more or less face each other in front of an oversized oak desk.

Sal nodded and set his Coke on the edge closest to him.

"Put a paper under that. I don't want another wet ring that doesn't come off," Tommy said from the doorway. "I'm leaving you two now. I'll be in the back. Yell if you need anything." This last was mostly said to Ben, Sal thought, as he put a magazine under the pop can.

"You ever work with that truth stuff?" Sal asked.

"Truth serum? Why do you ask that?" Ben looked genuinely surprised.

"Oh, I thought it might be helpful."

"In what way?"

Sal almost grinned. He really had Ben's attention now.

"Because I don't know if I saw what I think I saw. But maybe my brain remembers more than I think it does but can't tell me for sure without help." That was a lot for Sal to get out, but it was the truth, and he'd been giving it a lot of thought. Ben was the one who could help him—help his brain remember.

Ben frowned. "Let's talk first, then decide if we need to try something else. I'd like you to start at the beginning."

"The night Ahmed's body was found?"

"Yes."

But here Sal stopped. How much did this young man know about supernaturals? Would he believe him about the visits from Atoshle?

Sal started again slowly. "Atoshle, the ancient one, comes to visit me. He as much as told me about the death. To expect it." Sal glanced at Ben but couldn't read his expression.

"When does he visit?"

"At night. In dreams. Sometimes in person."

"Where exactly is he when you see him?"

"Looking in the windows of the trailer." Sal added softly, "Sometimes standing beside my bed."

"Don't you keep your doors locked?"

Sal shook his head. What difference would it make with supernaturals? A locked door wouldn't stop them. "Mostly

Atoshle, the ogre *kachina,* tries to scare me. I saw him that night.''

"The same night the body was found?"

Sal nodded. "He was outside my window."

"What does Atoshle look like?"

That was an odd thing for the Doc to ask, Sal thought, but he was acting like he believed him so he took a pen and sketched the mask on the back of the magazine under his drink, inking in the black slits for eyes and the fringe that covered the throat. Then he tore the corner away and handed it to Ben. He'd destroy the drawing after Ben looked at it.

Sal heard a quick intake of breath. Ben was studying the mask, but Sal could tell that it was familiar to him.

"What colors are on the mask?"

"Greens, reds, browns…"

"Tell me what Atoshle did that night."

"When I left the dining room I went back to my trailer. I laid on the bed and must have fallen asleep. I saw Atoshle standing at my kitchen window, the one above the sink. He stood there like he always does and watched me. But then I heard noises. I'd taken my hearing aid out, but I still heard something. There's never been any sound before. So, I was surprised."

"What kind of noise?"

"Grunting like a man weighted down. Atoshle disappeared, and I heard someone ask something."

"Did you hear what it was?"

"It was in English, but I didn't have my hearing aid in. Then I heard something hit the trailer."

"Someone could have dropped the body." Ben quickly sobered. "What happened next?"

"I went to the window, but Atoshle was gone. I couldn't see anything. So, I waited. Then I heard cries for help. I stepped outside but ducked back when I saw you. You know the rest."

"Why did you give Ahmed's widow the bag of amber?" Ben pulled his chair closer to Sal. "If you want me to believe you're innocent, tell me why you did that?"

Sal looked at the floor. Should he tell the Doc about the body on the hood? Or the amber rabbit left in its place? Maybe now was a good time to tell the truth about Ahmed's involvement in selling the yellow lies. But that would point a finger at Hannah. He couldn't do that. He didn't care so much what happened to himself, but .22 needed his mother.

"You were right when you said the trader looked like me. What if Atoshle made a mistake? Or killed Ahmed instead of me and left the body at my trailer to warn me? I had to make restitution with the widow."

"Why haven't you told Tommy this?"

"He'd think I was making it up."

"Maybe not." Ben told Sal about finding the mask only to have it disappear again. He added that .22 had said a masked person did the killing. "Is there any reason why someone might be wanting to scare you?"

Sal stared at the corner of the desk, pretended to be thinking. He knew the answer to this question. It was simple. If he'd never made amber, none of this would have happened. But who was trying to scare him? The ancient ones or another human who wanted the notebook? He didn't know. The only thing for certain was all this had something to do with the amber, the money it was bringing in, his copying nature; he was sure of it.

"Can't think of one." He didn't look at the Doc. Polite. He hoped his voice sounded strong. When Ben didn't say anything, he stole a glance at the man sitting opposite him. Ben seemed lost in thought. Sal waited, wondered what he could be thinking. A tap on the glass partition next to the desk broke the silence. Ben opened the door.

"I didn't think I'd have to bother you, but I need to make a couple calls and get rid of the drunks tonight if I can." Tommy had stuck his head in the door.

"No problem. We're just finishing up." Ben said. "I'll walk Sal back to his cell."

BEN SAT IN HIS PICKUP outside the jail, gathering his thoughts. He'd shared his suspicions with Tommy, told him how someone might be trying to scare Sal by impersonating a *kachina*, someone tied in with that mask that he'd seen hidden in the woods. Tommy appeared thoughtful. He said he'd do some checking too.

Ben was still vaguely uneasy. He couldn't really put a finger on what was bothering him. He didn't think Sal was suicidal, but he had complimented Tommy again on taking precautions. A jailer could never be careful enough. A small space, the embarrassment to a person's family, guilt… Guilt. That was part of his feeling of unrest. He'd bet his life Sal was telling him the truth about the supernatural. Sal had seen Atoshle. The *kachina* was real to him.

What he wasn't telling him the truth about was why he was being haunted. There was a reason, and Sal knew what it was. Ben could feel it. He didn't know how Sal's tribe viewed him. There could be some grudge, a payback, someone angry enough to have Sal witched. Ben should probably make some inquiries. Maybe Rose could be helpful. She knew the village, the gossip. He'd start there. It could be that Tommy should be looking for some disgruntled Hawikuh carver who had a beef with Sal. Someone who hid the body to make it look like Sal was involved…

The evening smelled fresh. Ben rolled down the window before he started the pickup, then pushed the sliding glass partition behind his head open all the way. The breeze promised rain. That was a good smell. A few drops had already smeared his windshield. But the scent lacked the acrid sharpness of water hitting limestone, one of those city smells that he didn't miss—wet cement.

This was probably the basic difference between Julie and him. He didn't want to live in a city. If he could help it, he never would again. And Julie? He couldn't imagine her anywhere else. As lonely as it was out here, he was drawn to the beauty, the quiet. So, wasn't he hoping for something that was highly unlikely to happen? That Julie would decide that no matter what, she couldn't live without him. He sighed. Life could get complicated. Ben pulled out of the parking lot and turned left onto the highway. He wasn't in a hurry and doubted that he'd see a car in the next five miles. There was time to think.

The headlights surprised him. He really hadn't expected traffic on this stretch of road, a minor artery between Hawikuh and Gallup. Ben was even more surprised when he recognized Dr. Lee's car. It must have taken a bunch of chocolate cake to keep a man until almost midnight when he'd have to be at the clinic by six. But maybe it was just the wiles of the landlady. Now there was a puzzle.

He replayed the conversation about prettiness. Some people just weren't meant to live so far from civilization. It made them strange. Hannah was strange. Could something like that happen to Julie? The thought jolted him. Was he just not facing reality? And why hadn't he made time to see her, talk, get caught up on her life, find out what this prince nonsense was all about? For starters, fear of rejection was pretty strong. The truth was, there didn't seem to be anywhere for the romance to go, and that hurt.

He was driving through an edge of forested land now. It had rained here earlier, and the coolness made him snap the window shut behind his head. He had reached the summit of the ridge and started down the winding highway that led to the boarding house. And a plan was forming. Not that he wanted to give shape to it quite yet, but he'd almost decided that if everyone was in bed when he got back, he'd do a little snooping in Sal's trailer. He had an excuse. He could be picking up some things that Sal had asked for. It was the perfect cover. He'd do it.

There were three vehicles parked in front of the boarding house—Hannah's Buick, Julie's rental and one other, some late model nondescript sedan parked along the rail, backed in to be more exact. He thought they must be vacationers who had pulled in for the night, judging from the Nevada license plate. His pickup made four. Not a busy night. Ben waited before he got out of the truck but didn't see a light in the house, only the hall night light, which stayed on. It would be a good time to take a look at the trailer.

The old Air Stream looked like it was straight out of the documentary on the Marlboro men—herders who used one-room portable shacks to hole up for the summer and stay within riding distance of the herd. Ben could remember seeing the trailers, high above logging roads hugging the timberline, tin smokestacks from potbellied wood burners standing tall; the chimneys towering over the silver rounded roofs as they dotted the mountains of Colorado and New Mexico exclaiming a solitary life.

This one looked fairly well cared for. A plate of siding had been tacked down where it had apparently peeled around the front window. The oblong white tank to the side suggested propane and not wood for heating. Someone had put skirting around the trailer and the steps leading to the only entrance or exit had a side rail.

Hadn't Sal said that it would be unlocked? Ben paused on the top step and took one last look at the house—no change, no lights indicating someone was up. He pulled open the trailer door, stepped inside, and snapped on his flashlight. The smell was old grease. He'd probably find a can of bacon drippings under the sink. And then there was the faint odor of mothballs—what a combination.

Two tree-shaped, pine air-fresheners, the kind you could buy in filling stations, hung suspended in the kitchen window. They hadn't been changed in a while or had wisely known when they were beaten and had given up, Ben thought.

The floor was linoleum, white with flecks of brown and scrubbed clean. Even the tiny cracks had been filled with wax. The flooring extended in one piece under the table, a Formica fold-down that separated two red vinyl covered seats and matching backs that faced each other and flanked the wide front window.

The sink was under a smaller window on the west. That must give it the distinction of being the "kitchen" window, Ben decided. There was an under-the-counter refrigerator on the left and a countertop stove, no oven, on the right. Six feet of knotty pine cupboards hung overhead.

A blue plastic drinking glass rested on the counter and a pair of jeans had been thrown across the top bunk opposite the table. That was it. Those were the only two things left "out"—the only clutter. Clutter was a luxury for people who lived in small spaces.

Ben wished he knew what he was looking for. It wasn't anything in particular or he would be able to give it a name. He had just sensed that he would be able to get a better idea of Sal—his interests, needs, who he was, some substantiation that he wasn't guilty. So far, nothing had caught his eye. He didn't think he could make a case for neat people not being murderers.

Where should he start? He hated opening cupboards and snooping, but that was what he was going to have to do. Ben took a step towards the back and almost dropped the flashlight. A soft moan came from the bottom bunk. He swept the bed with light. Whatever it was, it almost filled the space defined by plywood sides. Quickly, Ben stepped forward and pulled the quilt back.

A startled .22 blinked into the flashlight, pulled a reddened much-sucked thumb from his mouth and started to shriek in fright.

".22, it's Ben. I'm your friend, remember?"

"My friend gone," he managed to sputter between gulps for air and wiping his nose on his arm.

"Your friend will come back."

"After forever?"

"He won't be gone forever, maybe day after tomorrow."

"Promise?"

"Well,…" It certainly was easy to step into a trap with .22, and Ben didn't want to lie. "I'm pretty sure."

.22 swung both feet over the side of the bed and sat looking at Ben. He lightly tapped the heel of a sneaker against the wood paneling below the box springs, then stuck his thumb back in his mouth. He had been curled up in Sal's bed fully clothed. But for all Ben knew, maybe that's the way he slept every night, just another peculiarity.

"You sleep here?" .22's watery eyes searched Ben's face.

"No. I need to take some clothes to Sal." Ben took a guess and opened a cupboard above the top bunk and removed a pair of jeans and a tee shirt. "See. Shirt and jeans."

.22 loudly sucked his thumb but watched Ben intently.

"Me go see Sal?"

"Maybe. If he doesn't come home first. But you need to go to bed—your bed."

"Too loud."

"What's too loud?"

"My bed." Then .22 squinted his eyes, forced his head between raised shoulders and gave three realistic frog croaks— "Rrri-bit, rrri-bit, rrri-bit."

Frogs? In his bed? It probably wasn't out of the question. Ben smiled. "Come on, let's go back to the house. Chase that frog out. Tell him you need to get some sleep."

.22 giggled and slid down from the edge of the bunk tangling his feet in the quilt and pulling it with him.

"Careful. Let's put everything back like you found it." Ben bent over the bed to pull the sheets tight then turned to pick up the quilt. A tissue-wrapped package fell out of its folds and hit the floor. Ben leaned down to pick it up. The package was the size of money and had the feel of money. Someone had torn away the corner and the flashlight picked up the number one thousand—in every corner of about twelve bills.

"Money," .22 said.

"Yes." Ben tucked the packet into his jacket pocket. But what did he do that for? And in front of .22? He must be losing it. He guessed he'd learned not to leave something valuable and come back later hoping it would still be there.

"You keep?" .22 seemed overly interested.

"I'll keep it tonight. This is Sal's money and I'll take it to him in the morning."

"You buy ice cream?"

Ben laughed. "Yes, I'll buy ice cream. But not tonight. Now, let's go. I want to put this where it will be safe."

.22 followed Ben to his truck and stood sucking his thumb

as Ben unlocked the passenger-side door and tossed the packet in the glove compartment. He locked the compartment and the door—the money was making him nervous. Was he doing the right thing? It was obviously Sal's, and certainly made the bag of amber that Sal gave the widow look like chicken feed. Sal's worldly goods just took a big jump in value. It didn't make him guilty of murder, but it seemed to make him guilty of something. Twelve one-thousand-dollar bills. Where did you have to go to get currency in that denomination? Who would pay for something in bills that size? And what would they be buying?

SIX

THE NIGHT WAS creeping along on little cat feet—no, it was fog that was supposed to do that. But there wasn't much of that in the desert. Maybe, the night was slinking—that was something a cat could do, slink along on little velvet paws. Big velvet paws. Ben straightened the sheet, turned onto his back and looked at the ceiling.

He heard the grandfather clock in the hallway chime twice. He rolled over and checked his digital alarm clock on the nightstand—two and a couple zeros. This was getting him nowhere. He had put twelve thousand dollars in his truck. Why had he taken it? He could have left it in the trailer. To safeguard it—that's what he was telling himself. But he knew that he'd have to turn it in, hand it over to Tommy. Or give it to Sal. Or just ask Sal what he wanted done with it. What was he thinking? He had to give it to Sal and leave Tommy out of it. But where would Sal have gotten twelve, new one-thousand-dollar bills? He was a master carver. Could he have sold some work? Maybe. But what were the odds that the buyer or buyers would pay in thousand-dollar bills?

Ben sat up. He never had been any good at solving problems in the middle of the night. As long as he was awake, he'd just slip out to the truck and make sure it was still there. He'd be back in a flash and get a good night's sleep. He pulled on a pair of jeans and running shoes but didn't bother with a shirt. This wouldn't take long.

The night air was cool and muggy. He wished he'd slipped on a shirt. Lightning danced across the horizon to the west. There would probably be more rain before morning. Ben had used the back door off the porch and now rounded the house on the sidewalk that ran along the kitchen. The light was on. Ben slowed to look in the window. No one was in view. Someone must have come down for a snack and forgot the light. He'd turn it off on his way back.

He was feeling better about his decision to take the money to Sal in the morning. He could stop by the jail on his way to work, and he'd ask Sal what he wanted him to do with it. It wasn't Ben's business how he came by it. Maybe Sal would want him to put it in the bank, but he doubted that. But asking the owner was the right thing. He wouldn't go to Tommy first. Finding the money was unusual, but he didn't have any reason to suspect Sal of wrongdoing.

Two solar-cell yard lights illuminated the front of the boarding house and pushed the shadows to the back of the trading post. Ben glanced at Sal's trailer. It was dark. He doubted that .22 would have gone back. He hurried down the brick steps and felt a rush of relief when he reached his truck and tried the passenger-side door. All was secure—exactly like he'd left it. He turned towards the house. He'd go in the front since the house was always open. Nothing was ever locked out here—in its own way, that was reassuring. But he wasn't certain that he'd get used to it.

Hannah's rooms were at the top of the stairs above the parlor, and as he turned to shut the front door he heard voices. Angry voices. First Hannah in a tirade of what could have been expletives, then a second deep bass voice rising as a threat followed by silence. Had they heard the door close? Ben paused before continuing down the hall to the kitchen.

It had crossed his mind to knock on Hannah's door. But he

sensed that that might not be welcome. Maybe she was entertaining. He suppressed a laugh. That sounded stilted. If he believed rumors, she didn't have any problem hopping into bed with someone. So maybe the car he'd seen earlier belonged to a gentleman caller. He flipped off the kitchen light. One, it wasn't his business; and two, he was dead-tired. He needed to get some sleep before morning.

"Ben?" The knock on his door was insistent.

"What?" Ben sat up. What time was it? Six o'clock. He'd set the alarm for seven.

"Someone broke into your truck," Hannah said through the door.

"I'll be there in a minute." Ben bolted for his clothes. Broke in? He was trying to gather his thoughts. What did this mean? For one thing, the money wouldn't be there. He'd bet on that. Now what would he do?

"I've called Tommy. He should be here any minute. This has never happened before. It's always so safe out here. But first the murder, now this—who's going to want to buy the place now?" Hannah looked on the verge of tears when Ben opened the door.

"I'll see what's missing." He walked past her and hurried out the front door. He was being insensitive, but he'd have time later to reassure her—if he could. He couldn't deny that current events put the place in a bad light.

Ben could see the shattered window from the porch. Someone hadn't wanted to be neat about it; maybe he hadn't needed to be. The sound must have been muffled by the storm. Ben hadn't heard a thing but from the number of puddles, there had been a good sized gully-washer.

The first thing he saw as he looked in the passenger-side window was the open glove compartment. It looked like someone had taken a can opener to it but more likely a crowbar. The little interior light was still on, shining brightly on nothing. The truck's manuals, usually neatly stacked in the cubbyhole, were now on the floorboards. But the tissue paper package wasn't anywhere to be seen. He went around to the driver's side, opened the door and leaned in. His CD player was gone. They had left his CDs, about twenty-five of them—a halfway decent eclectic collection, if he did say so himself. A box of tools that he kept under the front seat was gone. Was there a chance that the thieves really did want the CD player and tools and found the money as a bonus? Maybe. Or it was a cover-up? But who knew about the money besides .22? Could some-one have watched him put something in the glove compartment and broke in on the odd chance it was of value?

"What'd you lose?" Tommy asked peering in the passenger-side window.

"The usual. Tools. CD player."

"We'll dust for prints but don't get your hopes up. We're starting to see more of this kind of thing out here. Hardly ever come up with a suspect. It's probably kids." Tommy stepped back. "We won't find a footprint or a decent set of tire tracks in this goo. Rain didn't do you any favors. I'm taking for granted it was locked." Tommy pointed to the window, "Looks like you made 'em work for it."

Ben nodded.

"You're too close to the highway—makes it easy for some-one to break in, grab what he wants and keep on moving."

Ben thought about the money. Should he say something? But what could he say? He wasn't about to tell Tommy about an-other bit of evidence that he had seen but wasn't to be found now. He'd done that once before. And he needed time to think.

"I got a surprise for you." Tommy pointed with his chin.

Ben looked towards the trading post. There was Sal with a broom in his hand, sweeping down the driveway like nothing had happened.

"Somebody make bail?" Ben asked.

"No bail. He was evicted." Tommy laughed uproariously, then gasped for breath. "They closed the jail, turned him out."

"How can a jail be closed?" Ben still thought Tommy was kidding.

"This time the plumbing did it. It didn't meet code. De-partment of Public Safety stepped in. Last time the fire escapes did us in. We didn't have any. Gets to be a real legal issue, prisoner's rights and all that. The lawyers get a hold of this kind of stuff and ask for the moon—last time they wanted individual towels, soap, a shower, nutritious meals... I draw the line at putting mints on their pillows.'' More laughter.

"How can you let someone suspected of murder just walk away?'' Ben was perplexed. He didn't believe Sal was guilty, but what if there had been an ax murderer in the jail? Would he be out walking around, too?

Tommy got serious. "What you said about the mask, how Atoshle appears to Sal, made me think that he's done something he shouldn't have and someone's putting a spell on him. That mask you found in the woods could have been part of a costume.'' They both watched Sal finish with the sweeping and go back into the trading post.

"He may be in danger,'' Ben said.

Tommy nodded soberly.

Ben felt another urge to share his knowledge of the twelve thousand dollars. But he didn't, and wasn't really sure why he didn't. Maybe this was a good opening, but he let it pass.

"Guess you'll need this for your insurance company.'' Tommy tore off the top sheet of the pad on his clipboard after he'd signed the bottom. "Robbery, locked cab, broken passenger-side window—that ought to do it.''

"Where's your office going to be while they're working on the jail?''

"More or less next to yours. They've given me a corner of the seniors center.''

"Lucky you. You'll have to sharpen up your checker-playing skills to stay there.''

Tommy laughed, "Could be,'' then abruptly added, "how's the redhead?''

Ben winced. "Okay, I guess.''

"You got that property staked out?''

"Not exactly. We were friends years ago but couldn't seem to make a go of things then, don't know that we'll try again.''

"Hmmmmm."

Ben waited, but Tommy didn't say any more.

TOMMY HAD DROPPED Sal off at the door of the trading post. Not open for business and here it was six-thirty. Sal didn't even go back to the trailer first, just took the keys from under a mat behind the deli, opened the back door, and picked up a broom on his way out front. He'd seen the For Sale signs, one up by the house and another in the window of the deli-mart. He wasn't sure he knew what that meant.

Would Hannah leave after all these years? Now that .22 was out of school and could travel? But where would she go? This was all she knew. But, she was Anglo. That made the difference. This wasn't her home. She didn't come from an ancient people who had lived in this area for hundreds of years, whose roots tugged at her heels like an anchor, bound her to the traditions, to her clan. No, in that way, she was free. And he'd told her he would stop making amber. Was he chasing her away? He stopped to unlock the cash register.

"I want you to go with me." Sal didn't turn around at the sound of Hannah's voice. She must have followed him in the back door but what was this nonsense she was saying? "I have to get away." She was standing beside him now. "What is there here for you? You've been threatened. Someone may have thought they killed you. Tommy may try to arrest you again." She had walked around the counter and put her arms around his neck; his chin rested on the top of her head as she nestled against his shoulder. "We should be together. We could go anywhere you want."

He didn't want to go anywhere. He couldn't go anywhere. Indians who left the reservation were never happy. His cousin Alfred had died a month after he left—run over by a school bus. He shifted slightly, but Hannah moved too, holding him tighter, her body now molded to his. Why was she coming on to him like this at this hour? He hoped she didn't want to do it in the walk-in freezer. They had tried that once, but it was just too cold—standing up, leaning against a couple dozen cartons of frozen Thanksgiving turkeys that had come in that morning. The cold had accentuated the blue veins just beneath Hannah's translucent skin giving her a sick, bluish-green cast and her nipples had turned maroon. But, so had his peter. He shuddered.

"What's wrong?" She had pulled back to ask.

"I need to think."

"What is there to think about? The business has made enough money to support the two of us. You know, you could continue..."

Sal knew that she meant the amber when she talked about "the business."

"Unless you want to share your little secret with me." She paused, "Once the house sells, I could pay you whatever you ask." She walked to the other side of the counter and began to straighten the cigarette displays.

This was better—breathing room. Sal sighed. "The recipe is not for sale."

"Not even for one hundred thousand dollars?" She whispered the number, but it seemed to bounce off of the shelves like an echo swirling around him.

"When the house and all this sells, I'll have it. Is that enough?"

"I won't sell."

"Then come with me."

She took a step forward; he braced himself and tried not to think of the freezer.

"One hundred thousand is a lot of money."

"I don't need money."

"You wouldn't have to live in some stupid, crummy trailer behind some stupid, crummy store out in the sticks." Her voice rose.

He ignored her anger. Since that wasn't his view of things, he didn't say anything. He had thought that if he went anywhere, he might take the trailer with him. It was his home.

"I don't mind."

"You're impossible." Now her voice was a shriek.

Sal stepped back; he knew what was coming. The first can

of soup hit the freezer door, the second knocked a calendar off the back wall. Hannah didn't take aim, just wildly threw the closest thing to her—in anger, frustration? Both, he guessed. She hated having to live with the word "no." Unlucky for him, she stood next to a three-tier display of Campbells. But then the pyramid tumbled to the floor. One can rolled to the front door, the others slumped together in a pile. It seemed to defuse things.

Hannah had jumped out of the way and stood with her back to him. There were a couple minutes of silence. Without turning around she said, "Clean this mess up and hose down the driveway; Gloria's bringing prospective buyers around eight." Her voice was calm, but hard.

She smoothed back her hair and straightened the jumper she was wearing over an old white shirt, taking the time to methodically roll up the sleeves. Then stepping gingerly over scattered cans of soup, she left, never glancing back.

Sal watched her go. They'd had three-for-a-dollar sales on dented cans before. There wouldn't be an apology. But she'd be okay later. This thing about him going with her or selling his recipe was a new twist. He didn't want to do either one and continuing to refuse would probably bring on another fit of temper. She seemed adamant. He'd wait. But what would he do? Ask Hannah about the trailer, he guessed, later, when things were calmer. He could put the trailer next to his sister's house. She didn't live in the village exactly, more like on one edge along the highway. But she had two bathrooms. That was a plus. Sal had helped dig the second septic tank.

What if he had one hundred thousand dollars? His wife would hound him to death, that was a sure thing, if she found out about that kind of money. And if he didn't give it to her, what would he do with it? His sister's oldest son had wanted to go to college, but then became a firefighter instead.

Sal had already given a few thousand to his sister around Christmas for new carpet and furniture. Then, he bought her that new van in February. He didn't think she needed anything else soon. No, the money would be a misery. He was a master

carver, and drew a disability check from the military. That was
enough for him. He never kept much more than pocket change
around and seldom needed much more. When he got a little
ahead, he gave it to Father Leget to continue with the restora-
tion of the Old Mission. If God meant him to make a larger
contribution, he'd give him a sign.

JULIE STOOD ON the front porch and watched Hannah and the
realtor give Ben's pickup a wide berth. She wondered what
excuse Hannah would come up with for the broken glass that
littered the parking area. Must have been good because no one
missed a beat, just continued to walk up the steps towards the
porch. The middle-aged couple, prospective buyers, looked like
they'd just sold the farm in Wakeegan. Julie got a distinct sense
of sitting ducks.

"Julie Conlin is with *Good Morning America*." Hannah was
using her exceptionally cheery voice, Julie thought.

"One of those perks of living in what has to be called a
natural wonder, a center of antiquity," the realtor chirped.
"Jackie Kennedy Onassis visited us once—you get all kinds of
important people out this way."

It was nice to be an important person this morning. Maybe
there'd be a cut in rent for posing on the porch for prospective
buyers, Julie mused.

"Will you be joining us for breakfast?" Hannah paused before following the others into the house.

"I'm giving Ben a ride to the office. I'll get something in
the village."

"Suit yourself. We're having peach blintzes," Hannah said
over her shoulder.

Even the fare had been bumped up a notch. No assortment
of dry cereals for this group. Hannah must really want to sell
this place. And why not? It must be a nightmare to maintain.

"Sure you don't want to break bread with Mr. and Mrs.
Sucker?" Ben had lowered his voice as he pushed open the
screen door. He must have passed Hannah's entourage in the
hall.

"It's not even tempting. I don't think I could handle an hour of chitchat about the 'center of antiquity.' "

"That bad?"

"Trust me," Julie said. "But why 'sucker'? That seems pretty harsh."

"Hannah's admitted to this place being an albatross."

"It would be for someone by herself. It's always easier if you have someone to share things with." Shit. She had rehearsed how she would keep their conversation away from talking about just this sort of thing and here, the second or third thing out of her mouth is something sappy about couples and sharing. And Ben was grinning.

"It sounds like you're beginning to see the light."

"Don't count on it, buster. It takes more than a couple days in the country to turn around the devoted city-dweller—no matter how interesting the lure is."

"As long as she doesn't mind my trying."

"I'm fair game."

"It's going to sound trite, but I'm glad you're here." Ben got in on the passenger's side before continuing, "Am I forgiven for ignoring you the last couple days?"

"If you tell me why you've been avoiding me." Julie slipped behind the wheel, then turned to face him. "Or explain how you've gotten to be on smooching terms with the landlady in such a short time. I'm sorry. I really have no right to pry. Forget I said that." She hadn't meant to admonish him. It really wasn't any of her business.

"Smooching terms?" Ben was grinning. "Like this?" He leaned across the bucket seats, drew her to him and gently tilted her head back, then with his lips an inch from hers said, "I'd rather be on smooching terms with you."

Her arms went around his neck in one automatic fluid motion, and she leaned into him. "I've—" His mouth blocked any more conversation. Hunger. That was the only way to describe it—on his part and hers. Did she appear too needy as she pressed against him, her mouth following his lead, open slightly, lips caressing, parting as his tongue pushed between?

He pulled back to nuzzle her ear, kiss her neck, trace the curve of her cheek with his finger.

"I've missed this. You," he corrected, and it was his turn to look embarrassed.

"I didn't know it was possible to fog up the car windows in June."

He laughed but left his hand on her shoulder as she turned to start the car. She didn't say any more—was she afraid of saying something too personal, or just saying too much? She was trying to breathe evenly, but it was difficult. What was that old saying about having your breath taken away? How could she have ever left this man—even in the name of youth and ideals?

"Can we start again? See where it leads?" he asked. He was watching her as she backed out and turned onto the highway. "Not that I could have stopped you, but I shouldn't have let you go four years ago—career or no career."

"No, you couldn't have stopped me, but I sort of hoped you would try."

"I've got a feeling that we need to work on our communication skills." He was laughing, and Julie relaxed. It felt right to be with Ben. Talking was easy. They discussed careers. Each fell back into the pattern of asking the other's opinion—and listened to it like close friends would. He continued to touch her, just the hand on the shoulder but she liked his closeness. It was reassuring and exciting all in one.

"I'd like your help," he said. "You want to know what has kept me preoccupied the last couple days?"

They were in the parking lot outside Ben's office, and he had turned towards her making no move to leave. He was so serious, she found herself nodding.

"I think Sal may be in danger." He told her what Sal had said about the visits from the *kachina,* Atoshle, on the night the body was found, and how .22 had shown him where a mask was hidden. And he told her about the money, the twelve one-thousand-dollar bills he'd put in the glove compartment.

"Having that much money doesn't make him guilty of anything. Are you sure it was his?"

"I don't think it belonged to .22 if that's what you're thinking. All he talked about was getting ice cream. The question is, what do I do now? I've managed to lose twelve thousand dollars of another man's money."

"Okay," Julie said. "Let's say that's what has happened. You took money belonging to Sal and lost it to whomever. If the money was payment for some kind of contraband, no one is going to say anything—like if someone hid the money in Sal's trailer knowing he was gone—"

"What are you suggesting I do?"

"Maybe nothing. Why not wait until someone says something—gives himself away. Or you could question Sal in a roundabout way and watch his reaction." Julie paused. "Maybe I could ask him, approach the topic of money in general—in relation to his work. I've scheduled another interview with him. Let me do it."

"That might be better," Ben said.

"Has anyone found the murder weapon yet? The trader was stabbed, wasn't he? Someone said the wound looked like it was caused by some kind of knife."

"Tommy should be getting a copy of the autopsy from the Office of Medical Investigation any day now. I'll ask to see it. My best guess is it was a narrow, single blade knife, stiletto type, like a switchblade. And I'd guess he'd been dead a good twenty-four hours before his body was found. Tommy's pretty certain he was killed somewhere else and dumped behind the trailer later."

"It's possible," Julie said thoughtfully, "that the trader was involved in something he shouldn't have been. Maybe with Sal."

"Could be. I know Sal is holding something back. I thought he was going to tell me the other night at the jail, but he didn't."

"You know, whoever scalped the guy had to know Indian customs, and know how Sal would react. The person who washed that scalp knew he'd have an audience—knew what Sal would do on the fourth day, where he'd go.''

"I've thought of that," Ben said. "Indian ritual is fairly predictable.''

"Does Sal have any enemies in the village?"

"I'm hoping the caseworker at the clinic can answer that.''

"You know this could be nothing more than a family dispute gone wrong," Julie sighed. "But I've been doing my homework on the tribe. Hallucinations are the disease of supernatural origin.''

The killing seemed out of place, Julie thought, a knifing, to be exact, something almost unheard of in the tribe. Witches caused bodily harm, illness, but by remote control—they seldom took the initiative.

"Have I lost you?''

"Sorry." Julie looked up sheepishly. "I was going to ask why Tommy locked up Sal in the first place. He didn't confess?''

"Not in so many words. Tommy feels circumstantial evidence implicates Sal. The fact that he gave this Ahmed's widow a bag of amber seems to indicate a pretty definite involvement.''

"He does a lot of work in amber," Julie said.

"Sort of his signature from what I gather. One of a handful in the village who can afford the stuff at thirty dollars an ounce.''

"Hannah carries supplies for carvers in the trading post. I wonder if she's the one who sells it to him?''

"Or trades it out for work. That might make it accessible.''

Ben glanced at his watch then reached for her hand. "This has been great.''

"How does that line go—'just like old times'?''

"Better," Ben said.

"Better?''

"Now I may have some idea of what might be important to me in life." One big grin and he opened the car door but didn't get out.

"What was all that about a prince?"

"Got me out of kissing a frog. I told .22 I already had a prince."

Ben laughed, "Maybe I should make an honest woman out of you." The kiss this time was tender and loving, almost chaste—but it still left Julie trying to catch her breath.

SEVEN

THE MOLDS WERE made out of rubber as heavy and thick as treadless tires. Sal had experimented with metal and plastic, but the first was too rigid and the second melted. He moved the tray holding a rubber mat that contained over a hundred indentations to better light. He needed good light when he poured. The fluorescent bulb above his head was fizzling and popping. He snapped it a couple times with his thumb and middle finger. The two other banks of lights gleamed a soft yellow. Hannah had thought of everything for his underground workshop—the lights emitted vitamin D, like the sun. Only these were grow lights for humans. It was supposed to keep him from becoming depressed. They had tested them on people in Alaska. Sal wondered how they had worked.

It was comfortable down here, cool, fairly well ventilated. Hannah had moved in a straight-backed chair and a cot. Not that he was the napping type, but it made the place seem more homey. And he was going to spend a lot of time down here, afternoons, evenings over the next couple months when he wasn't needed at the store. In two months he'd produce enough amber to pay off all Hannah's bills. Then, he was finished.

The heat from the Bunsen burner warmed his face. The open flame wasn't a problem. There was good air circulation. If he could just get over feeling trapped. He had a hunch that he'd test the ability of those lights. It would take some getting used to, working underground, living like a mole.

He straightened the rubber mold in front of him. It was pliable; he never had to fear breaking the nuggets. He filled the holes with molten amber and switched on the timer; their cooling time was crucial. He seldom had throwaways.

Hannah had treated his being in jail like he'd taken off on vacation. But she was right. It had been over a month since he'd produced any amber. The house painter wanted the second half of his payment, and the school had called. She was being pressured. She had an order for fifty pounds, half of it had to be plain. Those were her instructions, her orders. He didn't really mind. This would be the last of it. The last made under their business agreement.

The fifty pounds would pay off everything—the school, the painting of the house, the plumbing. Sal agreed that the boarding house needed renovation in order to attract a buyer. Hannah was right to invest in its upkeep in order to get top dollar. It was .22's inheritance as well as Hannah's—maybe the only money he'd ever have in life. He deserved a fair start.

Twenty-five pounds would go quickly without enclosures. Besides, most of the beetles had died. It was hard keeping insects alive in jars even with a good food source. He hadn't been here to look after them. And he could always get more.

He looked around the lab. In three short months, maybe less, all this wouldn't exist. Would he miss it? A little. Aside from helping .22, he liked the challenge. He proved something—did something that no one else could—he rivaled nature. But his deceit had brought him trouble. And he'd never had a clear conscience. That's why he sold very little of the carved fake locally. Ninety-nine percent of his amber carvings went out of state or were sold to tourists. People from Nebraska or Illinois or Alabama—people he'd never see. Nameless, faceless dupes who wouldn't remember that he was the carver of their treasure, their supposed gem.

Still, he'd put in a lot of work—tested recipe after recipe, adding something here, deleting it there. He wondered if people would believe him if he told them he combined tree sap with clear, melted plastic? To be more exact polyurethane, polyester and resin. The resin added color and sheen.

But the resin had been the difficult part. First, he had ordered mastic, an aromatic, astringent resin from a small anacardiaceous evergreen native to the Mediterranean. That had been expensive. And he'd had to drive into Albuquerque to find someone who could order it for him. Next, he tried copal, a highly lustrous resin from tropical trees. But, if anything, it made the amber look too shiny, too fake.

He then learned to distill the oil of turpentine from the crude oleoresin of the piñon pine and produce a hard, brittle resin of deep yellow-brown. Closer. But the color was still too dark— too much like Haitian amber and it didn't bring top dollar. Then he read that the resin could be manufactured by the polymerization of simple molecules like they did for varnishes. And he knew he had stumbled upon an important piece of the puzzle. He went to see his niece's husband.

His niece was married to a chemist, a professor at the University of New Mexico. It was his analysis that helped him decide the amounts, the ratios. But the clever part, the trick, was in the cooling—cooling the amber so that it wouldn't crack—that and keeping the color pure. His amber wouldn't turn dark or streak if left in the sun. He came up with a product that would stand up to the heat of polishing and drilling. The chunks were hard without being brittle. His product never lost its unique transparency under high powered buffing and would never feel slightly tacky if forgotten on the dash of the car in hundred degree weather. It even stood up nicely to the old-fashioned, hand operated bow-drill.

And it wasn't just that he had mastered the amber. His inserts were lifelike, perfectly encapsulated specimens of nature. That was another tricky part, a challenging part. The better the insert, the higher the price a piece could command. Hannah had gotten seven hundred dollars, wholesale, for a one-inch oblong with a housefly.

He didn't use them very often. Houseflies were difficult to work with—and too common. But they were safe. Flies preserved for 40 million years appeared as lifelike as modern houseflies, Musca domestica. He'd read that somewhere, in a report on genetic research on prehistoric organisms, then he'd seen a piece of 40 million year old amber in the Museum of Natural History in Albuquerque, and it was like staring at his own work.

Amber had suddenly become popular to study. Thanks to the movies, everyone wanted to believe that you could reconstruct dinosaur DNA from blood-sucking insects found in amber. But science was worried about pathogenic microbes. They feared the accidental release of ancient bacteria found in beetles which might defoliate a modern forest or wipe out a species.

Sal wasn't sure about that, but the article had reassured him that encapsulating the scavenger beetle was a good idea. Beetles had been around for a long time and they hadn't changed much in appearance. And they looked good. If he placed them just right, their pinchers stood out like weapons. He'd also come close to mastering leg placement. Seldom did he allow a specimen to rest with legs doubled back under its body. He was proudest of those whose wings flared slightly revealing an iridescent body poised on six legs. One time he had managed a mosquito right in the center of a two inch cube. He liked it so much he carved a frog around it. An amber frog with a mosquito in its stomach had gotten a lot of attention—and a big price.

It would be funny if someday a million or so years from now, entomologists would search his amber for viable bacteria. Or today. Would one of his nuggets find its way into a lab? Then what? Could he be found out? Sal didn't want to dwell on that. He'd been lucky so far.

He wondered what would happen to the drying chambers when the lab was dismantled—the vacuum tubes that sucked the juices from the insects, twigs and leaves until all that remained was a shell, an opaque hull, a shadowy outline of veins, hairy legs, pinchers in shades of brown. He laughed. Placing the inserts had been tedious—more error than success at first. But then he learned to pour a base in a tiny mold, place the insect—seldom in the middle, more often to one side—then fill the remaining area with cooling amber. The trick again was temperature but the result was almost always stunning. He had discovered that if he dipped the dried insect in liquid resin and allowed it to semidry it would hold its shape. The resin melded with its surroundings so that this original bubble was never detected.

Amber was expensive, much in demand. Good carvers like Rhoda Quam, Annette Tsikewa and Eddington Hannaweeke preferred amber. All purchased amber from the trading post. Even those who used to go into Albuquerque and buy African amber trade beads paid the extra for his and saved themselves a trip. And there was never very much available for the local carvers, never enough to arouse suspicion. Hannah knew her market, he always gave her that.

The timer went off. He switched on the fans, circulating air, equal distribution, and poked the chunks from the mat, letting each roll onto the wire rack and made certain that none was touching another. Their color was perfect. Each nugget glowed a warm, fiery gold. He had experimented with the color on this batch. A touch more resin, a mixture this time from Chinese elm. The formula was complicated, intricate, and constantly evolving.

It would take the better part of two months to make fifty pounds. He couldn't make more than sixteen ounces at a time. Slow. Hannah always tried to rush him. But he would finish before they left, before new people would take over the trading post. The result was the most important thing, like the nuggets in front of him. They were above suspicion. Wasn't that what she had insisted upon? He wondered what she would say if she knew that he was also able to make tortoiseshell?

The work almost always took his mind off of his problems. Lulled him into believing that all was well. Once was he could get lost in its intensity—the making of amber, the shaping of fetishes. Today, he had some thinking he had to do. He was almost sorry that the jail was closed. He had felt safe—had wanted to be there because Atoshle wouldn't find him there, wouldn't come to him. Now? He was worried. Atoshle was here; he felt his presence—was it an omen of his death? Unless he could figure out how to stop him, find out what he wanted, who had sent him—Sal would die. But that meant a ceremony and cost.

He checked the nuggets and turned each on the rack. He liked the unusual depth of bronze-gold color that each nugget emitted from its center. He reached in his pocket; he'd make a note of the addition of elm. It was never far away from him now, his notebook, small enough to fit into a hip pocket, top of his boot, under a buttoned flap in his shirt pocket. All his notes, the trial and error approaches to what was cooling on the racks in front of him were contained, crammed onto those pages. He hadn't always carried it. But something told him to now. Anything worth one hundred thousand dollars probably needed to be protected. Sal looked around the room. There was a fortune in front of him, but the key was his notebook. Without that, everything else was worthless. No one would be able to duplicate his work—not without the recipe.

Sal turned the nuggets one last time. Perfect. The batch was uniform, striking in color, excellent consistency. Next, he did what he should have done when this underground lab was first completed; he placed his own personal fetishes on a shelf above the cot: a piece of elk antler that resembled a snake; a red pipestone badger; an alabaster wolf with bands of sinew around its middle securing a lightning bolt of abalone, an eagle feather and tuft of hair from the undercoat of a bear; and the quarter-sized flat obsidian circle resembling a turtle.

When he felt his life's energies sputter like a drowning candle flame, he would call upon Wiloloane, the spirit of lightning personified in the snake—the spirit that would intensify the power of the other fetishes. Sal took the twisted piece of horn in his hands and breathed in its essence. The snake was a reminder that he was mortal but connected with the supernatural—those who had gone before. It reminded him that he wasn't alone, that feelings of isolation were a figment of his coyote nature, the trickster whose weaknesses of selfishness and arrogance could invade Sal's being, setting him up to be the prey of others.

He thought of the little silver pin he had seen at the trading post—a coyote, legs spraddled, bandanna around its neck and a set of perfectly etched tire tracks across its abdomen—the Santa Fe coyote as roadkill. Now, that was a sense of humor he liked. Maybe he should have bought it. It could have been just the medicine he needed.

He adjusted the white wolf to face east. Not that this fetish would see the sun rise from its basement home, but facing the direction of "new light" would help it to generate ideas and truth. Sal leaned forward and breathed in the air surrounding this white figure streaked with orange; its downward pointing tail and sharp pricked ears lending it an air of realism. This fetish had brought his grandfather and father good hunting and had been blessed by the ceremony to give it strength, then later dipped in the blood of the kill to say thank-you. But now, the abalone arrow secured by the turquoise bead on its back would help the wolf give him insights, flashes of light, that would show Sal the truth.

The pipestone badger was the guardian of the south and the summer people. Sal picked it up and absently rubbed its smooth sides. The symbol of his clan—if one fetish seemed to keep him in touch with self, with his surroundings, it was the badger. Aggressive when defending what is his, the badger reminded Sal that all humans have a destructive side—one that can erode good qualities and tempt one to follow base instincts—to put competitiveness or vengeance or physical harm above reason. He placed it back on the shelf and turned its head to the south.

The turtle meant long life. Sal smiled and felt calmer with the thumbnail sized circular piece of obsidian in his hand. Hannah had gotten a sack of "worry rocks" to put in a box by the cash register at the trading post, twenty-five cents each. At first, Sal had thought they wouldn't sell. Then he watched as tourists would pick one up, rub it, roll it around in their hands and buy it. Attracted by the smoothness, how it would take on the warmth of one's skin; the customers found them irresistible. He had carried the turtle in his pocket for years and enjoyed it in the same way. This ancient symbol of the mother earth never sought to go where it could not navigate in the water or on land. And always it was tenacious, cautious—achieving where others would fail. It was a good symbol to have with him at all times.

Sal stood back and surveyed the shelf of fetishes, then prayed that his guardians liked their new home. He held a leather pouch of cornmeal above his head and asked that this sustenance honor and keep them from hunger. He placed a pinch in front of each fetish, and felt relief flood his body. He should have brought these amulets out before. Their home was a fetish jar which he kept secure in the trailer. But this seemed better; they were in a position to do good here. He would let them get used to their new surroundings before he placed them back into the jar lined with feathers and sprinkled with powdered turquoise and shell.

JULIE HAD SUNG the entire musical score from *West Side Story*, well, at least the most popular numbers, without accompaniment by the time she got back to the boarding house after dropping Ben off at the clinic. Luckily her audience had been an open road, bright sunshine, and two ground squirrels sitting on a rock because she was tone-deaf. But she felt incredible. Would she have believed it? After all this time? Her feelings for Ben were stronger than ever. And his for her? The same, if she could believe that kiss. And he'd sounded sincere. Maybe, she should reconsider career versus commitment.

She'd try to talk with Sal after lunch, try to find out if he was missing any money. She'd promised to do that much for Ben, but she didn't have a clue how to go about it. She could see Hannah, real estate agent and prospects talking on the steps of the boarding house as she pulled in. From the smiles it looked like all had gone well. So well, in fact, Julie watched the agent walk over to the For Sale sign and smooth a Sold sticker diagonally across it. Sold. That was fast. Must have been the peach blintz.

Hannah was waving for her to join them. Why not? What was there to lose. Julie couldn't be overly excited about a transaction she knew little about. But if she loved it out here, why wouldn't someone else?

"Isn't it wonderful? We never thought we'd find just exactly what we've been looking for so fast." The woman gushed on, "Albert just sold both of our McDonalds in Oklahoma City. If I never see another pair of golden arches, it'll be too soon."

Polite laughter, then the agent broke in, "Miss Conlin, it's my understanding that *Good Morning America* might like to do some filming from here?"

My God. Had she used that to help make a sale? "A tentative filming date has been set for mid-August. Will that be a problem?" Julie anticipated the answer.

"Oh, my goodness, no." The new owner could barely contain herself. "Albert and I both feel so fortunate to get that kind of publicity. And we just want you to know that we'll honor all the arrangements that you've made with Mrs. Rawlings."

"Harold and I will be gone by August first."

"That's just a month." Julie looked at Hannah.

There was a smugness about Hannah, Julie thought. Maybe she should look for canary feathers hanging out of her mouth. This had to be a coup to sell the place that fast—and leave so quickly.

"Albert and I won't be back until then. Albert may come on ahead without me. It will take me the next two months to dig my way out of that house of ours. We've been there twenty-three years. Do you have any sense of what you can accumulate in that time?"

Julie wasn't certain whom she was addressing, but guessed the woman didn't expect an answer. Then she turned to Julie.

"If you need to plan any shots ahead of time, you'll be pleased to know that almost everything will remain the same."

"Everything?" Julie had no idea what the woman was talking about.

"Pictures stay, the ones in the parlor, and the grand piano— Mrs. Rawlings is selling all the original artifacts that came from her husband's family. All the old four-poster beds will stay, oak commodes, dressers, the grandfather clock in the hall. If you need to know the layout, it will be pretty much the same.''

How odd. They were just walking away. That explained how they could be ready to leave in a month. But how could someone just walk away from a lifetime of memories—and not just Hannah's. This was .22's heritage. Julie glanced at Hannah and got a sweet smile in affirmation.

''That's very helpful to know. I will be planning some of the shots in advance.'' In fact, she'd planned on putting the entire twelve-member crew up at Hannah's, use the boarding house as headquarters, as well as a backdrop. She probably couldn't fault the agent for using already booked rooms as a sales tool.

''That's wonderful. We have so much to look forward to.''

Julie looked at the husband. Hadn't someone called him Albert? Hopefully, he had a mind of his own. Surely, you couldn't own a McDonalds if you didn't talk, but maybe it was easier this way—let the little woman take center stage. He seemed to be from that ''little woman'' era—funny how men's reactions to women could be defined by eras. If a woman's hairstyle could place her within five years of her high school graduation, then how a man reacted to women was just as accurate an indicator of age. Albert had probably graduated in the early fifties.

''If you have any questions in the meantime, give me a call. Our office will be acting as representatives for the Scotts until they take possession of the property.'' The real estate agent seemed anxious to herd her newest profits back to the car. Hannah and Julie watched them leave.

''Where's .22?''

''Harold is in his room. This is all too hard on him. It's the only real home he's ever known.''

Then why not take some of the reminders of his father and grandfather, Julie wondered.

''What will you do?'' Julie hadn't meant to come out with it like that. But she was curious.

''Me?'' Hannah had swung sharply toward her then turned

back to gaze at the trading post. "I've thought I might go back to school. Do you think that's stupid? At my age?"

"No, not at all. You have a background in—archeology, isn't it?"

"Anthropology."

"It would make perfect sense. Your years out here. It would give you an advantage, I'd think."

"Maybe."

"Will you stay in New Mexico?"

"Never."

Julie was surprised at the vehemence. Why would you stay somewhere for twenty odd years if you didn't like it?

"I've promised myself greener pastures," Hannah added. "Literally. I want to go where the woods are filled with pines that shoot up into the sky—not like those scrubby, ten foot tall make-believe trees. That isn't a forest. That's a joke." Julie followed the sweep of Hannah's arm as it took in the wooded area behind the deli-mart and Sal's trailer. "I was born in Maine."

Julie waited, but that seemed to sum up Hannah's feelings, her reasons for wanting to leave.

"Will .22, ah, Harold, go back to school?"

"I'm hoping he can get some vocational training wherever we end up. Don't you think he could work in a restaurant? Salad maker? Dishwasher?"

Julie had never thought about it but couldn't see someone with that little motor control handle knives or slippery plates.

"He seems so good with wildlife; maybe he could work with animals somewhere."

"How do you know he's good with animals?" Hannah stared at Julie.

"The toads. He showed me the toads that he keeps in his room."

"You were in his room?" Hannah blanched. The absolute whiteness of her face matched the fury in her voice. "He's retarded but that doesn't mean he isn't old enough to want what he can't have." She took a breath and lowered her voice.

"You're a tease. I've watched you with men. Tommy, Ben, Sal. You just can't get enough of them panting all over you, undressing you with their eyes, their thoughts. Little Miss High and Mighty, plays awhile and then moves on. I know your type."

Julie watched Hannah's chest work to fill with air. "I can't protect him from everything. God knows, I've tried. You're evil taking advantage of someone so helpless. Do you know that?" Then Hannah stopped. A snide smile played around the corners of her mouth. "Did you keep your clothes on? Or show him what he couldn't have?"

"How can you say—" Julie started, but broke off when she heard someone coming down the walk to the side of the steps. Hannah leaned over the rail, then straightened and turned to Julie. Her voice suddenly level, cool, without any hint of malice.

"Perhaps, I've miscalculated. I'll take your word that nothing happened. But I'm warning you," Hannah lowered her voice and leaned close enough to spray Julie with spittle, "I better not have a reason to suspect you. Stay away from my son." This last was said with aspirated force and clipped enunciation. Then she was gone, up the steps, with the soft flap of her sandals as the insoles struck her heels.

"Would you have time to talk now?" Sal asked from the bottom of the steps.

"Sure. Now would be fine." But Julie must have appeared ruffled because Sal followed up by saying, "Don't be too hard on Hannah. She doesn't mean what she says. She just flies off, doesn't stop to think. She'll be okay later."

"Does she know what a champion she has in you?" Julie asked as she followed Sal towards his shed. At least there would be some privacy there.

"I don't know. Is that how you see me?" Sal didn't look over at her, just continued to walk, but he was smiling, a slight upturn at the corner of his mouth.

"I see you as one of her only friends," Julie said. On impulse she glanced towards the house and thought she saw a lace curtain at the dining room window flutter into place. Had Hannah added spying to her repertoire? Wasn't this exactly what Hannah had accused her of—being chummy with men? Here she was trotting across the lawn with Hannah's boyfriend. But, was he? Boyfriend seemed a little strong.

"Can you blame her for wanting to protect her son?" Sal asked.

Sal must have heard more of their conversation than she'd thought.

"Probably not. But I didn't do anything suspect."

"Maybe you don't see it that way. But a few years back there was a problem at his school. Someone got pregnant. It isn't like he doesn't have feelings, needs." Sal unlocked the shed and went in first to open the series of narrow windows on the east wall. ".22 has been a burden. He was sickly as a child. She's lucky that he's alive."

"You like her, don't you? I mean, it seems like the two of you are close." If he was bothered by her nosiness, Sal didn't show it. He simply pulled a chair up to the workbench for her and one for him.

"Maybe."

Maybe he liked her? Maybe they were close? Julie couldn't tell. And it appeared that Sal wasn't going to add anything.

"What will you do now that this place is sold?" Perhaps, that would shake some answers loose about the money.

"Go back to the village."

"Would you ever think of leaving—of going with Hannah and .22?"

"My life is here."

"Wouldn't it be possible to earn more money off the reservation?"

"Money?" Sal studied a box of antlers in front of him, setting one small branched pair on the table. "I have clothes on my back, food, a livelihood, a home, family…ancestors. What more should I want?"

"I realize I'm risking sounding like a raving capitalist, but haven't you ever wanted to get rich?"

"Is that what you want in life?" Sal had leaned back in his chair.

"No." Julie smiled. He was worming away from her again. "But couldn't you make more money with your carvings if you—oh, I don't know, got more exposure?"

"Thought you were going to help me with that, put me on TV and make me famous."

He was teasing. She was getting absolutely nowhere questioning him about money. She had no reason not to believe him—he was an Indian artist with simple needs, and Julie was finding it difficult to believe that the twelve thousand had belonged to him.

"I could pay you for these interviews. The program usually pays reasonable expenses—time lost from work—that sort of thing."

Sal waved her off and seemed almost offended by her offer, then he said, "You could do me a favor, though."

Julie watched as he went to the chest along the back wall.

"Would you put this in a safe place, a locker at the Greyhound terminal in Gallup? I'd appreciate it if you could rent a space in your name and bring me the key. The clutch is out in my truck." He placed a jar on the workbench. A pottery jar whose mouth was sealed with cork waxed securely around its edges for an airtight closure. Another hole, somewhat larger than a fifty cent piece, halfway down the side had been treated in the same way. The sides were rough with speckles of ground turquoise and shell and leather thongs held beads and feathers around its neck.

"It's a fetish jar." Julie was pleased that she could sound knowledgeable.

Sal nodded. "It belonged to my great-grandfather. I want it to be safe." He added after a pause, "I trust you."

"Of course I can help. I'm flattered." And she was. This was obviously something that meant a lot to him and he had asked her instead of going to Hannah. "I'll do it this afternoon." She watched as he wrapped it in newspaper and placed it in a box, then wrapped that in plain brown pieces of grocery bags and used reinforced tape at the seams.

EIGHT

"DON'T YOU THINK men who live alone get weird?" Rose snapped the lid off of the round Tupperware container of *bischochitos* and held it out to Ben.

"Did Sal ever marry?" Ben asked.

"Actually, he's still married. My aunt's husband's sister. But they haven't lived together for maybe ten, fifteen years."

"They never divorced?"

"No need to. He'd still have to support her."

"There were no children?"

"No."

"Would you say that Sal has a lot of money? By tribal standards, maybe, from his carvings?"

Rose helped herself to a *bischochito* and chewed one of the soft flat cookies filled with anise seeds. "Not rich. He gave his sister a new van first of the year. What would that set him back? Twenty-five, twenty-eight thousand, maybe thirty?"

"That's a lot of money."

Rose shrugged. "He's one of the best carvers. He doesn't pay rent or buy groceries. He trades out work and maybe some other things for most of what he needs." Rose was looking at the floor, but Ben could see the smile.

"Those other things being sexual favors for the landlady?"

"So the story goes."

"I wonder what he'll do when the trading post sells? That will certainly impact his current way of life."

"He'll move in with his sister; her husband died a few years back. Sal helps them out, mostly big stuff like the van. The kids are gone now. He'll get his meals cooked and laundry done."

Was there a hint of sarcasm? Rose seemed to be more liberated than most of the Indian women in her age group.

"Can you think of anyone who might want to cause Sal harm—put a spell on him?" Ben asked. "Or just plain steal from him?"

No, but I could do some checking." Rose stood and picked up the cookie container.

"I'd appreciate that." Ben looked at his calendar. "Am I double-booked at eleven?"

"Not really. Sylvester won't take long."

"Sylvester? I don't remember seeing him before."

"He usually sees Dr. Lee, but he's turning him over to you."

"Is his problem physical or mental?"

"Mental, but Sylvester thinks it's physical."

"Just what is the problem?"

"He comes in once a month to have the air let out of his balls."

"Rose, you're pulling my leg."

"Nope. He thinks he has ovaries, too."

"So what does Dr. Lee usually do?"

"He puts a blood pressure cuff around his arm, pumps it up and then lets the air out."

"And that's worked on his...problem?"

"Seems to."

"Then why doesn't he continue to see Dr. Lee?"

"Yellow Skin say we have head doctor now. You crazy, you see booga booga man, not medicine man." Rose ended her exaggeration by tapping her temple. "You smart. You think of something." Ben could hear her laughter as she walked back to her desk.

Ben hadn't been looking forward to eleven o'clock but he was intrigued by Sylvester. His granddaughter brought him to the door of his office at exactly five till and promised to be back in fifteen minutes. Not much time, but everyone seemed to treat these visits as routine.

Sylvester took a chair facing Ben's desk and didn't say anything, just stared at Ben. He had that disheveled look of someone challenged by dressing himself. His sweater was one button off; the Fruit of the Loom tag stuck out the front of his tee shirt. But he was clean and his hair was combed. Someone took good care of him, probably the granddaughter, Ben thought.

"What seems to be the problem, Sylvester?" Ben scooted his chair around the edge of the desk to appear less formidable.

"Got the pains again, Doc."

"Where are these pains?"

Sylvester waved his hand below his waist in the general direction of lower intestine and genitals.

"Can you describe the pains?" Ben reached for a yellow pad and pencil.

"It's my ovaries. They make my balls swole up." Sylvester puffed out his cheeks and held his breath, finally exhaling in a swoosh.

"I'm not sure it's your ovaries, Sylvester. You see, you're not supposed—"

"I know. I'm not supposed to have any. Dr. Lee said that. But…" Sylvester leaned to within two feet of Ben and whispered, "They came in the mail." Then he sat back.

"How did they come in the mail?"

"Cardboard box." His hands formed an imaginary square about five inches across.

That was a literal answer and not what Ben had hoped for. He guessed he'd have to try again. "Did you order them?" God, Ben hoped his room wasn't bugged and watched as Sylvester shook his head.

"Every time there's going to be a round moon, I need to let the air out of 'em though. Think they're defective?"

Now it was Ben's turn to look thoughtful. Once a month. It wasn't like he hadn't been warned. But he had an idea…

"You got a machine like Dr. Lee?" Sylvester was glancing around the still-bare office.

"No. We're not going to use the machine today. I'm going to teach you to do it yourself." This was either an unbelievable inspiration or just plain dumb. Nothing in between, Ben thought.

"Wouldn't you like to save your granddaughter the trip to the clinic once a month?" Sylvester nodded. Ben had his attention. Now, if this would only work.

"Sylvester, I want you to watch closely."

Ben pulled his chair closer to sit squarely facing Sylvester. Then Ben opened his mouth wide, inserted an index finger and pulled it quickly forward along his cheek and made a loud popping noise. With his eyes still on Sylvester, Ben did the same thing on the left side of his face. Sylvester began to smile.

"Let me try."

With Ben's guidance, Sylvester put his index finger in his mouth and on the third try made a respectable pop. After the second try on the left side of his mouth the pop resounded in the small office.

"That's great. How do you feel?"

Sylvester held up his hand, palm outward and looked pensive. Then he leaned back in the chair and closed his eyes. Ben waited. Afraid that he had dozed, Ben gently tapped Sylvester's knee.

Sylvester smiled, showing brown incisors and a missing first molar. "No pressure. That was real good, Doc. Better than Dr. Lee."

Ben grinned. This wouldn't exactly go down in the annals of psychology, but he felt good. It sure beat a blood pressure cuff once a month. And it was always good to get a patient to take responsibility for his own health.

Sylvester was so taken with his cure that he demonstrated for Rose and the granddaughter in the waiting room. Rose gave Ben a thumbs-up and large wink when they had turned to go.

"You're going to do okay, Doc. Passed your first test with flying colors." Rose was beaming. "Your other appointment at eleven no-showed. Oh, I almost forgot. This came for you. Tommy brought it over."

Was it a copy of the autopsy? Ben tore open the envelope as he walked back to his office. There were copies of both the autopsy and the police report. He thumbed through the autopsy first. It was more or less what he had expected, no surprises.

Ahmed's death occurred before scalping. Would that be a relief for the widow? Less gruesome, somehow? The weapon used was a blade about five inches in length with an odd knob at the base, a part of the handle, probably a stationery blade. It ruled out switchblades and most kitchen knives. The report used the word, "stiletto."

Ahmed had two wounds—both in the vicinity of the heart. One damaging thrust pierced the intercostal tissue between T4 and T5 vertebrae, penetrating the right ventricle. Did someone know what he was doing or was this done suddenly, without thought? Ben couldn't control a shudder.

The next three pages were discussions of organs, and the victim's general condition. The lungs were bruised. That was to be expected. The man was slightly underweight for his age and height. Unfortunately not something in his favor—he lacked the depth of tissue that might have kept the wounds from being fatal. Ben flipped to the last few pages.

Ben had been right. Ahmed had been dead approximately twenty-four hours when found. The scalp wound measured four inches by three inches. It was the opinion of the pathologist that these cuts were not made with the murder weapon but with a razor—one continuous rounded cut and a straight slice across the hairline. Ben put down the report. Certainly, the trader's death suggested preparedness, an element of planning on someone's part. But who would kill a man and then decide to scalp him later? Or were two people involved?

Ben turned to the police report. There was no blood in the vicinity of where the body was found to indicate that he'd been murdered behind Sal's trailer. But there was evidence that the scalping had been done there. Bits of tissue found under the head bore this out. If Sal wasn't the murderer, could he be the one who scalped Ahmed? No, that's too bizarre. What was Ben thinking of? Sal was a bit taciturn now and then but there was no indication that he'd be capable of taking a scalp. Still, it was Sal who led them to the scalp itself.

Ben continued to read. The skirting on the trailer had been removed, the body dragged out, lifted and deposited some ten feet from the dwelling. The body had been hidden there for the previous twenty-four hours.

Ben flipped to the list of effects. Ahmed had been dressed in shirt and jeans, billfold and watch intact, an amber rabbit fetish in his front shirt pocket. There was that rabbit fetish thing again. The tourist had wanted one. Sal seemed spooked by them. Was it some kind of talisman? A lucky charm for the trader—or unlucky, Ben amended.

According to a notation in the margin, the rabbit was in a gift box with a sales slip that electronically recorded the time of sale as 7:10 p.m. Maybe twenty minutes, twenty-five at the most, before the body was found. Ben leaned forward. It was obvious that the trader hadn't made a purchase. Could the husband of the tourist have gone back to the trading post in search of a gift for his wife? In a lucid moment he bought a rabbit fetish—but from whom? Who would know how to open the cash register? For that matter, the trading post itself? Sal. Sal would have had the keys. But during the interrogation, Sal steadfastly said he was resting in the trailer with his hearing aid out—from the time he left the kitchen to the time Ben found the body. Why'd he lie? Had he been, in fact, out back dragging a body—and how did the fetish end up in the trader's pocket?

"I took a chance that you'd be knee-deep in that." Tommy stood in the doorway. "Interesting, no? It sure suggests a whole new line of questioning for our pal Sal."

"What's this about a rabbit fetish? I'm assuming that the tourist purchased it, but who could have sold it to him?"

"Sal, more than likely. Then the old guy goes back to the trailer a little later to talk to his new friend and finds more than he bargained for."

"Was there anything special about the fetish?"

"It was one of Sal's. Small, but well done."

"Have you questioned Hannah?"

"This morning. She tried to cover for Sal. She said someone could have found the keys under the back mat, helped themselves and opened the trading post."

"Wouldn't the cash register have been locked? Sal wouldn't leave the keys to that under a mat."

"You're right. I asked her, and she didn't have an answer."

"Who besides Sal and Hannah would be able to ring up a sale? Did you ever ask him if he was in the trading post that night?"

"I assumed he'd tell me if he hadda been." Tommy paused and looked at Ben. "And don't give me any shit about what 'assume' stands for."

"Wouldn't think of it," Ben smiled. "Guess this means another visit with Sal."

JULIE HADN'T EXPECTED to see Ben back at the house for lunch but since he was with Tommy, it was probably business. Something to do with the break-in, maybe. So, she was surprised to hear them ask about Sal.

"I think he's down at the shed," Julie offered, then decided to tag along. She liked Sal. She even had her own ideas about his involvement in the murder—mainly, that he was innocent. Hadn't he trusted her with one of his most prized possessions, which was sitting in the trunk of her car until she could get into Gallup later?

No one said she couldn't go with them. Ben, in fact, seemed to encourage it. It was Tommy who seemed reluctant. But he couldn't keep his eyes off of her. She'd have to turn him down if he asked her out. Hadn't Ben done everything but promise to give their relationship another try? Tommy's lusting was just a little unnerving. And it wasn't like Hannah said—she didn't encourage this. With Tommy it wouldn't take much inviting. He was barely past the hormone surge of an eighteen-year-old.

"Hi." Sal stood in the doorway to his shed, a rough, unpolished chunk of azurite in his hand.

God, we must look like the avengers swooping down on a victim, Julie thought. It wasn't her imagination. She thought Sal's eyes had temporarily darted past her seeking escape. But he stood his ground.

"I think we need to talk." This from Tommy in a no-

nonsense voice. Whatever it was, Tommy was put out. Thought he shouldn't have to be here, probably. "I don't think you've told me all there is to tell about the night Ahmed's body was found," he said.

So that was it. It must be something big. Sal stared at the ground, not a yes, not a no, didn't even blink, just turned and walked back into the shed with three people following and sat at his workbench.

"If your memory needs a little refresher, read the last item that was found on the body. What does it say that they found in a box with tissue and a sales slip?" Tommy held out a sheet of paper.

Sal read slowly, then looked up. "A fetish? Who would have sold him a fetish?"

"I bet that's what we'd like to know. It's a good question because the man had been dead for about twenty-four hours, which makes it real difficult to go shopping." Tommy pulled up a chair, and dropped the snideness as he continued. "I want you to think, Sal. Any reason you know of that an amber rabbit fetish should be found on the deceased? One of your carvings?"

Sal wet his lips. He knows something, Ben thought, something he's not going to share. Was that a tremor in Sal's right hand as he pushed away from his workbench?

"Maybe the tourist bought the rabbit. His wife had wanted one earlier."

"And we're right back where we started. Who could have sold the tourist a fetish? Who was outside, maybe dragging a body behind a trailer—"

"I don't know."

"Is that your last word on this?"

Sal nodded.

Clearly exasperated, Tommy stood and bent over Sal. "You're in a heap of doo doo, pal. If I were you, I'd work on improving that memory." Tommy walked towards the door. "Were the keys under the mat that evening?" If Tommy had thought to catch Sal off guard, he did a good job, Ben thought as Sal stammered, "They were in my pocket."

"Key to the cash register, too?"

Sal nodded.

"Anyone have a duplicate set?"

"Hannah, I guess."

"When you left the kitchen earlier—"

"I went to the trailer, got a drink of water, took out my hearing aid and laid on the bed." Sal leaned back against the shed wall and closed his eyes. "That's when I saw Atoshle. I went to the window. His back was hunched, and he was bent over. Then I heard voices. Someone was talking to the *kachina*."

"Did you recognize either voice?" Tommy had returned to sit opposite him.

"One was deep, a man's voice I'd never heard before."

"The other?" Tommy asked.

"The old man, the tourist."

Tommy rocked back in his chair and stared at Sal. Obviously, this was the first that Tommy had heard this part of the testimony from the look on his face.

"You know that for a fact?"

"I'd swear to it."

"But you have no idea who the other voice belonged to?"

"I'd never heard it before—or since," Sal volunteered.

Julie fully expected some admonishment of, "Why didn't you tell me this earlier?" But, to his credit, Tommy kept quiet, then he leaned forward.

"Sal, you're smart enough to know what this looks like. The skirting on your trailer had been removed, a body which had been under there for twenty-four hours was dragged out and scalped while an old man with Alzheimer's is off shopping in the trading post, being helped by some stranger who just happens to have keys." Tommy raked the sides of his burr haircut with both hands. "If you can help me on this one, explain how all these things happened, you give me a call."

"So what do you think?" Ben asked. The three of them walked back to the house.

"It doesn't look good that Sal didn't come forward with this stuff about hearing voices and seeing something from his window. And the rabbit fetish seems to place him outside when he swears he was dozing," Tommy said.

"Why do you think he might be lying about the fetish?" Julie asked.

"Why don't you ask me how I think he could have missed a body being dragged in and out from under the trailer." Tommy shrugged. "*¿Quien Sabe?* I just hope he doesn't come up with any more surprises. I really don't want to find this man guilty."

GALLUP WOULDN'T have been her choice of destination on a hundred degree day but the rental's air conditioning worked, thank God! She'd be glad of that when she was out of the mountains and in the lower elevation of the plains in the hot, dry heat that radiated off the pavement. But, Julie didn't mind helping Sal. For whatever reason, he felt he couldn't ask Hannah to do it—or a relative, and that struck her as odd now that she thought about it. Hannah could have easily gone. She went into Gallup for supplies once a week. But maybe he didn't want anyone local to know that he was hiding a family artifact. Maybe he was breaking some kind of taboo.

But why didn't he trust Hannah? Unless he knew that someone had been in his trailer while he was in jail, had taken the twelve thousand dollars, and he wanted to play it safe but not arouse suspicion. Maybe, he did suspect Hannah. No, that didn't make sense. He seemed to genuinely like her. He always stood up for her, anyway.

Julie drove the length of Gallup's main street, one of those Out West kind of main drags that divided commerce into two sides of the street that could be called a downtown. Malls had appeared later sometime in the fifties. And it was across from one of these strips of green concrete buildings that housed an insurance company, Furr's supermarket, bible bookstore, Goodwill, and pawnshop that she saw the depot.

Out here, if you didn't have a car, a bus could make the difference between getting to places like Joseph City or Winona, Arizona, or staying home. There were no planes. The largest airport of any size would be in Albuquerque. The Santa Fe Railroad had only two trains a day—the east-bound Amtrak and the west-bound. No, Greyhound was alive and well in Gallup, New Mexico, with good reason.

Julie parked to the side of the building. There were four buses under a covered area connected to the terminal. Two were charters promising the South Rim of the Grand Canyon with stops in the Painted Desert and Flagstaff. One looked to be full of elderly tourists. Another bus was still loading; its luggage compartment filled quickly with boxes, grocery sacks and plastic-sided luggage. The message strip in the bus' front window read Window Rock, Ft. Defiance, Chinle, Lukachukai.

Navajo women in long tiered dark skirts and velvet blouses waited to board. The strings of turquoise around their necks gleamed softly beside large round silver pins of small, polished, individually set stones. Most wore moccasins. Young Indian women in jeans and tee shirts balanced round-faced, diapered but naked, chubby babies on hips and supervised the baggage. They wore very little jewelry and seemed to favor Nikes or Adidas. Good examples of the contrast one could find on any present-day reservation, Julie thought.

The heat from the idling buses was intense. The overhead trapped the fumes and held them shimmering under the steel corrugated roof. Julie walked a little faster towards the lounge. She could feel prickling sweat dotting her shoulder blades and gathering between her breasts. But the blast of refrigerated air that greeted her when she pulled the door open did little to offer relief.

Two degrees above a temperature that would preserve Fudge-sicles, the air was not only frigid but stale—cigarettes, the butts in a canister beside the door, baby formula, diapers, booze—two men stretched out on benches next to the restrooms appeared to be sleeping off the effects of alcohol rather than just napping. But the office personnel were friendly and polite. Julie placed Sal's package on the counter while a young man checked his book to determine what locker was available then asked her to follow him into a hallway that led away from the waiting area.

She fit the package into number fifty-seven, one of many narrow upright metal boxes embedded in the wall and closed and locked the metal door. Then at the attendant's urging opened the lock again with the key he'd provided just to make sure. It worked easily. She followed him back to the office.

"How long will you be needing the locker?"

"Thirty days." Julie made that up. She'd forgotten to ask Sal. She'd remind him of the time limit. But again it struck her as odd that this was so temporary. He must know about the stolen money and is using this as a stopgap measure. He's afraid the burglar might come back.

"Will that be all?" Julie could tell that the young man must have asked her twice because he was looking at her strangely.

"Yes." She smiled and signed the paper on the line where the man had put an X before she pulled her billfold out of her purse.

She hesitated, "Is it possible to have two keys?" Why was she doing that? She heard a little internal voice whisper "safe-guard." But against what? She sighed. It was done now as the man turned to take another key from a locked drawer.

"This will be extra." He laid the matching key on the counter, small silver keys with a distinct cutout shank and the stenciled number fifty-seven underneath the hole that could secure them to a key ring.

"Yes, of course, no problem." She watched as he rang up the purchase of locker rental on the cash register. Thirty dollars plus two for the extra key. About a dollar a day for peace of mind. She supposed that it was worth it. She assumed that the sealed jar held fetishes—relics from the past that had guided Sal's family—how could anyone put a dollar value on that?

She walked back out into the heat. Two of the buses had

pulled out, but that did little to make the boarding area more pleasant. She continued around the front of the building and eyed the pawnshop across the street. A part of her strategy for the show on Native American symbols was to film "old pawn"—jewelry and fetishes left to secure loans in shops such as the one in front of her. She'd use this tactic to give some perspective on how the Indian used his art as money, the liquidity of his talent. As long as she was in Gallup, she might as well make the most of the afternoon.

A jangle of bells announced that she had opened the front door. In moments a once-tall man from somewhere in back pushed through a curtained doorway but not before Julie's eyes had adjusted to the dim lighting coming from one long, dusty hanging fluorescent fixture with four yellowing bulbs. Much of the large room's light came from smaller tubes suspended from the underside of shelves in the countless number of glass cases that lined the walls and formed a horseshoe in the center.

Brown-edged posters announcing Indian events—pow wows, dances, markets—from years past attested to the longevity of the shop. Wooden support columns reaching to the ceiling were carved totems from the Pacific Northwest. There were shelves everywhere overloaded with pottery, *kachinas,* and sand paintings. It was more of a museum than a place of business and Julie was congratulating herself on the find.

"What can I help you with?" The man had to be the owner. He was the same vintage as the posters. What had the sign said out front? Morley's Wagon Wheel Trading Post and Pawn? Something like that, and this had to be Morley. He loomed over her and adjusted his glasses with a gnarled finger, pushing them to rest lower on his bulbous nose as he leaned against a counter. The man had probably been six-four before age had compacted disks and pulled shoulders forward.

Julie explained her reason for doing research in the area, pausing to show him her ABC identification card. And that was all it took. A somewhat grumpy Morley instantly threw down the proverbial red carpet.

"My wife died last year. God rest her soul. Wouldn't she be

excited to see me now. That show of yours was always her favorite. Even when she couldn't get out of bed, she'd have me prop her up to watch morning television. She'd be just tickled pink to meet you. Why, you could make a celebrity out of the old Wagon Wheel.''

"I would like to consider filming here. Your store is a wonderful slice of history.''

"All of it true. I can't tell a lie as good as this stuff can tell the truth.'' He motioned for her to follow as he made his way to a shelf of *kachinas*. "This wolf dancer and this eagle dancer bought a year's worth of dialysis for Dolly Honani. This watchband,…'' Morley hobbled towards a jewelry case, "bought Daniel Manygoats books and tuition at Ganado college.''

"But these pieces are marked 'not for sale.' ''

"I've made my money on lesser items. Kept the good ones. Ones that meant something.'' Morley looked around. "I've been offered a lot for all this. Smithsonian's interested.'' He sighed. "All in due time. Almost shut her down when the wife died. But couldn't think of another career that would be worth taking up at eighty-six.'' A deep bass laugh ended in a coughing spell. "I've been like this ever since I gave up stogies— never had a cough while I smoked.''

Julie waited while he unfolded a large handkerchief and turned his head to blow his nose. "I'm gonna have to sit down over here. I get winded anymore just standing up. You go ahead and look around. You got a question, just boom it out. My ears still work.''

She smiled her thanks and started with the jewelry cases along the north wall. Belt buckles, bolos, shirt collar tips, money clips—the glass shelves were crowded with sterling silver, most of it Navajo. Some of the better pieces were grouped as to artist on trays lined in blue velvet, the artist's name in gold done by a calligrapher, maybe the wife.

She worked her way along the cases passing a three tier presentation of Hopi silver distinct for its treatment of Kokopeli, the flute player, and surreal stalks of corn on bolos next to a belt buckle that mirrored life's maze. The next four cases held fetishes. Some of the best she'd seen. She knelt to get a look at the second shelf and almost lost her balance. There as the center piece of a thirty-inch fetish necklace was her corn maiden. Only this time it was two inches tall instead of four and one of a dozen other amber figures—frogs, coyotes, bears, an eagle—all intricately carved with inlaid obsidian, coral, turquoise used to define fur or feathers or corn shucks. The beads between the figures were rounded stones matching the ones used to outline the figures and interspersed with amber nuggets.

"Find something you like?" Morley called out.

"Yes. Could I see a necklace in this case?"

"I don't have to even go over there to know you're looking at Sal Zuni's work. He just brought it in, too, less than a month ago—more like a couple weeks back to be exact." Morley shuffled behind the row of cases carrying a ring of keys. "One of the best I've ever seen—in fifty-some years. And all in amber. I heard tell that a new vein has opened up. Time back, carvers couldn't get good Baltic. But look at the quality of this." He had spread a white velvet cloth on the top of the counter and laid the necklace out, reverently straightening each fetish. Then he switched on a crookneck lamp clamped to the counter's edge and pushed the covered bulb closer to shine directly on the amber.

"See that color. Rich gold. See how it catches the light? Here orange-gold, there golden-brown. But look. Twigs. There's a couple of bugs caught up here in one of them, too." Morley was turning the pieces under the lamp. "Here. Look at this. Perfect beetle. You ever think what the world must have looked like when this little guy was out crawling around? Whole hell of a lot different than it does today. That's for sure. But I wouldn't go back—even to swing in a tree." Morley ended in a loud guffaw, steadying himself by clasping the counter edge.

Julie moved the light closer. Man hadn't made an appearance yet when this "little guy" was alive. Yet, the beetle looked familiar. She would swear it was the same kind that was caught in her corn maiden, only this time it rested just above the hind foot of a bear—a bear with a turquoise heart line and coral eyes.

"Jumping Sumac beetle," Julie blurted.

"Beg pardon?"

"The beetle. That's what kind it is. I've seen one before." And she wasn't sure what surprised her most, finding an identical beetle encased in amber or the fact that Sal had sold this piece recently making it seem like he was in need of money when twelve thousand dollars was found in his trailer. Could he have earned the twelve thousand? Not unless he had sold a half-dozen necklaces lately and where would he find that amount of amber? Or a market close by that could take on that many? There was something she wasn't seeing. She could sense it. It was right here under her nose. But what was it?

"Is this piece for sale?"

"I haven't decided, might not ever get another like it. Sal's not as young as he used to be. He doesn't do as much carving anymore. This is the first piece of this magnitude he's brought in…in, gosh, must be five years now." He touched it fondly. "This took months to complete, maybe longer."

Julie slipped the necklace around her neck and looked at her reflection in a round hand mirror that Morley held.

"Sure does suit you. Matches your hair."

"Since I know Mr. Zuni, I'd like to feature this piece on the show. I'd planned to interview the carver and highlight his work. This would be a wonderful piece to showcase. I would be glad to buy it." Morley put the mirror down as she slipped the necklace off.

"I was thinking the price tag would be in the neighborhood of twenty-four hundred." He peered at her.

Julie didn't flinch but mentally tried to remember if her Visa could take on a load like that and was afraid it couldn't. She could use the show's expense account but that wouldn't be exactly fair. She wanted this piece for herself.

"Or tell you what I could do." Morley studied her before continuing. "Sees as how you'll be giving the Wagon Wheel some free publicity, let's say I could knock off a thousand or so. How's twelve hundred and fifty sound?''

"Much better." It wasn't like she treated herself to gifts like this everyday, but it was for the show. Guaranteed her interview with Sal would capture interest. And it was exquisite. A great reminder of her summer out here. That is, if no better reminders came along—like a little romance with one Ben Pecos. And that might not happen. She shouldn't get her hopes up. And this was better than eating a bag of chocolate brownies. Not that she'd ever done that but it was always a possibility in some moment of utter discouragement. She slipped the necklace back on and reached into her purse for her billfold.

SHE HAD ALMOST talked herself into believing that this was the best purchase of her life until she met Sal at the door to his shed, and he had roughly pulled her inside.

"Morley's. You got that at Morley's."

Sal sounded angry, and she was hurt. She had expected him to be flattered. It was a lot of money even discounted, and she wasn't certain she would have bought it if she hadn't known Sal.

"It's beautiful. Why are you angry? I've never seen work like this. I'm going to highlight it in the show. And look how it picks up the color of my hair. It was made for me."

"You didn't need to buy it. I could have made you one. And for a lot less than that old reprobate charged."

"In a month? And, besides, I got a deal. I'll give Morley free publicity for the Wagon Wheel."

"Whatever you paid, it was too much."

Sal reached out and unfastened the necklace from around her neck and took it to his workbench, switched on a work light and began to go over each fetish.

"It's not my best work. This is sloppy." He paused with the bear in his hand and stared at the Jumping Sumac beetle.

"I don't believe you. It's exquisite. How could it be any better? Pure amber with other semiprecious stones, all carved into figures that will forever remind me of my time out here— remind me of the artist.''

Sal jerked his head up. ''This isn't the way I want to be remembered.''

''I don't understand. I bought a thing of beauty. What have I done wrong?''

Sal ran a hand through his hair and leaned back in his chair. ''You haven't.'' His anger seemed to have dissipated. ''Most of my work is sold out of state. I needed some money for truck repairs a couple weeks ago, or I wouldn't have let it go. I hate to think what you paid for this. I just don't want you to ever feel that you were taken.''

''Never. I'll cherish the necklace. I'll never think it wasn't worth it.''

Sal didn't look convinced. What an odd man. Artist's temperament wasn't just an Anglo thing, she guessed and tried to smile reassuringly.

''Could you do me a favor and not wear it in front of Hannah?''

Aha. That was it. Hannah would think he'd given it to her. He probably got in trouble over the original corn maiden. She hadn't stopped to think.

''No problem.'' She smiled and patted his arm, coaxing a reluctant grin in return. ''Oh, the receipt and key for the locker.'' Julie fumbled in her purse. It crossed her mind to produce both keys but she didn't. She left one hidden in a coin purse. ''I wasn't sure how long you'd need the locker. I took it for thirty days.''

''That should be long enough. Things will be different by then.''

Julie suddenly snapped—Hannah would be gone by then. That's what he probably wanted to say. So, he must suspect Hannah of trying to steal from him. If not, why all this secrecy?

''Thanks for your help. I'm sorry about earlier. I never think my art is worth what people pay for it.'' Sal looked truly contrite.

''Forget it. I love the necklace. It's the most wonderful piece of jewelry I own. And mum's the word." Julie put the necklace into the velvet drawstring bag that Morley had provided and dropped it in her purse.

SAL STOOD IN the shed's doorway and watched Julie walk back to the house. He was troubled. Because he may have put her in danger by asking her to store the fetish jar? No. He couldn't believe that Hannah would try to take the notebook by force. Others might, but not Hannah. And Julie didn't know what was in the fetish jar. She was innocent, just a messenger. The thirty days rental was perfect. Hannah would be gone by then. In the meantime he would be careful.

It was the amber that troubled him. Someone he knew and liked had bought a fake. She probably paid a couple thousand and believed it to be an ancient semiprecious stone. It was okay when nameless tourists bought his work or someone a thousand miles away purchased nuggets. His corn maiden gift to Julie was more for what the fetish could do for her life than the value of the material it was made of. He had breathed power into the maiden—the power for Julie to get what she wanted. The amber was secondary.

Back when he started, he should have tagged the amber as synthetic. But that wouldn't have solved anything. Somewhere, someplace, the unscrupulous would mark it as real and perpetuate the lie. And wasn't it a Federal offense to dupe the public? Wasn't he already a candidate for prison? The Government had cracked down on the makers and sellers of fake turquoise. Why would he be any different?

Was he in too deep to turn it all around? Could he just walk away in a couple months with no repercussions? He just needed his luck to hold out a little longer. Then he'd destroy the notebook, the recipe, all his equipment. But for now his secret was safe.

"SMILE, YOU'RE ON Candid Camera." Rose was sitting behind her desk when Ben walked through the sliding glass door into the waiting room at the hospital.

"What are you talking about?"

"There." Rose was pointing to the corner of the ceiling above her head. "Hidden camera. We're going to nail those jokers who've been hitting the pop machines for change once and for all."

Ben looked at the two red and white vending machines against the opposite wall.

"Someone's been stealing?"

"This morning makes the fourth time in a month. All they get is a handful of quarters. It's probably kids. But it's the principle. Tribe wants to nip juvenile delinquency in the bud. But, you gotta catch 'em first. So, we got ol' one-eye. Now, all I have to do is remember to turn it on when I leave." She laughed. Ben liked Rose's laugh, hearty and robust; the sound made by someone who's not easily intimidated.

"You may have a little surprise in your office." Her voice suddenly dropped to a conspiratorial level. "Yellow Skin has called a staff meeting—just the two of you. Don't let him pull that 'I'm the boss' shit. You don't have anything to worry about. Everyone in the village knows you're the one who taught Sylvester how to let the air out of his balls. You're a hero." Rose couldn't keep a teasing grin from spreading across her face. Ben smiled as he headed towards his office. It could be worse. He could be remembered by something negative. He should probably feel thankful that Dr. Lee had sent Sylvester to him. It had given his reputation the boost it needed in the village.

"Do you know what time it is?" Ben hadn't stepped inside the room before Dr. Lee had jumped to his feet and pointed at his watch. "Second week on the job and you feel you can take liberties with the Government lunch hour. A while back I had problems with a new group of nurses. I had to put in a time clock, and it was just the answer. Maybe, that wouldn't be such a bad idea again."

Ben didn't say anything. He hated punitive, narrow thinkers.

He was ten minutes late from dropping his truck off to get the window fixed, but had been in thirty minutes early the last three mornings—where was Yellow Skin then? Ben smiled, walked around Dr. Lee, pulled out his chair and sat down. He wasn't going to be bullied into bringing a lunch and eating at his desk.

"Can I help you with something?" Ben tried to sound friendly.

"Feeling a little superior, aren't we? But then maybe a doctor who encourages a man to go around the village making popping noises with his cheeks has a right to."

Ben laughed along with Dr. Lee's maniacal cackle. "It seems to be working. I believe the patient has reported feeling better," Ben said, then waited. Neither his lateness nor the cure of Sylvester seemed to be the reason for this meeting. He waited as Dr. Lee cleared his throat.

"I've granted a favor to a dear friend, old friend, actually. And I believe that you're the one best qualified to help." Dr. Lee rose to close the door. "I don't know how much you know about Mrs. Rawlings', uh, Hannah's, affairs, but I would guess very little. It isn't like her to take a stranger into her confidence. She asked me to come out to dinner the other night to discuss her problem. And we both agree that you would be the logical choice."

For what, Ben wondered but sensed he shouldn't interrupt.

"I'm assuming that this knowledge is just between us. That is understood?" Dr. Lee paused, then acknowledged Ben's nod with a wave of his hand. "Well, it's like this. Ed Rawlings, Hannah's husband, had inherited the trading post, boarding house, deli-mart from his father, handed down from his grandfather and so on back to about 1912. It's never been out of the family. Ed Rawlings is before my time. But I understand the man was a perfectionist, a tight perfectionist, always pinching pennies, put everything—life's blood—into the running of the family enterprise. His marrying Hannah was a surprise. She was twenty-three years his junior, a student who spent weekends out here, someone who played chess, talked intelligently—you can imagine how it must have been." Dr. Lee glanced at Ben.

"A little blond oasis. Well, before long Ed Rawlings had fallen in love. But with his eye ever on the dime, he insisted on a prenuptial agreement. If Hannah decided to leave him, she would have nothing. She'd have no claim on the inheritance."

"Did that include his son?" Ben asked.

"I'm coming to that. Harold didn't make an appearance until ten years into the marriage—Ed was in his middle to late fifties, Hannah early thirties. The baby was a complete surprise. Ed insisted that the baby be named after his grandfather. I'm sure you've heard that stupid story about Ed shooting a .22 in the air." Dr. Lee paused. "Well, it wasn't apparent right away that something might be wrong with the baby. But when it was, Hannah suffered a nervous breakdown." Dr. Lee glanced at Ben and seemed to sense his objection. "No, no, I know it's not a clinical term but for lack of a better diagnosis, that's what Hannah calls it. She just 'lost it'—those are her words. Out here in nowhere, saddled with an aging husband and a retarded child…well, I'm sure you can imagine.

"And the child changed everything. Ed was besotted. A boy to carry on the family name. He refused to see, acknowledge, his son's shortcomings. When Harold had difficulty walking, when he didn't start to talk—Ed kept saying that there were schools that could turn the child around." Dr. Lee stood up. "I hope I have your confidence on this. I mean, what I'm about to say could be taken the wrong way." He sat back down. Whatever it was, he was reluctant to share, Ben thought, as he watched Dr. Lee pause to gather his thoughts.

"As if things weren't bad enough, there was an accident. I want you to know that I believe that it was just that—an accident. I know Hannah. Some might think her strange, but she's not malicious. I'd swear under oath to that." He licked his lips. "When Harold was a toddler, maybe three and a half, just starting to crawl around good, he got away from Hannah down by the river, and, well, fell in. It had been a big runoff year—river was up, formed deep pockets of water close to the edge. Harold was pulled under quickly. Hannah tried to reach him. But she doesn't swim. Anyway, her housekeeper happened along, Tommy's mother. Maybe you've met her?'' Dr. Lee looked at Ben.

"I knew she worked at the boarding house in the past, but I haven't met her.''

"Tommy was just a few years older than Harold. The boys played together. Well, as much as Harold could play with anyone. He really needed special attention—constant supervision, that is.''

"How does Tommy's mother figure in the accident?''

"Ah, yes, well, she said it wasn't an accident. She told Ed Rawlings that when she came along Hannah was holding the child under. There had been no struggle or screams for help. She said that Hannah was trying to drown the child.''

"My God. What did she do?''

"To hear her tell it, she had to fight with Hannah to get Harold away from her. It was Tommy's mother who took Harold back to the house and called a doctor. He was barely breathing. Tommy's mother resuscitated him.''

"Where was Hannah?''

"Well, this is the part that makes her look guilty. She ran. They found her a day later, incoherent, wandering along the highway to Ramah.''

"Whatever happened, it must have been the shock,'' Ben said.

"Yes. Shock.'' Dr. Lee seemed to be considering something. "It changed everything, ruined what little marriage there was. Ed never trusted Hannah with the child again. He got a full-time nurse and sent Hannah away for a while—to stay with her sister, I think.''

"How long?'' Ben asked.

"Oh, six months or so. When she came back, Ed was cold to her, distant, wouldn't talk. And Harold was still weak. He didn't have the reserves to bounce back—not from a near drowning. He suffered from numerous upper respiratory illnesses; in general, there was diminished lung capacity, the result of the accident, no doubt. Ed sent him off that fall to a children's hospital in Albuquerque. It must have cost him a fortune. The next spring Ed had his heart attack.''

"Tragic story. But I don't see how I can be helpful.''

"I'm coming to that. Before he died, just after Hannah came back from her rest; Ed drew up a new will. He didn't trust Hannah so this time he put in a provision to protect his son. If anything happened to Harold, if he were to die or fall prey to some new accident, Hannah would get nothing. Not one penny. Whether it was her fault or not. Furthermore, to ensure that Hannah would give Harold the best of care, in order to inherit, she had to wait until Harold was twenty-one. He had to attain manhood unscathed.''

That explains remaining out here when she hated it, Ben thought.

"In addition, in order to inherit anything; Harold must prove to be trainable—vocationally. He must demonstrate the ability to learn a trade, hold a job, fend for himself eventually, that sort of thing. It was Ed's hope that Harold would enter the work force and be able to support himself. Maybe not a normal life, but then what's a definition of 'normal'?'' Dr. Lee looked at Ben and laughed. "I bet you can't come up with one.''

Ben shrugged. He wasn't going to get into an argument on that one—not now, anyway. This was getting interesting.

"Hannah hasn't spent much time with Harold over the past ten years. She's kept him in schools, kept her part of the bargain, only visited him once a year but done her best to see that he's prepared for life. So, now he's home. And you know the rest. The property has sold. The proceeds will either go to Hannah as guardian for Harold or to Harold alone with a guardian appointed by the estate depending...''

"Depending?'' Ben asked.

"On whether she's kept her part of the bargain, which old Ed felt would be proved if Harold reached twenty-one and could be trained to earn a living.''

"And who's going to determine that?''

"Exactly.'' Dr. Lee beamed. "This is where you come in. Hannah asked me to do it, to test Harold—just a preliminary thing before he goes before a panel of judges made up of psychiatrists, psychologists, doctors, the like—the ones appointed by the estate. He has to prove he can be a contributing member of society."

"Ed Rawlings must have been convinced that Hannah would hurt the child—holding the money over Hannah's head and tying her to the land for sixteen years before she could even be eligible for any part of it after all her work. Well, it seems extreme." Ben said.

"It assured him a legacy. The Rawlings' investment would be cared for—land and child. It's logical."

Ben wasn't certain how much "logic" played in all this compared to possibly vindictiveness. But why was he ruling out that Hannah might be just what Ed Rawlings suspected—capable of murder? He shivered.

"Will you do it?" Dr. Lee leaned forward.

"Do what?"

"Test Harold. Give him the same battery of tests that he might expect from the panel next week. Do it as a dress rehearsal, make Harold feel at ease with being questioned. He likes you. Hannah said that. And I'm limited. I'll do a medical examination but since we have a psychologist onboard, I suggested you do the testing. It makes it more real."

"Wasn't there something done before he was released from school? Exit exams? Tests to show capabilities?"

"You'd think so. But...well, I..." Dr. Lee looked up nervously, "hope I can trust you."

"Go on," Ben said.

"Hannah took Harold out of school when he was fifteen. There was some incident involving sex—teenager stuff, some boys knocked up one of the kitchen help; and she found out that the hospital had him on drugs, saltpeter, she says. Anyway, she threw a fit and wouldn't have it. She won a court order to take him out of the school and send him to her sister's in Maine. She gave him a 'country life,' she calls it. And it certainly seems to have worked. Harold is robust. There are no more asthma attacks. He seems well adjusted—as much as he can be, of course.''

''And that didn't negate a provision in the will?''

''Not really. This final test is what counts. He's got to prove that he can cope. Then Hannah will enroll him in school this fall after the settlement, a vocational school. What do you think?''

''I don't know. I'm not sure I'm comfortable doing preliminary work that might clearly prejudice the situation.''

''You're not coaching him for God's sake. I know the kind of questions you'll ask. You're not giving him the answers.'' Dr. Lee didn't hide his exasperation. Then, after a deep breath, he continued, ''Look, you'll do it after hours or on the weekend. I'm giving my permission to use hospital facilities. Hannah thinks it would be best if it were done in a clinical setting— someplace he's not been before—replicate what he'll face with the appointed board. I think it's important—crucial—to how well he'll do from the standpoint of comfort. I look at it this way, without this 'rehearsal,' he could fail if only from nerves. Now, is that fair?'' Dr. Lee waited.

''How soon does it have to be done?'' Ben asked.

''In the next few days. I know, I know, not much notice. But now that the property has sold, time is of the essence, as they say. Hannah didn't think it would sell so quickly.''

Ben leaned back propping his straight-legged chair against the wall. What was he about to agree to? It certainly wasn't something that he hadn't done before, maybe, a hundred times before. It wouldn't be that difficult. And he could see that a trial run would be helpful. He would want .22 to succeed. So, why was he reluctant? Was he worried about the ethics? But what really was unethical? What was real was how he hated to be manipulated—have his credentials ''used.'' Yet, if Hannah was innocent as Dr. Lee believed, shouldn't he try to help?

''Okay,'' Ben said.

''Great. I knew you'd be willing to help.'' Dr. Lee jumped up. ''I'll call Hannah. She may want to go over details with you tonight, set a date, that sort of thing. Let me know so that

I can coordinate the physical—maybe the same day—not too much stress on our young man, get everything out of the way at once.

"Well," Dr. Lee stood and held out his hand, "thank you."

And then he was gone. But the handshake had surprised Ben. Testing .22 must mean a lot to Yellow Skin. Ben checked his calendar. Tomorrow, Saturday morning, might be a good time to do it, over the Fourth of July weekend very few people would be at the clinic. He'd ask Hannah tonight. Ben glanced at his watch. He needed to call Chu's automotive. They had promised his truck would have new glass in an hour. But something told him that might not happen—unless he reminded them. He needed it by four-thirty and hoped he wouldn't have to wait.

But he did have to wait. Not a lot happened on time on the reservation—not on Anglo time. So when he got back to the boarding house, Hannah was just serving supper to a gathering that included the new owners and the real estate agent. It was obvious that Hannah was pleased. Dr. Lee sat a few spaces to Ben's right and beamed down the table at him every now and then. What an odd way to win approval, Ben thought, agree to test a young man with severe handicaps. But there was no doubt that he was getting special treatment. The slab of prime rib that Hannah plopped on Ben's plate almost dragged down the table.

"What slaughter is she fattening you up for?" Julie whispered and pointed to the meat that had crowded his baked potato onto a side plate.

"Do I detect there's no love lost between you two?" Ben asked, keeping his voice low.

"Uh-huh." Julie leaned towards him. "Landlady and I are allergic to each other."

"Let me have your attention." Hannah tapped the edge of her knife sharply on her water glass. "I've opened a few bottles of wine. I think a toast is in order." Hannah finished filling everyone's glass. "To the new owners. May their joy abound."

There was polite applause. .22 tried to take his mother's wine glass. She poured apple juice into a stemmed goblet, handed it to him, and he quieted. They were sitting side by side tonight. Hannah probably thought it looked more loving. In fact, she seemed more loving towards him—straightened his bib, wiped spittle from the corner of his mouth, cut up his steak—even brushed his forehead with a kiss before she began to hand around the bowls of vegetables.

Ben couldn't imagine how Hannah must feel to be this close to leaving a prison; yes, that was a good word for it. She was caught up by the binding words of a husband who held her captive with a piece of paper long after his death—deserved or not, this had been her prison.

"One glass of wine and you're blitzed. You've been staring at the centerpiece for five minutes," Julie whispered.

"Not so. Maybe two minutes."

"Three," Julie said.

Ben grinned and passed on a bowl of mixed yellow and green summer squash. Why didn't he mind that she got the last word in—always. Probably because he realized he could be in love. But was he ready to share that yet? Maybe not. First, he'd make sure they had time together, lots of it, and soon.

"What a sparkling conversationalist. I had my choice of sitting by you or by .22—I'm beginning to think I chose the wrong dinner partner," Julie teased.

"Sorry. Guess I'm a little preoccupied."

"Any chance of getting you to take a stroll in the moonlight after dinner?"

"A big chance." Ben grinned.

But dessert was some intricate flaming thing that took extra production time, and was well worth it. Then the new owners begged him to pair with Julie and round out a foursome for bridge. Hannah and Dr. Lee had reneged and retired to the parlor. But not before Hannah had reminded Ben that the two of them needed to talk. Ben knew Julie had overheard. She didn't say anything just pulled her lower lip over her teeth and feigned interest in one of the watercolors on the dining room wall.

"What was that all about?" Julie asked, but didn't wait for

his answer before adding, "You don't need to tell me. I'm just being snoopy. But I don't trust her. Promise me you'll be careful?" Her hand was on his arm, lightly detaining him. He heard an earnestness in her voice.

"Will the two of you quit mooning around and get this game started," the woman called out good-naturedly. "We're ready for a challenge."

It was after midnight before the game broke up. Hannah had walked Dr. Lee to the door and asked Ben to join them.

"Let's talk outside. I think Harold's asleep but I can never be sure. I don't want him to be more upset by all this than he has to be."

"Did you check your calendar?" Dr. Lee asked Ben.

"Tomorrow morning is best for me," Ben said.

"Good. I think that will be fine for us, but what should I tell him? I don't want him to sense the importance of what you'll be doing and get nervous, overreact or something," Hannah said.

"I think if you tell him he's going to visit me, it should go all right. I wouldn't use the word 'test,' say that we're going to talk."

Hannah nodded.

"How soon will you know anything?" Ben noted the anxiety in her voice. This was pretty important to her. It sort of validated the last sixteen years or...

"I mean, if he fails, will you know right away? Will you have suggestions for things he could do to make it better when he's tested by the examiners?"

"Are you suggesting that I prompt him into passing?" Ben asked a little coolly. Wasn't this what he had dreaded? That he'd be asked to do a little coaching?

"She doesn't mean any such thing." Dr. Lee took Hannah's arm. "This is a trying time for her. So much is at stake."

"Forgive me." Hannah's cheeks glistened in the soft yellowish glow of the yard light. She dabbed at her eyes with a Kleenex. "I didn't mean that."

She was distraught. There was good reason for it. Ben suspected that .22 might not do well. What would it be like to have your fortune riding on the answers of someone retarded? Someone who had caused you grief but bound you to him by the very fact that he was impaired? Ben felt real empathy for Hannah. Whatever weirdness there was, wasn't there a good explanation for it?

The silence became awkward; Hannah blew her nose. Maybe, if he reassured her.

"Are you familiar with the type of questions that I'll be asking?" Hannah shook her head. "We'll cover a variety of topics," Ben began. "I need to test his vocabulary, general information, verbal comprehension, memory—things like that. We'll do simple arithmetic, some reading. We may have time for puzzles or picture assembly." Ben paused, "I'll probably have him go through a few simple neuropsych exercises."

"What do you mean?" Hannah's eyes were wide with alarm.

"Oh, nothing out of the ordinary—repeating sounds, copying geometric figures, tracing numbers—that sort of thing. I'll be as complete as I can be. I don't know exactly what he'll be asked by the panel but I'll come close."

This seemed to appease her and she managed a smile. "I can't tell you how much I appreciate this. It will mean so much to Harold. He won't be frightened with strangers if he knows what to expect."

Dr. Lee nodded vigorously. "This will be perfect. Shall we say nine-thirty tomorrow?" This time Hannah shook Ben's hand, maybe squeezed was a better description. But she looked relieved, even happy. That made him feel good. Ben excused himself and walked back into the house. He hoped Julie might still be up. As he reached the door to his room, he heard the front porch screen slam shut and the soft hurried steps of someone coming towards him. He was almost knocked off balance when Hannah threw her arms around his shoulders.

"I don't think you can know what this means to me." She was standing on tiptoe, her head buried in his chest. "It seems like I've waited for this moment all my life. I just get sick when I think he might blow it. Can you understand that?" She pulled away to look into his eyes. "Yes, of course, you can. I knew the minute I saw you that there was compassion and it wasn't put on. You have real feeling for others. It's rare, that. I haven't found it very often." She slid her arms up to circle his neck. "How can I thank you? Anything. You can ask anything." Before he could pull away, she brought his head down and found his mouth with hers. Her lips were soft. She moaned in an eagerness that quickened a response in him. He hadn't planned this, wanted this. "Anything," she whispered, her voice husky with sexual innuendo as she pulled back to look into his eyes then leaned forward again seeking his mouth.

"Hope I'm not interrupting anything?" Julie called out from the stairs.

Hannah sprang away from him. Ben could see the front of her shirt rise and fall with her rapid breathing. And, he could feel the anger—catfight came to mind. He was caught between two felines, one circling, one guarding her prey.

"Now that you've finished the—what would I call it? Warm-up act? I'll take over from here." Julie walked around Hannah to stand next to Ben.

Hannah was furious. In a flash Ben got the distinct feeling that she might try to get even, retaliate, literally lash out attacking Julie. But the moment evaporated. Hannah laughed.

"I can imagine what this looks like. But it's just a little thank-you to a special human being for his incredible thoughtfulness." She gazed up at him and took his hand. "I'll be forever grateful." She looked ethereal and waiflike standing in the subdued light of the hall, vulnerable even, as a warm breeze from the open front door played with a strand of white-blond hair at her neck. And then with a sweetness and light smile meant just for him, Hannah pushed past Julie and went up the stairs.

They waited until they heard the door to her room close.

"Near miss." Julie sounded ticked. "It seems like I can't leave you alone around that woman."

"You're making it out to be more than—"

"Bullshit." He'd never seen Julie this mad. She was spitting the words out. "She's evil. She uses sex. Uses people."

"I think you're wrong. I think I could prove you're wrong."

"I think you're under some kind of spell. The kind that starts about eight inches below the belt buckle."

"If you want to keep me off the streets, marry me," Ben said. For a moment he could hear the tick of the grandfather clock at the end of the hall. Then Julie said, "You always get the lines mixed up. You're supposed to keep me off the streets." But she was laughing, leaning against the opposite wall, arms folded across her chest. She seemed calmer.

"You think the next time Tommy Spottedhorse hints around about asking you out, I won't deck him? I don't think either one of us is safe on the streets."

"And your solution is to get married?" She was still teasing, but Ben thought he detected a hint of seriousness.

"Yup." He watched her.

She stared back. Considering her answer? He couldn't tell, but plunged ahead. "You're doing research now for the program. Why couldn't you continue to do that? You could put in an appearance on the show every now and then. Nothing says that you have to be in New York all the time, live there. Modems and fax machines have changed that. Unless you prefer New York?…" He stopped. Unlike Hannah, Julie's living out here didn't mean being caught out here. She could fly back East, tape a series of shows, then come back. But, would it be enough?

"You've given this some thought," Julie said.

Ben nodded. The ticking of the clock bounced off the walls as the silence stretched on. Finally, she said, "Where are you going to get a ring out here?" She was teasing again.

"Give me until tomorrow night."

"Okay."

"Okay as in yes?" Was he hearing correctly?

"This will teach me to accept a fertility fetish. Then even buy more of them," Julie laughed.

It crossed his mind to ask her what she was talking about,

but he didn't. He stopped thinking of anything else but how happy she looked as she threw her arms around his neck. And then he kissed her, quickly and lightly on her eyes, forehead, nose—then lingering on her mouth. Getting lost in her warmth and eagerness, he pulled her close. With all his being, he wanted this relationship to work.

NINE

IT HAD BEEN STUPID to promise a ring in twenty-four hours, but Rose helped him. Her brother did fine inlay jewelry and knew where to go in Gallup to pick up a half-carat diamond of good quality for the center—and didn't mind doing it on a Saturday morning. Ben gave him the money after looking at a number of settings and deciding on a wide gold band superimposed with a narrow raised band of polished slivers of turquoise, coral, shell, obsidian and pipestone—all the colors of the Southwest set to look like bright multicolored stripes. One of a kind. Wasn't that what Rose called it? And if her brother worked on it for the next eight hours, it would be ready by that evening.

Hannah and .22 were already waiting on him when he got back to the clinic. Dr. Lee was talking with Hannah; .22 had dumped a box of toys in the middle of the waiting room floor and was making revving noises for the engine of a red plastic Ferrari before he sent it spinning across the waxed tile. Ben had never seen him play before. .22 mentioned something about frogs, but there were no toys that Ben could think of at the boarding house—or books, or dogs and cats. Those things would be stimulating and helpful, encouraging him to use his faculties. He'd remember to suggest a few acquisitions to Hannah. In fact, he wondered what .22 did all day. Surely setting the table three times a day didn't take up all his time.

"My car fast." .22 looked up at him.

"I can see that." Ben stepped to one side as .22 crawled

after the toy. "Would you like to bring your car with you? We're going to visit in my office."

"Where's that?" .22 sat on the floor, the corner of his mouth twitching spasmodically.

"At the end of the hall." Ben pointed through an archway next to the receptionist's desk.

"Okay." .22 struggled to his feet, but paying attention to Ben was short-lived when he spied the pop machines. "Me want orange."

"Would it be all right? Or too much sugar under the circumstances?" Hannah turned to Dr. Lee.

"It shouldn't make a difference. Let me."

Ben waited while Dr. Lee found two quarters and produced an orange soda. .22 made car noises all the way down the hall when he wasn't slurping his drink. Some were quite realistic. One would think .22 had lived next to a raceway. But then maybe he'd watched television. There weren't any sets at the house, but, perhaps, there had been one where he had been staying. Not that Ben was a proponent of TV, but under the circumstances it might be something else Hannah could add. There were programs on the educational channels that could be helpful.

"Here we are." Ben held the door open.

"We play now?"

Hannah must have described what they were going to do as "play." It seemed a good enough explanation. .22 appeared comfortable.

"Yes." Ben had set up a card table and two chairs in front of his desk and pulled out one of these chairs now and motioned for .22 to sit. Ben wished he'd thought to bring a box of Kleenex as a sneeze produced lots of nose wiping on .22's shirtsleeve.

".22, I want you to listen carefully. I'm going to give you a word, and I want you to tell me what it means. Are you ready?"

.22 nodded vigorously.

"Winter," Ben said.

"Cold." Ben waited, but that seemed to be all that was coming.

"Breakfast."

"Morning eat."

"Good. Now let's try 'calendar.'"

.22 looked around the room, then became agitated, stood and walked behind Ben's desk. "On wall. On wall." He was pointing but couldn't see one.

"You're right. A calendar is usually hanging on the wall. I don't have a calendar, do I?"

.22 shook his head and walked back to his chair.

Ben made a notation on a yellow legal pad. "Now I'm going to ask you some questions. I want you to think carefully before you answer." Ben waited until .22 had settled down.

"What color is the American flag?"

"Red. Blue," .22 blurted out.

So much for careful thought. "Is there another color?" Ben prompted.

.22 shook his head, then brightened and said, "Stars."

"How many months in a year?"

"Birthday month, Santa Claus month, firecracker month."

"How many eggs in a dozen?"

.22 rocked gently and stared at the table.

Ben waited, then asked again, "Do you know how many eggs are in a dozen?"

Finally, .22 shook his head but didn't look up; his thumb had crept into his mouth.

"Do you know why we cook our food?"

"Tastes good." His head came up and the grin was ear to ear. His thumb left a moist trail along the edge of the table.

"Why do we wash our clothes?"

"Socks smell." .22 put a tennis shoe on the table and pointed to the ragged top of a stained red sock.

"That's good. But we need to keep our feet on the floor."

.22 obeyed immediately plopping his foot down then looked up to stare, mouth slack, eyes slightly watering but eagerly fixed on Ben. He's starting to enjoy this, Ben thought.

"Why shouldn't we fight with others?" Ben asked.

"Black eyes."

Ben smiled. .22 seemed to be relaxed now. Each answer that he considered right elicited a little bounce in his chair or the clapping of hands.

"What would you do if you saw a fire in your house?"

"FIRE. FIRE," .22 shrieked and pushed to his feet tipping his chair over before he opened the office door and yelled one more "FIRE" into the hallway.

Ben had no idea what Hannah and Dr. Lee thought, but no one came running down the hall. Ben closed the door and waited until .22 had returned to sit at the table.

"If I had ten apples and you ate three, how many would I have left?"

"Me sick." .22 rubbed his stomach. "Apples hurt tummy."

"Let's play with a puzzle." Math didn't appear to be a long suit and Ben decided to try something else. He put an opaque plastic screen between them and then dumped a half dozen large wooden pieces—the legs, body, head, and tail of a goat onto the table arranging them in mixed order before he lifted the screen.

"Can you put these together to make an animal?"

.22 leaned forward. A spasm in his right forearm scattered three of the pieces, but he grabbed the back legs and put them on the front of the body, the front legs on the back and then put the tail under the goat's chin.

Not bad, a basic understanding of goatees, Ben thought, but not exactly what the test asked for. Ben then used flash cards for colors and numbers. .22 did fairly well. He couldn't remember more than three digits, but Ben had suspected that. His reading was barely beyond preprimer and caused agitation, but he figured out "dog" and "run" and "red" and "boy" among others. And did better than Ben had anticipated on the Dolch list.

Ben then put three story cards on the table—a child standing in the snow, a child rolling a ball of snow, and a child standing beside a three-ball snowman—in reverse order and asked .22

to tell the story. He was quick and correct and very pleased with himself, pausing long enough to gulp the rest of the can of orange pop, some of which dribbled down the front of his shirt.

He failed two other picture-story tests—in one .22 had a man with a flat open the trunk after he had used the jack. But he copied three geometric figures correctly only going outside the lines when he was asked to put a circle inside a square. He could repeat certain tapping sounds made by drumming fingers against the tabletop and follow-the-leader when Ben held out his own hands and opened and closed his fists or turned his hands palms down, then back to supine. .22's hand strength was awesome; he tied and untied his shoes, hopped on one foot, but couldn't stand on one foot with his eyes closed.

He drew the arms coming out of the head in a picture of himself; produced a respectable "Harold" with the d and r reversed; but excelled at putting round pegs in round holes, nuts on bolts and matching green wires with other green wires.

"So what does all this mean?" Hannah nervously picked at her cuticles. Ben had asked .22 to wait in the reception area while he talked with his mother.

"I'm sure you've heard some of this before, and I think you want me to be honest. Harold is impaired. We both knew this before we tested, a 60-65 IQ, somewhere in there. He will always need supervision. But group homes would offer this. The positive side is how well he did on the vocational screening. Harold would be a good candidate for any number of assembly line jobs—simple tasks, nothing intricate—things that take matching, some concentration, moving large objects...he's amazingly strong. He may not always make the right decision if left on his own, but in a controlled atmosphere, he'll do fine." Ben paused. "I do think he lacks stimulation. He needs to practice putting things together, taking them apart—to play with toys that provide problem solving. I don't know what he does with his time all day, but he could watch television—educational channels."

"I've never let him watch TV. Violence and sex didn't seem to be the sort of thing I'd want to encourage."

"I understand. But some programs would give him an idea of the outside world, how people react to different situations."

"He does have a hobby. A few years back he began to collect frogs. He takes care of them, does all the feeding, cleaning of the aquariums. He's even earned some pocket money by selling some of the big ones to restaurants."

"Really?" Ben remembered .22's comment about his bedroom being too loud. He hadn't made that up.

"Would information like this help in the evaluation? Should I tell the examiners?"

"Of course. Anything that indicates he can adjust."

"Dr. Pecos, will you be perfectly honest with me. Do you think he'll pass the other test? Do you think other examiners will find him trainable, too?" Hannah was grasping the edge of his desk, knuckles white.

"I would be shocked if they didn't. I really don't think you have anything to worry about."

If he had thought there might be another emotional outburst like the night before, he shouldn't have worried. Hannah simply began to sob, her head in her hands, shoulders convulsing, almost no sound except for her gasps for air. Ben tried to comfort her, but she pulled away. It was obvious that all the years of wondering had taken their toll.

BEN CHECKED the picnic basket one more time. Champagne, a wedge of Camembert, crackers, a cold pasta and shrimp salad from the deli at Furr's in Gallup—Rose had done a pretty good job of following his list but not without a lot of teasing. Had he forgotten anything? The ring was in his pocket. He'd told Julie that they were eating out. Out wasn't a misnomer. He'd planned an evening under the stars, a dinner on a mesa. It would be different, romantic. He'd even thought to pack candles.

For once, it hadn't rained that afternoon. The temperature had risen to the mid-eighties by four p.m. and would drop into the forties that night. Maybe, they'd need another blanket. Which meant he wasn't planning on returning to the boarding house much before dawn. He hadn't consulted Julie. And maybe he was assuming too much, but instinct told him it would be all right.

And it was. When she met him at the door in heels and strapless sundress and he'd said they might need a blanket, she'd simply asked him to wait a minute and she returned in hiking boots, jeans, and flannel shirt, with two blankets under her arm.

"More like the dress code of this special restaurant?" Julie asked. She had tied her hair back with a green ribbon that matched the shirt's Black Watch pattern, but red-gold wisps escaped and softly framed her face. And she looked eager as she slipped a hand in his. In a rush he realized that he was going to make promises to this bright, vivacious woman—had, already. It made him feel good. He fought a temptation to kiss her; he knew the hall had eyes of its own. Instead he simply said, "I think you'll pass," and grinned.

Ben had remembered a road that left the main highway some five miles back and disappeared into the El Malpais, the badlands to the south. The rough terrain was dotted with huge humps of hills that reared out of the desert. If his timing was right, they'd be able to climb to a rock outcropping overlooking the valley and have dinner while the sun was setting. He put an arm around her and pointed out their destination in the distance, a wide, level expanse of basalt a quarter of the way up a towering mesa already turning rose-purple in the late afternoon light. And then he shared his day—an old habit—but it felt comfortable.

"I know you don't want to believe anything good about Hannah but I think you've misjudged her." Ben shared how .22 had done that morning, explained the circumstances and the test.

"Poor woman. What a tyrant her husband must have been. So you think .22 will do all right in front of strangers?"

"He should. He may not be as socially awkward as I think.

Of all things, Hannah said he collected frogs. He must have more than one or two in his room; she mentioned something about his cleaning aquariums."

"I've seen them. I was treated to a tour. It's a horrible place. I don't see how he sleeps in there, but believe me, he has more like two hundred."

"Two hundred frogs?"

"I'm not a good judge, but most seem to be toads."

"People don't eat toad's legs, do they?"

"What?" She grimaced.

"Hannah said that .22 has sold to restaurants. I just assumed that his collection was all frogs."

"Hmmm. Most of the ones I saw had bumps on their backs, warty protrusions—"

"Yuck. Let's think of something a little more appetizing to talk about."

Julie laughed, kissed him lightly on the cheek, then sitting close, comfortably slouched so that their shoulders touched.

He left the highway at the county marker, and they bounced along a barely discernible two-track road. Buffalo grass caught at the bumper and crunched under the tires. The windshield was coated with dust by the time he pulled the truck close to the base of the sloping wall and parked beside a clump of piñon. Green and brown, vegetation and dirt, a person had to see the beauty of the desert to like it out here. He looked over at Julie and felt a twinge of fear. Was he expecting too much? Slip a ring on her finger and she'd become a homesteader? Was he being foolish?

Julie stepped out of the truck and stood gazing up at the flat-topped mountain.

"Any guarantee my deodorant won't fail before we get there?" Julie had shaded her eyes and was studying the sheer rock climb in front of them.

"Hold that romantic thought," Ben laughed. "There could be a path around to the right—if we're lucky we'll find stepping stones right to the top."

"You're putting me on."

But he wasn't; they walked to the back side and there they were, steps winding upwards disappearing among the boulders. The first inhabitants of this land considered the area sacred and regularly made pilgrimages, wearing moccasin-smooth niches along the rock face. Hideouts like these had been lifesavers when the Spaniards had attacked. Where the going was steep, the old ones had flinted away grooves in the stone forming footholds as the path wound among shoulder-high boulders, making ascent fast when it had needed to be.

Ben took the picnic basket, Julie the blankets. They climbed in silence.

"This is perfect," Julie said, a little out of breath, but almost reverently as they reached the level outcropping of rock. Ben watched as she walked near the edge to enjoy the panoramic view. They were only a hundred feet above the truck and still some three hundred feet from the actual top, but the valley rolled out from the base of the mesa and stretched as far as they could see—a sharp contrast of emerald squares to rough, black eruptions that had burst through the earth's bubbling surface in some prehistoric age. In fact, these odds and ends of mountains were *huerfanos,* orphans and outcasts, stranded edifices destined to stand alone, separated from what was called the Rockies.

"I want this to be your home." It wasn't what he had planned to say. But it was the truth. They stood together and he turned her towards him tipping her head back to look him in the eye. "But I want you to be happy," he said.

"I haven't had second thoughts if you're worried. I know what I'm doing. And I'm marrying you not the landscape."

"I worry that you'll be too isolated. These aren't skyscrapers." His hand swept across the view to the west. Pinnacles of rock worn wind-smooth to a pale tan striated sandstone, some towering hundreds of feet in the air, jutted out from the base of the mesa.

"What happened to the man who had it all figured out last night? How I'll commute, tape a show, fly back home for a few months...?"

"I just want you to be sure."

"Is this the place where I say I'll show you how sure I am?" Julie was teasing but had unbuttoned the flannel shirt letting it slip to the ground. He watched as she propped a foot on a rock and unlaced first one boot and then the other kicking them to one side. Next came the bra and jeans.

"Should I ask to see the ring before I let this go too far?" Her thumb was hooked under the elastic waist of her panties. The ribbon had slipped from her hair and she tried to keep the red-gold strands from drifting across her face, finally giving up and pushing them behind her ears. There was a smattering of dark rose freckles across her chest. And he liked the way she stood there—assured, confident of her body, inviting him to view it, knowing she could excite him. He laughed. "You're so good at shedding clothing, why don't you help me with mine?"

"Great idea." She paused in front of him. "I want you. I want to be with you. I wasn't ready four years ago. The time wasn't right. It is now." She put her arms around his neck and started to say something else, but he kissed her—mouth, eyes, nose. With a little help his boots and shirt and jeans slipped to a pile at his feet.

The warmth of the granite slab felt good against his back. Her hair smelled like rain as she snuggled into him. There wasn't any talking now. So much for wanting to go slow. Abstinence had fueled a hunger that surprised him in its intensity. And he heard each of them say "I love you" in their slippery frenzy, both breathless, moaning, pushing and thrusting until his body shattered into liquid pieces and he felt her slump against him.

In the quiet that followed, he stroked her back, her hair and listened to the wind whistle flute notes around the base of their rock haven. Had he ever felt this good? Or knew that what he was doing was so right?

"Does this qualify us for the mile-high club?" Julie rolled to the side then slipped to the ground.

"Probably not." He laughed, then stooped to fish the ring

box from a jeans pocket. "But something tells me I better keep my promise. One ring in less than twenty-four hours." He took it out and slipped it on her finger. "If you'd like something different—"

"It's perfect." She sounded awed. "It looks like out here. Your landscape will never leave me." She held her hand out from her body so that the sun gave the diamond dots of color and the raised band of inlay stripes sparkled against the gold.

"It looks good with what you're wearing." Ben had started to dress but hadn't taken his eyes off of Julie's nakedness. Julie suddenly looked self-conscious. "Hey, no complaints." He pulled her to him. "You have a choice—seconds, or champagne." He thought the decision had already been made as her arms went around his neck.

"HAS ANYONE SEEN Salvador?" Hannah asked. "He didn't show up for work this morning."

So that's why there's an assortment of dry cereals on the table and a note to help yourself, Ben thought as he watched Julie pick up the box of Special K. Hannah had to open the trading post.

"He might have gone into Gallup," Ben said.

"I think he would have told me. He's always dependable. Besides, his truck is here. You don't think Tommy picked him up again? For more questioning, maybe?"

"I'll check when I get to the office. Tommy's still in the temporary offices next door."

"I understand that congratulations are in order." Hannah smiled at Julie. "Rose's brother does the best inlay work in the village." Hannah studied the ring on Julie's finger.

This is going well, Ben thought. Absolutely no animosity. He began to relax.

"Is this an engagement or wedding ring?" Hannah asked.

Odd question, Ben thought, as he watched Julie hesitate.

"We're engaged. We haven't set a date yet, maybe, at Christmas." She glanced at Ben.

"It's my understanding that all Indians are married under the blanket. At least, that's what Ed used to say. And since the two of you carried enough blankets out of here night before last—'' Hannah was looking at Ben. There was a smile but he thought it was snide, meant to be hurtful.

"Does it make any difference?" Ben cut her off. He didn't know whether he was reacting to being lumped into the racist "all Indian" reference or he hated to see anyone make light of their happiness. Ben put his arm around Julie.

Hannah shrugged and turned away. Her interest in them as sport seemed short-lived. "I'll be at the trading post. If you see Salvador send him over." She refilled a pitcher of milk, set it on the table then walked out the back door.

"Every time I feel sorry for her, she ruins it." Julie started to say something else but stopped as .22 pushed open the dining room door.

"Me hungry," .22 mumbled. He looked half-asleep as he picked up two bowls from the stack at the end of the table and filled both with Cheerios, scattering a generous cup or so on the table.

"Hey, pal, why don't you eat one bowl at a time." Ben leaned across the table but .22, apparently afraid that Ben would take one of the bowls, swept them towards him spilling still more of the little round oat O's.

"Me hungry." This time it was pronounced clearly and a couple decibels louder.

Ben decided upon a different tactic. "What are you going to do today?"

"Go to river."

"Is Sal going with you?" Julie asked.

"Maybe yes."

"Will the two of you fish?" Julie poured milk on one bowl of Cheerios for him.

"Catch frogs." At this point .22 slouched down in his chair, leaned over the table and began to snag Cheerios from the tabletop with the tip of his tongue, flicking them quickly into his mouth and stopping only to belch or emit a lifelike, "rrrri-bit."

"That's pretty good," Julie laughed.

"I hate to leave all this wildlife, but I'm running late." Ben pushed back from the table then bent down and kissed Julie.

"Me, too. Me, too." .22 leaned across the table towards Julie, eyes closed, lips puckered.

"I don't kiss frogs, remember? Unless it's like this." Julie kissed her fingers and pressed them to his forehead.

THE WATCH WAS CHEAP, a Timex. The silver band with chunks of spider web turquoise set on either side of the face had been won in a poker game—a long time ago from a Navajo. But the watch worked and its dial glowed in the dark. He never thought he'd be thankful for that. Sal looked at the watch's face and felt a tongue of panic lick up his spine when he realized he didn't know whether it was eight a.m. or eight p.m. He practiced slowing his pulse by taking deep breaths. It must be morning. And this would be the start of his third full day in the lab—locked in the lab. He was buried underground in a place that no one knew existed. But he couldn't think that way. This was only a test. Of wills? Or of winning? But weren't they the same?

He'd argued with Hannah on Friday. It had started out innocently enough. She had come down to check his progress, pick up what amber he'd finished. She'd had a port-a-potty put in. Said she thought he would be pleased. Now he wouldn't have to leave, interrupt his work, just to take a leak. She seemed pleased with herself—almost manic in her effusive praise of his work, picking up nuggets holding them under the bench lights, ooing and ahhing, saying this was some of the best color he'd ever produced.

And then she had seen the boxes. He was in the process of dismantling the lab, taking apart the dryers, the heating elements. He had enough inserts to finish the last twenty-five pounds. The liquids would be last. He'd take the resins outside to destroy, treat them as potential toxic waste, make certain they didn't find their way into the river. He was being careful.

"What are you doing?" She walked among the crates next to the bench. Her voice was flat, soft.

"Just getting a head start on shutting down. I imagine I'm going to have to be out of here soon, with the place sold." He stood watching her back as she moved along the bench picking up a nugget, putting it down, moving on. Her shoulders stiffened and her movements became jerky. She knew he was quitting. So, what was wrong? He braced himself.

Then she came to the tortoiseshell. He hadn't meant for that to happen. He had forgotten the two test pieces that he'd tossed on top of the convection dryer. At first she was quiet turning them over and over in her hand, studying them before she said anything.

"So this is why you can just quit making amber. You've found something you like to do better, something just as valuable, something that you care so much about that you've hidden it from me." Her back was still to him. She held the tortoiseshell under the bench light.

Sal didn't say anything. He simply had to let her anger run its course. Like always. Only maybe this time it was going to be worse. Her voice was so quiet. He almost wished she'd do something, turn around, confront him.

"Who said you could waste time on this cheap shit? I think our bargain was for amber, only amber." Then she seemed to reconsider, "Actually, this does make sense. It's not so bad, good, really. It'll pass and you'll have something to make after you sell me the recipe for amber."

"I'm not selling, Hannah. Tortoiseshell or no tortoiseshell. I'm not making anything fake anymore. Can you understand that? We've made the money you needed. Harold completed school, the house renovations got you a buyer. I've been able to help my family. All and all I'd say we've been successful. I'm stopping while we're ahead, before we're found out."

"But tortoiseshell—"

"No." Sal thought his voice boomed across the room. He thought it sounded unnatural. She ought to know the risk of selling tortoise. At least amber wasn't on an endangered species list. He was sorry he had even experimented now. He'd never try to sell tortoise. He hadn't made the pieces with sales in mind—it had been just one more challenge.

"Is it because I never said that I love you? Never let you live in the big house? Or are you punishing me because I'm leaving?" Hannah now stood two feet in front of him. Her white skin was splotched, angry red smudges colored her cheeks and her eyes glittered. He could handle her anger better than this. Where was she leading?

"Why are you tormenting me? Refusing me? You're going to make me do something I don't want to do," she said.

She had reached out to caress his face, letting her hand trail down the front of his shirt before dropping to her side. He willed himself not to flinch, to stand quietly, to wait. Her lips parted and small, even white teeth peeked out. He watched as she ran her tongue along their lower edge.

"Do you love me?" Luckily, he didn't have to answer because she went on. "Or was it just sex? All those years only meant a roll in the hay now and then, didn't they? There was no commitment, just air that thing out every once in a while, and everything would be all right. Harold meant nothing to you. All those years I struggled alone."

She let her fingers trace the bulge at his crotch. Still, he willed himself to stand without emotion. He knew he wouldn't get a hard on. All his senses were on alert, on caution. His skin prickled. She'd never acted like this before. Maybe if he said something, explained…

"We were adults. There was never any talk of my getting a divorce. That wasn't what we were all about," Sal ventured.

"What were we all about?" She tipped his head back to make eye contact, and her fingers were like ice.

"About friendship and caring—helping one another."

"And good friends do this to one another? I'm not asking for you to give me the recipe. I've offered to buy it."

"No one will get the recipe. I won't perpetuate a lie."

"Why don't you just call the authorities and report what you've done if your conscience is bothering you so bad?"

Sal had thought of it, but didn't because he wasn't the only one involved. He cared that much, and maybe lots more once upon a time. But that was gone now.

"Harold loves me. Are you jealous?"

"How can I be jealous of your son? You've been a good mother considering—"

"Considering that I tried to kill him, is that what you were going to say?" She bristled.

"Considering that you've been alone."

This seemed to appease her. She looked away, seemed calmer.

"I'm going to miss you. But maybe you'll be with me in spirit. Maybe I'll be able to keep you with me always." She looked up, her eyes begging for reassurance. Sal smiled. So all this was just due to jitters over moving, leaving behind everything she'd known for thirty years. He guessed he'd feel the same.

"I'll never be that far away from you." He held his index finger and thumb one inch apart. "Think of me and I'll be there."

She smiled back, a wan, nervous smile and then she leaned forward and hugged him.

"Forgive me. I haven't always been fair. But I do things that are the best for all of us. Do you believe me when I say that?" She pulled back and searched his face.

"I do." Then he started to add, "There was a time—" She put a finger to his lips to silence him then snuggled against his chest.

Sal smoothed her hair, buried his nose in its woodsy fragrance. He held her like that. A minute. Two minutes. Then she stepped back and walked towards the stairs. She hadn't said anything when she left. There were no more threats about the amber, no offers to buy his secret. She just left. He hadn't suspected then that she would lock the trap door, bolt and secure it so that he couldn't leave. And when he did discover it, he'd laughed. It was like her. A harmless threat. Like a kid who takes away the ladder to the tree house but brings it back later after the point has been made.

By the next morning it wasn't funny any longer. And she had turned the lights off, probably from the electrical box outside. Or maybe a fuse had blown. He could give her the benefit of the doubt. But that was becoming difficult. He had turned everything off—bench lights, overheads, fans—before going to sleep and when he woke up, the lights simply didn't work. He was in the dark. The pitch blackness that smelled slightly of dampness and mold pushed in upon him. He had fits of sneezing and his eyes watered. Then the fans had come on—fans only—circulating the air, lifting his spirits until he had tried the lights and found he still had no power.

And then he had heard the snap of an opening somewhere. A sliver of light played at the top of the stairs, but the wedge of a door had closed before he reached the top step. There was a flashlight and a sack of food, a banana and two boxes of dry cereal.

He didn't need to dwell on the fact that there was a dumbwaiter opening to deliver food, a narrow slot built into the heavy insulated door. He had never noticed it before. He should have suspected something when she insisted on putting in a cot and table, let alone a port-a-potty. This was calculated, planned in detail. If he hadn't seen it coming, it only magnified the fact that he didn't have a clue as to how it would end.

He couldn't let himself think that she would kill him. Wasn't this all because of the amber? Wouldn't he be safe as long as he didn't give up the recipe? Probably. He thought of his notebook and how he'd hidden it and not kept it with him. It would be safe, this one bargaining chip that might save his life.

But people would look for him. He felt a flood of relief. Yes. He wasn't thinking straight. He would be missed. He needed to meet with Julie about the show. It was a stroke of genius that he'd asked her to help him hide the fetish jar—she'd know he'd never leave it behind.

And .22, he'd promised to help him catch frogs. They were going to the river this morning. .22 would whine until Hannah released him. And Tommy Spottedhorse. He knew that Sal wouldn't skip out. Tommy hadn't jailed him again, sent him to Gallup for lock-up because he knew Sal was honest and wasn't going to go anywhere. Tommy would try to find him. And his sister expected him for dinner. Yes. He'd almost forgotten a celebration dinner on the Fourth. They were going to see the fireworks. It would be all right. Hannah couldn't get away with it. She couldn't leave him there to die.

"ROSE SAID YOU WERE coming in over the holiday weekend. I thought I'd make myself comfortable. If you call this comfort." Tommy indicated the straight-backed metal chair next to Ben's desk. "This is just one step above prison-issue."

"Is there a difference between prison-issue and regular Government-Issue?" Ben laughed. "At least it matches the desk and filing cabinet." He pointed to his coffee mug. "Can I get you some? It'll be instant, but I just need to heat some water." Tommy shook his head, "I don't have long."

"What's up?"

"For starters, I'm kicking myself. I think I've been an ace idiot. Here take a look." Tommy tossed two Polaroid snapshots on Ben's desk. "Old camera but best I could come up with."

Ben picked up one, then the other. "Looks like a knife."

"Is a knife. I found it on my desk Friday wrapped in that morning's newspaper, Albuquerque Tribune, and stuffed into a reinforced Manila envelope."

"Something tells me I don't have to ask what it is," Ben said.

"You're right. It's the murder weapon. That's the stiletto that killed Ahmed. Lab guys confirmed it this morning."

"Why would someone leave it on your desk?"

"Why would one person leave it, you mean. One good set of fingerprints on the handle belong to our pal."

"Sal?" Ben couldn't believe it.

"None other."

"Have you brought him in?"

"I was out there a half hour ago, just missed you. Hannah

says he's disappeared. She hasn't seen him since Friday. How 'bout you?''

"The same, I guess. Hannah was ticked that she had to open the trading post this morning. But where would Sal disappear to?''

"Who knows? The only sure thing is I'm up to my ass in a homicide, and I let the guy who did it go.''

"Are you thinking that Sal left you the knife and then skipped out?''

"That's my best guess. He could be halfway to Mexico City by now.''

"His truck's still at his trailer," Ben said. "It looks like he's been working on it recently.''

"I saw it. That's what makes me think he took off for the badlands on foot or borrowed a car.''

"El Malpais?''

"Yeah. He could hole up for a while, do penance, then work his way towards the border.''

"But why would he give himself away? Give you the murder weapon?''

Tommy shrugged. "He could have been told to do it—to come clean. Probably had a ceremony and according to Indian ways, the priest told him to get rid of anything having to do with the dead man. Maybe he was being bugged by the old ones. Sal was complaining of bad dreams when he was in jail. He told us he saw supernaturals. It could be, he just needed relief.''

Ben nodded. But it bothered him. Sal seemed too honest. When they had questioned him, Ben thought Sal seemed uneasy—who wouldn't be under the circumstances. But taking off? That certainly hadn't been Ben's impression of what he might do.

"Now what?'' Ben asked.

"I put out an all points. Luckily, we got some mug shots when he was in jail a couple weeks ago. We'll get a packet out. One thing's for sure, he's a hundred or so miles away from here by now.''

"BOY, ARE YOU POPULAR. So much for your trying to catch up on any work over the long weekend." Rose had stepped into his office just as Tommy was leaving. "I had hoped that we might have a minute to talk but they said it was an emergency."

"Who's they?"

Rose waited until Tommy was out of hearing. "Sal's sister and wife."

"What do they want? Have they found Sal?"

"I don't know. They seem pretty upset."

"Send them back."

The first thing that struck Ben was how old the two women seemed. Yet, both were probably in their early fifties—the same as Hannah, but there the comparison stopped. These were matrons—women who got their short hair regularly permed, let the gray show, and chose navy polyester slacks, anklets, flat-heeled oxfords, and plain blouses that pulled taut across ample bosoms and rounded abdomens. Each held an oversized vinyl purse on her lap, across plump legs that dangled over the edge of the chair, feet just brushing the floor.

Sal's sister introduced herself as Daisy Sandoval and seemed to be the spokesperson, indicating that Sal's wife might want to see him by herself later on. But when Ben looked over inquiringly, the other woman stared resolutely at the floor. Some sixth sense nudged him that this wasn't going to be easy.

"There's something very wrong," Sal's sister began. "Sal was supposed to have dinner with us last night. My son just returned from California. I had invited Mary," Daisy gestured towards Sal's wife with her chin, "and my son's girlfriend. I had fixed paper bread. Sal's favorite. After dinner we were going to watch the fireworks at the civic center. He never showed up."

"If something had come up, would he have called?" Ben asked.

"More likely, he'd drop by. He's always coming over. I saw him Friday morning. Sometimes I help him with his laundry. They live apart, you know." Once again, Daisy indicated the woman beside her. "So, he doesn't have anyone to take care of him."

Ben couldn't help compare the picture being painted of a helpless Sal with his own situation. There was no way he thought that Julie would take care of him, well, at least, not in the way Daisy was describing. That wasn't his definition of a wife—laundress and cook—but old ways die hard on the reservation.

"He hasn't come back for his clothes. He left three pairs of jeans, six tee shirts, socks and the sheets off of his bed. Now, you tell me, what did he sleep on Friday night?"

Sal's wife nodded. Obviously, it was common knowledge between the two that Sal only had one set of bed linen.

"I see why you're concerned." What else could Ben say? Should he broach the subject of Sal's being implicated in a murder? He really couldn't say anything until Tommy gave him the okay. But maybe if he asked general questions...

"Do you have any reason to think he might have left the village?"

"And gone where?" Daisy scoffed. "You don't know Sal very well. He'd never leave. He takes what you'd call a vacation not five miles from here and meditates but that's more for cleansing, ritual reasons before a ceremony."

"I dreamed he was buried," Sal's wife said.

Daisy's head jerked abruptly in her direction.

"What?" Ben thought he had misunderstood.

"He sent a messenger to me in a dream. He's been buried alive."

Ben realized he was staring, what an attention grabber. Daisy was the first to speak.

"When was this?" Her tone was sharp.

"Last night."

"Tell us what you saw," Ben said. It wasn't that he believed in this type of telepathic communication. But, then again, he didn't rule it out. He noticed Daisy's brows knit in a frown. This must be news to her, too. And he sensed she didn't like to be surprised.

Mary moistened her lips. She's enjoying this, Ben thought, center stage, all eyes focused on her. Would she fabricate a story for this attention? He'd watch for clues.

"I didn't go to bed until after the news. I always watch channel seven." She shifted her purse and methodically folded the handles inside the flap of a pocket attached on the outside of the bag before continuing. "I usually can't get to sleep easily. Sometimes I get up and down three or four times. I live by myself. I, that is, we, Sal and I never had children. I live in Sal's parent's house to the right of the plaza." She paused to glance quickly at Ben. "Sal has lived at the trading post since he started working there."

There was no indication of how long ago that was, but Ben seemed to remember someone saying Sal had been there for fifteen years, a long time to be separated without divorce. He wasn't sure how important this was to the story; he had the distinct feeling that his Indian listening habits were being tested.

"But the house that comes from his family has his spirit. He is of the badger clan, one of the thirteen matrilineal clans of the village."

Did he need a history lesson? Better yet, could he get out of one? Ben relaxed. This wouldn't go any faster with urging—even if he could give it.

"Sal's spirit called me by my Indian name, *Maiatitsa*, little bluebird, and warned me of the snowy owl." She paused for effect. The owl was a portent of death, Ben knew, but why the winter color of white, an absence of any hue in the middle of summer? What was even more interesting was that her voice had taken on onerous tones and she was rocking, ever so slightly, back and forth.

"Look to that which reflects the light of day, has no color of its own and keeps the sun from penetrating below the ground by blanketing the earth, deadening the spirit." She droned on staring from under lidded eyes. "And be wary of the snow maiden who lives to keep green shoots from reaching the warm rays, who guards against life escaping from her watchful eye, whose hoary breath can paralyze—numb the stinger of the bee, the claws of the bear, the heart of the hunter.'' She paused for emphasis, then shook her head, blinked her eyes and suddenly returned to normal. Yet, Ben had the distinct feeling that he had experienced the spirit that had spoken through her. It was eerie. He felt shaken.

''Sal's spirit cried out to me. He's being held underground by the snowy maiden.'' She indicated she was finished and slumped back in her chair, eyes averted.

No one spoke. Ben wasn't real good at metaphors but you didn't have to be an English major to think of Hannah. He couldn't check an involuntary shudder. But wouldn't Sal's wife naturally suspect Hannah? Want to implicate her, get her in trouble? Could you lose your husband to another woman and not feel some animosity—an anger that even years couldn't erase? Ben stole a look at Daisy. If anything, her frown had gotten deeper. She seemed speechless, just stared at Sal's wife. Wasn't it truly possible that all this was just for attention as he first suspected? And as far as that went, hadn't it worked?

''We must consult the priests,'' Daisy said.

Not ''I believe you'' exactly. But she wasn't saying that she didn't either. How tactful, Ben thought. Both women stood. Daisy thanked him for his time and then they left. He heard himself making lame promises to keep in touch, let them know if anything came up and for them to be on guard.

And then he sat back down at his desk. He couldn't stop himself from putting some credence in what Sal's wife had said. At least, he was certain that she was telling the truth. The truth as she saw it. The supernatural so easily intertwined with life sometimes. If his grandmother were still alive—

''I always hate to interrupt a trance.'' Rose was kidding, but she must have been standing in the door for a moment.

''Come in.'' Ben blinked then pushed his hair back off his forehead with two hands. It was difficult to dispel the mood Sal's wife had created. And he was irritated at having to talk to someone right now. ''What's up?''

"Well, this may be nothing. I probably shouldn't be bothering you—"

"Hey, I'm already bothered." He tried to sound like he was joking but saw Rose hesitate. "No, really. Here's a chair." He walked around his desk and pulled one of the chairs closer to his desk. "Now what's all this about?" He sat down across from her.

"This, I guess." She held a videotape in her hands. "Yesterday, we caught the kids who had been raiding the pop machines."

"That's great. Was it someone after some firecracker money?"

"More like cigs and beer, or pot." She gave him a look that said he might be out of touch with teens. She was probably right.

"But that's not exactly why I'm here."

Ben waited. Rose was fidgeting with the tape, reluctant to talk. But why?

"You know, it might be easier if I show you what I saw. Let you see for yourself, decide for yourself." She grinned. "See if you think I'm 'round the bend."

He followed her to the nurse's lounge, which held a TV and VCR. Lunch seemed to go faster for some with the soaps on. Funny how civilization intruded upon the reservation. Did that mean *As the World Turns* might have universal application? He didn't know. It just seemed so incongruous out here.

He watched as Rose pushed the cassette into the machine and fiddled with the knobs. The screen came up a fuzzy gray drizzle then snapped to a clear picture of the reception area. He watched a still life of the pop machine, the six straight-backed chairs, the hanging pots of wandering Jew and philodendron, the Yei rug, tile surfaced coffee table, magazines haphazardly tossed on top…all in black and white. So what was he supposed to see? He started to say something. Rose shushed him and pointed.

He could just make out Hannah and .22 walking up to the front door, pushing it open. This must be Saturday morning before the testing. Then Dr. Lee came out from the back. As Ben watched, Dr. Lee bussed Hannah on the cheek. A kiss. Now that was interesting. Suddenly, Rose put the tape on Fast-forward.

''Not that that isn't worth watching but let's get to the good stuff.'' She released the Fast-forward and the tape slowed to normal speed.

''What am I looking for?''

''You'll see. Or, at least, I hope you will.''

Now it was Hannah alone, Hannah chewing her cuticles, pulling at a hangnail, Hannah looking out the window, suddenly hopping up as .22 enters from the back with Ben. Ben motions for .22 to stay and Hannah to go back to his office with him. Now there's only .22 playing on the floor. He picks up the Ferrari and runs it back and forth along his leg.

Looking around he lets the toy car fall. And then he stretches. Fingers clasped, he pushes his arms above his head and yawns, then digs in his pocket and bounding upright walks to the pop machine.

''Stop the tape.'' Ben didn't mean to yell. ''Can you replay that part—start with the yawn?''

''It gets better. Let me continue and then we can go back, okay?''

Ben nodded and then sat forward leaning against the conference table, trying to stop his brain from whirling in confusion, stop the questions, just watch…

.22 puts one quarter in the slot but drops the other, which rolls back into the center of the room. He deftly turns, retrieves the quarter and then flips it. With thumb and forefinger he sends it spiraling into the air, catches it and smacks the coin against the back of his hand. Heads or tails? Ben couldn't tell which. But did it matter? Because…but wait. Suddenly, .22 appears to go limp; his arm jerks forward. The soda is obviously forgotten as he slumps to the floor all the while nervously facing the camera. Did he hear someone coming?

Ben watches .22 wet his lips, reach in his pocket, then rub at his eyes, which suddenly water. As if in slow motion, .22's jaw falls open and his upper lip starts to twitch just as Dr. Lee reenters the picture to squat beside him. Dr. Lee's back is to the camera blocking most of .22's face, but it's obvious that he's asking questions from the way .22 nods or shakes his head. He ends by patting .22 on the shoulder before leaving the room.

"That's about it," Rose said just as the screen went fuzzy. "Replay?"

"You bet. But I'd like to stop a couple places, mind if I man the controls?"

Rose handed him the remote after pushing Rewind.

"I'm so relieved that you think something's fishy, too. I don't always check the tapes in detail, just record over; but I needed to adjust the camera and figure out why Friday's tape kept jumping around—see if I'd gotten it fixed by Saturday. It's like watching two different people, one retarded, one okay—even if only for a couple seconds."

Ben nodded. He probably couldn't say it better himself and he wasn't thinking multiple personality.

"Do you know .22?" Ben asked.

"Not really. Everyone knows about him, how his mother tried to kill him and Tommy's mother saved him. Tommy's mother used to call Hannah the Indian word for evil. She used to swear she could prove Hannah tried to kill the boy and not just once."

"Why wasn't anything done?"

"I guess it was, sort of. Ed Rawlings sent his wife away. So, what do you make of all this? Why would .22 pretend to be more incapacitated than he is?"

Ben didn't answer, just shook his head. He was looking at a replay of .22 letting the plastic car slip from his lap. He slowed the tape.

"Do you mind if I have a copy made?"

"No problem, but you can keep the original."

"Thanks, and thanks for saving it. It brings up some questions, that's for sure."

"You would know. Didn't you test .22 on Saturday? Yellow Skin said you planned on it."

"Yeah. And I'm not sure my findings match what I'm see-ing."

"There's probably some medical explanation. I'm sure you'll figure it out. I better get back to work. Yell if you need me." Rose walked back out front.

Ben pressed Play. He was engrossed in what he saw. He knew what he suspected. But what did he really have? One minute—probably less than one minute of tape that showed a young man going from impaired motor control to what ap-peared to be more normal in the blink of an eye, and then slip backwards again. Now he struggled with movement, controlling his tics, his arm; now he was tossing a coin in the air, perfectly in control; now he was slumped on the floor, eyes watering, lip twitching. Ben switched off the VCR and leaned his chair back against the wall.

He had either watched an Academy Award-winning perfor-mance or…or what? What explanation was there for this ap-parent respite, however brief, from affliction? And would others agree with him? Rose saw a difference. But was it big enough to do something about? Was it documented anywhere that .22 didn't have normal moments, times when he was more in con-trol? Was there proof that he couldn't have flipped a coin or stood upright, tall, head not thrust forward? And did it say anywhere that he couldn't bend over, pick up a coin and not lose his balance?

But wasn't it more his facial expressions? For a few seconds, his face lacked any reminder of the Cheerio-eating frog dem-onstration Ben had watched at breakfast. For those few seconds on the tape Ben had seen the eyes of an intelligent human being, not someone who struggled with a sixty-five IQ, but a man who—if you ignored his shaved head, the scabs covered by ointment, the pimpled chin and watering eyes—might be handsome. But again, who was to say that .22 couldn't go in and out of his impairment—waver—lucid moments with good motor control then back to struggling. Had anyone documented that? And who could he ask? Not Hannah. But maybe someone at the school; or, perhaps, Dr. Lee.

Ben sat quietly. He had to face it. Was this just his own ego struggling to find an answer—help Ben save a little face, since he had been the one to test .22? What was it Rose had said, if anyone would know, he would? Could he have been so thoroughly duped? Wouldn't he have suspected? He had been complete in the testing. Just because it was a trial run to assure that Hannah wouldn't be cheated out of her inheritance didn't mean...

Ben let the chair crash forward. The inheritance. Of course. There were a few hundred thousand dollars riding on .22's abilities, or lack of which as the case might be. Why couldn't Hannah have gotten someone, an actor, to impersonate .22? But, damn it, he looked like Hannah—those same watery blue eyes, blond hair—wouldn't that have been hard to match?

So why couldn't Ben shake the feeling that he had been used? If he wasn't who Hannah said he was, wasn't it a stroke of genius to set up a test of his skills? Didn't they need to make sure that .22 would pass—but not just in skills, in believability? What better way than run the act by a shrink ahead of time.

But didn't that raise questions about the real .22? Was there a real .22 still alive and well somewhere? Ben cursed the holiday. Tomorrow he'd call every institution in Albuquerque that might have had as its ward one Harold Rawlings about ten years ago.

"Want me to have a copy made for you? My son gets tapes done at the high school. They've got some pretty good equipment." He hadn't heard Rose return.

"That would be great if he has the time."

"As upset as you look, there's no way I wouldn't make him have the time." Rose smiled. "I'll leave both on your desk after lunch tomorrow."

Ben thanked her and walked back to his office. What should he do? What reason did he have to check hospitals? Did he really have enough to go on? He was suspicious, but that was about all. And actually what crime had been committed? .22 wouldn't go for testing before the board until Thursday. Hadn't Hannah said the appointment was Thursday in Albuquerque?

Then if all this was a charade, and the inheritance was gotten under false pretenses, there would be a crime and it would be time to bring in the authorities. But Ben felt an urgency. He needed to do something now. Three days. Could he come up with more evidence in that time? He knew he was going to try. And he knew he would ask Julie's help.

TEN

JULIE HAD WALKED Ben to his pickup after breakfast. There would be more fireworks that evening, and they made plans to go. She hoped her day would be productive. She had wanted to talk with Sal and map out what she'd like him to say on camera. It wasn't too early for that—talk about it a month ahead and rehearse until the on-air moment arrived. She'd worked with the uninitiated before. Everything would be fine, then add a couple cameras, a crew and suddenly the prize interviewee would become tongue-tied. She'd even seen them bolt—right off the set at airtime.

The toes of her sandals were stained dark brown from walking across the lawn. Someone had watered. Hannah probably, but she must have gotten up at dawn. Julie could see her pumping gas in front of the trading post. She wouldn't have to do that much longer, one month, maybe less.

Julie wandered towards Sal's shed and trailer. It wouldn't hurt to check, but everything was closed tight. Locked. Julie rattled the doorknob on the trailer, then peered in the eight inch square window in the door. It was a tiny space but uncommonly neat for a man. But wasn't that sexist and unfair? Julie admonished herself.

Next, she tried the shed. This time the door was padlocked shut with no windows to peek through. There seemed to be such a finality about Sal's being gone—like he planned on staying away for a while, took precautions, didn't just disappear. But that was odd. He'd known that they needed to spend time together, how important it was that they continue to meet, discuss how he wanted his art presented. Why wouldn't he have said something to her?

And the package, the fetish jar—she hadn't thought about that. There had been too many opportunities for him to tell her he was planning on a trip—that that was why he needed to keep the jar safe. But maybe he'd picked up the package. He certainly wouldn't disappear without it. He had seemed so earnest taking her into his confidence. Yet, he'd been gone three days without telling anyone.

She shaded her eyes and looked back towards the boarding house. There were so many good angles. She needed to get to work on a shot script—at least, patch in some background around the interviews she had planned. She needed some fade-in, montage stuff for the opening to set the stage and capture the Southwest in color. Possibly a river shot would do that—river with bluffs rising out of the desert, the seeming contradiction of water in an arid setting.

Today might be a good time to check out the river—to make some preliminary decisions, mark areas that would get the desired results—the interest of the audience, the oohs and ahhs that would keep viewers from flipping to another channel. She was beginning to feel a little pressured. She needed to get the blessing of the producer, and soon. In fact, it would be better to spend the extra money and send whatever pictures she got by overnight mail. Just in case her thinking didn't mesh with those in charge.

She needed to change shoes, throw on jeans, grab the camera bag—if she hiked to the bluffs and followed the curve of the river back, she wouldn't miss lunch.

A breeze dried the perspiration that dotted her hairline, neck, and tops of her shoulders—evaporative cooling—the thing that made the desert livable, pleasant even, in the summer. She had rolled up the sleeves on her cotton shirt and pulled the tail out. Another "do" for the desert was to wear natural fiber clothing. She liked it out here. It wasn't really a matter of Ben talking her into it. There weren't too many places in New York that she could hike to—and be alone.

And there was the beauty. A number of flowering cacti lined the path—little pincushions of green with two-to-three inch red or yellow trumpets. She felt lucky to have found them; the flowers would be gone by tomorrow. Some things in the desert just didn't last—one brief burst of color or scent and then oblivion.

It hadn't rained for days and the ground was crusty again— a mixture of sand and fine dirt that crunched underfoot. It made a mockery of the swath of rich, black earth across the Midwest that produced the food staples for the country. By rights this land shouldn't produce at all. But if you knew where to look and waited for a rain, it came alive.

The river had probably flooded this area fairly recently— maybe last season—replenished the minerals, enriched the soil. Julie thought she recognized marks on boulders that could have been made by standing water. The river was thirty feet in front of her now, the last twenty were covered by a stand of young cottonwood. She paused to aim the Nikon, then switched lens deciding on the small zoom, and took three good pictures, towards the river, away from the river and one of the bluffs.

If the riverbed was shallow and gravel-lined through this area, she'd wade. It would feel good, and she could get some spectacular shots walking downstream unobstructed by the trees. The coldness of the water almost made her reconsider. But the bottom was smooth with pea-sized bits of granite and an occasional marble-round piece of pumice, and she decided to brave it.

When she first saw the cages in the shallows, it didn't make sense. Why were there twenty-odd galvanized wire cages two by four by one foot ringing a man-made pool, rock-lined and two feet deep but closed to the current of the river? In fact, the pond was carefully constructed so as not to have running water infiltrate the basin at all but to rely on a pump attached to a gasoline generator that whirred and chugged spewing water through a recycling tube some four feet in the air. It was a fountain, but not a very pretty one. There was no statuary, maidens dumping water from their urns and there was no vegetation, lily pads with flowers; but the pond was clear, free of debris.

Heavy black plastic trapped the water and its inhabitants should they escape, but that seemed unlikely as each cage was skewered to a stake by a short length of chain that let it stray a foot but no farther and each fist-sized door was clipped snugly shut.

Julie knelt at the pond's edge and studied the arrangement before leaning over the cage closest to her. She had been right. If toads were the ones with warts, then these were toads—all of them. And they looked exactly alike. This wasn't a varied collection but a large assembly of the same species.

The toads could choose to be immersed or retire to the drier part of their wire-mesh homes. Most, it seemed, preferred the shallow water. It wasn't the purposeful placement of the toads that intrigued her; it was the smell. The strong, unmistakable odor of tea. And not just any tea—Earl Grey.

She cupped her hand and let the water from the pond trickle through her fingers. It was tea, light golden brown, aromatic, sun-brewed to perfection. The toads were having a tea party. She couldn't stifle a giggle. Feeling somewhat like the Mad Hatter, she retrieved a wad of tea bags that had been tied to a stake allowing them to float towards the center where they would get sun and checked the tags. For whatever it was worth, she had been right. It was Earl Grey.

The toads certainly seemed to have good taste. But that might be all they had. Even though the pond was full of some kind of water flea that flitted in and out of the cages almost sitting on the toads' noses, no one was eating. Some of the ones who had chosen to pig-pile in the dry end of their cages looked lethargic. A white mucous trailed across their backs oozing, it appeared, from their small hornlike row of points. Had these toads been injured?

Automatically Julie raised the camera—a shot of the pool, a change of lens and a close-up of the toads. There must be some explanation. Of course, she was assuming that these were the toads she'd seen in .22's room—part of the hobby that Hannah told Ben about. But he wouldn't be selling the legs of these guys to any restaurants. And he would have needed help building this pool, adding a generator, the filters and water spout. He wouldn't have known how to do all this.

And why were they all alike? Where would anyone get a hundred or so toads all alike? Trap them? Is that what she was looking at? Julie didn't think so. This arrangement seemed more for exercise—take everyone out of the aquariums in the darkened bedroom and let them frolic in nature, eat in the wild, reproduce… Only none was doing any of that.

Suddenly, Julie didn't feel very comfortable. She didn't want to run into .22 out here and be discovered yet again by his overprotective mother. Better to leave toad farming or whatever it was to others. But Earl Grey tea…that was a puzzle.

She didn't meet anyone on the way back and used two rolls of 24 exposures getting just the shots she wanted. She thought the guys in New York would be pleased. And it might save time to just send the film. If she had the film developed here, it would waste another week—driving into Gallup, leaving the film, going back for the pictures, and then having to mail them. No, the studio would get the film quicker than she'd get pictures back. It would be just as easy for the studio to develop the film in the first place.

The mail would be picked up at the trading post in the morning. Sending it overnight delivery assumed it would get there by the end of the week, maybe sooner. She'd stop by the corner of the trading post marked Post Office when she got back.

BREAKFAST HAD BEEN peanut butter and jelly on whole wheat—with lettuce and mayo. That last addition bothered Sal. Unless .22 had helped and Hannah had left it that way, didn't want to hurt .22's feelings. It was just another queer twist to being imprisoned in the first place. But, the lights were on. He'd worked last night—to keep his mind off of things and not just because there had been a note from Hannah saying it was in his best interests to do so.

He could play along. He'd unpacked everything, set up the workbench, the miniature chemistry lab, the fans and dryers. He wouldn't work very hard. But he knew she could spy on him. He felt her watching from somewhere in the darkness. So maybe it would impress her that he could change his mind and do things her way.

He smiled. Maybe, if she thought profits would lag, she'd let him out. He tried not to dwell on that—the out part. He thought of positive things, how his sister had expected him for Sunday dinner. Then they were going to view the fireworks at the civic center. That was yesterday. Her son was back from fighting a fire in California. She would be upset. But she'd know that Sal wouldn't have left—never without telling her— no matter what. But would her concerns be enough? And where would anyone go to look?

He'd tried thumping against the trap door with a leg from the bench but could tell from the sound that extra insulation had been placed above the opening. The sound seemed to stop and fall back around his ears. He'd had to take out his hearing aid in order to continue. But wasn't the opening in the pantry to begin with? Not some place anyone other than Hannah was allowed.

Pounding was wasting his time. What an interesting thought. When he had nothing but time, he thought of squandering it. Sal had marked each day on the wall in pencil—the day, a slash, and a number. He wasn't sure why he was doing this, but it seemed important. He was in control of something. That was what was important.

JULIE HAD GOTTEN BACK to the boarding house in time for lunch and a message from Ben saying he was still at the clinic but would be home in time to pick her up for fireworks. She had looked forward to spending the afternoon with him. It was a holiday, after all. And then she'd laughed at her peevishness. She was probably more upset at finding two tourist buses blocking the drive and seventy-some people roaming the grounds and lining up for a ham sandwich and potato salad. So much for eating—it would take a couple hours to feed that mob.

It was midafternoon before the tourists went on to whatever the next stop was. The house was quiet. From her bedroom window she could see a young man from the village sweeping down the drive in front of the trading post, mounding what looked to be discarded junk food wrappers along with a healthy amount of dirt that had sifted across the cement—the same young man who had seemed impressed when she'd handed him the package for New York. He had asked her about her job, said that he'd like to leave someday but probably wouldn't get much farther than an art school in Santa Fe. They had both laughed. It hadn't taken Hannah long to replace Sal. Julie watched as the kid hosed the drive around the pumps, stopping to refill the reservoirs of windshield cleaner, even wiping the squeegees. She hated to think anyone could take Sal's place so quickly.

She missed Sal—it wasn't only that she was beginning to worry about the show. He was a friend. But Julie felt she had lost her star, literally lost the main attraction. He would have been good. But why was she thinking in the past tense? Wouldn't he turn up? She just wasn't sure. She should probably start working on a backup plan. Maybe she should interview another carver, not wait too long. But she had a very expensive fetish necklace that she'd hoped to feature. What would she do about that? She turned from the window. Now might be a good time to make a sandwich.

The kitchen was empty. Five large heavy-gauge black plastic garbage bags were lined up by the back door—stuffed to overflowing with discarded paper plates. What a mess. What a lot of work. It was little wonder that Hannah wouldn't miss this.

There was a plate of ham slices on the second shelf in the fridge and she'd seen a loaf of whole wheat next to the sink. Julie collected mustard and mayonnaise and put them on the counter. What she couldn't seem to find was the potato salad. She rearranged a few jars, knelt to look in the back and popped the lids off of three containers that held assorted leftovers from last night's dinner but no potato salad. Oh well, chips might be nice.

For some reason she was giving herself license to chomp down a few nitrates and fat calories. All this because she was missing Ben? Maybe. But the trek to the river must have burned enough calories to compensate. She opened the cupboards next to the sink, a nice assortment of condiments but no chips. Where else would Hannah keep food? Hadn't she seen a pantry? Of course, the door around the corner to the left of the upright freezer.

At first Julie thought the door was locked. It was heavy and didn't want to budge. Humidity might make it stick but there wasn't much of that. Julie turned the knob and put her shoulder against the panel of knotty pine closest to the casement and pushed. It burst open and Julie stumbled forward struggling to recover her balance.

The light from the kitchen illuminated a totally bizarre scene—Hannah held a plate with a ham sandwich, and stood over .22, who was cowering at her ankles. Light had been provided by a flashlight on a shelf above Hannah's head. Then swiftly, barely acknowledging Julie, Hannah put the plate on the shelf and smacked .22 across the face. Two red welts rose immediately and .22 started to whimper, then cry.

Hannah glared at her, "I don't know what you're staring at. It's called discipline—a little time-out with no lunch." Hannah picked up the plate and turned back to her son. "See this? This is what you can't have. Bad boys have to wait till dinner and then they won't get dinner unless they've been good. Does a certain bad boy understand that?"

.22 stopped blubbering, and he nodded before tentatively reaching up towards the plate. Hannah gave his hand a resounding slap. "That doesn't look like understanding to me." Hannah loomed over him. "Don't you want to show Julie what a good boy you can be?"

"Me good." .22 looked up at Julie with a tearstained face,

and she fought an impulse to drop to her knees and hug him. He looked so forlorn. What could he have done to warrant this?

"Me hungry." This time .22 lunged upward towards the plate knocking it from Hannah's hand. The sandwich scattered and .22 grabbed up a slice of bread stuffing the entire piece into his mouth.

Hannah was seething. Julie saw Hannah's hand come up from her side, and she grabbed Hannah's wrist and held on hard, keeping Hannah from striking the hungry young man again.

"I don't believe in corporal punishment," Julie said and didn't loosen her grip even when Hannah struggled.

"I don't see that this is any of your business."

"There are other ways to discipline that don't include with-holding food or hitting children."

"Well, I'm just sure that you would know all about it," Hannah sneered.

"I know right from wrong." Julie let loose of Hannah's wrist.

"I love you." .22 looked up at Julie, then threw his arms around her, shackling her at the knees and buried his head in her thighs inadvertently wiping his nose on her jeans.

Couldn't he have thought of anything else to say, Julie groaned inwardly as she watched color creep up Hannah's neck.

"Let go." Hannah was not pleased. She roughly twisted .22's ear, pulling his head back.

Was it Julie's imagination or did .22 look gleeful? Was he smiling as he pulled away from Hannah and burrowed his face deeper into her legs? And the bear hug was in earnest—she had lost feeling in her right leg. Suddenly, he released her as his left arm jerked uncontrollably. .22 fell forward and Julie lost her balance sitting back hard on the floor. Thank God for spasms. But if it hadn't been for the thick carpeting, I could have been bruised, she thought and struggled to her knees. And new carpeting at that, she decided as she choked back a sneeze from the sizing, must be a cosmetic touch for the new owners.

"Harold is sorry. I hope you're not injured." Hannah leaned over her, then straightened and turned back to .22. "Tell Julie you're sorry."

.22 seemed hesitant and still cowered on the floor covering his head with his hands. He's scared to death that she's going to hit him again, Julie thought.

"He doesn't know his own strength. He really doesn't mean to do things like this. His judgment simply isn't like ours." Hannah seemed to be seeking approval. Then she held out her hand to help Julie up.

For a split second Julie considered not accepting the gesture. But, for what? Couldn't she be magnanimous? A little forgive and forget never hurt.

"I'm positive Harold didn't mean to harm me." Julie stood.

"Me sorry."

"I know that and I appreciate your apology." Julie smiled at him. "Well, my looking for chips started all this; would I be likely to find any in here?"

Hannah picked up the flashlight and turned the beam to a shelf above Julie's head.

"The lights are out. I need Sal to check the breaker box when he gets back. But you have your choice—corn or potato?"

Julie grabbed the corn chips and walked back out to the kitchen to retrieve her sandwich feeling more relief than she wanted to admit.

"I DON'T BELIEVE IT. I know I haven't seen the tape but you didn't see him this afternoon, either." Julie and Ben were watching the fireworks from his truck at the edge of the civic center's parking lot. She had told Ben what had happened and could tell he was upset that .22 had been physical with her. And she hadn't even told him that his strength had scared her— just for a second when he wouldn't let go. She didn't consider herself a wimp but there was a brute force, animal strength about him and that coupled with his impaired reasoning...could he be dangerous? A sexual assault, maybe? If she were being honest, that had crossed her mind when he was burying his face in her thighs.

"Who can cry on demand complete with snot?" Julie asked.

"A good actor."

"And you think that Hannah may have hired such an actor when something happened to her son?"

"It's not as far-fetched as it sounds," Ben said.

"But still, the risk and all. It doesn't seem very plausible."

"But worth it if he passes. He got past me."

"I still think you're jumping to conclusions."

"Will you agree that the situation is strange? That there seems to be a lot that we don't know about?" Ben asked.

Julie nodded. They sat in silence.

"I don't want you around him when I'm not there," Ben added abruptly. "If he isn't who we think, then, who knows? Anything could happen."

"I don't need protection. I've lived twenty-seven years without your being around to run interference." She didn't try to keep the anger out of her voice.

"I'm not asking. I'm telling. I believe he could be dangerous. Are you forgetting that there's an unsolved murder? And that Sal has disappeared?"

Julie fought back an angry retort. Ben seemed to be over-reacting, and ordering her around. She hadn't meant to sound harsh, but she wouldn't be cloistered, kept on a leash. She could see Ben's jaw working as a starburst of light rained from the sky. Three more Roman candle explosions—fiery balls in pink, green and gold shot upward before shattering in an umbrella of trailing comets.

"I can take care of myself."

"I haven't seen a lot of proof of that."

Was he referring to .22 or four years ago when she had been abducted by her boss? She'd gotten out of that, hadn't she?

"I'm sorry you're angry. But that's no excuse to come down on me. I'm an adult and I'm able to make adult decisions. I refuse to believe that I could be injured by .22—are you sure you aren't more angry because you think .22 may have tricked

you? Isn't all this just a reaction to a bruised professional ego?
Which I don't think you have to worry about in the first place.
.22 is retarded—sometimes more, sometimes less in control but
nonetheless impaired.''

Ben didn't answer. And maybe it hadn't been the most tactful
thing to say. But she was irritated. He didn't own her. That
wasn't the meaning of the ring on her finger. And a doctorate
didn't mean he had to be right. He hadn't been in that pantry.
It was that simple. She didn't think she could be tricked very
easily, either.

''I think we need to talk with Tommy's mother,'' Julie said
after a pause. When there was no reaction from Ben, she continued. ''Maybe I'll look her up in the morning. I'll ask Tommy
to run me by, help me find the place and do the introductions.''
She saw Ben's fingers tighten around the steering wheel. Stupid. She hadn't been thinking. Under the circumstances men-
tioning Tommy must have seemed like a taunt. How could the
evening have gone so wrong? Julie leaned out the window to
watch a group of children waving sparklers and playing tag not
far from the truck.

''I'd like to go with you to see Tommy's mother.'' Ben
nosed the pickup between two parked cars in front of the boarding house and pulled on the emergency brake. They had hardly
spoken after the firework display, or on the ride back.

''Sure. I'd like that. Shall I pick you up at the clinic around
lunch?''

''That'll be fine.''

God, how formal. The goodnight kiss was only slightly better. Oh well, maybe in the morning everything would look different, Julie mused. She wouldn't run the risk of saying anything else that might be misunderstood. She couldn't even coax
a half-hearted smile from Ben before she walked back to her
room. He looked tired. He took things so seriously. Sal's disappearance was bugging him as much as it was her. And he
was conscientious. If someone had taken advantage of his professional opinion, used him, he wouldn't get over it easily.

She got ready for bed but then found she was too restless to sleep. Had she been unfair? What if .22 really was an impostor? What if they both had been taken in by an actor? And the first .22? Dead? Maybe with a little help? Maybe the second time there hadn't been a Tommy's mother around to save him. She shivered. This certainly put a sinister spin on things.

She turned out the light. She'd picked up a Hillerman mystery at the trading post earlier, but this didn't seem like a good night to start it. She lay back on top of the covers after fluffing her pillow. A breeze had sprung up. At least it had waited until after the fireworks. She watched the lace panels at the window billow stiffly into the room. And there was a full moon—almost full, maybe two nights shy of perfect roundness but big enough to cast shadows that played across the patchwork quilt.

Didn't this tiff with Ben only play up her worst fears? That she was too unbending—that they both were—to make it work? She lived in New York for Christ's sake. Didn't he take that into consideration? Didn't that give her some badge of courage—or at least prove that she was able to take care of herself?

They'd decided on a wedding at Christmas, six months, less than six months away. She'd called her parents and had sat through fifteen minutes of, ''I know we have no right to interfere, but...'' And the concerns had all been ones Julie had faced—her career, what she might have to give up living in a rural area, how would she be accepted by ''his people,'' and then her mother had reminded her that her engagement to Wayne had lasted two years and wasn't that smart planning because it hadn't worked out in the long run—so, wasn't Christmas just a little sudden? Shouldn't she take her time? After all, what was the rush?

And then her mother ended by saying that she always worried that Julie was ''committed to commit''—that maybe the engagement was all the closure she really sought, that a marriage... Julie had abruptly hung up, used the excuse that someone was waiting to use the phone, that she'd call back. But she hadn't, and wouldn't real soon.

The first thump made her catch her breath. It had come from the corner near the armoire. She listened but there was nothing

more, no sound that she didn't recognize. Branches from a
nearby cottonwood scraped the side of the house; the breeze
played with a set of wind chimes at the far end of the porch.

Then suddenly there were three more thumps, evenly spaced
in rapid succession, but closer to the bed this time. She sat up,
then reached for the lamp on the nightstand. This was going to
take incredible nerve, but she had to check it out. She switched
on the light and crawled to the foot of the bed. Taking a breath
she looked towards the armoire, then to the throw rug between
the big chest and the bed and burst out laughing. There in the
middle of inch-deep green shag sat the biggest toad she'd ever
seen. Easily seven or eight inches across, he sat unblinking,
stunned by the light, and hesitated before he hopped towards
the bed.

"Oh no you don't." Julie jumped up and grabbed a towel
from the bathroom, threw it over the toad, then slipped on sandals and a robe, scooped up her errant visitor and started out
the door. She was reluctant to just put it outside—what if it
was part of a collection? It looked exactly like the ones she'd
seen at the river bunched in cages, staked in the shallow pond.
And this old guy was the granddaddy of them all.

She hesitated but knew she should take it back to .22—if it
wasn't his, he'd know what to do with it. Hopefully, the door
to his room would be unlocked, and she could just nudge it
inside and hurry away.

The hall was quiet. The grandfather clock had just struck
one. From the "Do Not Disturb" signs on the room next to
hers and the one across the hall, it appeared that Hannah had
guests for the night. .22's room was at the end, kitty-corner
from Hannah's. Julie dropped to her knees and tried to look
through the keyhole. There was a light on, night-light judging
from the amount of illumination, in addition to that weird glow
from the aquariums. And that was about all that was in her line
of sight.

Still crouching, she tried the door handle. Open. Now, she
needed to concentrate on not making any noise. She placed the
toad on the floor beside her and loosened the towel. Then she

turned her attention to the doorknob, turning it slowly to the right, a click, faint but she paused. Was .22 asleep? He should be at this hour. She continued to turn—another half-revolution, and it was ready to push open.

Holding the knob secure in her left hand, she reached down and dragged the towel and toad closer, then pushed the door open three inches. It was the voice that caught her attention first before her eyes had adjusted to the dimness—the deep masculine voice whispering, quieting an obviously upset Hannah. The man appeared to be gruffly pleading with Hannah. Julie was just too far away to distinguish the words. She leaned forward, peeked, and caught a glimpse of a tall man with his hands on Hannah's shoulders.

Was it Ben? She thought so. Something about the deep bass voice, and the posture reminded her of him. She wiggled forward again trying to see if .22 was in bed, but the heavy wooden frame obscured her view. She wished she wasn't so jealous. But hearing Ben with Hannah just pushed her buttons.

Julie slowly released the doorknob, let it turn back making no sound cradled within her sweating palm. She felt sick like someone had pounded the air out of her. She sank back on her heels. She certainly hadn't expected to find this. But then she roused herself. It wouldn't be a good idea to have Ben or Hannah find her on her knees in the hall looking in the door.

The toad forgotten she grabbed the towel and inched backwards before she stood, not really trusting her legs to bear her weight. Reality shivered down her spine. Ben seemed to be a lot more friendly with the landlady than he wanted her to know. But was she jumping to conclusions? Couldn't it truly be someone else? A border, perhaps?

First, she needed to prove it wasn't Ben. No one had come to the door of .22's room. She hadn't been noticed. Her breathing was more even now and mastering her fright of creaking boards, she walked towards the stairs and crept down pausing on the bottom step to listen. The house was quiet. The wind whistled across the porch, through the screen to fluff her hair and tickle along her neck, but even it seemed subdued.

She was feeling stronger. She continued past the kitchen to the back. She needed, desperately needed to find Ben in bed, his own—and put these green demons behind her. She knocked softly. No answer. He was probably sound asleep. She turned the knob and pushed the door open. A lamp on the nightstand gave out hooded light; its pleated shade directed all the illumination towards the floor, but there was no one in the bed. The bed hadn't been slept in—sat on, even. She stepped into the room. The bathroom door was open.

"Ben?"

No answer. But she hadn't really expected one. The room felt empty. It was obvious that no one was there—hadn't been for a while. She couldn't stop the feeling of alarm that pushed into her consciousness. And that sinking feeling almost of nausea when her mind strayed to what she'd seen upstairs. She would just have to face it—Ben cared for Hannah. It crossed her mind to sit and wait for him to come back. But, then, what if he didn't? What if she had seen the prelude to a night together?

But wasn't she jumping to conclusions? Unfounded, so far. She didn't have proof. They'd sort of had a fight. Would this be Ben's way of getting back. No. He didn't think like that. It couldn't have been Ben upstairs... Maybe he'd gone back to the clinic, or somewhere in his truck. She'd check out front. She hurried into the hall, out the front door, across the porch pausing to catch the screen to keep it from slamming. His truck was there parked where they had left it earlier. She slumped back against the railing. Now what? But something was wrong. The driver-side door was open. She looked around. She couldn't see Ben, or anyone, for that matter. There was simply the truck sitting at the curb with its interior light shining through the windshield attesting to its emptiness. But now that she was out here, it wouldn't hurt to check, at least close the truck's door. There were fewer cars than just an hour ago. Hadn't Ben parked between two cars earlier?

She saw Ben's legs, then his body as she rounded the front of the cab—the blood didn't register until she had knelt beside him cradling his head, trying to rouse him. The welt at his crown was separated down the middle by a jagged cut mushed by hair and clotted blood.

"Ben." Her voice sounded strange. Because she was crying? Probably. Relief, fright—emotions tumbled over one another. She wouldn't let herself think he was dying. She took off her robe, wadded it and placed it under his head then rummaged behind the truck's front seat, found a towel, ran to the closest spigot on the side of the trading post and soaked it in cold water. The compress seemed to work. Ben moaned, turned his head towards her and tried to open his eyes.

ELEVEN

"I DON'T NEED STITCHES." Ben was sitting on the edge of his bed next to Julie who was holding a bag of ice wrapped in a towel.

"You just don't want your head shaved. I detect a little vanity," Julie answered.

"We already have one shaved head around here."

"You should never take a chance with a head wound."

"I'll be at the clinic in four hours. I'll have someone look at it then."

"At least call Tommy."

"And what? Say I was hit on the head in the parking lot and don't remember much else?"

"I'm not going to win, am I?"

"No." Ben laughed.

"You're impossible." Julie fell backwards on the bed.

"We both are. Headstrong and impossible. Think this relationship has any hope of working?" Ben was teasing but Julie thought there was an underlying seriousness.

"I want to give it a chance. How about you?" She propped herself up on one elbow.

"I'm committed."

"Ugh. You sound like my mother talking about me."

"I'm in love. Sound any better?"

"Lots." Julie threw her arms around Ben. "This whole thing is getting dangerous."

"Past tense." Ben gestured toward his head.

"And you have no idea who it was or why?"

"None. After the fireworks tonight I pulled in beside a car I thought I recognized. The night I locked the money in my glove compartment, there was a car with Nevada plates parked next to the truck—same car. I'd swear to it."

"So you decided to investigate?"

"Something like that. I guess I found out it was more than a coincidence."

"And you don't remember anything?"

"Nothing that makes sense. The trunk was open. I leaned down to take a look…"

"And, then what?"

"I thought I saw trays of vials. Lab setup, sort of."

"Maybe the guy's in pharmaceutical sales."

"It wasn't like that. I don't know how to explain it. All the test tubes had rubber stoppers like they were being delivered to a lab."

"Couldn't that be it? A collection of samples on its way to a university or hospital?"

"But what of? They all looked the same. All held some kind of white liquid."

"A medium, maybe? Something could have been incubating in the tubes. The person could drive around the Southwest picking up whatever it is for testing."

"It wasn't in dry ice or a cold container of any kind. Whatever it was, he or she didn't want me to see it."

"How can you be sure that the owner of the car whacked you on the head?"

"I can't. But the car was gone when you got there. And the last thing I remember is looking in the trunk."

"It's probably a good assumption."

Ben shrugged. "I vote for trying to get some sleep." He pulled the quilt back. "It'll be nice to have company tonight."

"There's no way I'm going back to my room."

"I'm beginning to think that head wounds come in handy."

Julie gave him her best withering look and pulled up the quilt.

BEN PICKED UP a handful of patient folders. The first day back after a long weekend and the cases seemed to pile up. He hoped he would have time to call around Albuquerque and find out more about .22 as a child.

"You look like lukewarm death. Something happen to your head?" Rose asked.

"Had a little tussle with a car part."

"I don't think you were the winner. Want one of the docs to take a look?"

"I'll do it later."

"The tapes are on your desk. I made two copies. I thought you might need an extra."

"Thanks." First thing he'd do would be lock the original in a file cabinet. And the others? He wasn't sure how he'd use them. He'd toyed with sending a copy to the board of examiners. He could find out who was performing the tests easily enough. He could probably just ask Hannah without arousing suspicion, use some pretext of sending them his findings, which wasn't a lie. Only his "findings" wouldn't be what she thought they were. He had a break at nine after his first patient.

Ben hoped his eagerness to finish the session wasn't apparent. But he found his mind wandering. Not that a husband's beating up on a boyfriend in a bar wasn't interesting, he simply couldn't concentrate. At ten till the hour, he fibbed that he was expecting a call and rescheduled the woman with her husband for a continuation on Friday at four and promised himself he'd be more attentive.

He'd checked into hospitals or homes that would have taken children on a boarding basis—treating any mental as well as physical problems, and he had come up with three possibilities. At least the three had been in operation for fifteen years or more. Didn't Dr. Lee say Hannah had taken .22 out of the school or hospital over some sexual misconduct when he was fifteen? Maybe someone would remember what that was all about. And wouldn't it prove that .22 could have more normal moments? That maybe the tape wasn't an aberration after all? He dialed the first number on his list.

The receptionist in records at the children's hospital said they had only had boarding facilities for five years and didn't accept teens, only children birth to twelve. Probably smart, Ben thought as he dialed the second number on his list, Woods Memorial Children's Home and Psychiatric Hospital. He was kept on hold and listened to elevator music for what seemed like five minutes.

"How can I help you?" The older woman's voice was brusque, businesslike and sounded like she had more to do than chat with Ben.

"I'm Dr. Benson Pecos, Hawikuh Clinic. I recently completed an exam on a young man who may have been a resident at Woods. If he was, I'd like to speak with the supervising physician. His name is Harold Rawlings. He would have been fifteen when he left and that was about six years ago."

"Rawlings?"

Ben wasn't sure but he thought he detected a note of curiosity.

"Yes. His father, Edward Rawlings, first placed him in the home. His mother visited once a year or so. Hannah Rawlings."

"Tell me again why you need this information."

Ben reiterated his part in the testing. He was requesting a history that would help him build a case for the boy's trainability. He added that the young man needed to be able to enter a vocational school in the fall and would not receive the money to do so unless his success was assured.

"The board of examiners has requested a profile of his teen years, a history of setbacks, behavioral regression, as well as successes, that sort of thing. A review of previous testing might be enough." It wasn't that much of a fib. He expected the examiners to do just that.

Ben couldn't read the silence that followed.

"I'm afraid you're a little late. Those records have been released to the current consulting physician, closing the file here. You would have to direct any questions to him."

"And his name?"

"Dr. Leland Marcos, Indian Health Service, Hawikuh, New Mexico." There was a pause.

"Isn't that where you said you worked?"

"Yes." Ben noted her suspicious tone and hoped he hadn't sounded too curt before hanging up.

Dr. Lee. A player unaccounted for. Ben leaned back in his chair. What was the good doctor's part in all this? Was he just trying to help out, unaware of the possibility of duplicity on Hannah's part? Or was he an instigator, a mastermind who knew how to work the system and could grease the wheels of the medical community to get .22 through? His urging had certainly helped Ben make up his mind to test. Dr. Lee could be persuasive.

But hadn't he seen them together, .22 and Dr. Lee? Certainly at Hannah's dinners Ben had never suspected Dr. Lee was anything other than what he seemed to be—a concerned friend. If Ben remembered correctly, on the tape .22 sat on the floor when Dr. Lee entered the waiting room and kept his back to the camera. Was there anything that indicated .22 was reacting differently with him? It was difficult to tell. .22's face was blocked by Dr. Lee's back.

Ben could always give a copy of the tape to Dr. Lee. And then what? If he's innocent, he'll investigate, be thankful for Ben's concern. If not? Ben didn't have a good feeling about what that might mean. He couldn't help but feel Hannah was desperate enough to try to get the inheritance any way she could. If .22 had died, foul play or not, she'd have to come up with a plan like this or lose out on everything she'd worked to protect. And didn't it come down to what business was it of his anyway? Even after Thursday, why would he get involved at all? But there was an issue of ethics, and his reputation—if .22 were ever proved to be an impostor. There was probably no way around it. Even based upon the flimsiest of suspicions, he needed to seek the truth. How to reach the truth was the only real issue.

THERE WERE SIX CHILDREN around the kitchen table ranging in age from ten to eighteen. The noise was deafening—yells, laughter, screams when an older child took something away from a younger—all this in a room no larger than twelve by twenty. Two of the younger children grabbed a bag of potato chips at the same time pulling until it burst amid squeals of accusations. Tommy's mother, a short woman with long black hair caught in back of her head by two beaded barrettes worked at her kitchen counter fixing yet another sandwich—this time for her oldest, Tommy—totally oblivious to the cacophony of sound around her. Ben and Julie declined a sandwich. There was no way they would add to this person's lunchtime craziness.

"This was a terrible time to drop by," Julie apologized.

"They'll all go back to the summer recreation program down at the mission school in another fifteen minutes. Except for this one." His mother playfully punched Tommy on the arm as she put the sandwich in front of him. "Then we'll have peace and quiet. Besides, he promised to bring you over. I was beginning to think he'd forgotten."

"I bet she's asked me every other day since you got here." Tommy ducked another playful blow from his mother before she picked up an empty pitcher that had held Kool-Aid and carried it to the sink to mix a refill.

Against Ben and Julie's protests, Tommy made two of his brothers take their sandwiches into the living room to make room at the table.

"At least have a cup of coffee." Tommy's mother put two bright blue ceramic cups down next to a thermos, both had the insignia of the Hawikuh Wildcats on the side. "It keeps fresh this way. I fixed a thermos of coffee every morning when Tommy's father was alive. He worked road construction for the state. I guess habits are hard to break." She smiled and pulled up a chair next to Tommy.

Julie found herself murmuring something supportive.

"Don't get her going. Next she'll tell you it's been easy raising this mob by herself." Tommy indicated the kids at the table, most of whom were leaving, some with a half-eaten sandwich in one hand, chips in the other. The screen door banged after each exit.

"Peace and quiet. Finally." Tommy's mother got up to clear the table. Julie offered to help but was waved away.

"Julie and Ben would like to ask you some questions about when you worked for Hannah Rawlings," Tommy said.

Julie saw his mother pause before she resumed wiping the counter.

"And here I thought she was going to ask me to star in her show." His mother turned from the sink and smiled.

"I'm going to ask you to help me," Julie said. That wasn't a lie. She needed someone from the village to show her what could be photographed and what couldn't, what could be said without offending. "I don't want to overstep boundaries. I'd like to show you what I'm planning and get your opinion."

"I could do that." She sat back down at the table and poured herself a glass of grape Kool-Aid. "Why do you want to know about Hannah Rawlings?"

"Ben is doing a profile—testing .22's proficiency—has to in order for him to continue at school." Tommy went on to tell his mother what Ben had shared with him, about the inheritance, about why Ben was involved. Ben had indicated that he would be making the decision about .22's future, but he hadn't mentioned the board of examiners in Albuquerque. And nothing had been said to Tommy about their suspicions—that .22 might be an impostor. Ben didn't feel that they had enough to go on yet. Julie knew he didn't want to make it a police matter when it wasn't one, or influence whatever Tommy's mother might be able to add.

"I don't think it's my place to get involved," Tommy's mother said.

"I think you can be helpful. Fill me in on what he was like as a child. His shortcomings—I need to know how much he's improved—if he has, or whether he's regressed."

The silence stretched so long that Julie was afraid Tommy's mother wouldn't say anything. Wasn't going to help them at all; then without raising her eyes from the table, she said, "All this about inheritance? It shouldn't even make a difference. .22 wasn't Ed Rawlings' son."

"Are you sure? How do you know that?" Ben sat forward.

"Hannah. She came to me about aborting the child. She really didn't want the pregnancy. This was before Ed knew. She was far enough along to be sure—maybe two months. She wanted the name of a woman in Ramah who performed such operations. The marriage had turned sour. She would have left if she could have. Some said there was already a boyfriend."

"The father of the baby?" Tommy asked.

"Maybe. I never knew. Wasn't my business."

"Did she decide against the abortion?" Julie asked.

"No. She had one. It didn't work; something went wrong. The woman in Ramah told someone the baby was a problem, impossible to dislodge. After the baby was born, and it was apparent that the child was not normal, Hannah went a little crazy. She wasn't religious, but she blamed herself. And Ed was so attached. That baby meant everything to him. It favored Hannah, light skin, eyes—he worshipped that child. It didn't take long for Hannah to realize that the baby chained her to Ed, made the bad marriage even worse."

"Then what happened?" Ben gently encouraged her.

"I was offered a job more or less full time at the trading post. I could bring my own babies as long as I gave adequate time to .22 and Hannah."

"How long did this go on?" Ben asked.

"Three and a half, four years."

"Until the accident," Tommy added. "Everyone here knows about that?" Ben and Julie nodded.

"I wanted to quit before the 'accident,' as you call it. I couldn't take it any more. She was mean to the baby. Any little thing was an excuse for a spanking or locking him in the closet. Hannah was devious. She'd 'lose' the baby. Put .22 somewhere and then pretend, I think, that she couldn't remember where. We would find him in the cellar, the walk-in freezer, under the porch—it was too much. She put him in the root cellar under the pantry so many times, Ed had the place boarded up. Finally, he took the child away. It was the best thing for all of us. I couldn't promise that I could protect him anymore. And the asthma attacks were terrible."

"It's surprising that he survived," Julie said.

"And got so big." Tommy's mother added.

"Have you seen him recently?" Ben asked.

"Hannah brought him over to the house when he first came home in June. I thought she was trying to show me that he had grown up in spite of her, somehow prove to me, or just make amends, I don't know. I had to admit that he had done well, looked healthy, better able…" Julie thought she looked pensive and seemed to be choosing her words before she continued. "I wouldn't have believed that it was .22 if he hadn't crawled over to the closet looking for the toy box. Sometimes I would bring him home with me for the night—when things got bad with the asthma and all." She paused. "He called me 'Ne-Ma.' Don't ask me what that means, it was just his name for me. He remembered."

"If he hadn't remembered those things, you said you might not have believed that it was .22?" Julie asked and felt Ben's silent approval. Tommy's mother seemed to have doubts—or were they too eager to find something that would support their theory?

"He was born with a double caul," she said. "I was the midwife."

"A double what?" The term seemed familiar. Julie tried to remember what it meant.

"The caul is a part of the amnion that can cover the child's head at birth. Correct me if I'm wrong," Ben turned to Tommy's mother, "it brings good luck and is supposed to be an infallible preservative against drowning. Guess we know that part worked. But a double caul? I'm not sure."

"It promises that the child will have special sight. Inward sight but more than just intuition. The child will be gifted as a, a…what do you call it when they can see things that happen in someone else's mind?"

"Mind reader? Perhaps, a clairvoyant?" Julie offered.

"Something like that. It's a special gift. .22 couldn't speak—but he could read my mind. It happened lots. I'd be thinking of something and he'd show me that he could see what was here." She paused to touch her forehead. "It became our game.

I'd think of Cheerios and he'd crawl to the table and bring me the box.''

"And the grown-up .22?" Ben asked.

"Nothing. I tried, but there was nothing. I don't think he even had a hint of what I wanted him to do. When Hannah was in the kitchen getting a drink of water, I asked him to tell me what I was thinking. I swear he didn't know what I was talking about, just looked confused, stuck his thumb in his mouth and started to rock back and forth on his heels. That part reminded me of the old .22, all right. It used to be exasperating. When he didn't want to do something, he'd just close everybody out. He could suck his thumb and rock for hours.''

"Could he lose his special power as he grew up? Would that be common?" Tommy asked.

"It should get stronger. That's why I was surprised. But I believe that it was .22—if anything, he looked even more like his mother than he did as a child. And his head always needed medicating because of the itching even then. We could never keep him from scratching, even if we tied his hands at his side. One winter I kept them bandaged. He wore big gauze mittens and still found a way to scratch the sores. It was awful.''

"Do you remember what you used to keep the itching down?" Julie asked.

"Bag balm.'' She looked up. "You know, udder cream. Same stuff I put on Tommy's goat after milking. Hannah asked me the same thing—if I remembered what we used to apply to his head when he was young. Maybe that's the reason she stopped by.''

Julie felt elated. She hadn't realized that she had had her hopes up, wanted .22 to be who he appeared to be, no more, no less. For Ben's sake. And now it looked like Ben had been exonerated—his first diagnosis was correct. Even Ben would have to agree it would be difficult to fool someone who had been so close to .22. Professional reputation was intact. But he didn't look happy.

On the way out, Julie asked Tommy if there was any word on Sal. But there had been nothing, not even a false lead from someone thinking he could identify Sal from the posters. What was even stranger, Tommy hadn't been able to prove that Sal had had any kind of local ceremony—"a demon-chaser" in Tommy's words—at least, no one was admitting to knowing anything about one. Sal appeared to have vanished.

"I need to talk to Daisy again," Tommy said.

"Daisy?" Julie had no idea who he was talking about.

"Sal's sister, Daisy Sandoval. Not a particularly pleasant woman—especially when she's upset—but she's close to her brother, and, of anyone, should know where Sal might have gone. He'd get in touch with her first, probably. Maybe if I keep after her—in school they taught us that perseverance could be everything. But that's going to be harder on me than on Daisy." He grinned, then waved good-bye to his mother.

Julie dropped Ben off at the clinic. If she had hoped he would be feeling better now that Tommy's mother had strengthened the case that .22 was, in fact, who he said he was, she was disappointed. Ben seemed morose. And she wasn't any good at reversing his mood.

THE DRUG HADN'T taken effect immediately. Sal remembered that much. He'd felt sleepy—was having difficulty standing, keeping his legs from crumbling underneath him until finally he'd slumped to the floor by the cot unable to even crawl under the covers. He rested against the cot's metal rail side wondering what time it was. He didn't have the energy to check his watch.

He couldn't with the lead weights that seemed tied to each wrist mooring them to the floor. And his head hurt if he tried to think too much—like wondering who had turned on the lights that now blazed above his workbench.

It was then that the trap door had opened. Hannah. Hannah came down the steps first with…with Atoshle behind her. Atoshle in his grand mask and white robes, tall, towering above him in his majesty, just like all the times he had visited before and had stood beside Sal's bed looking down at him or peeked in the windows of the trailer, or followed him to the river to leave the amber rabbit on the hood of his truck after taking the body…

Sal had tried to rise but only fell to one side to rest on his shoulder, head lolling backwards. He wanted to cry out. What had he done to deserve a visit from this *kachina?* Would the ogre hurt him? Was it time for his death?

Sal struggled again but instead of rising, rolled backwards to lie flat on the floor staring upward at this monster—the personage that parents called upon to scare children into behaving. But Sal wasn't a child. Was there some mistake? What could Atoshle possibly want from him?

"Salvador, we need your recipe for amber." It was Hannah speaking but the sound came from a tunnel, hollow with an echo. A voice over a voice, only one was just a split second slower. He must have started to shake his head because she went on. "It's no good trying to say you don't know what we want. Remember, I know you have a notebook filled with your experiments. A notebook that will tell us how to make the amber."

She was kneeling beside him now; Atoshle looked miles away, floating above him as high as the ceiling. And Atoshle just hovered, swaying side to side.

"Salvador, where is the notebook?"

He thought he shook his head.

"Do you want Atoshle to beat you?"

Sal thought he saw a club in the great *kachina*'s hand. Could he shake his head "no" again? He tried.

"It's no use. You gave him too much. We're not going to scare him into telling us anything. He's a zombie," Atoshle boomed out but let the club drop to the floor.

"It's here. I know it is. We've looked in the trailer and the shed. Where else could it be? Look in his toolbox." Hannah addressed Atoshle. At this order Atoshle moved to the workbench and then out of Sal's sight. He could hear the crashing and banging that meant things were being turned over, thrown to one side when the notebook wasn't found.

"Go through his pockets." Atoshle called out from somewhere across the room.

The bass voice was familiar. Yet, that didn't seem like something Atoshle would say. Hannah roughly checked his shirt pocket, nothing, then pulled his keys, and a three-inch comb from a front pocket in his jeans. Reaching underneath him she slipped his billfold out of a hip pocket.

"Nothing." Hannah had sat back on her heels. "This would go so much easier for you if you'd cooperate." She was peering at Sal, unhappy with him, he thought. Her lips were pulled tight against her teeth making her mouth a long pink line that stretched out straight then zigzagged in slow motion across her face when she spoke. He concentrated on her mouth.

"Let me see the billfold." As if from out of nowhere, Atoshle swooped down, bent over Hannah and took the billfold.

A thought tried to surface, push and thrust and swim to the forefront of a brain turned to mush. Sal strained, some warning. He almost had it. Yes. There was something in his billfold. Something that would tell... Get someone in trouble. A secret. His secret with Julie.

"Well look at this." The bass voice again, muffled behind the mask. "A claim check, receipt for a locker at the Greyhound terminal in Gallup. But guess whose name it's in? Your boyfriend has been fucking around with the little redhead."

"Give me that." Hannah jumped up, but Atoshle held it out of her reach.

"So old Salvador was just devoted to you. Wouldn't change his shorts without you. But went right out when you weren't looking and got a little help. And what do you think could be in that locker? Do I have to give you more than one guess?" Atoshle was laughing. But not in fun, more in meanness, Sal thought. And Hannah was frenzied, leaping at the paper, then beating her fists against the *kachina*'s chest, which made him laugh louder.

"Better save some of that energy. We don't have the notebook yet." He caught Hannah's arms and held her stationary.

Hannah jerked backward. "Let me go. This is serious. Stop fooling around."

"I don't think I'm the only fool in this room." Atoshle let her go, then handed over the receipt.

"What should we do?" Hannah held the receipt out in front of her to read before wadding it into a ball.

"Make Sal open the locker. Take him to Gallup—" Atoshle said.

"Don't be stupid. We can't risk letting him out of here."

"Then, look for a key." Sal thought Atoshle sounded impatient.

"Won't someone have to sign for whatever's inside?"

"Probably. So, you've got one possibility left."

"I'll get Julie to open it for us. That should be simple enough," Hannah said.

"I doubt if she'll just volunteer. Maybe I—" Atoshle began.

"I don't want you near her." Sal could feel the vehemence in Hannah's voice without understanding what she was saying. "I've watched the two of you—you'll give yourself away. Tell me you didn't enjoy burying your head in her crotch this afternoon in the pantry. I frankly thought that was a little much."

Atoshle gave a short laugh. "I'd call that one of my better performances, impromptu, but perfect."

"You didn't think your little act was just a tiny bit too realistic?" Hannah's mouth pulled back into the pink straight line.

"Hey, how were we to know she'd walk in on us trying to feed Sal?"

"Well, I don't want you 'performing' with Miss *Good Morning America* again."

"Fine by me. After Thursday, we're out of here. I've been limping and slobbering for two months. Enough is enough. I couldn't care less about your little notebook."

"It means a lot to me." Suddenly her voice was a purr.

"Probably a lot of money. But I think we'll have enough without it."

"And if something goes wrong? If we don't get the inheritance?"

"Hey, that's almost a done deal. Did I fool that Doc, or what?"

"There's one more hurdle. Are you forgetting that?"

"Damn, this thing is hot."

Sal watched as Atoshle's head flew upward, off his shoulders and out into space, spinning end over end before crashing to the floor. Multicolored feathers fanned out from the top then broke upon impact. His wooden beak splintered and bounced towards Sal.

"Why did you do that? Do you know how much this is worth? It's ruined." Hannah dropped to her knees, swept the pieces toward her, then cradled the mask before setting it on the workbench. "Didn't we agree that no one would see you without a cover-up?" She nodded towards Sal.

"He's as good as dead. Don't you have what you want?" Sal saw a finger pointing to the receipt still wadded in Hannah's hand. But the only word he heard was "dead, dead, dead." It seemed to be circling in his head, a banner pulled around and around just behind his eyes.

"Maybe the notebook is in the locker, maybe it isn't. We'll have to see." Hannah smoothed the receipt and put it in her pocket.

If Sal could have laughed he would have and not just made the sputtering noises that left saliva trailing down his chin. As his eyes focused, he could see that the supernaturals were playing tricks. Instead of the mask of Atoshle, the head of .22 sat on the shoulders that were encased in white flowing robes. .22? Yes, it was .22. The ancient ones enjoyed a joke, and this was a good one. They had even given .22 a booming voice, and made him stand up straight.

"What's wrong with him? Looks like he's foaming at the mouth." The toe of a sneaker pushed out from the hem of Atoshle's robe and nudged him.

"He'll be all right," Hannah said.

"You have a weird sense of 'all right.' Left to die in an underground room isn't my idea of 'all right.'"

"Losing your nerve?"

"Maybe. I just want this to be over." .22 bent over Sal, and Sal looked up into watery, deep blue eyes, familiar eyes, eyes he knew as well as his own only they belonged to .22—the gods hadn't overlooked detail.

"I liked this man," .22 said.

"What does that have to do with anything?"

"Maybe I don't want anything to do with his murder."

"Don't you think it's a little late to show concern? Want me to remind you who killed Ahmed? Then dragged him all over kingdom come—and almost got caught. If that tourist hadn't been crazy, you would have. You took a chance selling him that rabbit. That wasn't too bright."

"Shut up. It was a pretty good idea to kill Ahmed by the river, scare the shit out of Sal—and who thought up the scalping?"

"Well, not until after you came back to the house with the body and asked my opinion."

Quickly Hannah stood on tiptoe and kissed .22's cheek. "Let's not fight. We're in this together. I couldn't have done it without you. I owe all of our success to you. There, is that better? And, we'll be rich—just one tiny hurdle left. But after Thursday, we've won."

"Why don't you forget about the amber? After Thursday, you're right, we'll be rich. Why press our luck? Why do this?" .22 motioned towards Sal.

"I don't expect you to understand. It was a business deal. He owes me. All this was my idea. He would never have thought of it on his own. I bankrolled him; I was the quality control; I kept on top of the market. I found Ahmed, got him to sell back East, made sure we didn't saturate any one area…all that's worth something." Hannah walked along the workbench. "If anything should go wrong Thursday—if for whatever reason the board doesn't believe you—I have to know I have enough money…"

"You worry too much. Hasn't it gone all right so far? Running the act by Ben was brilliant. We could practice and practice and still not have had an honest-to-God real-life test."

"Yes, we have Leland to thank for that. But amber's my ace in the hole. There's a good solid market out there, worldwide, that won't change anytime soon—worth about a hundred and twenty thousand a year."

Sal heard .22's low whistle.

"That much?" .22 asked.

"Impressed?" Hannah had begun to straighten things on the workbench. "And to think Salvador was having second thoughts. He didn't want to make anything fake anymore. I honestly thought he might turn himself in, and me.'' She walked back within Sal's line of sight. ''If anyone could understand the need for a little extra money, I'd think it would be you. How many of those frogs do you have now?''

''Toads. Colorado River toads. A hundred seventy-five. More than I want to milk in one afternoon again soon.''

''Did Delbert pay you for the venom last night?''

''Yeah, he made me a good deal on the toads, too.''

''Just don't lose the money.'' Hannah said. ''You were lucky to get it back last time.''

Toads. Frogs. .22 liked frogs. Took care of them in his room in glass houses. Sal had helped him feed the amphibians all the leftover flies and beetles. So what was this about venom and money? But Sal suddenly couldn't keep his eyes open and the voices above him drifted farther and farther away until there was just a faint rustling of people moving around him, putting him on the cot, then nothing before he fell into a deep sleep.

JULIE'S BEDROOM was hot when she got back to the boarding house. Barely two in the afternoon and there was no air circulation, just an unbearable stuffiness. Another midsummer day without rain. Everyone was reluctant to use the word ''drought,'' but she had overheard locals at the trading post refer to the rain as ''behind schedule, a late monsoon season, a crop blaster.'' Temperatures were usually in the eighties. But according to the radio, this was the eleventh consecutive day in the mid-nineties. So far, this was the hottest summer on record. The porch was the only inviting place. She could spread out her notes on the table in the corner, and if there were any breeze at all, she'd feel it.

''Come on out. I'm just finishing up here.'' Hannah was seated at the table shelling peas. ''Our growing season is usually about a month behind those at a lower altitude. Most years, peas would be doing great about now. But there's been too much heat.''

''I can work inside. I don't want to make you move,'' Julie offered.

"Don't be silly. I've been wanting to talk with you."

Against her better judgment, Julie found herself curious.

"Can I trust you?" Hannah lowered her voice.

The question took Julie off guard. What did she mean by that? Could she know that they suspected something? That they had tried to prove her son wasn't who she said he was?

"How do you mean that?"

"Let's sit on the steps." Hannah moved across the porch and pushed the screen open for Julie to follow. "Years ago, Ed and I used to sit out here and watch the garden grow." Hannah had tucked the long skirt of her gingham sundress under her knees and seated on the top step, leaned against the railing. "It all seems so long ago." Abruptly, she turned to Julie. "Do you garden?"

"About as well as I carry a tune. Horribly."

"It's soothing. It's the one thing I'll miss."

"Surely gardening will be easier someplace else. Isn't it a challenge in the desert? Poor soil, scanty rain?..." Julie didn't know where this was leading, but she doubted that Hannah wanted to talk about raising vegetables.

"Maybe, when I get paid for the house and all, I won't have to grow my food just to make ends meet. I don't ever want to be in that position again."

Julie didn't comment. She always found herself on guard around Hannah. Julie repressed a shiver and watched Hannah leave the porch to rearrange a watering wand, drag it to a patch of melons along a fence sporting a jumble of vines, some covered with four-inch-long cukes. No one could say Hannah didn't have a green thumb.

"I may be leaving sooner than I expected." Hannah resumed her perch on the top step. "I'd like you to water the garden for me. I couldn't bear to think of it withering away just because I wasn't here. Would you mind?" Hannah turned to face her and Julie could feel the scrutinizing gaze of the deep, steel-blue eyes. But what did watering the garden have to do with trust?

"I'd be glad to. If you'd feel better, you could leave instructions. I'm not exactly a natural at this."

Hannah smiled. She was being genuinely nice, Julie decided, but had the distinct feeling Hannah wasn't being chummy over a garden. There must be something else.

"I need to take you into my confidence and, well, frankly, I'm not sure I should. I'm not sure whose side you're on." Hannah was twisting the hem of her dress, absently, a nervous habit, as she looked at Julie straight on, unblinking, the color rising in blotches on her neck.

"Try me." What else was there to say?

"I got a letter from Salvador." Again, that unblinking lock-on eye contact. She's trying to second-guess my reaction, Julie decided as Hannah paused before going on.

"I know what you're thinking. I should hand over the letter to Tommy," Hannah said. "I shouldn't even have kept it."

That hadn't entered Julie's mind, but it was probably the right thing to do.

"Could you understand if I told you I couldn't do that? Not ever. I don't believe that Salvador could kill anyone. I don't care what evidence they think they have. I know the man." Hannah turned to stare at the garden. "I won't turn him in. He deserves a fair chance. That's why he's left, not just to get away, but to let things die down. Tommy's a hothead, and he'll go after him, drag him back, accuse him…" She took a deep breath then added, "He'll make him stand trial for the murder even if the evidence is only circumstantial."

Julie watched as tears welled then spilled to roll down Hannah's cheeks.

"Sal needs our help. Your help. You've proved that you're a friend. You've helped him before. He trusts you. We're the only friends he has." Hannah pulled a tissue from her pocket and blew her nose.

Where was this leading? How could she help Sal?

"He feels terrible that all this has happened, and he can't be on your show. His word is his life, and now he's backing out," Hannah said.

"Are you sure? Did he say he wouldn't be coming back?"

"Julie, he can't come back. Maybe it isn't the way you or I

might handle the problem—to run away—but to Sal he's just stepping aside until things get all figured out. He trusts that as long as he's innocent, he won't be prosecuted. He just needs to stay out of the way of justice. Let things take their course.''

Julie's first reaction was anger. She had counted on him to be her focus, as a master carver he was the pivotal person in presenting fetishes of the Southwest. Now, in under a month, she had to change the script—all of it—not to mention she had spent twelve hundred dollars for a necklace that might not be appropriate to display if she used another carver... But could she understand Sal's reaction? Yes. Tommy seemed convinced that he was a murderer. He'd blanketed a three-state area with posters. She knew Tommy had the murder weapon, but still there was room for doubt. She just didn't think Sal could have killed someone. In that, she agreed with Hannah.

"He sent me this.'' Hannah reached into her pocket. Julie recognized the slip immediately even before Hannah had smoothed it against her dress and handed it to her. It was the receipt she had given Sal after storing his package. "He needs you to get his belongings for him and cancel the locker rental.''

"Did he say where I was to take the package?'' Julie asked.

"Here. I'm to give his sister a call—maybe run it by. She's close, first house on the right just after you enter reservation land.''

Julie could understand that Sal would want the fetish jar to remain in the family. It would be important to him. Maybe there was some ceremonial importance, something coming up. But why hadn't he just given it to his sister in the first place? Who knew? She was sure that Sal had had his reasons. "I'll go to Gallup in the morning,'' she said.

"One more thing. I think Salvador's sister knows where he is. Please don't say anything to Tommy or Ben. I suspect Daisy was the one who mailed the letter to me. But I don't want Tommy to know. I don't want her badgered by him. Can you understand that? Can this be our secret?''

It was true. Tommy was planning to talk with Daisy—had admitted to trying to pressure her.

"Yes. I don't have a problem with that." She hated keeping secrets from Ben, but just this once it wouldn't hurt. He'd want to tell Tommy...

"Thank you. Salvador will be forever grateful. His spirit can rest easy now." Hannah gave Julie a quick hug then stood. "I may not come back after the testing on Thursday. I promised my sister in Maine a long overdue visit. She hasn't seen Harold since June. He's anxious to see her, too. Will you remember to water? Just do the garden and the flowers along the sides of the house. It'll need it twice a day if that isn't too much. Gloria from Century 21 will manage the rest."

Julie nodded.

"Thanks." Hannah picked up the colander of peas and went back into the house.

WOULD HE HAVE eaten had there been food? Sal didn't know. He knew he was afraid of being drugged again. He was still wobbly and couldn't trust his memory of events for the last two days. He continued to hallucinate but no more Atoshle. That image was gone.

He had straightened the lab, but he hadn't worked. Probably didn't need to because it wouldn't save his life. The thing he knew for certain was that the claim slip was gone. Hannah had taken the receipt out of his billfold and that as much as told her the notebook was in a locker at the bus terminal. She hadn't found the key in his shoe, but she had won. There would be no reason to let him out. She could duplicate everything, the rubber molds, the dryers, the chemistry—she would be able to make amber. Maybe not as good as he could at first, but in time...

It was difficult not to be depressed even with the lights on. How would Hannah get the fetish jar without Julie's help? And then what would she do to Julie? And why did he remember .22 as a tall man in Atoshle's robes? He sat down at his workbench and held his throbbing head. Did he let this happen? Could he have done something differently? He cursed the am-

ber and his own stupidity for being sucked into a plan to help
Hannah…to help .22.

TWELVE

A SUMMER SQUALL had blown across the mountains in the night
bringing the rain everyone had hoped for, and the morning was
decidedly cool. Overcast and muggy, if Julie remembered what
humidity felt like. Keeping her word, Julie hadn't shared with
Ben her part in retrieving the fetish jar. She felt guilty, but he
had been preoccupied during the evening. Still trying to decide
what to do with the tape that gave .22 thirty seconds of nor-
malcy, she guessed.

And Julie had to admit that she was a little irked that he was
hanging onto something she felt had been proved impossible.
.22 wasn't normal. He had improved somewhat since child-
hood, learned to speak, dress himself, but that was the extent
of it. Hadn't Tommy's mother put Ben's doubts to rest?

As usual, Ben left for the clinic at seven. She had walked
him to his truck, and he'd promised to be a human being that
evening. Suggested a movie in Gallup, dinner too, if she
wanted. She did. Maybe they needed to get away, take a break.
There had been just a little too much Sal, and .22. and Hannah
lately.

She hummed as she gathered up her notebooks and a recorder. She had meant to stop by and talk with Morley at the
pawnshop and a quick call had even gotten her an offer of
lunch. She doubted if she'd have time, but she didn't want to
disappoint the old man. He was so happy to hear from her. She
had the key to the locker in her pocket along with the receipt.
Funny that Sal hadn't sent his key. He didn't know that she
had one, but it could have just slipped his mind. It wasn't like
he didn't have other things to worry about.

She had to admit she hadn't felt this good in days. She was
back to work on the script—had spent the evening on a new
idea that would include a lot more of Morley and the pawnshop

and maybe a couple other shops in Gallup. And she was doing something for Sal. That made her feel good. She truly wanted to help him. She thought of the amber maiden and how much it meant to her. She wouldn't forget his kindness—and the least she could do was be helpful when he needed it.

Hannah held the front door open for her, offering to help carry something.

"Thanks, but I'm used to lugging equipment around. This is no where close to my usual poundage."

"Are you taking all this to Gallup?" Hannah asked.

"Combining business with business in this case. I'm including Gallup in my piece on Southwest symbols—" Julie stopped. Earlier, she had pulled her car up to the railing just below the steps to make it easier to load, and there was .22 strapped into the front seat.

"Look, I can't take .22 with me. As I started to say, I have an interview set up."

"Please. He's such a good traveler. I can't get away now that Salvador's gone, and I promised him a trip."

"Ice cream. Me want ice cream." .22 was jiggling up and down in the seat. She could hear him through the closed window.

"No. I can't be responsible. You'll have to get him out of the car." Julie was adamant and using her best no-nonsense voice.

At this .22 began to cry.

"See what you've done. I've thought you had a mean streak. I can't believe you could say no to him. He likes you—considers you a friend. This is such a simple thing to do for him."

"Friendship has nothing to do with it. This is a workday for me." Julie chose to ignore the part about being mean.

Hannah walked towards the car, opened the door, told her son to "shut up," waited a split second for results, then slapped him, reached across, unsnapped the seat belt, and angrily jerked on his arm. .22 slipped from Hannah's grasp and rolled to the ground, his face wet with tears, wailing uncontrollably and hiccuping, "Me go, me go, me go" between gulps for air.

"It would be the simplest of kindnesses to take him with

you. He'll sit quietly. He's really well behaved.'' Hannah's voice rose above the din.

''I'm sure he would be.'' Julie was starting to reconsider as .22 waved a finger towards her and took up the chant of, ''You take, you take, you take.'' It would be a simple thing to take him. The exposure would do him good. But still, the responsibility, the interruptions; she needed to work.

''It's only thirty miles into town. Here's some money; just buy him something at McDonalds—he'll be fine.'' Julie stepped back as Hannah thrust a five dollar bill towards her.

''Hannah, please understand. I'm not letting him tag along on an interview. I can't. There'd be nothing for him to do.''

''Leave him at the bus station after you pick up the package. He loves to watch the buses pull in and out. He's got to learn how to take care of himself. Someday soon he'll be living in a group home, cooking, working—walking to a bus stop all on his own…''

''Hannah, please, it's just impossible. I don't want to hurt his feelings but maybe some other time.'' Julie tossed her equipment in the backseat, quickly slipped behind the wheel and tried not to look at .22's forlorn expression as he smeared tears hit and miss across his face. She mouthed one more ''I'm sorry'' and put the car in reverse.

Her conscience kicked in about five miles down the road and Julie had second thoughts. What harm would there be in taking .22 into Gallup? It was true that he had to learn to fend for himself. Wouldn't this be good for him—a little booster in self-confidence? And with this trip right before the test, maybe he'd feel more at ease about the trip to Albuquerque. He'd appear better able to handle himself on his own. If she remembered correctly, that was a criterion for being awarded the money.

But the real reason she'd play babysitter was to prove to Ben—once and for all—that .22 was retarded. She wasn't certain how she'd do that, but she would. It was the least that she could do. And then she'd have Ben's attention again—not share it with self-doubts about his competency and watch him brood over what he viewed as a possible professional error. Not that she liked to play heroine, but she was in a position to help. He would be thankful for that. And she wasn't afraid—not really. How could she fear someone who wore udder cream smeared across his head?

She slowed. She had just entered reservation land and there was a house on the right. Didn't Hannah say that's where Sal's sister lived? And why shouldn't this Daisy Sandoval be responsible for picking up the fetish jar? Cut out the middleman—in this case herself. It would give Julie that much more time to spend with Morley and .22 for that matter.

Since Sal wanted his sister to have it, Julie could leave the claim check and key with a note giving this woman the right to cancel the locker. Then Daisy could do anything she wanted—involve Tommy or not involve him, but it would be her decision. And Julie wouldn't necessarily be keeping information from the authorities. The decision might come under the heading of "passing the buck," but there was a good argument for keeping any involvement within Sal's family.

Julie was definitely pleased with herself as she pulled in front of the house, a pitched roof structure with a picket fence. Please God, make Daisy be home. This would only work if she could hand the key and receipt off—she'd never leave it otherwise.

"Yes?" The door opened at the first knock.

"I'm Julie Conlin. I'm looking for Daisy Sandoval." When the woman nodded, Julie launched into who she was and where she lived but Daisy stopped her with a terse, "I know who you are," then softened when Julie explained about the locker and what it held. Daisy was jubilant to retrieve the fetish jar and thanked Julie profusely, saying Sal would be pleased.

This had turned out perfectly. Julie pulled a tire-screeching U-turn and headed back to pick up .22. She didn't have a clue as to what she'd do with him, but she'd find something—and hopefully someway to prove he was who he said he was.

BEN MADE A DECISION. And now that he'd made it, he felt better, felt it was the right one. He'd give the tape to the examiners once he found out how the testing was going to be handled. He'd let the board decide how to use it. He'd called the real estate agent around eight and gotten the name of the lawyer handling the "particulars," as she had called them. Ben had explained his part in the testing of .22, and she seemed comfortable with giving him information. The same for the lawyer—they were encouraging, in fact.

The examination would be done by the University of New Mexico psych department at ten a.m. the next day. Ben compiled his notes on .22, including random observations, edited the report, and wrote an introduction to the tape expressing his concerns and asking for the team's evaluation. He sealed everything into a Manila envelope; it was almost eleven.

He'd toyed with the idea of delivering the materials himself and when Rose said he had three cancellations for the afternoon, his mind was made up. He'd drive into Albuquerque, deliver the packet of materials to UNM and then stop by the Indian Hospital and visit old friends. He felt guilty that he'd been in New Mexico over a month and hadn't at least called. He was counting on his old mentor, Dr. Black, to understand what it was like to start a new job. He was sure Sandy could remember being in this position himself.

And he'd take Julie. That would be a treat. He was feeling guilty about ignoring her, not being very good company lately. Dinner, movie—maybe stay overnight in Albuquerque, drive to Santa Fe for the weekend. He'd "X" himself out for Friday on the clinic schedule.

He didn't see Julie's rental car when he pulled up in front of the boarding house, only Hannah's maroon Buick. The car was backed in and the trunk was open like someone was packing for a trip. Maybe Hannah and .22 were going into Albuquerque tonight, ahead of time.

He pushed open the front screen and ignored the first four rings of the phone as he walked back to his room, then turned and on the sixth ring picked it up. Where was everybody?

"Julie Conlin there?" The man's voice sounded young.

Ben explained who he was, and, no, he hadn't seen Julie, was there a message?

"Tell her I took a look at the two rolls of prints and I'm impressed. I'm sending out my ideas for some other shots and how we can get a story out of the landscape—sorry, I know this doesn't mean anything to you. Just tell her to expect a package. Oh, one other thing. Do you know if she's planning some kind of story on the toads?''

''Toads?'' Ben didn't think he'd heard correctly.

''Colorado River toads. Latest craze. People are raising them, milking them for their venom. Then they dry the stuff for smoking. Supposed to be some kind of psychedelic high. And it's legal at least for now. Can you imagine sitting around squeezing juice out of toads? But it looks like she found a pretty good-sized farming operation out your way. Whoever owns them knows their stuff, too—using tea to revive them and keep a live food supply fresh after harvest.''

Toads. Venom. Ben didn't even remember hanging up. Where was this operation? Why did Julie have a picture of it? Wait. .22 had toads. Julie had seen them in his bedroom. But why had she taken a picture of them? Did she suspect—

''Who was on the phone?'' Hannah came out of the kitchen.

''New York reminding Julie of a deadline. Have you seen her?''

''She left early this morning.'' Something was trying to surface, dig its way up through his memory…something about venom.

''Did she say where she was going?''

''Do some interviews, I think. I don't remember her saying where exactly. I know she didn't say when she'd get back.''

Venom. Vials and vials of a white, milky substance in the trunk of a car. The trunk he was looking into the night someone pounded on the back of his head. The packet of money—had it fallen out of .22's pocket? That wasn't just possible, it was probable. The money never had anything to do with Sal. And wasn't that why it had been stolen back so quickly? The owner knew who had it, watched him put it in the glove compartment.

''Anything else?'' Hannah was frowning, peering at him.

He quickly collected himself. ''Sorry, I just remembered something I need to tell Rose before I leave,'' he lied. ''I have a meeting at IHS in Albuquerque. Can you tell Julie I'll be back by six?''

And then Ben impulsively said, ''Let me take .22 into Albuquerque with me. He might like the ride. It might be a good idea to make a fun trip out of it—before he goes in tomorrow.'' And it just might give me the time to flip a few coins, and discuss toad farming, Ben thought. There would be no better way to settle this once and for all than face to face. He wasn't afraid of .22—at worst, he was some kid Hannah hired to help her and would bolt at the first accusation.

Hannah looked surprised, caught off guard. Suspicious? Or was that his imagination? Quickly, she recovered and said, ''I don't think so. He hates long trips. Sometimes he isn't very good for long periods of time—when he has to sit still.''

''All the more reason for a practice run. Where is he? Let's let him decide.''

''He's taking a nap. And I don't want him disturbed. I think rest is more important for him today than getting him all excited before the test.''

THEY HAD JUST FINISHED the fifth chorus of ''Old MacDonald Had a Farm''—not that .22 could sing all the words, he couldn't; it was the ''ee ii ee ii ooo's'' that made him jump up and down, squealing with delight. And he did fairly well carrying a tune. Someone had taught him the song, and it seemed to be the only one that he knew. Julie had tried ''Ninety-Nine Bottles of Beer On the Wall.'' Nothing. There was a lukewarm response to ''Mary Had a Little Lamb,'' but no real interest. So, it was back to Old MacDonald—and back and back—the repetition was driving her nuts. But .22 seemed happy.

She glanced over at him and got a wide-mouthed grin. She'd stopped at the Allsups on the edge of Gallup and picked up a soft drink telling herself in advance that she'd get the upholstery shampooed if he spilled any. And surprisingly, he didn't. He sucked noisily on a straw but kept the cup upright.

She parked in front of Morley's and painstakingly explained that they were going ''to visit.'' But .22 twisted around and leaned over the back seat and pointed to the bus station.

''Big car.'' Even his voice sounded awestruck.

''Bus. It's like a big car.''

''Me go.''

"Not today. Remember, we have to visit Morley."

"No. Me go." His fingers dug into the back of the seat.

Oh God, Julie had visions of a tantrum. She didn't have to go to the bus station, but maybe just a walk over by the ones under the roofed area. That wouldn't hurt anything.

She had to admit that .22 walked beside her perfectly behaved as they crossed the street, didn't bolt or dash into traffic, and it was apparent that he was enraptured with the buses. He kept repeating "Wow" in rapid succession. When they neared the loading bay, he had broken into that halting run of his.

Then he stopped, breathed in the exhaust fumes telling anyone who would listen, "Smells good." Julie watched from a distance. .22 was beside himself with joy, hopping up and down trying to look into the high windows—once even looking under the nearest bus, scrambling as close as he thought was safe to peer into the baggage compartments.

"That's enough. We need to see Morley." Julie pointed across the street. .22 seemed surprised and hung back.

"Me go inside?"

"Not today." Julie started toward the street.

"Me go pee."

Of course, shouldn't she have anticipated this? "Okay. This way."

She pushed open the door to the lounge and pointed to the restrooms. How stupid, she didn't know whether he could read. She grabbed his hand and walked with him to the back and pointed to the door marked "Senor."

"I'll wait here."

.22 wasn't gone long but long enough to dribble water down the front of his slacks. And his hands were dripping wet. When she tried to hand him a wad of Kleenex, he pulled away and ran around the corner. Since hide and seek wasn't on her agenda, she resolved to corral him and make it back across the street to Morley's without any more delays.

At first, she couldn't tell where he'd gone. A quick survey of the benches of people in the lounge didn't give him up even after she squatted to check for him crouched underneath. He simply wasn't in the open area.

"Your pal's over here." A man behind the counter gestured towards the back where the lockers were.

As Julie rounded the corner, she could see .22 trying every handle on every locker. Well, maybe that's what she'd do, too—if she thought like .22. He was just completing his rounds when number fifty-seven swung open after a strong tug, much to .22's glee.

"Hidey place." He stuck his head in. "No stuff." He pulled back and looked genuinely disappointed. "Where stuff go?" He stuck his head back in.

He seemed to have the concept of lockers, Julie thought. And Sal's sister must have left right after Julie dropped the key off in order to beat them here, but Julie was relieved. Sal's package was in the right hands. It was safe. Whatever happened to his grandfather's fetish jar, it wasn't her responsibility any longer.

"I don't want this to be taken wrong. I mean I'm as willing to help the handicapped as the next person, but I can't have this young man banging on the lockers. Believe it or not, these locks are pretty fragile." The attendant stood to her left and stared at .22, who had slipped to the floor and cowered with his thumb in his mouth. "Are the two of you waiting for transportation?"

"No, I, uh, we just stepped inside to use the facilities."

"And you're finished now?" Julie saw his eyes take in .22's damp fly.

"Yes." There wasn't anything else to say. Few people were comfortable around those who were so markedly different. ".22, we need to go now." Julie was firm.

She held out her hand to help him up and tried not to flinch when he grasped with his wet thumb sliding along the inside of her palm.

"Thank you for being so cooperative." The attendant beamed but walked behind them to the door in a barely veiled shooing movement. "And understanding." He lowered his voice. "It's a terrible shame, isn't it?" He inclined his head towards .22 and if he'd clucked his tongue, Julie wouldn't have been surprised. "Is he a relative of yours?" he asked in a whisper.

Suddenly she felt a rush of feeling for .22—he had faced discrimination all his life. She smiled at him, but he seemed completely subdued by the incident at the lockers. Probably had no idea why he couldn't stay and play with number fifty-seven.

"I'm his caretaker for the day. It's important that he takes advantage of every opportunity to interact with the world around him. It's been so good of you to indulge us." There. That had a nice snotty ring to it. Seemed to work, too, she decided, as the attendant murmured something and retreated behind the counter.

She was glad to be back outside. Fresh air was preferable even in ninety-six degree heat to the unnatural coldness of the terminal lounge. She had expected some reluctance, but .22 held her hand without prompting as they crossed the street. She waved to Morley, who was waiting on the curb. He'd just rolled a faded green canvas awning to a half-mast position above the wide front display window, but Julie thought the shading device was overkill seeing that the windows were lined with cracked and peeling, yellow see-through plastic as it was.

"Who's your friend?" Morley looked down on .22 from a height made considerable only because of .22's slump. It dawned on Julie that .22 would be almost as tall as Morley if he stood upright.

"Hannah Rawlings' son. She runs the trading post by Hawikuh." Julie pulled her recorder and briefcase from the rental's backseat before joining him.

"Of course. I used to do business with Ed Rawlings. That was some years back. How long's he been gone now? Ten, twelve years?"

"More like sixteen or seventeen."

"Don't say. And what's this youngster's name?"

".22." The answer was gleefully shouted out and Julie hurried to amend with, "That's a nickname. This is Harold. Harold, can you shake Morley's hand?"

Suddenly .22 seemed shy and shuffled behind Julie.

"That's okay, big fellow, don't want to take up with strangers too fast. Tell you what, I've got some coloring books inside and some crayons that could keep a guy busy for some time. Let's me and you go take a look.''

Julie smiled as .22 reached out to take Morley's hand. Once inside, Morley cleared a space at a roll-top desk and took coloring books and crayons from a bottom drawer.

"You think he'd like those watercolor pens better? I got a box of them around here, can't say as I remember where right offhand.''

"The crayons should be fine." Julie watched as .22 peeled the paper off the magenta. At least, he wasn't sticking them in his mouth.

"We can work over here." Morley motioned towards a card table behind the glass counter that held some old pawn. "I thought these pieces might interest you.''

Julie picked up a concho belt, each round, etched section finished in the center with a piece of coral. "This is exactly what I had in mind." Then she pulled out the recorder and her notebook. "I'd like you to give me the history of each of these pieces—and any interesting stories, if you think of any. I don't promise I can use everything so I'll reserve the right to edit.''

They worked quickly together even with the half dozen interruptions caused by the phone and customers. She'd already narrowed Morley's seemingly endless supply of anecdotes to three and had decided to put him on camera for the show when a tourist bus unloaded thirty people at the door, and Morley excused himself to act as proprietor. She wasn't watching closely, but it seemed like he sold a number of things—at least two big pieces, a squash blossom necklace and a pair of beaded moccasins, followed by the usual trinkets.

The tourists hovered over the counters as Morley pulled first one, then another tray from underneath and switched on the crookneck lamp clamped to each cabinet's edge. She noticed .22 had stopped coloring and had begun to rub his stomach. He must be famished. She'd lost all track of time. It was already twelve-thirty. She really needed to get him something to eat. She'd probably be asking for trouble if she kept him waiting too much longer. He had been so good, no whining. He'd sat in one place and stayed out from underfoot. That had earned him a hamburger and then some.

She told Morley that she needed to get .22 some lunch and then get home, said she'd take a rain check on their lunch together but maybe when she brought the edited version of her notes—the part of the script that would deal with the pawnshop for him to review on Monday, they could go then. Morley promised he'd close between eleven and one—he allowed as how he wasn't going to miss out on a date with the "prettiest gal in Gallup." Then she gathered up her materials and taking .22's hand went out to the car.

"Bus." .22 stood on the curb and watched a charter pull out and head north.

"Yes," Julie answered and hoped with fingers crossed that he wouldn't want to go back to the terminal. "Are you hungry?"

"Me eat." At the mention of food he clamored into the car and held quiet while she pulled the seat belt across his chest and snapped it in place. The scent of udder cream almost gagged her. His head seemed more thickly coated than usual. Poor thing, the sores looked icky. He'd had to put up with so much in his young life.

"Booger. Me want booger."

"Ham-bur-ger," she enunciated clearly. "We'll stop and get hamburgers on our way home."

She was saving the bribe of ice cream until she really needed it. And so far, so good. She was amazed and feeling more than a little self-righteous about her good deed. It had really been pleasant—taking .22 with her had been a super idea, good for both of them. It taught her some patience and gave him some quality time in the real world. She slipped behind the wheel and started the engine.

"PHONE'S FOR YOU." Hannah leaned into the kitchen.

Damn. Ben had taken the time to grab a sandwich before he took off for Albuquerque, and now it looked like he was going to be delayed even longer—unless it was Julie... He bounded for the hallway.

"Rose?" He hoped the disappointment didn't show.

"You've got to get back here." He started to interrupt but she cut him off. "I know you have other plans. But believe me, you'll want to take a look at this. I can't say any more. Please, trust me." Then she hung up.

Ben stood a minute by the phone. He'd never known Rose to exaggerate. If she said it was important, it was. He just couldn't think of what patient might be causing the crisis. Someone must have been brought in who needed hospitalization—maybe needed to be taken to Gallup. He'd have to go back.

"THEY'RE IN YOUR OFFICE." Rose met him at the front door.

"They?"

"Daisy and Mary."

Suddenly, Ben was angry. "You dragged me back here because of two women who probably have nothing more than a good case of premonition—"

"This is serious. I think they know something about Sal. And Julie."

Ben felt a wave of dread. "Julie?" He pushed past Rose. Julie? What could she have to do with this?

The two women sat next to each other exactly as they had on Monday. Only there was a package on his desk opened at the top, its wrappings torn back to reveal a large piece of pottery.

"She killed Sal." This from Mary who seemed agitated as she folded and unfolded a white handkerchief bordered with pink flowers.

"You don't know that for certain," Daisy snapped. "It's the girl that I'm worried about after what Rose told us."

"Wait. Someone start at the beginning." Ben sat down.

"Your friend Julie stopped by my house this morning with a receipt and key to a locker at the bus terminal in Gallup. Sal, sometime back, had asked her to store a package for him there." She paused to indicate the box on his desk. "She told me it held the fetish jar of our grandfather. She said she had no idea why he didn't just bring it to me in the first place because in a letter to Hannah, he'd said I would pick it up—''

''He never wrote a letter. She killed him. So now she has to lie,'' Mary interrupted.

''Let me finish.'' Daisy scowled in the general direction of Mary, who was staring at the floor. ''Your Julie thought to bring the key and receipt to me, have me go into Gallup and pick up the box. She said she would be more comfortable if I had it. I told her that would be fine. Then the more I thought about it, I knew it had something to do with Sal's—''

''Death,'' Mary finished her sentence.

''Disappearance.'' Daisy shot her a glance.

''When we got the package home, we opened it. It was great-grandfather's fetish jar all right, but it was sealed shut. That wasn't right. I couldn't imagine why Sal would do such a thing.''

''We opened it,'' Mary added.

''And look.'' Daisy handed him a small notebook, blue cover, three inches by five, spiral bound across the top and about a half inch thick.

Ben flipped it open and couldn't understand the notations. There was page after page of what looked like experiments. First there was a formula, then a list of ingredients—things like resin and tree sap in addition to poly something or others, synthetics, then cooling times, sketches of insects and things labeled dryers—suddenly, his eye caught the word, amber. Ben looked at Daisy.

''Sal was making amber?'' he asked.

She nodded. ''I, we, should have guessed before. He always had access to perfect pieces. Amber's expensive, but I thought that Hannah got it for him. And he always helped his family. Gave us money when we needed things. I should have known that his carvings couldn't have paid for a new van—not in one lump. And he had to hide it from us.'' Daisy paused. ''Could he go to jail?''

''Not if he's dead,'' Mary said, but Ben could tell that Daisy was ignoring her and wanted his opinion.

''It's illegal. The Government has cracked down on those

producing fake turquoise. It depends on how far he carried the scam—where he sold it. If he kept it for himself and only carved fetishes that he sold, then it's probably not as serious.''

"Hannah sold amber. The kid who works at the trading post, the one who helped out Sal, said she shipped twenty-five pounds last week. And that trader, Ahmed? The kid says he used to pick up boxes of what could have been the same stuff.'' Daisy paused. "That much amber was worth a lot of money. Hannah wanted this notebook. I know that she did, and she's put Sal in danger to get it.''

Ben noted that Daisy didn't say that she believed Sal had been killed. But could that be possible? The recipe was equivalent to a small fortune. People had killed for less. And it seemed obvious that taking Julie into his confidence meant that Sal was trying to hide the notebook from somebody.

"Did you say that Hannah told Julie that she'd gotten a letter from Sal with the receipt—a letter that asked Julie to get the jar and then turn it over to you?'' Ben asked.

"Julie said that Hannah thought I was helping Sal—that he was hiding out somewhere with my help. But that's not so. I haven't seen him. And I don't believe he'd write a letter. Sal wouldn't do that. And he wouldn't run. First of all, he wouldn't leave the village. He'd stay until this murder thing was all cleared up.'' Daisy folded her arms across her chest. "I know my brother.''

One thing seemed certain. Hannah knew much more about Sal's disappearance than she had admitted. So, if Hannah got the locker receipt from Sal and tricked Julie into going after the package...

"Why did you say earlier that you were worried about Julie?'' Ben felt his palms grow moist. Somehow he knew he wasn't going to like the answer.

"We went into town right after she left, and we saw her and that retarded boy—Hannah's child—by the bus station. She had mentioned to me that she was interviewing Morley from the pawnshop but didn't say anything about taking .22 with her.''

"In Gallup? .22 was with Julie?'' Ben was standing.

"And then when Rose said you might have doubts about .22 even being .22…"

"Hope it was okay to tell." He hadn't seen Rose in the doorway. He nodded, or he meant to nod. His mind was racing—thoughts of Sal and toads and amber were jumbled together but all implicated Hannah and whoever .22 really was. Hannah had lied to him not an hour ago as to her son's whereabouts and Julie's. He fought a wave of nausea. Hannah had sent .22 with Julie thinking she was going to pick up the package. Julie was in danger. He knew it; he had to think.

"Rose, get Morley on the phone. Find out if she's still there. If she is, don't upset her but tell her not to leave. Then call Tommy and fill him in. I'm on my way to Gallup."

THIRTEEN

"Booger good. Me eat hundred boogers."

.22 clutched a wad of French fries in a greasy fist, then stuffed the last few bites of the third hamburger into his mouth with his other hand—a two-fisted eater. She was glad she had opted to eat outside. Without a bib .22 splattered ketchup and mustard down his shirt and onto the table. She had some cleanup to do, but it was better than eating in the car or inside. Bob's Drive-In at the edge of town had been a good idea.

But they attracted attention. That part was difficult to get used to. Diners inside peeked out the window between bites and let their eyes wander to .22. She had wanted to scream at them that he couldn't help it. Did they have to stare? This wasn't a freak show. She could never get used to this sort of thing.

There was always so much promise, hope, during a pregnancy and no warning sometimes that things could go wrong. What would she do—she and Ben do—if they had such a child? They hadn't talked about children, not in any concrete way. Both seemed to take for granted that there would be some, one or two. And if she were asked when, she knew the answer would be vague. Sometime. Some future time when everything was perfect. Jobs secure. A house of their own—not something temporary supplied by IHS out in nowhere.

But when were things ever going to be perfect? She was signing on to follow Ben around—and it would be just that for a few years before he might land a job in a metropolitan area if he ever did. But would that be so bad for a family? Living in settings with minimal threats of gang involvement, or drugs? A reservation might prove the best place to raise a family. It could provide the kind of diversity that enriched children, in addition to keeping them safe.

She opened another package of ketchup and squirted it onto the plastic lid from the shake. .22 stopped dunking his fries in his ''berry-milk'' but put his five fingers in the ketchup one at a time and then loudly sucked the thick red condiment off of each one. Julie ignored him. He was quiet and getting nourished.

A young child rode by on a bike chanting, ''Dumbo, Dumbo, Dumbo...'' Twenty-two stuck out his tongue and left it there until Julie was afraid that he'd pulled a jaw muscle. She couldn't really reprimand him; it was the other child's fault.

And the child's lack of manners didn't seem to faze .22— with a little coaching he even ordered another strawberry shake on his own. She gave him the money, and he went inside the diner and waited at the counter behind two other people before placing his order. She'd have to tell Hannah. Julie doubted if he'd ever done that before. And he was proud of himself. He actually glowed and kept patting the sweating sides of the shake cup and repeating, ''Mine. I got berry-milk.'' Then he would break into a grin.

He was being so good. There had been the hint of a hassle when she hadn't let him take the shake or any of the food in the car. She was anxious to get back, but she sat with him until he finished, which seemed to take forever. She could remember her parents' exasperation when she and her brother dawdled over food. But it was a beautiful summer's day, and their table was under an old cottonwood whose natural canopy offered shade. She really wasn't in a hurry.

Julie relaxed and watched .22 drag his fries through the ketchup and make loud sucking noises with his straw when he reached the bottom of his shake. And then she thought of it— why couldn't she test .22? He trusted her; he'd try for her. Couldn't she find out if he could flip a coin on demand? That would be helpful. Give Ben some idea of whether what he saw was a fluke or not.

".22, watch this, because I want you to try to do the same thing." Julie dug a quarter out of her coin purse. "Now, watch carefully." She cradled the coin on the side of her index finger and slipped the tip of her thumb underneath, pausing, then thrusting upward in a quick release action that sent the coin careening into the air, heads, tails, head, tails, heads, tails before it toppled back to the table, to spin crazily and roll to a stop against an uneven plank in the wood top.

.22 was mesmerized. His eyes had followed every move of the coin.

"Here. It's your turn." She held the coin out.

Suddenly he began to shake his head faster and faster, eyes closed, fists pounding on the table.

"Stop." Julie leaned across the table and grabbed him by the shoulders. "Please, .22, tell me what's wrong." What a strange reaction. She'd never expected this. He pulled away and stuck his hands in his pockets. But at least he quieted. "You don't have to do this if you don't want to."

"Can't do. Can't do." He was rocking now. That side to side movement that often preceded a bout of howling.

".22, I know that you can do it. I watched you on videotape, in the waiting room at the doctor's office. You put a coin into the pop machine, it fell out, you picked it up and flipped it. Do you remember?"

He was deathly still, staring at her. She heard the happy squeals of children playing on the swings in a park across the highway. A breeze fluffed a tuft of .22's hair as a fly investigated the udder cream. He didn't move. She started to push back from the table.

"Sit down."

Where did that voice come from? She didn't know that voice.

Resonant, bass, commanding... But she couldn't sit. She needed to run. Instinct screamed in her head to get away. Before she was able to articulate, even isolate what it was, all her senses had gathered to warn her, to scream at her. This was danger. This man—this wasn't .22 in front of her. Run. She tried to move.

"I said sit." The hand that clamped onto her wrist had shot with lightning quickness from under the table to nail her, hold her. "There's a gun pointed at your gut. I suggest that you do what I say."

She sank back to the bench.

"Say, is everything all right out here?" The man who had served them was standing at the side door, peering over at them, leaning on a broom.

"You don't want people hurt, do you?" The threat was hissed before .22 let loose of her wrist and started beating the shake cup on the table. She noticed that one hand stayed out of view.

"We're fine. Just a little misunderstanding over having another shake," Julie called back, hoping her voice didn't quiver.

The man nodded and walked back inside.

"We've got to get out of here. I'm going to get up first. You walk ahead of me. Don't get cute. I've killed before. You won't make any difference." The voice belonged to someone else, but it was .22 who stumbled getting up, thrust his head forward and dangled one arm at his side before assuming that familiar disjointed gait that made him walk haltingly beside her.

He brushed against her as she stepped back pulling the car door open. Not that she hadn't believed him, but she caught a glimpse of the small revolver above the pocket of his slacks. The barrel was pointed at her; his hand was steady.

"Now, open the back door." When she hesitated, he added with a short laugh, "Thought I'd let you out of my sight and go around to the other side? Get real, bitch."

She did as she was told, then slipped behind the wheel. She was trying to think, but the words "killed before" echoed, demanded attention. Had it been Sal? Yes. That made sense. But couldn't it have been Ahmed? Or both of them?

"What are we waiting for?" The coldness of the gun's barrel surprised her as it pressed into her neck. She started the car.

THEY LEFT HERE about twelve-thirty. We had to end our interview when a busload of tourists stopped in. Some lady called asking the same question. I hope Julie and the boy aren't in some kind of trouble." Morley was waiting for an answer, but Ben didn't want to say too much.

"I hope not, too." He knew that wasn't going to satisfy Morley but that was all he wanted to say for the present. "Were they going straight home?" Maybe, if he kept him answering questions.

"They could have been. I don't think she had any other interviews."

Ben tried to remain calm. He hadn't passed Julie's car on the highway. Did she have other errands, ones she didn't mention to Morley? And wasn't Tommy out on the road somewhere right now setting up a roadblock a few miles north of the reservation?

"Oh, wait a minute. The youngster was hungry. Julie said she needed to get him some lunch."

"Do you have any idea where they might have stopped?"

Morley shook his head. "My guess would be some burger place. You got about ten to choose from."

"Could I borrow a phone book?"

Morley shuffled behind the counter and handed one over.

"Last year's. You can have this one. It don't make no difference; nothing ever changes around here."

Ben sat in his truck and looked up drive-in food vendors. Morley was right, there were nine and all more or less clumped together along the south end of the main drag. He'd drive by and look for Julie's car.

But there was nothing—one trip up then down the street, a couple detours around the back of a McDonalds and a Whopper Burger to check parked cars, but none was Julie's. There was no trace of them. Yet, he felt that they couldn't be that far ahead of him.

If they were on their way back, he should be able to catch

up with them. But what if something had gone wrong—.22 had
accosted Julie, threatened her over the package… He had no
way of knowing. He headed across town to pick up Highway
32 and passed an independent burger place, Bob's. On a whim
he pulled into the parking area. It wouldn't hurt to check.

"Good-looking woman with a retarded kid? Big kid, close
to full grown? Yeah, they just left. Maybe, fifteen minutes ago.
Headed out 32." The man at the counter remembered them
well. "Is that kid safe?"

Ben felt his knees wobble. "Why do you ask?"

"Well, I thought she was having a problem with him at one
point. It looked to me like he was trying to strong-arm her. He
sure had her locked in a grip all right. I bet that young fellow's
strong as an ox. They are sometimes, and they don't know their
own strength. Now, take for example my wife's cousin—"

"What happened to the woman?" Ben gripped the counter.

"Nothing. I asked, but she said everything was all right. She
sure was good with him. She cleaned him up after he ate a
couple burgers and fries, then she entertained him out there on
the park bench. It looked like she was trying to teach him how
to flip a coin."

"Flip a coin?" At first he couldn't believe what he'd heard.
But, no, that was just like Julie. She'd try to prove that .22
either could or couldn't. And it was for him. Ben knew that.
She probably took .22 with her in the first place because she
thought she could help. Ben ran outside and jumped in his
truck. Fifteen minutes. She was alive and well fifteen minutes
ago. But maybe just barely if .22 had grabbed her like the man
said. The coin toss must have given it away. .22 must have
known that he'd blown his cover. And that meant he was dangerous. Ben peeled out and gunned the truck up an embank-
ment and onto 32.

.22 WAS SWEATING. The sun glistened on the red-gold stubble
that outlined a square, prominent jaw. She studied him in the
rear-view mirror as he leaned over her shoulder, the muzzle of
the gun still buried in her neck. Who was this man? Who would
pick at sores to keep them scabbed over so that he could pre-

tend to be someone else? And for what? What would he get out of all this? Money? Was he being paid to impersonate the real .22? It would give Julie time to think if she could get him to talk.

"Do you have a name? I can't continue to call you .22 or Harold."

His legs were bent, one knee pushing into the back of the front seat. He looked cramped and nervous. Julie adjusted the rear view mirror. He glanced out the window. Would he tell her who he was? Curiosity was almost calming as she pushed the gas pedal down. Fifty-five, sixty, seventy—hopefully, some of Tommy's men would be patrolling.

"Hey. Don't get smart. Drive the speed limit."

He worked the gun's muzzle up under the occipital ridge behind her ear. She dropped back to sixty-five.

"If you won't tell me your name, will you tell me if you're an actor by trade?" She watched as he made eye contact in the mirror. She had his attention. "You were perfect. You fooled the best. If you hadn't been caught by a hidden camera, no one would have ever known."

"Yeah." For a minute she thought it wasn't going to work. Then she caught the sneer, the thin smile that reeked of bravado and heard it in his voice when he said, "I could be an actor if I wanted. I'm good. And you can call me Carl."

"How did you meet Hannah, Carl?"

"I've known her all my life, dear old Auntie Hanny."

"You're her nephew? You're doing this for your aunt?" My God, Hannah had involved a relative. Was he her sister's son? "Which means the original .22 is probably dead?" Julie hadn't meant to ask that and bit her lip when she saw the flare of rage.

"Why don't you shut up?"

She needed to try a different tactic. "Why don't you wise up and not get into more trouble? You really haven't done anything wrong. You haven't committed fraud, haven't been examined by the board and collected any money. You could still get out of all this."

"Nope. A dead man says I can't turn things around now."

She felt him lower the gun as a car passed going in the

opposite direction. It hadn't been anyone she knew. But what would she have done if she'd recognized the driver? What could she do? Swerve? Lay on the horn? Her only hope was somehow getting back to civilization.

"So what do you want to do?"

"When I grow up? Isn't that the way that goes?" He leaned forward; his breath tickled her ear. "Well, between you and me, I've grown up just fine. Hannah and me are going to get the fuck out of this shit hole. You're not going to stop us." The menacing tone made her cringe. "You want to know what happened to .22? He died of a cold. After all that fucking attention—'baby Harold can't do this, baby Harold can't eat that, baby Harold is worth all that fucking money'—all those years I took care of him, he just up and dies—one month before he would have graduated from that special education program. That little fucker owed me."

"And Hannah thought up a plan to get the money anyway."

"Yeah. With a new baby Harold." He let his mouth go slack, then sucked loudly on his thumb while she watched in the rear-view. Carl to Harold, Harold to Carl. It really was a remarkable acting job.

"So whom did you kill, Carl?" Go for it. He seemed willing to brag. Maybe she could get some answers. What did she have to lose?

"Wouldn't you like to know?" That snarl again.

"Did you kill the trader?"

His eyes gave it away before he said, "What if I did? He was butting into things where he didn't belong, getting greedy, thought his cut should have been as big as ours. And then he tells Hannah that he knows the stuff is fake—threatens to get us all locked up unless we can come up with $500,000. Can you imagine? Here he was getting a sweet little cut of the action but no he has to go and ruin it. I was smart to off him. I knew I could pin it all on Sal, use the scalping to pressure him into giving up the—"

They saw the flashing lights at the same time—a barricade of patrol cars across the highway about two miles ahead. She sucked in her breath. Could she dare to hope that Tommy knew? That he was looking for her? Was Ben with them? She took her foot off the gas.

Then her eyes locked with the hard, cool blue ones in the rear-view mirror and his animal fright bore into her, seemed to travel down the muzzle of the gun. There was nothing to keep him from killing her, too.

"Take the side road. There. And fucking step on it."

Her breathing was shallow. She was so close to safety. If she could only get someone's attention. She grabbed at the steering wheel as it jerked through her fingers when she left the highway and jolted down the gravel incline. She reacted quickly and steered the car onto the jutted dirt, two-track drive that led around, then up and through an outcropping of rock to God-knew-what on the other side. Ben called these cart trails "rescuers ruts" barely kept passable by ranchers needing access to areas that might hide livestock in need of help—areas that were rough and remote and a part of the badlands and would only give up their secrets if you had a four-wheel drive vehicle.

The car bottomed out twice before the tires grasped enough gravel to propel it forward and upward, the floorboarded engine whining a protest even after she'd rammed it into Drive 3. She was afraid of careening off the side to hang precariously before rolling down among the boulders or breaking an axle in the foot-deep ruts that banged both of them against the car's interior. The going was slow, and the car was already overheating. Julie watched the needle climb.

"Stop here."

She put on the brake, turned off the engine and pulled the emergency. They were on an incline, behind a boulder nestled between two overhanging outcroppings of rock—and hidden from view. Julie was certain of that. Hidden and out of range of hearing but she laid on the horn anyway. In case Tommy's men were scouting—

The pistol butt crashed into the side of her head snapping her neck to the side.

"Don't do that again. I've told you. I have no reason not to kill you."

She watched as Carl lit a cigarette. The smoke seemed to dance and skip over the seat between them, and she realized how dizzy she was. The force of the blow had blurred her vision. She shook her head to clear it. There was no doubt that he would do what he threatened. It wasn't just the blow to the head, she felt numb trying to think, figure out some way to get away. The lump was already pushing up into a good sized knot just above her ear.

He sat immobile but still holding the gun to her head. Was he trying to decide what to do? Probably. It was obvious that a roadblock wasn't in his plan. But was it meant for them? Julie allowed a glimmer of hope. It had to be. She needed to believe that. A couple more long sucking drags on the cigarette and .22 tossed it out the window.

"Open the trunk." .22 got out of the car.

"No. You can't make me get in the trunk. I'm claustrophobic. Gag me. Tie me up somewhere. But not the trunk." She had locked the driver's side door. Her voice sounded shrill, thin and wavering and she clutched the steering wheel in some kind of death grip hoping he couldn't pry her fingers loose.

"You stupid bitch. We're through playing around. I need the package. Sal's package. The one you took out of the locker. You following me? You must have gotten up real early to drive over here and back. So I just bet it's still somewhere in this car."

He grabbed a handful of her hair and forced her head back against the seat, then over it as far as her neck would extend and gave her hair a yank. "Are you paying attention to me? I don't need any more of your games. Now, unlock that door. Step out real slow and walk to the trunk."

He released her hair, and Julie did as she was told. She wasn't sure he wouldn't throw her in the trunk, but he could have broken her neck just then. And the package? What was his interest in Sal's package? Better yet, what should she tell him? The truth? But then he might kill her. Should she stall? Lie? Say she forgot? But they were in the bus station, he saw the empty locker...maybe, she had forgotten it, maybe she left it at Morley's.

"It's not in the trunk."

"I'll tell you whether it is or not."

He made her stand beside him as he leaned into the trunk pulling out mats, dismantling the tool kit, tossing tire iron and jack to one side. He ran his free hand under and over and between every two pieces of matting. It seemed to Julie that he was looking for something awfully small. He wasn't acting like it was a fetish jar that he was after.

"Empty your purse." He grabbed her arm and propelled her around the side of the car, tucked the gun in his belt, scooped the purse off the front seat and tossed it to her. She dumped everything on the hood and Carl went through the same motions—opened her cosmetics case, looked carefully at her address book, ripped the lining around an inside pocket.

"It's in your fucking equipment, isn't it?"

"No. It's at Morley's. I wanted his opinion."

Could she keep up this charade not knowing exactly what he was looking for? Her life probably depended on it. But what had been in the fetish jar? A piece of jewelry? A one-of-a-kind artifact worth some ungodly sum?

She wasn't prepared for Carl's reaction—he was laughing. Was she wrong to mention Morley's? Did he know that she didn't have a clue as to the jar's contents?

"I just bet you did. Getting the old coot's opinion was pretty sly. You were going to steal it, weren't you? How long was Sal's notebook even in the locker? Long enough to get a receipt and a key and figure out that Sal wasn't coming back? Or did you even put it there in the first place?"

She didn't say anything, just shrugged. Did she look guilty? And a notebook? All this, her death, maybe Sal's, over a notebook. Was it some kind of blackmail? Yes. That had to be it. Sal knew something about Carl being a fake. He had written something incriminating. But then, what would that have to do with Morley?

"Do you think all this is worth killing over?" Me, the trader, not to mention Sal, she thought, but went on. "How can the contents of that notebook justify taking a life?"

"Because, beautiful, it's going to make Aunt Hanny and me

a whole hell of a lot of money. It's a little investment for the rest of our lives. I got a feeling that I don't have to tell you that. Now, why don't you just get in the car real slow and throw all your crap out for me to take a look at.''

He pushed her ahead of him and into the back seat. The recorder and notebooks were in two bags on the floor behind the passenger seat.

''Is Sal dead?'' Maybe if she distracted him…and then what? She needed to buy time. Think. She had to think.

''Bet you'd like to know, wouldn't you? Let's just say that he's alive but not very well and not likely to see the light of day anytime soon.'' More laughter.

Julie opened the opposite door. Thank God, she'd rented a four-door.

''Hey, let's toss those out on this side.''

She pulled the car door closed but didn't latch it before she tossed the recorder in his direction. But Carl wasn't paying attention. He had moved to rummage in the trunk. Then stepping back where she could see him, he began wiping his head with a towel, smearing the udder cream and cursing when it didn't come off easily, ducking down to study his image in the outside mirror.

''Jesus, this stuff is crap.'' He scrubbed at his head. ''But I guess it was worth it. Not a bad way to earn a few hundred thousand, if you look at it that way.'' He chuckled, but it wasn't a happy sound. He had removed a stocking cap from a back pocket. A couple more swipes and he'd be done, Julie thought. She needed to make a decision.

Julie eyed the gun still tucked in his belt. She had edged closer to the opposite door while she gathered up the cloth bag of notes and tried to see past the jumble of waist-high rocks to her right. They had climbed about fifty feet into the outcropping of rock that rose from the edge of a field. But it wasn't a shear drop from where they were parked, rather a gradual sloping descent into a field of corn. If she ran, zigzagging, keeping her body low, she might have a chance. The gun was a revolver, small caliber, meant to be shot at close range, not very accurate beyond fifteen feet. Did she have the guts to risk injury but foil sure death?

"Check the inside pocket in my bag." Then she heaved the bag out the door and didn't look back. She simply dove through the passenger-side door, stumbled, gained her balance, scrambled over the first boulder, rolled, righted herself in time to hear the ping of a bullet glance sharply off the rock to her left followed by his angry curses; then bent over she slipped, fell, leaped up in a crashing descent towards the field of waist-high tassels—not much camouflage, but better than nothing. The second and third pings sent bits of rock spraying across her neck. Close.

She could hear him panting, grunting with the exertion. Just another twenty-five feet and then she could run towards the highway. She could find help, flag down a car. Traffic was slowing because of the roadblock. Maybe someone would see her from the road. She didn't stop to think that he might catch up with her before she reached safety. She just knew that she had to try. That it was probably her only chance. He was close. He fell, cursed, shouted at her, then in a rain of pebbles, crashed forward. Another bullet missed. Four down. Two more. Waste two more, she prayed.

She didn't allow herself to look back. Her jeans were torn at the knees, her hands bleeding, palms scraped and raw. The next bullet grazed her shoulder. In a reflex motion she grabbed her arm but kept going. Fifteen feet to the bottom. Just fifteen feet. She could make it to the field and to the highway. She had to make it to the highway.

She hopped, twisted, stubbed her toe, jumped over a rock. The ground was more even now. He only had one bullet left. But the small avalanche of rock told her he was still in pursuit, and almost on top of her. He hadn't stopped to reload. But if he missed with the last bullet, he could do enough damage with his bare hands. She could hear his breathing. Could she make it?

She wouldn't allow herself to think otherwise.

When he swiped at her arm, she deftly ducked and dodged left. More cursing, then a lunge that knocked her flat. The breath whooshed from her lungs and she gasped, struggling to refill them. She rolled over to see him at her feet, on all fours, breathing hard, then he slammed his knee down pinning her ankle and pointed the pistol. She had almost made it—had almost made flat ground and the highway. He was trying to catch his breath. His knees and hands were as torn up as hers.

"You stupid bitch." He gulped air before continuing. "You thought you'd get away."

He straightened, then pushed to his feet standing over her, chest heaving, the pistol surprisingly steady. The crack of sound followed by an echo of percussion pierced the air and seemed to coincide with .22's suddenly being jerked upward and back to lie just out of reach, blood already foaming from the hole above his eye. He lifted his head, the hand holding the pistol wavered but was still pointed her direction.

Julie didn't wait to see more; she bolted upright, and ran, not looking, not caring, just forward out along the side of the field into shoulder-high brush, falling, staggering to her feet only to slip again, dreading to feel the burning sting of Carl's last bullet.

"Julie, Julie. It's okay. .22's dead. It's me. Look at me; it's Ben." Strong arms had caught her, pinned her as she flailed about. But Ben?... Was she safe? Was it true she had escaped? She burst into tears as the scent of his after-shave engulfed her. He smoothed her hair and tightened his hold all the time whispering his love.

Suddenly all feeling drained from her body, and she slumped against him as he lowered her to the ground in the midst of trampled chamisa. Ben cradled her as she tried to catch her breath between sobs of relief, and he kissed her and said he'd never been so frightened in all his life. Then they both laughed when she said she thought she had the corner on fright, thank you very much.

"Looks like you're going to live." Tommy stood at the edge of the rocks, a deer rifle slung over his shoulder.

"Thanks to you," Ben called back. "You ever put in some time on a SWAT team?"

"Used to keep the family in venison every winter. That's about all." But he grinned his appreciation of Ben's admiration.

Julie thought Tommy was being overly modest, remembering the single, life-ending bullet in Carl's head.

"If you want to go back to the village, have that arm looked at, I'll meet you at the clinic in about an hour," Tommy said then turned away as one of his patrolmen walked up.

"I don't think I'm really hurt. Cuts, bruises, a crease in my shoulder—"

"How'd this happen?" Ben gently tipped her head sideways to look at the discolored bump above her ear.

"You don't want to know. Have you found Sal?" She changed the subject and struggled to her feet with Ben's help. Better to get him off the topic of her injuries. In fact, she felt a little ridiculous. She was the one who had insisted that .22 was who he said he was. She was the bright one who thought she could tell the difference—even went back to the house to pick him up in order to help Ben—or prove that she was right, probably, more of the latter.

"Not a trace. Did .22 say anything?"

"His name's Carl. He's Hannah's nephew. He killed the trader who was in on some kind of deal. He also said that Sal is alive, but not well—I think that's how he put it. Oh yeah, said Sal wasn't going to see daylight again, something like that."

"Hannah's nephew. That puts a twist in things. But explains how he could resemble her. It's obvious that they've gotten Sal out of the way in order to get the notebook."

"What's all this about a notebook?" After Ben finished telling her what Daisy had discovered in the fetish jar, Julie stood quietly and thought of the corn maiden with its perfect Jumping Sumac beetle and the necklace with an identical beetle stuck in the bear. She should have known that the odds of one man finding two such perfect specimens of the same insect were improbable.

"I feel so stupid. It was right there in front of me. And he tried to tell me. He was so mad that I'd paid all that money for a fetish necklace that wasn't even real."

"Am I going to be mad, too, at how much you paid?" Ben was teasing as he put his arm around her and guided her towards his pickup.

"Listen, buster, separate checking accounts are more important than two bathrooms in any marriage," she teased back but loved the feel of being alive, of having her life ahead of her, of being able to lean against Ben, draw on his strength. She felt almost drunk with the prospect of having a future. She got into the truck with probably more help from Ben than she needed, then slipped across the seat, ignored the pain in her shoulder and put her arms around his neck as he swung behind the steering wheel.

"I love you." Anything else she had wanted to say was cut off by his kiss.

"If I didn't think you needed medical attention, I could suggest one or two activities—" he began.

"There's always later." She snuggled against him, then became pensive. "Can you imagine someone keeping his head raw and covered with salve all this time? And he fooled a lot of people." Julie noticed Ben grimace. Oops. Foot in her mouth again, but she wasn't thinking about Ben's testing him; she was thinking of Tommy's mother.

"Has Hannah been picked up?"

"Tommy sent a patrol car out to the trading post. I don't know if she's under arrest. I was a little more concerned about someone else." He reached over to put an arm back around her shoulders after he'd pulled out onto the highway.

"You know, I can't help but feel that Sal's whereabouts is right under our noses, too. I should have been smarter about the amber, should have snapped to its being too perfect. And I should have believed you about .22—I have the same feeling about Sal; I should know where he is. That I do know if I can only put it together," Julie said.

SAL DREW A HASH MARK on the wall. Number six. Then snapped off the flashlight. He had to conserve the batteries. Friday, Saturday, Sunday, Monday, Tuesday, Wednesday. Six days. Five nights. But not that he could tell the difference. He sat down heavily on the cot. His strength was going. How long could he last? He had water. The sink in the corner had been put in for the lab. It was well water, unfiltered and tasted slightly metallic. But it was wet. He could drink and wash. Was it comforting to think someone would find a clean body? If anyone ever found him.

He slept most of the time now. Years ago he'd read a study on cave dwelling, about an experiment at Carlsbad Caverns. After a couple weeks underground, a person's perception of time became warped. There was no difference between night and day. A person began to sleep ten, twelve even fourteen hours at a time. Sal had started doing that, sleeping like he was still drugged.

He stretched out on the cot. He no longer fought the darkness. He'd found some candles in his toolbox, but they were long spent. He thought he could detect a lingering scent of bayberry. Whatever that was. The flashlight was his only illumination. He turned towards the wall after bunching his pillow and tucked the round cylinder under the mattress. The flashlight was important to him. It would be like losing his sight if anything happened to it thrusting him into a blindness that he didn't think his sanity could recover from.

He dozed but couldn't drift off into the black bottomless sleep he was used to. There had been no visitors—no Atoshles in his dreams threatening him. But didn't the visits by Atoshle have something to do with .22 and Hannah? Hadn't they been trying to scare him? To make him give up the amber? .22 who wasn't .22 after all? And Atoshle who wasn't Atoshle but was .22? It made his head hurt.

He knew Hannah planned to move, just up and go and leave him underground. And he had exhausted himself trying to find a chink—one weak link in his underground cell that would let him escape. But there was none. Noise didn't seem to carry. He had banged on the metal workbench, on the sink, on the pipes exposed for two feet before they disappeared behind the rock wall. No one came, but his head had rung for hours, even with his hearing aid in his pocket.

He had tried to force the bit of a hand drill through the trap door but struck what was probably half-inch metal. He was in a fortress. And maybe he had just given up. Finally, he simply resigned himself to whatever was to be. He put his trust in his guardian fetishes that still perched above the cot. He carried the obsidian turtle in his pocket now and often drew it out to run his thumb over its cool smoothness. Long life. The turtle could give him that. Did he dare hope?

At first the scraping didn't register. The sound was muffled and sounded far away. But the ray of light that flooded the top of the stairs was real. Someone was opening the trap door. Sal pushed to his feet as it clanged shut leaving darkness surrounding the single beam of a flashlight.

"Stay where you are."

"Hannah?"

What could this mean? He tried to keep down the joy that bubbled up, burst through his being sending shock waves to his brain. She'd relented. She'd come for him. "Hannah, yes, I knew you'd come. You couldn't kill me. I knew that. I—"

"Shut up."

"Let's go now. There's no need to wait. Let's leave." He heard himself babbling, but couldn't stop. "I need to get something to eat—"

Sal heard her cock the semiautomatic, and he stumbled back and sat down hard on the cot and closed his mouth. He wasn't going anywhere. But why was she going to shoot him?

"Two cop cars pulled in. They've got him. I know they do." Her voice was quivering, and she seemed to be talking to herself. She was on the verge of tears or already crying, he couldn't tell which.

"Who? Got who?" he asked.

"Carl. I didn't want him to go with Julie. But he was so sure. Said it was the only way we'd get the notebook. I knew it was trouble. Something must have gone wrong."

"This Carl is .22? Where's the real .22?"

"Dead. And don't think I murdered him. I didn't have to. He died of pneumonia in the spring he was nineteen."

"So who is Carl?"

"Good, isn't he? I don't think I'd have ever thought of having him impersonate Harold if I hadn't seen what a good mimic Carl was. When they were younger, it was cruel. Carl would follow Harold everywhere, two steps behind walking just like him. At the table he would torment Harold by eating like he did. And they looked alike through the eyes. Carl was only three years older.''

"Your sister's son?"

"Yes. After Harold died, it seemed a simple thing to do…" Her voice was flat. She stopped, then added wistfully. "We were going home, to Maine. I'd live with my sister and make amber. There would have been enough money for all of us."

"Until Carl killed the trader?"

"He had to. Ahmed was getting in the way, demanded that we include him as a partner—threatened to go to the police because he knew the amber was fake. It was my idea to scalp him and pin the murder on you. But even then, we could have gotten away. It was you. You and your stubbornness. Your refusal to give up the recipe. You made Carl risk his life."

Sal flipped on his flashlight. The beam crisscrossed the light from Hannah's flashlight, but there was a gun all right. Light reflected off the barrel. She was standing three feet in front of him now. The gun was a semiautomatic, petite, maybe a Lady something-or-other but deadly.

"Hannah—"

"We've talked too much. I have to do this now, then wait until everyone's gone and leave after it gets dark. Nobody remembers that this cellar is here."

"Wait. Hannah, please—"

"HAVE YOU FOUND Hannah?" Ben asked as Tommy walked through the door to the clinic's emergency room.

"Nothing yet."

He looked tired, Julie thought. The nurse was bandaging her shoulder and reminding her again about how lucky she'd been.

"Hannah's car is still there. I think she sensed something was wrong when you and .22 didn't come back, or maybe she saw the patrol car and took off on foot. We'll find her. It's only a matter of time. She couldn't have gone far."

"Can we go back to the boarding house?" Julie was thinking about changing clothes—what wasn't torn was dirt streaked, stiff or discolored with blood.

"It should be okay. My men have searched the house. I've left them out there just in case she tries to come back."

"I'm going with you. After the death of Harold, she'll need someone. I think she'd rather hear about the death from me," Dr. Lee said from the doorway. "But I must tell you, I find it very difficult to believe what I've been hearing—all this about Harold being someone else. This could look bad for all of us if—"

"Harold was an impostor. It appears that he was her sister's son. Hannah perpetuated the sham and meant to profit from it. Miss Conlin is alive because Ben saw the dust kicked up by her car going up the side of that outcropping of rock between here and Gallup. There was no mistake about what this .22 intended to do. The young man was killed in the act of threatening the life of Miss Conlin. My report will reflect this." Tommy sounded terse and not in a mood to take anything from anybody—especially an overbearing doctor, Julie thought.

"Ah, well, yes, but I would like to verify this information on my own," Dr. Lee countered.

"We have every reason to believe that Hannah Rawlings could be armed and dangerous."

"You've got to be joking. I've known Hannah for five years. I've never found her to be anything but a loving mother, accomplished anthropologist, and dedicated to maintaining her place of business." Dr. Lee sounded exasperated.

"I am not asking you to stay out of this investigation; I am ordering you to do so. I will accept your offer to stand by as a physician. That is the extent of your involvement that will be approved by my office." Tommy looked at his clipboard as much as dismissing Dr. Lee who then turned to Ben.

"I'll follow the two of you in my car. I think we need to be going."

After Dr. Lee had left the room, Ben shrugged and helped Julie off the examining table.

"What do you think, Tommy? Is it okay if he tags along?"

"It's difficult to turn down your boss."

"LET'S GO THROUGH what we know about Sal's disappearance one more time." Julie said. She sat forward on the front seat of the truck, legs tucked under her, facing Ben, her cuts and bruises forgotten.

"For starters, we know why he was abducted," Ben said as he pulled onto the highway that would take them back to the boarding house.

"True. We have the motive. Now, if I could just think like Hannah…"

"I'm kinda glad you don't."

"Be serious. Maybe, I can figure out where he is."

".22, or Carl, said that he wouldn't see the light of day. Believe it or not, that supports what Sal's wife says. She thinks Hannah buried him alive." Ben said.

"Underground? Wait. That's it." Julie was bouncing up and down. "Remember what Tommy's mother said about Hannah leaving .22 in different places—she left him so many times in the root cellar under the pantry that Ed Rawlings had it boarded up?" She was almost shrieking with excitement. "I knew if I could just think like she does. When I burst into the pantry yesterday, Hannah had a ham sandwich. Obviously, we know now that she wasn't disciplining .22 like she said. Ben, that sandwich had to have been for Sal. .22 was on the floor getting ready to open a trap door—and the floor had just been carpeted. The carpet was thick and new so that it would trap sound. I wondered who would carpet a pantry." She was beside herself now. "Ben, hurry. We've got to get Sal out."

FOURTEEN

JULIE JUMPED FROM the truck as it rolled to the curb in front of the house and raced up the brick steps, Ben close behind.

"What's going on?" Dr. Lee yelled out his car window.

"We may know where Sal is," Ben called back.

"What if we're not in time?" Julie said out loud but didn't want an answer. She hadn't even put that into words before. They had to be in time. She simply couldn't think otherwise. But what if Hannah had killed Sal first and simply hidden the body in the cellar? No, Carl had sounded like Sal was still alive, and they were about to feed him just yesterday. He was alive.

The two policemen stood by the front door reluctant to let Ben and Julie by but after being briefed, one pulled his revolver and led the way to the kitchen.

"Stand back." The younger of the two policemen had opened the pantry. The thick new carpet was already pushed to the side to reveal a steel reinforced door. He gave a tug to the ring and the door lifted easily. "It must be spring-loaded. I can't see a thing, though. Is there a light switch anywhere?"

"The lights aren't working," Julie said.

"Who's got a flashlight?" Ben asked.

"I do. It's in the car. I'll be right back." The first policeman hurriedly left.

"Hello. Anybody down there?" The second policeman leaned over the opening.

"Oh, for God's sake, there's no one down there. Who'd you expect to find?" Dr. Lee pushed to the front and striking a match started down the steps.

"Wait, I'm coming, too." The policeman descended and was quickly swallowed by darkness.

"She's got a gun." The voice was Sal's, weak, wavering as it carried up the stairs, but Sal's nonetheless. They were in time. But it was too soon to feel relief.

"Hannah. Oh, my God, Hannah's hiding in the pantry." Julie couldn't stop Ben as he bounded down the steps. She didn't have to think before following him. Sal. She had to reach Sal.

The beam of Sal's flashlight was dim, but Julie could see Hannah in front of Sal, the gun pointing at the group on the stairs.

"Hannah. There's been some error. This is absurd. Put down that gun." Dr. Lee took another step downward.

"Stop right there. I'll kill all of you if I have to. Where's Carl? You killed Carl." Julie felt a shiver. Hannah was losing it, waving the gun towards them. She was on the edge. And the detective was frozen, his gun now in his holster, his hands in the air.

"We had to, Hannah. He went a little crazy when he knew we'd found him out," Ben called out.

"You bastards."

The shot exploded around them. Dr. Lee's scream was the only indication that someone had been hit. The basement flared into blackness and a tangle of movement. Julie saw Sal's flashlight careen off the cot and hit the floor as the cop on the stairs dropped to a crouch to rush forward. Then there was the sound of a scuffle. Hannah screamed and Sal yelled, "I got her."

"What the...?" The second policeman appeared with a flashlight, stumbled down the stairs, gun pulled. "Hold it right there. Nobody move."

"It's okay. There won't be anymore shooting. Here's her gun. But somebody needs to call an ambulance," Sal said.

"Is THERE ANY MORE coffee?" Sal held his cup out, and Julie didn't mind waiting on him. It was a miracle that he was sitting at the kitchen table. He was weak but had found the strength to tackle Hannah after she'd shot Dr. Lee.

"More scrambled eggs, too?" she asked. He'd just eaten a half-dozen with diced ham and four slices of whole wheat toast. He'd refused to go to the clinic when the ambulance came for Dr. Lee. He just said that good food and sunlight would fix him up. Maybe he was right.

"What are you running out here? A soup kitchen for just any old Indian we happen to dig up?" Tommy crossed the room and scooted a chair up to the table. It was obvious that he was pleased to see Sal.

Sal grinned and returned to his eggs.

"Any word on Dr. Lee?" Ben asked.

"Bullet shattered the femur. He'll be hobbled for a while. But so will his ego, I'd imagine. Self-centered little prick. Oops, sorry." Tommy looked over at Julie.

"And Hannah?" she asked.

"Already on her way to Albuquerque with an escort. Armed,

I might add. But I don't think she's going to give anyone any trouble. She was pretty torn up about .22, or Carl what's his name, her nephew,'' Tommy said.

"And the plan could have worked. Came that close.'' Tommy held his two hands about a half-inch apart in front of his face. "Pinning Ahmed's murder on Sal, the scalping and all—that was ingenious. After I got that knife with your prints on it, I knew for sure you were out tearing around the badlands, old man.''

"She knew what my reaction would be,'' Sal added. "Right down to watching her wash that scalp. I believe she'd decided to lock me up a long time back or make me go crazy from seeing Atoshle. She knew I wouldn't give up the notebook. Making sure I was implicated in a murder and setting it up to look like I'd run really covered her tracks.''

"Remember when .22 told us the masked man did it? He even showed me where the mask was buried. It was a pretty clever way to confuse the issue,'' Ben said.

"What will happen to Hannah now, Tommy?'' Julie asked.

"She was more than an accomplice to a murder—''

"And an attempted one,'' Sal added, "but I won't testify against her.''

"Why not?'' Julie couldn't believe what she was hearing.

"I don't know legal terms, but it seems to me there were 'special' circumstances. She was cornered, about to lose everything she'd ever worked for. She was pressured into the situation. Old Ed had her by the throat—even from the grave. You can't blame an animal for taking care of itself, lashing out in order to escape.''

"I'd call it a little more than 'lashing out.' You're forgetting that she aimed a gun at two police officers and shot Dr. Lee,'' Tommy said. Julie could tell he was getting irked with Sal. "She could have done more. Should we just forget that? And the fact that you were being killed so that she'd get rich? That doesn't fit your animal analogy. The law might be limited in what can be chalked up in the poor wronged widow category.''

Tommy paused and his voice was gruff when he added, "The sex couldn't have been that good.''

Sal carefully placed his fork on the table and stared at Tommy. Julie thought if a room could hold its collective breath that was what was happening now. No one moved.

"If I were you, I wouldn't pass judgment on something unless I'd been there myself." Sal struggled to hold his deadpan expression, but couldn't. He grinned and then broke into a laugh.

Male posturing...that's all it was; the tension melted. But she knew she wasn't the only one who sighed in relief.

"You know, I agree a little with each of you," Ben said. "On one hand a case can be made for Hannah's being cornered—yet, it can't be an excuse. I'd like to see her get psychiatric help. I've recommended that she be sent to the state hospital in Las Vegas for evaluation. If she's found competent, she'll stand trial. Even for a first time offense, the charges are serious. One way or the other, she'll be locked up for life."

Sal shrugged and took a drink of coffee. What would he really do when he was called to testify? Julie didn't know, but she was curious about his future. "What are you going to do now, Sal?" she asked.

"Move back to the reservation. Maybe buy the trailer from the new owners. Put it at Daisy's."

"Guess the only loose end is this amber thing. Got any ideas on how we can make that right?" Tommy had turned to Sal.

"Report it. Call the authorities. Then see if we can find a list of Hannah's buyers, put out a statement of content. I'll offer to make restitution." Sal didn't flinch.

"Under the circumstances that may be enough. Carved pieces would have a value because of the art. So, we'd mostly be talking the raw stuff." Tommy looked over at Sal. "You know your fake stuff was damned good."

"Too good." Sal returned to his eggs.

"You acting Clinic Director until Dr. Lee gets back?" Tommy turned to Ben.

"Not until Monday. In the meantime I'm taking a little well-earned R and R in Santa Fe for the next four days." Grinning, he pulled Julie onto his lap.

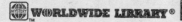